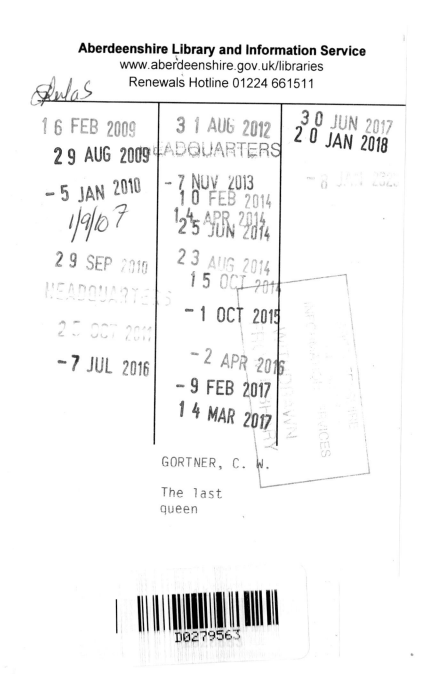

the LAST QUEEN

ABOUT THE AUTHOR

C.W. Gortner is half-Spanish by birth and his formative years were spent in southern Spain, where he began his lifelong fascination with history. After years of working as a fashion marketer and editor, C.W. returned to college to pursue a Masters in Fine Arts in Writing. He lives in Northern California with his partner of thirteen years and their Welsh Pembroke Corgi, and welcomes visitors at: http://www.leonibus.com.

the LAST QUEEN

C. W. GORTNER

HODDER &
STOUGHTON

Published in the United States of America in 2008 by Ballantine, and originally published in a different form by Two Bridges Press, Berkeley, CA, 2006.

First published in Great Britain in 2008 by Hodder & Stoughton
An Hachette Livre UK company

1

A CIP catalogue record for this title is available from the British Library

Hardback ISBN 978-0-340-96292-3
Trade paperback ISBN 978-0-340-96293-0

Typeset in Monotype Fournier

Printed and bound by Mackays of Chatham Ltd, Chatham, Kent

Hodder & Stoughton policy is to use papers that are natural, renewable and recyclable products and made from wood grown in sustainable forests. The logging and manufacturing processes are expected to conform to the environmental regulations of the country of origin.

Hodder & Stoughton Ltd
338 Euston Road
London NW1 3BH

www.hodder.co.uk

To my mother, Maravillas Blanco,
and my late father, Willis Always Gortner II,
for Spain, a lifelong infatuation with books,
and the courage to persevere.

. . .

And to Erik, for always believing.

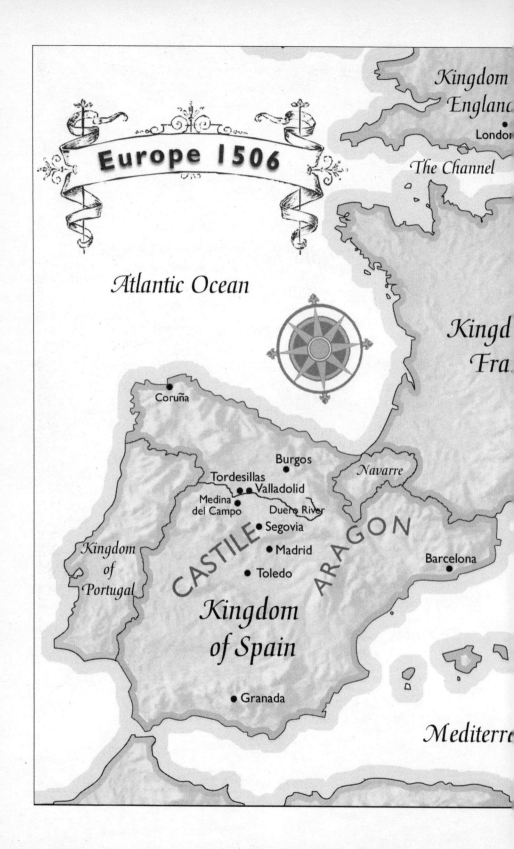

the
LAST QUEEN

TORDESILLAS,

1550

*M*idnight has become my favorite hour.

The sounds of the night are less intrusive, the shadows like a familiar embrace. By the light of a single candle, my world seems much larger than it is, as large as it once was. I suppose it is the bane of mortality to suffer time as it narrows and confines, to know that never again will anything seem as wide, as open, as attainable as it did in our youth.

I have had more occasion than most to reflect on the passage of the years. But it is only now, in this quiet hour, when all those who surround me have surrendered to sleep, that I can see clearly. It is a consolation, the knowledge, a gift I do not wish to squander on recrimination or vain regret. History may not forgive, but I must.

Hence, this blank page, the sharpened feather and the pot of ink. My hand does not tremble as much; my legs do not pain me so that I cannot sit in this grand, if somewhat frayed, chair. The memories tonight are vivid, not evanescent; they evoke and entice. They do not haunt. If I close my eyes, I can smell the smoke and jasmine, the fire and rose; I can see the vermilion walls of my beloved palace, mirrored in a child's eyes. Thus did it begin, all of it, in the fall of Granada.

And so tonight, I will bear witness to the past. I will inscribe everything I have lived and seen, everything I have done, every secret I have hidden.

I will remember, because a queen can never forget.

1492–1500

INFANTA

...

PRINCES DO NOT MARRY

FOR LOVE.

— GATTINARA

ONE

...

I was thirteen years old when my parents conquered Granada. It was 1492, the year of miracles, when three hundred years of Moorish supremacy fell to the might of our armies, and the fractured kingdoms of Spain were united at last.

I had been on crusade since my birth. Indeed, I'd often been told of how the pangs had overcome my mother as she prepared to join my father on siege, forcing her to take to her childbed in Toledo—an unseemly interruption she did not relish, for within hours she had entrusted me to a nursemaid and resumed her battles. Together with my brother, Juan, and my three sisters, I had always known the chaos of a peripatetic court, which shifted according to the demands of the Reconquest, the crusade against the Moors. I slept and awoke to the deafening clamor of thousands of souls in armor; to beasts of burden dragging catapults, siege towers, and primitive cannon; to endless carts piled with clothing, furnishings, supplies, and utensils. Rarely had I enjoyed the feel of marble underfoot or eaves overhead. Life consisted of a series of pavilions staked on stony ground, of anxious tutors gabbling lessons and cringing as flaming arrows whooshed overhead and crashing boulders decimated a stronghold in the distance.

The conquest of Granada changed everything—for me and for Spain. That coveted mountain citadel was the most opulent jewel in the Moors' vanishing world; and my parents, Isabel and Fernando, their Catholic Majesties of Castile and Aragón, vowed to reduce it to rubble rather than suffer the heretics' continuing defiance.

I can still see it as if I were standing at the pavilion entrance: the lines of soldiers flanking the road, winter sunlight sparking off their battered breastplates and lances. They stood as if they had never known hardship, gaunt faces lifted, forgetting in that moment the countless privations and countless dead of these ten long years of battle.

A thrill ran through me. From the safety of the hilltop where our tents were, I had watched Granada fall. I followed the trajectory of the tar-soaked, flaming stones hurled into the city walls and beheld the digging of trenches filled with poisonous water so no one could breach them. Sometimes, when the wind blew just right, I even heard the moans of the wounded and the dying. At night while the city smoldered, an eerie interplay of shadow and light shivered across the pavilion's cloth walls; and we awoke every morning to find cinder dust on our faces, our pillows, our plates—everything we ate or touched.

I could scarcely believe it was over. Turning back inside, I saw with a scowl that my sisters still struggled with their raiment. I had been the first to wake and don the new scarlet brocades my mother had ordered for us. I stood tapping my feet, as our duenna, Doña Ana, shook out the opaque silk veils we always had to wear in public.

"A curse on this dust," she said. "It has seeped even into the linen. Oh, but I cannot wait for the hour when this war is at an end."

I laughed. "That hour has come! Today, Boabdil surrenders the keys to the city. Mamá already awaits us in the field and—" I paused. "By the saints, Isabella, surely you don't plan to wear mourning today of all days?"

From under her black coif, my elder sister's blue eyes flared. "What do you, a mere child, know of my grief? To lose a husband is the worst tragedy a woman can endure. I will never stop mourning my beloved Alfonso."

Isabella had a flare for the dramatic, and I refused to let her get away with it. "You were married less than six months to your beloved prince before he fell off his horse and broke his neck. You only say that because Mamá has mentioned betrothing you to his cousin—if you ever stop acting the bereaved widow, that is."

Prim Maria, a year younger than I and possessed of a humorless maturity, interposed herself. "Juana, please. You must show Isabella respect."

I gave a toss of my head. "Let her first show respect for Spain. What will Boabdil think when he sees an infanta of Castile dressed like a crow?"

Doña Ana snapped, "Boabdil is a heretic. His opinion is of no account." She thrust a veil into my hands. "Cease your chatter and go help Catalina."

Sour as curdled cheese our duenna was, though I suppose I should have spared a thought for the trials the crusade had wrought on her aged bones. I went to my youngest sister, Catalina. Like Isabella, our brother, Juan, and, to some extent, Maria, Catalina resembled our mother: plump and short, with beautiful pale skin and fair hair, and eyes the color of the sea.

"You look lovely," I told her, tucking the scalloped veil about her face. Little Catalina whispered in return, "So do you. *Eres la más bonita.*"

I smiled. Catalina was eight. She had yet to master the art of the compliment. She couldn't have known her words eased my awareness that I was unique among my siblings. I had inherited my looks from my father's side of the family, down to the slight cast in one of my amber eyes and unfashionable olive complexion. I was also the tallest of my sisters, and the only one with a mass of curling coppery hair.

"No, you're the prettiest," I said, and I kissed Catalina's cheek, taking her hand in mine as the distant blast of trumpets sounded.

Doña Ana motioned. "Quick! Her Majesty waits."

Together, we went to a wide charred field, where a canopied dais had been erected.

My mother stood clad in her high-necked mauve robe, a diadem encircling her caul. As always in her presence, I found myself bending my knees slightly to conceal my budding height.

"Ah." She waved a ringed hand. "Come. Isabella and Juana, you stand to my right, Maria and Catalina to my left. You are late. I was beginning to worry."

"Forgive us, Your Majesty," said Doña Ana, with a deep reverence. "There was dust in the coffers. I had to air their Highnesses' gowns and veils."

My mother surveyed us. "They look splendid." A frown creased her brow. "Isabella, *hija mia*, black again?" She shifted her regard to me. "Juana, stand up straight."

As I did her bidding, another trumpet blast reached us, much closer now. My mother ascended the dais to her throne. The cavalcade of *grandes,* the high lords and nobles of Spain, materialized on the road in a fluttering of standards. I wanted to shout in excitement. My father rode at their head, his black doublet and signature red cape accentuating his broad shoulders. His Andalucian destrier pranced beneath him, caparisoned in Aragón's scarlet and gold colors. Behind him rode my brother, Juan, his white-gold hair tousled about his flushed, thin face.

Their appearance elicited spontaneous cheers from the soldiers. *"Viva el infante,"* cried the men, beating swords against shields. *"Viva el rey!"*

The solemn churchmen followed. Not until they reached the field did I catch sight of the prisoner in their midst. The men drew back. My father motioned, and the man on the donkey was made to dismount and forced forward, to raucous laughter. He stumbled.

My breath caught in my throat. His feet were bare, bloodied, but I marked his inherent regality as he unwound his soiled turban and cast it aside, revealing dark hair that tumbled to his shoulders. He was not what I expected, not the heretic caliph who'd haunted our dreams, whose hordes had poured boiling pitch and shot fiery arrows from Granada's ramparts against our army. He was tall and lean, with bronze skin. He might have been a Castilian lord as he crossed the field to where my mother waited, his steps measured, as if he crossed an audience hall clad in finery. When he fell to his knees before her throne, I caught a glimpse of his weary emerald eyes.

Boabdil lowered his head. From his neck, he removed an iron key on a gold chain and set it at my mother's feet, a symbolic symbol of defeat.

Jeering applause and insults came from the ranks. With an impassive countenance that conveyed both his inviolate disdain and infinite despair, Boabdil allowed the applause to fade before he lifted his practiced plea for tolerance. When he finished, he waited, as did everyone present, all eyes fixed on the queen.

My mother stood. Despite her short stature, slackened skin, and permanently shadowed eyes, her voice carried across the field, imbued with the authority of the ruler of Castile.

"I have heard this plea and accept the Moor's submission with humble grace. I've no desire to inflict further suffering on him or his people. They've fought bravely, and in reward I offer all those who convert to the True Faith baptism and acceptance into our Holy Church. Those who do not will be granted safe passage to Africa—providing they never return to Spain again."

My heart missed a beat when I saw Boabdil flinch. In that instant, I understood. This was worse than a death sentence. He'd surrendered Granada, thus bringing an end to centuries of Moorish dominion in Spain. He had failed to defend his citadel and now craved an honorable death. Instead, he was to be vanquished, to bear humiliation and exile till the end of his days.

I looked at my mother, marked the satisfaction in the hard set of her lips. She knew. She had planned this. By granting mercy when he least expected it, she had destroyed the Moor's soul.

His face ashen, Boabdil came to his feet. Burned earth clung to his knees.

The lords closed in around him, leading him away. I averted my eyes. I knew that if he'd been victorious he would not have hesitated to order the deaths of my father and my brother, of every noble and soldier on this field. He'd have enslaved my sisters and me, defamed and executed my mother. He and his kind had defiled Spain for too long. At last, our country was united under one throne, one church, one God. I should rejoice in his subjugation.

Yet what I most wanted to do was console him.

WE ENTERED GRANADA in resplendent procession, the battered crucifix sent by His Holiness to consecrate heretic mosques carried aloft before us, followed by the nobility and clergy.

Discordant wailing sundered the air. The Jewish warehouses were being impounded. Gorged with fragrant spices, yards of silk and velvet, and crates of medicinal herbs, the market represented Granada's true wealth, and my mother had ordered the wares secured against looting. Later, she would have them inventoried, tallied, and sold to replenish Castile's treasury.

Riding with my sisters and our ladies, I gazed in disbelief upon the ravaged city. Shattered buildings stood empty, seared by flame. Our catapults had leveled entire walls, and the stench of rotting flesh wafted from the mounds of broken stone. I saw an emaciated child standing motionless beside some dead rotting animal bound to a spit; as we passed, gaunt women knelt in the ruins. I met their impenetrable stares. I saw no hatred or fear, no remorse, as if the very life had been drained from them.

Then we started to ascend the road to the Alhambra—that legendary palace built by the Moors in their flush of glory. I couldn't resist rising in my saddle to peer through the gusts of dust kicked up by the horses, hoping to be the first to see its fabled walls.

Someone cried out.

Around me the women pulled their mounts to a halt. I looked about in bewilderment before returning my gaze to the road ahead.

I froze.

A high tower thrust into the sky like a mirage. On its parapet I could see a tiny group of figures, the wind snatching at their veils and flimsy wraps, light sparkling on the metallic threads woven through their gowns.

Behind me Doña Ana hissed, "Quick, cover the child's face. She must not see this."

I swiveled in my saddle to look at Catalina. My sister's eyes met mine in fearful confusion before one of the ladies pulled the veil over her face. I clenched at my reins, turning back around. A cry of warning hurtled up my throat as I saw, in paralyzing horror, the figures seeming to step out over the parapet, like birds about to take flight.

Around me, the ladies gasped in unison. The figures floated for an impossible moment in the air, weightless, shedding veils. Then they plummeted downward like stones.

I closed my eyes. I willed myself to breathe.

"See?" chortled Doña Ana. "Boabdil's harem. They refused to leave the palace. Now we know why. Those heathen whores will burn in hell for all eternity."

All eternity.

The words echoed in my head, a terrible punishment I could not imagine. Why had they done it? *How* could they have done it? I kept seeing those fragile forms in the pinpricked darkness behind my eyelids, and as we rode under the Alhambra's gateway, I did not point and laugh with the other women at the broken bodies strewn on the rocks below.

My parents, Juan, and Isabella swept ahead with the nobility. Maria, Catalina, and I remained behind with our women. Taking Catalina by the hand and hushing her anxious questions, for she knew something terrible had happened, I gazed at the citadel. With the afternoon light turning to vermilion on its tiled facade, it appeared blood-soaked, a place of death and destruction. And still I was overwhelmed by its exotic splendor.

The Alhambra was unlike any palace I'd ever seen. In Castile, royal residences doubled as fortresses, encircled by moats and enclosed by thick walls. The Moorish palace had the mountain gorge for protection, and so it sprawled like a lion on its plateau, sheltered by cypress and pine.

Doña Ana motioned to Maria; together with our ladies-in-waiting, we marched into the audience hall. With Catalina's hand still clutching mine, I took in everything at once, my heart beating fast as I began to see just how magnificent the Moor's world was.

An immense space of saffron and pearl opened before me. There were no scarred doors, no suffocating staircases or cramped passageways. Instead, carved archways welcomed me into rooms where honeycomb walls curved, and secret mosaic terraces could be glimpsed. Glazed porcelain vases held vigil under smoke-darkened hangings of every imaginable hue; quilted pillows and divans were strewn about as if their occupants had just retired. I looked down at my feet to a scarf coiled on the tiled floor. I feared to touch it, thinking it might have been dropped by one of the concubines on her doomed race to the tower.

I had dwelled in ignorance. No one had told me the heretic could create something so beautiful. I gazed up to an inverted cupola. About its perimeter, the painted faces of dead caliphs stared at me with laconic reproach. I swayed where I stood, overcome. I now understood why the concubines had chosen death. Like Boabdil, they could not bear to live without this Eden that had been their home.

The scent of musk crept past me. I heard water everywhere, a constant murmur as it flowed through rivulets carved in the marble floors, emptying into alabaster pools, set to dance in the patio fountains.

I paused. A sigh shifted through the pilasters, stirring the hair of my nape. Catalina whispered, "*Hermana*, what is it? What do you hear?"

I shook my head. I could not explain.

Who would have believed me if I said I could hear the Moor's lament?

TWO

. . .

For three magical years, Granada became our haven from the grueling pace of the court. With the end of the Reconquest, my mother turned her focus to strengthening Spain and forging alliances with other sovereigns. Travel still took up the majority of her annual schedule, but she deemed it best if we had a permanent household in the summer months, far from the pestilence and heat that plagued Castile.

My sister Catalina's betrothal to Henry VII of England's eldest son was celebrated the year after Granada's fall, reminding me that I too had been promised in my childhood to the Habsburg emperor's son, Philip of Flanders. I was not unduly concerned. The only one of my sisters to actually wed was Isabella, and several betrothals were mentioned for her before she went to Portugal and returned a widow less than a year later. I knew few princesses had a say in their destiny, but I didn't care to brood on a future that seemed distant and prone to change.

In Granada my world was full of youthful promise. After our daily lessons of history, mathematics, languages, music, and dance, my sisters and I often went to the lovely terraced patio at the edge of the gardens, where we practiced the ageless pastime of royal women: embroidery. Ours was a special task, however, for our simple cloths would be blessed and sent to adorn church altars throughout Spain as gifts from the infantas.

I loathed sewing. I had an impatient nature, and as I approached my sixteenth year I found it almost impossible to sit still for any length of time. My altar cloths were fit only for washing the church floor, riddled as they were with botched patterns and snarled threads. I usually pretended to embroider, while keeping close watch over Doña Ana, anticipating the time of my escape.

The duenna sat under the colonnade, a tome in her hands, from which she read aloud the passion of some martyred saint. It was never long before her head began to bob on her squat neck, her eyelids fluttering as she fought in vain against torpor.

When her eyes finally closed, I allowed a few more minutes to pass. Then I set aside my embroidery, slid my slippers from my feet, and inched up from my stool.

Maria and Isabella sat exchanging confidences. As I tiptoed past them, slippers in hand, Isabella hissed, "Juana, where do you think you're going?"

I ignored her, motioning to Catalina. My little sister leapt up, her embroidery falling unheeded to the ground. With a smile, I said, "Come, *pequeñita*. I've something to show you."

"Is it a surprise?" Catalina eagerly kicked off her slippers. She stopped, clapped a hand to her mouth, and glanced at Doña Ana. The duenna slumbered, oblivious. It would take an elephant's approach to wake her now, and I choked back a sudden giggle.

Naturally, Maria thought the world would come to an end if any of us deviated from our regimen. In a scandalized whisper she said, "Juana, you'll catch your death of cold running about barefoot. Sit down. You can't take Catalina into the gardens without a proper escort."

"Who says we don't have an escort?" I retorted, and I crooked my finger. From the terrace pillars behind us, a slight shadow uncoiled and approached.

She stood expectant, her hooded liquid-black eyes gleaming and curly hair the color of a raven's wing braided about her head. Though she wore a proper Castilian gown, the aura of cinnabar and jangling bracelets still clung to her. I smiled when I saw she too was barefoot.

Her name was Soraya. She had been found hiding in the Alhambra's harem, and no one knew if she was a slave left behind when the concubines committed suicide or the daughter of one of the caliph's lesser wives. She'd begged for mercy in her Arabic tongue and readily converted; no more than thirteen years old, it mattered little to her which god she venerated as long as she lived. I implored my father to let her serve me as a handmaiden and he agreed, despite my mother's objections. She never strayed far from my side, sleeping at the foot of my bed on a cot and padding behind me like a cat by day. I spent hours teaching her Spanish and she learned quickly, but more often than not she preferred to keep her silence. She had been baptized with the ubiquitous Christian name of Maria; she never responded to it, though, and so we all came to accept the name she'd come with.

I adored her.

"That heretic slave?" My sister Isabella now hissed. "She is not a proper escort!"

I tossed my head, clasped Catalina and Soraya by the hands, and crept off into the gardens.

Stifling laughter, we stole into a rose bower that had once been the caliphs' private retreat. Soraya knew the gardens like the palm of her hand: she had taken me here countless times on forbidden excursions and she knew where I wanted to go. Dusk had started to envelop the sky in a violet swirl. She made an urgent gesture; I dashed forward, nearly tugging Catalina off her feet. "Hurry! Soraya says we must get there before night falls."

I yanked Catalina forth, Soraya loping ahead. My sister gasped, "Juana, slow down. I can't run as fast as you two." She came to a stubborn halt. "My feet hurt." Dropping her slippers, she shoved her grass-stained feet back into them. "You tore your skirt when we went through those bushes," she added. "It's the third skirt you've ruined this week. Doña Ana will be furious."

I glanced at the tear. I could care less about Doña Ana's anger. We had reached the lower gardens; ahead a crumbling wall bordered the gorge's deep chasm. In the distance loomed the Sacromonte hills, pockmarked with caves. Soraya stood by the wall. She pointed upward.

I lifted my eyes to the amethyst sky. "Look!" A lone shape flittered above us. It was followed by another, then another and another, until myriad creatures weaved a leathery lattice, crisscrossing without touching, the swift beating of their wings invisible to the eye.

A shiver went through me. I knew they wouldn't harm us, but I couldn't help but feel some fear, though I had come to see them several times before.

Catalina pressed close to me. "What . . . what are they?"

"What I wanted to show you. Those, *pequeñita,* are bats."

"But—but bats are evil! Doña Ana says they nest in our hair."

"Nonsense. They're just animals." I could not look away, transfixed by their stealth, wishing suddenly that I too could soar through the air like that, dusk on my skin.

"Watch closely. See how they pass over us without a sound? Though it will soon be dark, they never lose their way." I glanced at Catalina. She was pale. I sighed, dropped to one knee. "I too was frightened the first time I saw them. But they ignored me as if I didn't exist." I gave her a reassuring smile. "You mustn't be afraid. Bats eat fruit, not people."

"How do you know?" she quavered.

"Because I've watched them before; I've seen them feed. Watch this." From my gown pocket I withdrew a pomegranate. I bit hard into its tough outer skin, exposing glistening ruby seeds. Digging the seeds out, I tossed them up into the air a short distance away.

A bat swooped down to catch the falling seeds. Catalina went wide-eyed as I took her by the hand and we crept forth, staring in awe at the wondrously hideous animal, its tiny body furred like a rat's and its leathery wings surprisingly agile. Soon, there were several more above us, so close we could feel them slice the air above our heads. They dipped close to the ground where the seeds had scattered, as if in a swoon of indecision, and I was about to throw out more seeds with my red-stained hands when I felt Catalina's hand tighten in mine.

"No," she whispered. "Don't."

"But they won't hurt you. I promise. You mustn't be afraid."

"I . . . I'm not. I just don't you want you to."

I longed to lure more of the creatures. I'd been experimenting with the seeds; I hadn't thought I could actually attract them. Yet even as I debated, the bats flew upward in a squall. Catalina and I squealed and leapt back, covering our heads. As they joined their companions in their strange aerial dance, I saw Soraya smile and I laughed.

Catalina glared. "You *were* scared! You thought they would hurt us."

I nodded. "I was. I guess I'm not so brave, after all."

The last drop of sunlight faded. The bats flitted to and fro, drawn to the moisture from the Alhambra's many fountains. Usually they stayed aloft until night had fallen, then veered in a cloud to the orchards spilling over the countryside, where ripe crops beckoned.

Not tonight. Observing their erratic pattern, they seemed restless, uncertain of their destination. Had our presence agitated them?

"Maybe they're not as indifferent to us as I'd thought," I said aloud. Catalina looked at me. Above us, the bats scattered like leaves dispersed by a sudden wind.

Disappointed, I turned to the palace. Soraya slid next to me, tugged at my sleeve. I followed her gaze to where the streak of flaming torches carried by slaves raced toward the keep.

"*La reina,*" Soraya whispered. "*La reina su madre está aquí.*"

I gave Catalina an uneasy smile. "We should go back now. Mamá is here."

The moment we returned, Doña Ana cried: "Where have you been? Her Majesty has arrived!" Grabbing Catalina by the hand and glowering at me she motioned Soraya back to our quarters and hustled us through the corridors to the Hall of Ambassadors.

Isabella and Maria were already there. Avoiding Isabella's pointed stare, I went to stand beside Maria. She said, "Doña Ana was beside herself. Why must you aggravate her so?"

I didn't answer, intent on the courtiers filing in from the keep, scanning their ranks for my father. My heart sank when I failed to find him. My mother had come to Granada alone.

I flinched when Archbishop Cisneros entered the hall, his Franciscan habit flaring about his skeletal bare feet in their leather sandals. He was Castile's most powerful ecclesiastic, head of the See of Toledo and our new inquisitor general; a protégé of Torquemada's, Cisneros, it was said, had walked all the way from Segovia to Seville in those sandals to thank God for our deliverance from the Moor.

I believed it. He had devoted himself with singular focus to the eradication of heresy from Spain, ordering all Jews and Moors to either convert or leave on pain of death. Many had chosen to flee rather than live under the threat of his spies and informants, dedicated to hunting out those *conversos* who continued to secretly practice their proscribed faith. My mother had had to put a rein on his tactics when he tried to investigate members of her household, several of whom had Jewish ancestry, but he'd still ordered the mass burning of more than a hundred heretics in a single *auto da fé,* a horrifying death for any living being, regardless of his faith. To me, he smelled of sulfur, and I was relieved when he passed without a glance, stalking into an antechamber.

Moments later, my mother emerged.

She moved through the bowing courtiers, the frontlets of her linen hood tied under her chin. She'd grown stout since the Reconquest and favored simple apparel, though today she wore her favorite sapphire jewel depicting the bundled arrows and yoke of her and my father's emblem.

We curtsied to the floor. She said, "Rise, *hijas.* Let me see you."

I remembered to keep my spine erect and eyes lowered.

"Isabella," my mother remarked, "you look pale. A little less prayer might do you good." She moved on to Catalina, who couldn't repress a spontaneous "Mamá!" followed by a flush when the queen rebuked, "Catalina, remember your manners."

Then, with Cisneros behind her, she stepped before me.

I felt her displeasure fall upon me like an anvil. "Juana, have you forgotten the order of precedence? As my third eldest, in the absence of your brother, you should be beside Isabella."

I raised my eyes. "Forgive me, Mamá—I mean, *Su Majestad.* I . . . I was late." As I spoke, I sought to hide my pomegranate-stained hands behind my back.

My mother's lips pursed. "So I see. We shall speak later." She stepped back, encompassing us with her next words. "I am pleased to be with my daughters again. You may now go to vespers and your supper. I'll visit with each of you once I've attended to my affairs."

We curtsied again and traversed the hall, the court bowing low as we passed. Before we left, I braved an anxious glance over my shoulder.

My mother had turned away.

I WAS SUMMONED after supper. I went with Soraya, and as I waited on a stool in the antechamber to the queen's apartments, she went to settle on a cushion in the corner with languid grace. Whenever she could, she opted for the floor instead of chairs.

I watched the trembling light cast by the oil lamps onto the intricate honeycomb ceiling, my hands plucking my skirts. Soraya had helped me squeeze into one of my stiff formal gowns, which seemed to have shrunk since I last wore it, the bodice straining across the swell of my breasts and the hem barely grazing my ankles. I'd shed my first blood in my thirteenth year and since then it was as if my body had developed a will of its own, my legs sprouting like a foal's and a fine reddish down materializing in places Doña Ana forbade me to touch. Soraya had coiled my hair in a beaded net and I scrubbed my face until my cheeks felt raw, trying in vain to get rid of the smattering of freckles that betrayed my frequent forays outside without a coif.

All the while, I wondered what awaited me. My mother rarely came to Granada this early in the year. That she was here in mid-June must mean something was amiss. I tried to reassure myself it couldn't have anything to do with me; I couldn't think of anything I had done wrong save for my occasional escapes into the gardens, which could only be a minor transgression. Still, I worried, as I always did when faced with my mother.

The queen's longtime friend and favorite lady, the Marquise de Moya, appeared at the entrance. She gave me a reassuring smile. "*Princesa,* Her Majesty will see you now."

The marquise had always been kind to me; she would have warned me if I faced censure. I walked with renewed confidence into my mother's apartments, where her other women paused in their unpacking of coffers to curtsy. When I came before her bedchamber door, I stopped. I could not enter without her spoken leave.

Her chamber was small, illumined by braziers and candelabra. A large window at the far wall overlooked the valley. Books and papers sat piled on the desk. The tarnished and chipped silver sword of the Reconquest, which my mother had had carried before her at every battle, hung prominently on the wall. Her bed was nestled in a corner, half-hidden by a carved sandalwood screen. In keeping with her personal asceticism, the marble floors were bare.

I knelt on the threshold. "I beg permission to enter Your Majesty's presence."

My mother emerged from the shadows by her desk. "You have my leave. Enter and close the door."

I could not see her face. Pausing at the appropriate distance, I curtsied again.

"You can come closer," she said dryly.

I stepped forward, wondering (as I had for as long as I could remember) if she liked what she saw. Though I stood almost a hand taller than her, I still felt like a little girl hoping for praise.

She moved into the light cast by the candles. My trepidation must have shown, for she said, "What do you see, *hija*, that you must stare at me thus?"

I immediately lowered my eyes.

"I wish you'd cease that habit. Since you were a babe, you've always stared at everything as if it were on display for your inspection." She motioned at the stool by her desk. Once I had sat, she regarded me again in silence. "Do you know why I've called for you?"

"No, Mamá," I said, in sudden dread.

"It should be to chastise you. Doña Ana informed me that you left your sisters and sewing this afternoon to take Catalina into the gardens. I understand you often disappear like that, without word or leave. What is the meaning of these excursions?"

Her question took me aback; she rarely expressed interest in my private thoughts. I said quietly, "I like to be alone sometimes, so I can observe things."

She took her seat on her upholstered chair before the desk. "What on earth could be so fascinating that you must be alone to observe it?"

I couldn't tell her about the bats. She'd never understand. "Nothing in particular," I said. "I like my solitude, is all. I'm always surrounded by servants and tutors and Doña Ana nagging at me."

"Juana, their duty is to guide you." She leaned to me, her voice firm. "When will you realize you cannot do as you please? First, it was your fascination with everything Moorish. You even insisted on having that slave girl serve you, and now this odd penchant for solitude. Surely, you must have a reason for such unusual behavior."

My shoulders tensed. "I don't think it's so unusual."

"Oh?" She arched her brow. "You are sixteen years old. When I was

your age, I was fighting for Castile. I didn't have time or inclination to indulge in pastimes that perturbed my elders. Nor, I should think, do you.
Doña Ana says you are rebellious and willful, and dispute her every
word. This is not the behavior of an infanta of the House of Trastámara.
You are a descendant of kings. You must behave according to your rank."

Her reprimand wasn't unfamiliar and still it stung, as she knew it
would. How could I compare my thus far insignificant life with her monumental achievements? Satisfied with my silence, she pulled a candle close,
opened a portfolio, and removed a sheet of vellum.

"This letter is for you."

I had to stop myself from snatching it out of her hand. "Is it from
Papá? Is he coming to visit us? Will he bring Juan with him?"

I regretted my words the moment they were uttered. Her voice tightened. "Your father and brother are still in Aragón. This letter is from the
archduke Philip." She handed it to me. "Pray, read it aloud. It's in French,
a language I prefer not to speak."

Had she come all this way to bring me another boring letter from the
Habsburg court? I began to feel relieved when it occurred to me that if
she'd come to Granada just for this, it must be important. In sudden concern, I studied the vellum in my hand. It was expensive, a supple skin
scraped and softened to the consistency of paper. Otherwise, it seemed
much like the other, periodic letters that had come over the years, until I
noticed sentences scratched out, denoting a clumsy hand with the quill. I
glanced at the signature: A scrolling *P*, stamped by the Habsburg eagle
insignia. This must be a letter from Philip himself.

"I am waiting," my mother said.

I started to read, translating the words into Spanish: "'I have received
the letter Your Highness lately sent to me, from which I perceive your affection. I assure you that your noble words could not be sweeter to any
man's ears, nor your promise more gratifying—'" I frowned. "What letter does he speak of? I've never written to him."

"No," she said. "I have. Go on."

I returned to the letter. "'More gratifying to one who shares your devotion. I must tell you what earnest love I feel knowing I shall soon see
Your Highness. I pray that your arrival here, and my sister Margaret's departure for Spain, may thus be hastened, so that the love between us and

our countries can be fulfilled.'" I looked up in sudden comprehension. "He . . . he speaks of marriage."

My mother reclined in her chair. "He does. It is time you go to Flanders to wed Philip and for his sister Margaret to come here as a bride for your brother." She paused. "Is that all he says?"

I found it difficult to breathe. The letter swam before my eyes. "There's a postscript here from someone named Besançon. He advises me to learn French, as it is the language spoken at the Flemish court."

"Besançon." My mother grimaced. "He may be Flanders's premier archbishop, but he is too French in his manner by far, though he knows how we feel about that nation of wolves." Her gaze turned distant. "No matter. France will be put in its place soon enough. That realm has bedeviled us for years, encroaching on Aragón and threatening your father's right to Naples. It's time we put an end to their effrontery."

A taut smile crossed her lips. "The emperor Maximilian and I have agreed to forgo any dowries, what with the cost of transport these days, but upon his death his son, Philip, will inherit his empire, while his daughter, Margaret, will inherit several important territories in Burgundy. And once your sister Catalina weds the English heir, we shall become an even greater power, with familial ties across Europe, and France will never dare meddle in our affairs again."

I sat rooted to my stool. How could she speak of politics when my entire existence had just been overturned? She expected me to leave my home, my family, for an unknown land and husband, so she could strike at France? This couldn't be happening, not to me.

My voice shook. "But why me? What have I done to deserve this?"

She gave an arid chuckle. "You speak as if it were a punishment. This cannot come as a surprise; you know you've been promised to Philip since you were three." She fixed me with her stare. "I trust you haven't forgotten the importance of doing your duty for Spain?"

I heard the warning in her tone, and for the first time in my life I forgot it was not wise, or beneficial, to argue with Isabel of Castile. All I could think of in that moment was that she would never have abandoned Spain. How could she expect me to?

I lifted my eyes. "I haven't forgotten. But I do not wish to marry Philip of Habsburg."

I saw her hands tighten upon her chair's chiseled armrests. "May I ask why?"

"Because I . . . I don't love him. He is a stranger to me."

"Is that all? I didn't know your father when we first wed, yet that didn't stop me from doing my duty. Through our marriage, Spain was united under God. Our duty came first, but love soon followed. Those whom God has joined will always find love."

"But Papá is Spanish, from Aragón. You didn't have to leave."

"Few royal women can wed their countrymen. I was blessed with your father, yes, but many of Castile's nobles fought our marriage at first, as you well know. They didn't believe Fernando was worthy to be my consort. The *grandes* wanted me to wed one of them instead and seize Aragón for Castile, so they could add to their power. Indeed, they almost forced me to it. But God's will prevailed. He brought Fernando and me together so Aragón and Castile could join against the heretic, and now he unites you and Philip for Spain."

I bristled. "Papá *was* worthy. He was a prince and became Aragón's king, as well as your king consort. What is Flanders but a paltry duchy and Philip a mere archduke?"

"He may be an archduke, but he's also the emperor's heir. And while Flanders is a duchy, it's far from paltry. As part of the Habsburg Empire, it oversees the Low Countries and guards their borders against the French. Moreover, it is prosperous and peaceful. Why, Philip's subjects are so devoted to him they call him 'the Fair.' And he is only a year older than you. Any princess would be overjoyed to wed such a man."

"Then send him another," I retorted, before I could stop myself. "Maria isn't promised to anyone. She could replace me and he'd never know the difference. It's not as if we've met."

"Replace you?" She sat upright. "If I didn't know better, I'd almost think you defy me."

I flinched. "I . . . I don't mean to, Mamá. But if I must wed, I'd prefer a Spanish lord."

The clap of her ringed hands on the chair rang out. "Enough! A Spanish lord, indeed. As if I'd ever give a daughter of mine to one of those vultures who call themselves *grandes*! They ruined Spain with their avarice and ambition; were it not for me, they'd still have us in chaos while they stuff their purses with Moorish gold. Have you not heard a word I've said? You will be a Habsburg empress. I have chosen you for this great task."

I should have been scared; I should have realized I had lost this battle. Instead, in a steely voice I hardly recognized I said, "I never asked for it."

She stood with an angry exhalation and paced to the window. The seconds passed like years. When she finally spoke, her voice cut through me. "You will do as you are told. Flanders is a respectable kingdom, which Philip has ruled since childhood. His lineage is impeccable, and his court renowned for its culture. I assure you, you'll find yourself right at home."

Tears burned behind my eyes. I saw my childhood vanishing before me like an illusion, my carefree afternoon in the gardens the last I'd ever enjoy again. I didn't care about Philip's reputation or his court. Nothing he had could ever equal the beauty of Spain.

A chasm opened inside me. "Mamá, please. Must I do this?"

She turned about. "The Cortes has given its consent, and the betrothal documents are signed. I cannot disregard the welfare of Castile because you wish it so."

The room keeled about me. I barely heard her as she returned to her desk. "You'll not go to Flanders alone. Doña Ana shall go with you as your head matron, and you'll have a household to attend you. And Philip will of course see to your well-being, as a good husband should. You will see these fears of yours are but the nerves of a new bride. We've all felt them in our time."

My entourage had been selected; she'd even determined how my husband would treat me. In that moment, I saw Boabdil as he kneeled in the charred earth before her.

I bit back a hot surge of tears. I would not grovel. "When?" I asked. "When must I go?"

"Not for a year at least, though we've much to do." Her tone turned brisk. "I know how advanced you are in your studies, yet seeing as you've little occasion to practice your French, I will find an experienced tutor to assist you. You must also continue to perfect your music and dance. It seems the Flemish value such skills."

There it was: my future laid out with the precision she'd shown in her battle against the Moors. I was but another soldier in her army, another cannon in her arsenal.

In that moment I hated her.

She inked her quill, drew her stack of papers close. "Now I've work to attend to. Tomorrow, after your lessons, we'll compose your reply to Philip. Give me a kiss and go say your prayers."

Tomorrow seemed a lifetime away. I could not feel my legs yet somehow I managed to graze her cheek with my lips, curtsy, and walk to the door. When I reached it, I paused with my hand on the latch. I thought she would relent, call me back, because she couldn't let me leave like this.

But she was already bent over her dispatches.

I walked out, past the women into the passageway, the letter gripped in my fingers. Soraya rose from her crouch with a questioning look. I couldn't return to my chambers. My sisters would be awake and waiting. They'd not let me alone until they pried the news from me and then—oh God, then I'd start bawling like a child, like an idiot, like Isabella in her endless grief! I couldn't face them. Not yet. I needed time alone, somewhere private to vent my rage and sorrow.

I yanked up my skirts and began to run, narrowly avoiding startled sentries and slave girls, who dropped into hasty curtsies, spilling baskets of sun-dried linens. I fled as if pursued, running and running until I burst, breathless, into an open courtyard, Soraya close behind.

The scent of jasmine washed over me. Above, a sickle moon hung suspended in a dazzling spangled night. I heard water spill from the stone lions ringing the fountain; my feet soaked in the waterways as I slowly turned about to stare at the Alhambra's curving arches, the intricate pediments and sculpted marble.

The silence was a presence. Everything had changed. This world I loved so much, it would not mourn me. It would not even feel my absence. It would continue on, agelessly indifferent in its beauty, its walls absorbing the echoes of its departed.

I felt Soraya at my side. As her hand enfolded mine, I let my tears fall in furious silence.

THREE

...

We departed Granada for Castile in the evening, to avoid the worst of the heat. The trip would be tedious, with weeks of riding on our hard-backed mules; and as we took the winding mountain road downward into the valleys of Andalucia, I stared over my shoulder.

The Alhambra reclined on its hill, tinted amethyst in the dusk. Above its towers, the sky unfurled like violet cloth, spangled with spun-glass stars. A few peasants lined the road to wave at us; in the many farms dotting the landscape, dogs barked. It was like the end of any summer, as though we'd return again next year as always. Then we rode past the tumble of stones by the roadside where it was said Boabdil had taken his last look at Granada and wept.

Like him, I wondered if I would ever see my cherished palace again.

...

THREE WEEKS LATER, WE REACHED THE ARID PLATEAU OF CASTILE and the city of Toledo. Perched on its cragged hill above the river Tagus, Toledo caught the sunset as we approached—a beautiful tumble of white and ocher buildings crowned by the cathedral. I'd always liked the narrow winding streets and the smell of baking bread in the morning, the burst of sudden flowers glimpsed in a courtyard from behind cloister gates, and the glorious Mudejar archways engraved with the secrets of the vanquished Moor.

Now I saw it as a prison, where my future had been decided without me. Toledo was the official gathering place of the Castilian Cortes, that advisory council of lords and officials elected by each major city in Castile. My mother had curtailed the flagrant power of the Cortes from the anarchy prior her reign; however, she still had to appeal to this body to sanction taxes and other major expenditures, as well as royal unions and investiture of her succession.

These same Cortes had approved my betrothal.

As we rode up the steep road toward the Alcázar, I compressed my lips. I'd barely spoken the entire trip, and my ill temper only increased once I found myself within that old castle, a cavernous warren with walls that were always damp to the touch. After the oleander-dusted patios of the Alhambra, it felt suffocating, and to make matters worse, here my French lessons began in earnest, supervised by a humorless tutor who subjected me to interminable lectures and the painstaking daily recitation of vowels.

He drilled me four hours a day, his accent as sour as his breath. I took cold comfort in deliberately mutilating my verbs and watching him turn white with anger; until one afternoon as he droned on and I sat with hands clenched, I heard the clatter of hooves entering the bailey.

I ran to the narrow embrasure. I could scarcely see into the bailey, craning my face against the window slit to catch a glimpse of the arrivals.

"Mademoiselle," the tutor rapped. *"Asseyez-vous, s'il vous plaît!"*

I ignored him. When I spied the tethered stallions caparisoned in scarlet, I promptly flew from the classroom, leaving him standing there, aghast.

I dashed down the stone staircase. A group of Castilian nobles appeared ahead, making their way to the *sala mayor*, the great hall. I spun around, yanking at my cumbersome skirts, and made haste to the minstrel gallery. If only I could reach him before my mother did, convince him to—

I cursed under my breath when I espied courtiers already assembled in the hall. I could not go in now without an escort, and I crouched instead behind the screen concealing the gallery from the *sala*, to watch as the lords of my father's court strode in.

When I saw my father with them, I sighed in relief.

His red cloak was flung over his shoulders. The wool would smell as he did, of horse and wine, and his own sweat. Mud-spattered boots hugged legs thick with the muscles of a lifetime spent in the saddle. He wasn't tall, but he seemed to tower over all as he swept his cap from his head, revealing close-cropped dark hair. With cap in fist and one hand cocked at his hip, he surveyed the ranks of Castile with a grin before he bellowed: "Isabel, *mi amor*, I am home!"

I clapped a hand to my mouth. How the nobles hated it when he yelled like that! His trademark entrance, it conveyed his ebullient love for his wife and disdain for Castile's rigid protocol. To the *grandes* of my mother's court, it was yet another sign of his uncouth Aragonese blood, and their faces hardened accordingly.

I didn't need my mother's reminder that her Castilian lords did not approve of her husband. Aragón and Castile had been separate kingdoms and sometime foes until my parents wed. Though smaller in size, Aragón had its Mediterranean holdings and a fierce independence, while Castile held most of central Spain and was therefore the greater power. My parents' union had joined the kingdoms, though their marriage treaty stipulated Aragón could retain its own body of elected representatives, its Cortes, and right of succession. Upon my parents' deaths, my brother, Juan, would succeed as the first ruler of both kingdoms; his dynasty would ensure Spain never separated again. Until then, my father was king consort of Castile and king of Aragón in his own right and he never let anyone forget it. The Castilian nobles' dislike of him was only augmented by the fact that my mother had allowed him this concession.

Over the years, I'd heard other tales, not meant for my ears. That my father had an eye for women was evident; my mother had brought his illegitimate daughter, Joanna, to court and made his illegitimate son an archbishop. Yet such peccadilloes hardly mattered in a marriage that was the envy of all who beheld it. My mother never raised an objection and their reunions were always joyous occasions. Papá was a merry companion, who relished a bawdy joke, a good cup of *jérez*, and the company of his children, none of whom loved him more than I.

I peered through the screen. He'd removed his cloak and was conversing with my mother's trusted adviser, the emaciated Cisneros. His noblemen stood apart from the Castilians, testament to their mutual antipathy. Then my mother entered with my sisters. My father immediately left Cisneros to go to her. Her pale cheeks flushed as he leaned in. To me, it seemed as if there was no one else in the hall, no other lovers in the world. They walked hand in hand to the dais. A smile played on my father's face as the Castilians came to bow before them.

I melted against the screen. If only I could wed a man like my—

My mother's voice echoed into the *sala:* "And where, pray tell, is Juana?"

Quickly smoothing my rumpled skirts, I descended into the *sala.*

My father grinned as I approached. He'd shaved his beard and his face was bronzed from his travels, giving him the air of an adventurer. I didn't dare look at my mother. Coming to the foot of the dais, I curtsied. *"Su Majestad,* I am overjoyed to see you."

"Your Majesty!" he exclaimed. "What is this, *madrecita?* I don't care for ceremony from you."

"Fernando," chided my mother. "Stop calling her that. She is not your little mother." As she spoke, she motioned the nobles aside, leaving me on my knees. Then she said, "You may rise. I'll not spoil your father's return by asking you where you've been."

Papá chuckled. "She was probably bribing the stable boy for a stallion, so she can ride back to Granada and hide in the hills like a bandit. Anything not to wed the Habsburg, eh?"

I couldn't help but smile.

"She is impossible," declared my mother. "She is headstrong and too temperamental by far, and you, my lord husband, only encourage it, when you should set an example."

Papá laughed. "She's as you were at her age, my love. Can you fault her? A Spaniard to her core, she no more wants traffic with foreigners than you would."

I wanted to laugh aloud. Papá would help me. He'd put an end to this odious betrothal.

He held out his hand. "Come, let us walk alone." He winked at my mother; her frown eased. She beckoned my sisters. "We'll wait for you in the solar," she said, and with my father at my side, I went out into the bailey.

THE WHITE-HOT SUN scorched the cobblestones. I winced, searching my pocket for a ribbon to tie back my hair. My father reached out to coil the heavy mass in a knot at my nape. "I used to do that for my mother," he murmured. "She had hair like yours, thick as a mare's mane. It was her only vanity—after her love for me, of course."

I threw myself into his arms. "I've missed you so."

"I missed you too, *madrecita*." As I felt his callused fingers stroke my neck, I had to bite back the humiliating tears that were never far from my eyes these days.

I drew back. "I didn't see Juan in the hall. Did he not come with you?"

"I left him resting in Segovia, though you'll be happy to know that while in Aragón, he made quite an impression. He so astonished my Cortes with his erudition, they were rendered speechless, a rare event for them. But the trip back to Castile has tired him."

I nodded in painful understanding. Juan's health was a constant concern. In Castile, a woman could inherit the throne, as my mother had, but Aragón abided by the statutes of Salic Law, which prohibited female succession. Should, God forbid, Juan die before he wed and sired a male heir, Castile and Aragón could be torn apart once again.

My father shielded his brow with his hand. "By the saints, it's hot as Hades. Let's go into the shade before you break out in freckles. We can't have a spotted bride on our hands."

I turned away. He took my chin, brought my face back to his. "Are those tears I see?"

I wiped at my eyes. "It must be the dust," I muttered. "I hate this time of year in Castile. There are dust and bugs everywhere."

"Indeed," he remarked, and he steered me to a bench under the portcullis's shadow. Perched beside him, I was acutely aware of his strength, which he exuded, like a bull.

He cleared his throat. "I must speak of an important matter." He looked at me intently. He had a puckered scar on his temple, and the cast in his eye that I had inherited—only his was pronounced—made it look as if he were squinting. I thought him the most handsome man I'd seen, nonetheless, because when he looked at me, it was as if I was all he wanted to see.

"I know this union with the archduke has brought you no joy," he said. "Your mother tells me you were most upset, and spend all your free time wandering about like a lost soul."

I grimaced. "What free time? I scarcely have a minute to go to the privy, I'm so busy trying to learn my French and perfect my music and dance."

"So, is that where you were earlier, learning your French? Come now, will you not open your heart to me? You know I won't chastise you."

His words softened the defenses I'd hidden behind since learning of my betrothal. "I don't mean to be difficult," I said with a catch in my voice. "I realize how important this marriage is."

"But you'd rather wed a Spaniard, or so your mother says."

"Spain is home. I can't imagine leaving. And if I marry the archduke, I will have to leave."

He sighed. "As different as you and your mother are, you share this one thing: Isabel also loves Spain, with all her heart. Sometimes, I think, more than anything else on this earth."

Hearing an old pain in his voice, I said, "Then we are not so alike, for I love you more than anything else."

His smile revealed uneven teeth. "You live up to your name. Not only do you look like my mother, but you are loyal, just like her."

"Am I really?" I liked being compared to my namesake, the late queen. Though she died before my birth, her passion for Aragón and my father was renowned. It was said she'd connived to have him wed my mother years before my parents met, foreseeing they would share a greater destiny together than if they ruled apart.

"You are. To my mother, devotion to country was the most important thing in life. She told me, it's the only love that lasts." He patted my hand. "That is why if you don't want to wed the archduke, we'll not force you. No matter how important this marriage may be, I'll not abide it if it makes you unhappy."

I sat in silence, pondering his words. When I failed to feel the overwhelming relief I'd expected, I asked, "Mamá spoke of France threatening Aragón and our need to prove our power. Is that true?"

"Ah, *madrecita*, what does it matter? If you do not wish it, it's as good as over."

"But it does matter. It matters to me. I want to understand."

He rubbed his chin. "Very well. You know that while your mother and I are titular monarchs of Spain, my kingdom of Aragón has kept its independence. But in truth, we must remain united for the good of our country. We have your brother to ensure this, but it wasn't too long ago that Aragón and Castile were avowed foes and the *grandes* conspired against the Crown and Cortes."

I nodded. "Yes, I know. But then Mamá and you wed and made Spain strong."

"We did, but there are some who would love to see us fail, so they can return us to the days of lawlessness. We took liberties from the nobility; we reduced their holdings, and we made them swear fealty to us before their own interests. And yet we couldn't have succeeded without their support, and not a few of them would conspire with Lucifer himself behind our back to achieve our downfall. Plus, Aragón once lost its claim to Naples to Charles of France."

"But you won it back. Naples is yours now, by treaty."

"Lamentably, treaties are only as good as those who sign them. While in Aragón, I received word that my old enemy Charles is dead. He named his cousin Louis d'Orléans as his successor. Louis is a true Valois, without scruple or conscience. He despises my hold on Naples and has proclaimed he'll fight me for it. Any war he starts over Naples will be a war with Spain."

I flared at once. "If he declares war, then we'll defeat him as we did the Moors!"

"Unfortunately, it's not that easy. Naples is the gateway to the African trade routes. It's far away and Louis knows we can't afford to wage war on two fronts without emptying our coffers and exposing Aragón to a French attack. Remember, Aragón shares a border with France and Italy. Louis can march his armies straight through my kingdom. And as soon as he's crowned, I fear he'll do just that. He'll make us divide our resources and we haven't the money or the men."

I clenched my fists at the image of the French swarming into my father's kingdom, as they had since time immemorial, implacable in their hunger for spoil and blood.

"It's quite simple, really," he went on. "Isabel and I expended our treasuries on the Moorish crusade, and both our Cortes refuse to sanction further taxes. They do have that right: they are the voice of the common people and unlike other rulers in Europe, we rule by their consent. Spain has given us all she has, and wars cost money, lots of it. Hence, the Habsburg marriages."

I frowned. "The Habsburgs will give us money to fight the French?"

"Not money. Security. Through the marriages, we'll be allied to them. Trust me when I say Louis will think twice about declaring against me if he thinks the Habsburgs will turn on him. The emperor is canny: he's a friend of everyone and confident of no one. For now, he sees the advantage in Spain, but should Louis convince him to join the French cause instead, together he and the Habsburgs could bring us no end of trouble."

I considered this. Unlike my sisters, who rarely looked beyond their apartment doors, I'd always had an ear for the goings-on at court. I'd often overheard nobles discussing the fact that while rich in land, Spain's treasury never overflowed, its deficit increased by the demands of the Reconquest.

"What about Admiral Colón's colonies?" I asked. "Isn't there gold to be had there?"

"That charlatan?" He blew air out of the side of his mouth. "A New World, he calls it, when all he's found is a parcel of mosquito-ridden isles. He may have earned himself a title for discovering land beyond the Ocean Sea, but whether there's any gold there remains to be seen."

I marveled at this disparity in my parents' characters. To my mother, Cristobal Colón's New World represented thousands of heathen souls awaiting the word of God; to my father, it was but an inordinate expense, better directed to the defense of Spain.

"Don't tell your mother I said that," he added with a wink, as if he'd read my thoughts. "She'd have my head. She's convinced one day Colón will discover a city paved in gold, filled with savages clamoring for Cisneros and his pyres."

As my laughter pealed out, I felt my cares lift from me for the first time in weeks.

"There," he said. "That is how I like to see you. You must laugh often, my daughter. It is good for the soul." He paused. "Do you now understand why the marriage is important?"

"I do. By marrying me to Philip, and Juan to his sister, the Habsburgs will lend us their power, and France will be forced to negotiate with us rather than simply declare war."

"Indeed. And who better to teach that Flemish archduke the way of the world than you?"

I had to contain my desire to please him. I'd hoped for release, and instead I now faced a difficult choice. "I'll do whatever I can to help Spain," I ventured.

"Yes, but you don't need to sacrifice yourself. We'll find you a Spanish husband instead and send—whom did you suggest? Ah, yes: we'll send your sister Maria. She's an infanta too, and as you told your mother, it's not as if Philip will know the difference."

"Maria!" I rolled my eyes. "She doesn't know the first thing about these matters. She'll try to soothe Philip with psalms and embroidery, and end up boring him to death."

He chuckled. "Am I to understand you could harbor a secret affection for our fair archduke?"

"Bah. He means nothing to me." I took my father's hand in mine. "But for Spain, Papá, I will do it. For Spain, I will marry him."

"*Madrecita,*" he murmured, and he kissed my lips. "You give me great pride this day."

WHEN WE ENTERED THE SOLAR, my mother glanced up from her chair. Isabella and Maria sewed nearby; at their feet, Catalina dangled yarns over the batting paws of a calico kitten.

My mother said, "There you are. Did you have a nice walk? Come join us, Juana. Your father hasn't had a chance to bathe or change his clothes yet. Let us leave him to his squire. We'll dine together later in my rooms as a family, yes?"

I nodded and went to a chair. Picking up my embroidery hoop, I began to thread my needle when Isabella bent to me and hissed, "Well? Are you going to marry him or not?"

"Yes, I am," I hissed back. "And I don't want to hear another word about it till my wedding."

FOUR

...

The bells of Valladolid clanged in unison, echoing into the brooding sky and ringing in my betrothal day. In my apartments in the *casa real*, I plucked at my white skirts, surrounded by ladies as I waited for my escort, the stalwart and handsome Don Fadriqué, admiral of Castile, who'd fought for my mother at her accession and been one of her most devoted supporters.

"I'm going to be late," I said, rising from my chair.

Doña Francisca de Ayala, one of my matrons of honor scheduled to travel with me to Flanders, replied, "His Excellency the admiral will be here soon enough, although if Your Highness doesn't sit still, the gown will be hopelessly wrinkled by then."

I curbed my retort. This wasn't a day to wield my temper. Today I was to be formally betrothed by proxy; joined by holy vows, at least on paper, to a man I had never met.

Philip was not here. My mother had informed me that a prince never fetched his bride, particularly as the royal wife—unless a sovereign queen—must live in her husband's country. All the same, I didn't like it. What kind of man did not attend his own betrothal ceremony?

I didn't dwell on it, however. I wanted to get through the ceremony without mishap. Turning from Doña Francisca, I beckoned to the young auburn-haired woman sitting on the window seat. "Beatriz, would you come loosen my stays? I feel like a trussed hen."

With a smile, Beatriz de Talavera came to me.

I'd taken to her the moment she was appointed to my service, the only one of my new attendants I felt any affinity toward. Younger than me by a year, Beatriz had a disposition that matched her lively looks, her dark eyes framed by curling lashes, her figure lithe and graceful. Born the niece of the Marquise de Moya, my mother's intimate head lady, Beatriz possessed all the requisite blood and skills of a royal lady-in-waiting, and a healthy wit most of these women lacked.

With nimble fingers, she loosened the stays. "Does that feel better, *mi princesa?*"

I leaned close. "It's not as if that fat old Flemish my husband sent as his proxy will care either way. Unless one happens to be a barrel of beer, he seems most oblivious."

Beatriz chuckled, turning me to the mirror. "Nevertheless, I vow the fat old Flemish has never seen a more beautiful bride."

I hadn't looked at myself yet, despite the hours others had spent primping and dressing me in my elaborate costume. Now I gazed in awe at my slim figure in its pearl-encrusted bodice, scalloped sleeves, and silver damask overskirt. About my throat I wore a large ruby given to me by my mother, one of the few jewels she hadn't sold or pawned to finance her wars. Yards of silvery veiling drifted from my coif; within this excess, my face shone pale as bone. To denote my virginity, my hair tumbled to my shoulders, a recent wash of ash and henna coloring it sinfully red.

"Blessed saints," I whispered. "I hardly recognize myself."

"Neither will the Flemish. He'll think the Virgin herself has descended from heaven."

"Then maybe if he thinks I'm the Virgin, he'll not make the same mistake our envoy did in Flanders during my brother's proxy wedding."

We giggled, recalling how the Spanish ambassador in Brussels had, during the symbolic laying of his bare leg over the archduchess Margaret, unfastened the wrong button of his hose and exposed himself to the Flemish court. The laughter helped ease my nerves, and I offered Doña Ana a smile when she bustled in moments later, plump as a partridge in her new velvets.

"His Excellency is coming down the corridor. Hurry, ladies, to your feet. Beatriz, cover the infanta's face with her veil and join the others."

Beatriz curtsied, though she couldn't stop her giggle when she saw me wink.

—

THE CEREMONY WAS interminable. As Archbishop Cisneros intoned High Mass, I felt myself collapsing before the altar like a cake in the sun, impaled by my finery, my headdress so heavy I marveled my spine didn't snap under its weight. As he escorted me here, the admiral had told me I looked lovely and I preened under his gentle gaze, steadfast manner, and lean, imposing height, which had set many a woman at court to sighs. But now all I felt was miserable and tired. All I wanted to do was take off these clothes and soak in a hot bath.

Beside me, the Flemish envoy's ale-saturated breath rasped. Incense billowed from the braziers, coalescing with the candle and votive smoke and the musk of nobles, courtiers, and envoys crammed into the pews. In their royal pew, my parents sat stiff as effigies.

Finally, Cisneros spoke the long-awaited vows. I choked back sudden laughter when the envoy repeated in his dreadful accent: "I, Philip of Habsburg, archduke of Burgundy and Flanders, take thee, Juana, infanta of Castile and the Indies, as my wife. . . ."

When my turn came, I reversed the ridiculous array of titles: "I, Juana, royal infanta of Castile and the Indies, take thee, Philip, archduke of Burgundy . . ."

Thus, with a few meaningless words, I was formally betrothed to the archduke Philip.

. . .

WINTER ROARED IN LIKE A BEAST. ICY STORMS TURNED THE SKIES black and coated the roads with frost, even as my mother traveled from one end of Castile to the other, dragging us with her.

She did not rest for a moment, nor did she allow me to. New duties were added to my already mind-numbing schedule, along with fittings for my trousseau and evening lectures on all the diplomatic issues I was expected to influence at Philip's court, the foremost of which was to never let him sign treaties with, negotiate with, or otherwise show any favor to France. Exactly how I was supposed to do this, my mother didn't explain, but it wouldn't have mattered if she had. Though I had resolved to do my duty, I still took to pummeling my pillows at night, loathing this marriage that seemed nothing more than a political stratagem.

Soon after the Feast of the Magi on January 6, word came that my maternal grandmother, the dowager queen, had fallen gravely ill. Defying the hellish weather, my mother rode straight to Avila in central Castile, accompanied by the Marquise de Moya and, to my surprise, by me.

I hadn't seen my grandmother since my early childhood; none of my siblings had. She had been twenty-three years old when her husband, my mother's father, King Juan, died, and had been obliged to retire from court, as befitted a widow. In the ensuing years, she succumbed to a grief-induced illness of the mind, eventually becoming so debilitated she could not travel or abide the presence of strangers. For forty-two years, she had dwelled in Arévalo; to me, it was as if she had died long ago. I did not understand my mother's explanation that as I would soon leave for Flanders, I had to bid my grandmother farewell. Surely if she was too ill to leave Arévalo she'd hardly remember a granddaughter she'd met once during a familial visit years ago. I certainly didn't recall much of her. I had only an obscure memory of distant eyes staring at me, and a spectral hand that reached out, ever so briefly, to caress my hair.

Peering through the snow-flecked wind, I caught sight of Arévalo like a lone bulwark on the plain, stark as the land surrounding it. The castle custodian and his portly wife hurried out to welcome us and hustle us into the *sala*. My mother went straight to consult with the physicians she'd sent ahead. Left alone, I accepted a goblet of warm cider and moved through the hall.

Woven rugs covered the plank floor, the furnishings of sturdy yew and oak. Wrought-iron candelabra illumined faded tapestries, their once-vibrant wools drained from years of light and dust. Though hardly luxurious by court standards, the castle seemed comfortable enough for one old woman and a handful of servants.

"I remember this hall well," the marquise said from behind me. "Her Majesty and I used to play here when we were girls, pretending we were captive damsels waiting to be rescued."

I'd forgotten that in their childhood, my mother and the marquise had lived in Arévalo with my grandmother. I could no more imagine my mother as a girl than I could the staid marquise, and I murmured, "It must have been lonely," for lack of anything else to say.

"Oh, it was," she replied. "Fortunately, Her Majesty and I had each other. We made up games, sewed together, and went riding. It was lovely in the summer, especially in fair weather, but the winter—brr! It was miserable, just like today. You could see your own breath."

A fire burned in the hearth, and braziers were scattered throughout the hall. Wrapped in my fleece-lined cloak, I didn't feel any chill, and yet a shiver went through me. I could imagine the night wind seeping through every window and wall crevice, whistling down the corridors like a phantom. What had my grandmother done during those long, bitter nights? Had she roamed the twisting passages with the wind, plagued by the penury and helplessness of a widowed queen? Or had she floated alone, forgotten, already caught up in her own inner labyrinth?

As if she could read my thoughts, the marquise said softly, "You mustn't fear. Her Grace the dowager is old and ill. She will do you no harm."

I frowned. "I do not fear—" I stopped when I saw my mother motion from the staircase.

"Your grandmother is upstairs," said the marquise. "You will meet with her there."

THE CHAMBER WAS DARK. Pausing on the threshold, I waited for my eyes to adjust while my mother strode in without pause, striking flint and lighting candles. A web of light flickered and spread. "Juana," she said, "come in and shut that door. I can feel a draft."

Steeling myself against an inexplicable thrill of fear, I stepped into the room.

In the interplay of shadow and light, I saw an old loom in the corner, a table and chairs, and a dilapidated throne. I'd expected a sickroom cluttered with medicine and the stench of illness, and I turned in relief to where my mother stood by the bed.

The moment lengthened. She stood in absolute silence, looking down at an almost indistinguishable figure under a mound of covers. Then I heard her say, "Mamá?"

It was a voice unlike any I'd heard from her before, little more than a sigh and laden with a profound sadness. Then she looked up at me, and with her hand beckoned me forward.

I moved to the bedside. I went still.

Only my grandmother's head and upper torso were visible, propped on pillows. Strands of colorless hair fell to a sunken chest without any visible breath. The bones of her face seemed etched under a waxen mold; her bruised eyelids closed. She looked so still, so insubstantial, I thought she must be dead. I forced myself to take a step closer. Something unheard, perhaps the brush of my fingers against the tester curtain or click of heel, awoke her. Eyes the hue of a frozen sea slowly opened, riveting me with their glassy stare. Her parched mouth moved, in a barely audible whisper: *"Eres mi alma."*

You are my soul.

"No," said my mother. "It's Juana, Mamá. It's your granddaughter." She added in a low voice to me, *"Hija,* come into the light. Let her see you."

I started around the bed, my nape crawling as my grandmother swiveled her head to me. I fought the urge to look away. I did not want to meet that probing gaze, did not want to see whatever horrors lurked there.

Then her frail voice reached me, as if from across an abyss. "Why are you afraid?"

I lifted my gaze. The pounding in my chest dissolved.

Never had I beheld such unspeakable anguish. In my grandmother's eyes I saw the toll of an eternal night, of a solitude that had ravaged without succor or release. Forced to suffer isolation no mortal being should endure, she now begged with her eyes for mercy, a swift end to an existence that had ceased to hold any meaning.

I dropped to my knees, fumbled under the furs. The hand I enclosed in mine felt brittle as a desiccated leaf. There were no more words. The dowager queen sighed. Her eyes closed in fitful sleep. After a long moment, I released her hand and stood. I turned to face my mother. She did not move, her face pallid, her chin lifted as if she were about to ride into battle.

"Why, Mamá?" I asked. "Why did you do this to her?"

"I did not do anything," she replied, but I heard the quaver in her voice, a gnawing edge I suspected had eaten at her for far longer than anyone suspected. "My mother was ill," she went on, too quickly, as if she sought to purge herself of a terrible burden. "She could no longer live in this world. I was only a child when she began having her first spells. Later, after I was queen, it became painfully clear she would never get well again. This was all I could do. This was the only place where she could be kept safe."

"Safe?" I echoed.

Quick anger flushed her tone. "Don't look at me like that. I assure you, no harm came to her. She had the services of her women and her custodians, a host of doctors, the entire castle to walk in, everything she could possibly want."

"Not everything. She was a queen once." I paused. "Wasn't she?"

My mother's eyes bore at me. I could almost smell her fear, her guilt. "I brought you to say goodbye, not to question. I told you, she was not harmed. Only once I'd been assured that her illness was beyond the remedy of any cure did I find myself forced to impose further restrictions. She . . . she could not be allowed out. She was not fit."

I clenched my fists at my sides. "Why did you bring me here? Why now?"

Her words came at me like vengeance. "So that you can see that I too have had to make sacrifices; that sometimes even a queen must act against her heart if she is to survive. I had no choice. I did it for Spain and for our blood. Think of what might have happened if the world had found out? I couldn't risk it. We had been through too much. My duty first was to protect Castile, above all else. Castile had to come first."

My throat closed on itself. She had done this. Isabel the queen had imposed this seclusion on Arévalo. It was simple, terrifyingly so. Her mother, the dowager, had become a hindrance. For the good of Spain, she had to be consigned to darkness, hidden away so no one would know that madness tainted our blood. What else was she capable of, this iron-hearted queen? What would she not do, not sacrifice, to safeguard her kingdom?

I bowed my head, unable to endure the terrible secret in my mother's eyes. "You should not have done it," I said. "She is our family, our flesh and blood. She belonged with us."

My mother gave a choked sound, almost a cry. "You dare judge me?

You do not know, you cannot know, the responsibility I faced, the enormous duty I had to shoulder on my own."

"Oh, but I do know, Mamá," I said quietly. "How could I ever forget?"

And I turned and walked from the room.

FIVE

. . .

I faced the windswept cauldron of Laredo Bay two months later. Sailors and deckhands rushed about on the galleon; the air throbbed with their cries, the rumble of coffers dragged to flatboats, and coarse voices lifted in command.

Behind me, my sisters and brother clustered together against the wind, regarding me in awe. I was the first of us to undertake such a trip, and at my mother's gesture, I turned and went to them. To my surprise, it was Isabella, newly betrothed to the Portuguese heir, who embraced me first. "I shall never see you again in this life, *hermana*," she whispered.

"Nonsense," I replied, even as her words moved through me. I drew back from her to allow Maria to kiss my cheek. "Be strong, Juana," she said, "as you always are."

Catalina was next. I saw at once that she was losing her struggle to contain her tears. One look at her brimming eyes, at the strands of gold escaping her cowl, and I held her close. "You must be brave when your time comes to go to England. Think of me, as I will of you, *mi pequeñita*."

Catalina clung to me until her governess, Doña Manuel, pried her away.

I curtsied before Juan. "May God keep you in good health, Your Highness."

"Will you be kind to Margaret when you see her?" he blurted, his face wan and eyes febrile from a recent attack of fever. "Will you be a friend to her until she comes to me?"

"I'll be like a sister to her and tell her she's the most fortunate woman in the world to have such a handsome husband-to-be."

"Oh, Juana, I am sad to see you go!" Juan embraced me. Against his frail body, I heard him say, "I will pray for you, my sister."

I set a hand briefly to his cheek before I turned to my father.

It was the moment I most dreaded. I feared it would cost me my last shred of painstaking composure and I resolved not to leave him with the memory of a tearful child. Yet as I saw him standing there by my mother, his cloak whipping about him and his face under its cap shadowed by his own hidden pain, I had a sudden vision of myself as a little girl, wrapping my arms about that strong body. All of a sudden, it hurt to breathe.

"Papá," I said. He swept me into his arms, enveloping me. "Be strong, *mi madrecita*. Be brave, as only you can be. Never let them think Spain doesn't rule in your heart."

"I will. I promise." I felt a vast emptiness when he drew back from me.

My mother stepped forth. "Come, Juana. I will see you to your ship."

AS THE SUN MELTED in a ball of scarlet fire into the horizon, my armada lumbered out to sea, propelled by vast billowing sails. The waters transformed from murky emerald to diamond azure; foam sprayed up against the prows as the ships plunged forward.

An algid wind tugged at my cloak. I did not move from my vigil on the deck, straining to keep the receding mountains in sight, even as night crept in, trailing shadows and mist. Soon Spain sank away into nothingness.

· · ·

THE TRIP TOOK THREE WEEKS LONGER THAN EXPECTED, AFTER A gale struck and separated my fleet. Exhausted by the close quarters, the lack of fresh food, and my women's ceaseless prayers for a safe arrival, on September 15 I gratefully set foot in Flanders.

A crowd waited to receive me, their resounding cheers scattering pigeons from rooftops. I waved as I rode through the town of Arnemuiden to a house prepared for me, where I fell into bed. I awoke the next morning to a headache, sore throat, and news that the carrack carrying my trousseau had scraped against a shoal and sunk. Everything, and everyone, aboard had been lost.

"What shall we do?" wailed Doña Ana. "All your gowns, your jewels, your slippers and headdresses: gone! You have nothing to wear for your meeting with the archduke."

I sneezed. Beatriz gave me a handkerchief. "Surely, there's something in my coffers," I said.

"Like what?" said Doña Ana. "You're not possibly thinking of one of those old wool gowns you insisted on bringing? They smell of dirt and smoke."

"They smell of Granada," I replied with an impatience born of too many hours on the sea with my duenna. "I also know we packed a red velvet and cloth of gold somewhere. Either should suffice. In the meantime, we'll just have to purchase some fabric to make new gowns. We're in Flanders, are we not? Cloth is this nation's trade."

"Your red velvet is inappropriate for travel, and the cloth of gold too extravagant. As for purchasing cloth, we're not merchants to debase ourselves thus."

By the Cross, she could be difficult! I sat up in bed. "If I need clothing, then we must pay for it." I paused. "And where in all this is the archduke?"

Tense silence ensued. Then Doña Ana said briskly, "You mustn't worry. His Highness the archduke has been apprised of our arrival and is—"

"Hunting," interjected Beatriz, with a wry smile. "When we failed to arrive as scheduled, he thought our departure had been delayed and he went to hunt boar. His sister, the archduchess Margaret, sent word while you slept. We are to proceed to Lierre, where she waits to receive us."

I stared at my lady for a moment before I pressed a hand to my lips in mirth. Here I was discussing my choice of raiment and my husband-to-be was off hunting! Not the most auspicious start to our union, I thought, even as I said, "Well, then it hardly matters what I wear, does it?"

Despite Doña Ana's protest, I chose one of my comfortable wool gowns, though I soon deduced the people of Flanders wouldn't have minded if I'd donned sackcloth. Lining the roads to Lierre, they cheered themselves hoarse and threw handfuls of flowers, clad in colorful costumes. Their sheer numbers astonished me, accustomed as I was to the vastness of Spain, where one could ride for days without encountering another soul.

Like its denizens, the land itself challenged my senses—a verdant monotony boasting nothing higher than a squat hill. There were no jagged mountains, no hilltops crowned by frowning stone castles or vast golden plains. Flanders looked like a garden bowl, green and inverted and soaking wet. There was water everywhere, a permanent presence sitting turgid in marshes, babbling in rivers, or flowing through canals; water dripping from the sky and water sloshing underfoot. Outside their picturesque hamlets, where it seemed even the dogs were well fed, luxuriant fields sprouted cabbages, legumes, and other vegetables, and gleaming livestock munched within grassy enclosures. Flanders teemed with abundance, a veritable heaven on earth, where it seemed no one had ever suffered war or famine or disease.

Flemish noblemen and their wives met my entourage halfway to Lierre. The women chattered nonstop, their low-cut gowns and hiked skirts revealing sturdy ankles in colored hose. By the time we rode into Lierre, Doña Ana sat rigid on her mule, her flinty expression indicating that, to her, Flanders was steeped in vice.

Built on the banks of the river Néthe, Lierre was dazzling, crowned by spires and crisscrossed with canals. Balconies were festooned with flower boxes and laundry; the cobblestone streets rang with the rattling of coins in velvet pouches as merchants went about their business. I stared in delight at street vendors peddling meat pies and sugary buns, and Beatriz laughed aloud when she spied market stalls piled high with bolts of brocade, velvet, tissues of every hue, satins, and fine-worked Brussels lace.

"It is paradise," she exclaimed.

"It is Babylon," snarled Doña Ana.

It is my new home, I thought, and I rode in a daze through gilded gates into the courtyard of the Habsburg palace of Berthout-Mechelen.

Philip's sister, Margaret, waited to greet me—a tall, rangy princess whose pronounced nose and equestrian jaw set off effervescent gray-blue eyes. After kissing me on the mouth as if we'd known each other our entire lives, Margaret led me through ostentatious passages into an antechamber hung entirely in blue satin. I could see a huge bed heaped with furs in the adjoining chamber. Venetian carpets covered the floor; a fire crackled in the marble hearth. In the corner stood a wood tub lined with sheets—for my toilette, explained Margaret.

"You do want to bathe, *oui*, after such a tiresome journey?" She did not seem to recall that as my brother's betrothed, she too would soon undertake the same voyage. Clapping her hands, she sent her women rushing at me.

I stood, stupefied, as the Flemish women stripped me of my clothing like a slave on the auction block. It took a few moments to locate my voice; when I did, my protest brought everyone to a halt. Margaret regarded me curiously as I clutched at my shift.

"I . . . I wish to bathe alone," I managed to say, in halting French, as Beatriz and my ladies came to flank me. Doña Ana and my other matrons stood frozen.

Margaret shrugged. "*Eh, bon.* I'll see to your supper." Kissing me again as if the matter were of no particular account, she swept out, her ladies chuckling behind her.

I gave a nervous laugh, hugging my arms about my chest. "They act like barbarians!"

Beatriz nodded. "Indeed. Her Majesty would be outraged."

"No doubt," I said, and I eyed the tub. "But I could use a bath. Come, help me."

To my matrons' horrified gasps I drew my shift over my head and tossed it aside. Doña Ana cried, "Absolutely not! I forbid it. That bath is not properly drawn. I can smell the perfume in the water from here. You'll smell like a heretic odalisque."

"Seeing as I smell more like a goat after weeks at sea, I hardly see the argument," I replied. Beatriz helped me into the tub. I reclined in the scented water. "*This* is paradise," I sighed, and Soraya slipped forth to massage my feet with aromatic oils she produced as if by magic from within her gown pockets.

Doña Ana glared, whirled about, and started barking orders at the other women, who were soon hauling in my surviving coffers, searching the contents for suitable garments.

My skin glowing, I was dressed in my crimson velvet with my mother's ruby about my throat. Against the blue room, I shone like flame. Doña Ana threw a veil over my head moments before Margaret and a group of nobles tromped in. Pushing in behind them were the men of my entourage, still clad in their soiled traveling gear, their expressions hard with anger that they'd not been offered so much as a room to rest in.

I resisted the urge to pull off the veil. Castilian tradition decreed only her husband could unveil a royal bride. I thought it absurd, echoing the Moors' habit of immuring their women, and I stood rigid as a sculpture when Margaret declared, "Such a lovely gown. And the ruby is gorgeous, my dear. May I present a few members of our court? They're most eager to pay their respects."

I nodded, starting slightly when the archduchess leaned to me and whispered, "All this ceremony is frightfully tedious, my dear, but they simply refuse to heed reason. We can only hope they'll make their speeches brief so you can sup in peace."

Not knowing what to say, I inclined my head as the archduchess introduced the nobles, as well as Margaret's former governess and matron, Madame de Halewin, a gaunt woman in jade silk. Most of the names flew from my head the moment they were uttered; I had an overall impression of well-fed sleekness and appraising eyes before a corpulent man in crimson robes strode into the room, his fleshy face beaming.

"His Eminence the archbishop of Besançon, Lord Chancellor," pronounced Margaret.

The Spanish company bowed in deference to the authority of the church. Besançon was the highest ecclesiastic in Flanders, his position equal to that of Cisneros in Spain. He was also the man whose postscript had displeased my mother. As I started to curtsy, he shot out a fat, ring-laden hand, detaining me.

"*Mais non,* madame. It is I who should bow to you." He did not bow, however; his head tilted at an angle before he turned his keen stare to Margaret and issued a curt babble of Flemish.

I looked in puzzlement at the archduchess. With a reddening of her cheeks, Margaret translated, "His Eminence wishes to know why Your Highness wears a veil."

"It is our custom," interjected Doña Ana, before I could reply. "In

Spain, a bride must remain hidden from all male eyes until she is wed by the church."

I spied the pinch in Besançon's mouth, belying his jocular smile. With a swift upsweep of my hand, I removed the offending cloth.

Silence fell. Then Besançon cried, *"Très belle!"* and as if on cue, the Flemish broke into applause. With a wave of his hand, the archbishop sent two pages speeding from the chamber. Doña Ana rumbled forth. "This is an outrage! How dare he disdain your privacy?"

"He did not disdain it," I said to her, through my teeth. "I did. I'll not have him question my suitability. And it seems I have pleased."

Doña Ana snapped, "He is no one to question! He's but a—"

The tromping of footsteps spun her around. While the Flemish grinned and the archduchess Margaret released a bray of laughter, the footsteps grew louder, coming closer and closer.

Besançon's pages ran back into the chamber and bowed to the floor.

A tall young man strode in.

He wore a leather jerkin fitted to his chest, his long legs encased in cordovan boots. As he whipped off his cap, he unleashed a wave of gold-auburn hair that fell to his shoulders. His prominent jaw, aquiline nose, and generous mouth were highlighted by close-set blue eyes that mirrored Margaret's, as did his unblemished white skin.

A slow smile curved his full lips.

I didn't need anyone to tell me who he was. There could be no doubt. This was the prince his subjects had dubbed Philip the Fair, and he was indeed that—the fairest man I'd seen, his beauty almost too perfect yet without a hint of femininity, like that of a bold young stag.

I felt a discomfiting sensation. He stood in the stunned silence with gloved hands on hips, studying me as if I were the only person in the room, his gaze intent on my face before it trailed to my breast, where it lingered, as if he espied my quickening pulse. It was an outrageous, brazen look, and yet to my confusion, I found it flattering. No man in Spain would ever dare look upon me, a woman of royal blood, like this. I knew I should retrieve my crumpled veil, but the candid approval in his gaze made my insides turn liquid warm.

Like his minister Besançon, Philip of Habsburg obviously liked what he saw.

"His Highness the archduke," said Archbishop Besançon with pompous redundancy, seeing as everyone had dropped into obeisance.

Philip yanked off his gauntlets and came to me. He seized my hand, raised it to his lips. His pungent scent teased my senses, a heady brew of sweat and horse, spiced with an unknown salty tang I had sometimes smelled on my father.

"Bienvenue, ma petite infanta," he said in a low voice. I glanced at the hand holding mine. He had lovely fingers, I thought in a haze, strong, tapered, without any visible scars. Those hands had probably never held anything more demanding than a hunting bow or sword.

I summoned a tremulous smile. Was this magnificent youth to be my husband? It seemed impossible. I'd prepared to tolerate him at best, disdain him at worst. I had anticipated a marriage without passion, an alliance of state for the good of Spain. I even thought I might hate him. I never for a moment imagined he might stir any sort of feeling in me. But this was unlike anything I had felt before, an inexplicable sensation like butterflies dancing in my veins.

I realized with a start that he waited for me to speak. I managed to murmur, "My lord honors me," and he gave a soft chuckle before turning to the assembly with an expansive smile. "I am delighted with my Spanish bride. We shall marry at once!"

His declaration rippled like catastrophe through my ranks. Doña Ana swayed as if she were about to swoon; the other matrons glowered. Even Beatriz looked discomfited. With a high-pitched laugh, Margaret said, "Brother dear, must you be so impatient? She has only just arrived here, after an exhausting voyage. Perhaps you might greet her entourage first?"

Philip waved his hand. "Yes, yes." He didn't relinquish his hold on me as the members of my household stepped to him. Pulling myself to attention, I introduced them by name, as Margaret had done for me. They filed past, followed by my matrons and ladies. I heard his boot tap, tap, tapping on the carpet. Not until the clergy's turn came did he display sudden interest.

"My professor of theology, the bishop of Jaén—"

"Bishop?" interrupted Philip. "As in, ordained by the church?"

The elderly bishop paused. "Yes, Your Highness. I am ordained."

"Splendid! Then you can marry us."

"I . . ." The bishop glanced at me. "Your Highness, I fear I cannot."

"Why not? Is there something wrong with your mouth, perhaps, that you can't recite a few vows?" Philip turned to me. "Is there something wrong with him, my sweet?"

There were flecks of white in the azure of his irises, like diamond shards. And he had the longest lashes I'd seen on a man, so fair they seemed spun of white gold.

"Well?" he said. Laughter rustled low in his throat. "Is there something wrong with him?"

I blurted, "No, my lord. But it's not fitting we should wed before—"

"Never mind that. Besançon!" The Flemish archbishop bustled forth. "Is there any reason the infanta and I should not wed here and now?"

Besançon chortled. "None. You need only repeat the vows in person to sanctify your union. Under canon law, Your Highnesses are already husband and wife."

Philip cupped my chin. "Can you think of any reason?"

Doña Ana cried, "By her honor, Her Highness must be wed by the church!"

He didn't glance at her. He stared at me as if he could compel me to his will, and quite to my disconcertion I found myself wanting to oblige. It was impulsive, scandalous even, for of course there were several reasons why we shouldn't wed like this, the primary one being that such events were supposed to be protracted affairs celebrated with pomp. Now, at the age of sixteen, I faced my first decision as a woman, independent of rank or protocol; and all of a sudden I thought that nothing about this marriage made any sense. I didn't know Philip and yet I'd been sent all this way to become his wife. Whether it happened today or next week, what could it matter?

"I see no reason, my lord," I finally said, and as Doña Ana groaned in dismay, I motioned to the bishop of Jaén. "My lord, if you wouldn't mind?"

He dared not refuse me. "A Bible," he quavered. "I must have a Bible."

Besançon produced the tome with premeditated haste. Glowering, my retinue knelt beside their Flemish counterparts. The archduchess Margaret joined the other ladies.

There in that antechamber, without incense or altar, I married Philip of Habsburg.

"May none tear asunder those whom God hath joined," concluded the bishop, and Philip bent to me and put his lips on mine. My first kiss; he tasted of wine. It wasn't unpleasant.

He drew back and with a triumphant grin said, "Now, to the feast!"

AS SOON AS WE entered the hall, I realized hours of advance preparation had been expended on this banquet.

Trestle tables stretched the hall's length to a canopied dais, where Philip and I took our seats. Musicians struck up a refrain. Servitors entered, carrying baked boars' heads stuffed with caramelized pears; winter peacocks sautéed in hippocras; glazed honeyed herons; haunches of cinnamon-roasted venison; and myriad unrecognizable dishes smothered in creamy sauces. I ventured an inquiring look at Philip, as each course was set before me. He recited the corresponding platter's name in French. I smiled, feigning understanding.

Throughout the feast, I couldn't help staring at him. I searched for but failed to find any arrogance beyond what was normal to his rank, none of the callousness or spoiled petulance I could expect from an heir to an empire. He was attentive, solicitous, as a well-bred prince should be. It wasn't until the desserts were finally served that he whispered, "You haven't recognized a thing you've eaten tonight, have you, *ma petite*?"

"No," I told him, "but I've had poultry before, my lord. I do know its taste."

"Do you?" He forked a piece of roast flesh from his silver plate and raised it to my lips. I glanced around, wishing we weren't so visible to the Flemish courtiers seated below us, several of whom were staring, smiling and nudging each other as if they knew something I did not.

I took the fork from him. "Delicious," I pronounced. "I believe it is quail, yes?"

He let out a hearty laugh. Then I felt his hand slip under the table to rest on my thigh. I went still. It took a moment for me to identify my fear.

He touched me as if I were a prized possession, a favorite hound or hawk.
I understood then that I was his now, to do with as he wished. I'd surrendered whatever little freedom I'd enjoyed as an infanta to become the
archduchess of Flanders, Philip of Habsburg's wife.

I regretted not having stood my ground earlier. I knew, of course,
what was expected of a bride on her wedding night, in general if not
specifics. I hadn't stopped to consider this was, in fact, *my* wedding night.
Was I prepared to give myself to a stranger? Unlike me, I doubted he was
a novice when it came to such matters. Men rarely were. I should have insisted we wait until a proper ceremony was arranged; I should have
pleaded exhaustion or another indisposition.

Yet even as I thought this, I knew I deluded myself. I had agreed because I had wanted to, because I had seen a challenge in him I could not
resist.

I reached for my goblet. Philip took up his at the same time. His gesture conveyed what he did not say, and so intense was the way he looked
at me that after we drank together Margaret leaned from her place at my
left side to whisper in my ear, "You mustn't worry, my dear. My brother
is like any man, but you'll have your cathedral wedding. My lord Besançon won't be deprived of the opportunity to show you to the people.
He considers our alliance with Spain his greatest achievement to date. Indeed, I'm surprised he hasn't sent me packing my coffers this very night,
so he can see me off all the quicker to your brother's bed."

I glanced past Philip at the archbishop. He nodded as Philip murmured to him but seemed more interested in his food, eating with his
hands like a serf. I thought there was something unpleasant about the
prelate but I was grateful for Margaret's reassurance. Perhaps now would
be the time to tell her about my brother and his many princely accomplishments.

Instead, I felt Philip take my hand and draw me to my feet. "Play a
bass dance," he called to the musicians as he led me to the floor. "A Flemish bass dance to celebrate my marriage."

His court yelled their approval, banging goblets on the tables, causing
cutlery and trenchers to jump. My entourages' brows arched even higher;
I could practically feel their stares boring into me. To them, my wedding

ceremony had been a farce. I shouldn't be here. I should be in virginal isolation with my women until I was wed by the church, with all the requisite trappings.

All thought of extolling Juan's virtues fled my mind. Surely, I couldn't dance with a man I'd just met, and whom, in my entourages' opinion, I had not yet officially wed?

As if he sensed my misgiving, Philip said, "Come, my infanta. Let us show them how Spain and Flanders can dance together."

He propelled me forward. As the drumbeats gathered force, I surrendered my inhibitions. I excelled at dancing, and the bass dance was one of my favorites, its fluid rhythm and intricate twists and bows requiring both stamina and grace. Philip too proved an excellent dancer, and I met his every move with ease, as if we'd danced together a hundred times before.

He whispered, "You are breathtaking," and my flush must have reached the roots of my hair when he disdained the courtly glance to kiss me instead on the mouth, quenching my breath. This time, it was more than pleasant. I felt his kiss down to the very tingling soles of my feet.

About us, the court turned boisterous. All of a sudden, the Flemish courtiers stood in an exuberant rush, sending platters crashing to the floor as they grabbed any available woman by the hand, including several of my ladies, and hauled them onto the floor. Within seconds, a mass of cavorting bodies surrounded us. Instinctively, I pressed closer against Philip, staring in disbelief as the Flemish whirled my horrified Spanish ladies about.

Philip chuckled. When I followed his gaze to where one of my women was fending off a drunken lout, I let out an unwitting, nervous laugh. I'd never beheld such unbridled enthusiasm before. Uncouth as they were, the Flemish certainly knew how to enjoy themselves.

Philip looked at me. His regard turned somber. "Your countrymen are not amused," he said, and my stomach sank when I saw the noblemen of my entourage, who'd come to accompany me here and bring Margaret back to Spain, stand in unison and march from the hall. "You must go now," Philip added. "I'd not be the cause of further reproach from that dragon duenna of yours."

He guided me through the crowd to where Doña Ana stood trembling with rage. My other women wrenched free of their uninvited partners to fence me in. My duenna gripped my arm. "It is time you retired, Your Highness," she said, in a tone that broached no argument. "Now."

I stared at her livid face and moved with my phalanx of women to the hall doors. As I walked out, I looked over my shoulder. Philip stood among his courtiers, his eyes fixed on me.

I knew it would take more than Doña Ana to keep him at bay.

...

SIX

The moment we reached my apartments, Doña Ana turned on me. "This is a disgrace! What would Her Majesty your mother think were she here to see this? She would most certainly tell you that a few vows in an antechamber do not a marriage make!"

At the mention of my mother, I went cold. "It was Her Majesty who sent me here. And the archduchess Margaret herself told me Besançon will hold this cathedral wedding you insist on."

"Hah! What does that French pig in his satin know? Did he not insist you remove your veil with no more ceremony than a pauper's daughter?" She wagged her finger at me, her jowls quivering. "I suppose you think it's perfectly acceptable for them to flaunt you like some trophy. You always did like to be the center of attention."

"By the Cross," I cried. My matrons gasped and genuflected. "Are you going to tell me there's something wrong with a simple dance between a wife and her husband?"

"He is not your husband! You were betrothed by proxy in Spain— betrothed, nothing more. By the law of God, what you wish to do with him tonight is a sin."

The matrons rustled, muttering. I said softly, "How do you know what I wish to do?"

"I can see it in you," she spat. "I see your wantonness. And as your matron, I forbid you to allow him into this chamber should he dare come to your door."

"You forbid me?" I met her hard stare. I took pleasure in her flinch, in wielding for once my own power over her after years of submitting to hers. "Careful, señora," I said. "I am no longer a child to be reprimanded by you."

"Would that you still were, for even as a child never did you dare go so far." Her face set like mortar. "If you let him come to you before the marriage is sanctified, I cannot be held responsible, nor can any of your ladies. We cannot serve you under such conditions."

I faltered. I'd never been without my ladies. All my life, they had been there to help me with the private tasks other women performed on their own.

I turned to my matrons. They looked away as if I'd been branded. "As you wish," I said quietly. "Those who disapprove should go." Even as I spoke, I wondered at my boldness. What would my mother say when she heard about this? Somehow the thought of defying her from across the sea gave me a small thrill.

My duenna drew herself to full height. "So be it." She stalked out, followed immediately by the matrons. I turned to find that only Beatriz and Soraya remained in the room.

Beatriz said, "We will not leave Your Highness on your wedding night."

I sighed in gratitude. "Please, help me undress."

I stood motionless as they replaced my finery with a linen bed gown that had surfaced unexpectedly in one of the coffers. Soraya went to prepare the bed. Beatriz draped a topaz silk robe about my shoulders. "I found this earlier while searching for your red gown," she said, and as I sat at the dressing table, she undid my braid and began brushing out my hair.

I stared unseeing into the polished glass. I had no doubt Philip would indeed come to me tonight and that I was about to take the final, irrevocable step into womanhood. It wasn't too late to change my mind. I could issue the order now, have the door bolted and have Beatriz send word that the day's events had exhausted me and I must rest.

I whispered, "Beatriz, do you think I am wed in the eyes of God?"

Beatriz paused in her brush strokes, met my gaze in the mirror. "Your Highness has nothing to be ashamed of. You are wed. It's just as well Doña Ana and that gaggle of crows aren't here to spoil your night. I vow they'd douse the lust of Lucifer himself."

I giggled. "You are incorrigible."

"I speak the truth as I see it. You are his wife, he is your husband, and that's the end of it." She leaned closer. "And providing you and the fair archduke do what comes natural to most married couples, you could be mother to a prince before the year is out."

I gasped, pinched her arm. Beatriz winked at me and turned to Soraya, who had paused with a pillow in her hands. "You! What are you doing standing there with your ears big as castles! Draw down those sheets. His Highness the archduke could be here at any moment and—"

She went still. I too paused as I heard a bawdy song echoing in the corridor. Beatriz started fussing over my hair again, running her hands over its fiery curls until I pushed her away. "I'm fine," I said, but I couldn't look in the glass anymore, my heart galloping in my chest as I stood.

A knock came at the door. Beatriz looked at me; I looked at her. Another knock came, louder this time. We didn't move. Four more bangs.

"Blessed Virgin, open it," I said, "before they bring it down."

Philip and three of his gentlemen stepped into the room, flushed from carousing, chemises open to their navels. As one of them made a playful grab at Soraya, Beatriz lunged. I stopped her, marched up to the fool, and slapped his hand away.

"What is the meaning of this intrusion?" I said, in a tone that would have made Doña Ana proud. They didn't seem to notice I was trembling under my robe.

The slim man who'd accosted Soraya leered. "It is Flemish custom to see the newlyweds put to bed, my pretty wench, unless you'd like us to christen it first."

The others roared. Had they actually forgotten whom it was they addressed? I looked at Philip. "My lord, your ways are not yet mine. I ask you to please send these lords away."

Philip nodded. "Of course. My lords, off with you."

The men moaned and tromped out. Beatriz started to move toward me when Philip said: "You and the girl too. I would be alone with my wife."

Beatriz curtsied, then took glowering Soraya by the arm and led her into the antechamber.

The door shut. In the slight draft, a candle by the bed went out.

Now that we were alone, he looked enormous, a giant with hands like platters. I was overwhelmed with longing for the chamber I'd shared with my sisters, for the susurration of their voices in the dark and quiet snores of our ladies on their pallet. What was I supposed to do? What did he *expect* me to do? I searched my mind for a nugget of useful advice among the stockpile imparted to me. I flashed on my mother. She always offered my father a goblet when he returned after an absence, and I said, somewhat breathlessly, "Would my lord care for wine?"

He gave a soft laugh. "I think I've had enough." His hand reached for me. "Come here."

I recoiled. My mouth went dry. His fingers caught at my wrist, tugging me to him. As he bent to me, I turned my head away. "My lord, please," I whispered. "I am afraid."

He paused. "You are afraid? I'd not have thought you capable of such an emotion, my fiery princess." As he spoke, his fingertips caressed the underside of my wrist. His touch was light as a feather tip and yet it felt like a thousand braziers lighting up inside me.

He was watching me intently. He smiled. "Ah, yes. You are not afraid. You are just unsure of yourself. But you can feel it, can't you, my sweet Juana? You can feel how much I desire you."

My heart sounded like horses galloping in my head. I drew a shallow breath, standing perfectly still as his other hand snaked to my waist and unbuckled my robe's jeweled clasp.

The robe slid from my shoulders, pliant as wings. *"Mon Dieu,"* he breathed, "you are more beautiful than I imagined." He lifted his eyes. "And me, my infanta? Do you find me beautiful?"

I couldn't speak a word, but as if he espied the answer in my silence his smile broadened and he began to tug at the tangled stays of his shirt.

A surge of unexpected confidence drove me to him. I pried his fingers aside, disentangled the knots, his breath hot on my brow as I peeled back the linen. His chest shone in the candlelight. I tentatively set my palms on him, marveling that skin so smooth could be so firm to the touch. He moaned. I watched his eyelids flutter and close. As abruptly as it appeared, my confidence vanished. I stepped back, flustered. What was I doing? He'd think me as wanton as Doña Ana had accused me of being.

His hand caught me again. "No. Don't stop. I promise, I will not hurt you."

He drew me to him, buried his hands in my hair and pulled it back from my temples. I felt his arousal press against my leg and I wanted to look, to see what made a man.

He brought my mouth to his. This time, his kiss was charged, demanding. I finally did what I had wanted to do from the moment I set eyes on him: my arms rose about his shoulders and I pressed my entire length against him, feeling him tug loose the stays of my bed gown.

Our bodies' innate language took over. I let my hands roam the planes of his torso with eager inexperience, finding the hidden places that made his skin twitch and him groan. He crushed me against him, raising the cloth of my gown up my body until it passed over me in a crumpled mist.

I stood before him. I'd never been naked in front of anyone save my women, but I wasn't ashamed. I knew I had a lovely body, my breasts high and firm, my waist slender and legs toned from years of riding. He confirmed this with his eyes, bowing his head to tease me with his mouth. I had never imagined such an intensity of pleasure. I threw back my head as he went lower, lower, rousing a hunger unlike any I had experienced.

In some distant part of my mind a warning clamored that this wasn't how it was supposed to be. I should be waiting for him in bed; he should blow out the candles, slip in beside me with his shirt still on. It was supposed to be brief, painful, then over. It should beget a child, not rouse such heat that it felt as though we might ignite and consume each other.

But now nothing could quell the desires he had awoken. When he grasped me by my waist and hoisted me up, I wrapped my legs about him with ferocity, our hips grinding in a primal dance. He whispered, scalding my thighs as he lowered me onto the bed.

He paused, his face in shadows. Watching. "Show me," he said, "show me everything."

I let out a sudden laugh, the audible release of my joy nearly as powerful as the euphoric sensation of lying naked under his gaze. Then I met his stare and reached to my thighs, parting my legs slowly, with a lasciviousness I hadn't known I possessed. He did not move at first. Then he undid his codpiece and untied his hose, removing his slashed breeches. His hose slipped to his groin, slid apart, and crumpled at his feet.

I had never seen anything so magnificent.

He was fashioned of sinew and muscle, his skin pure as white stone, his broad torso narrowing into lean hips, his sculpted thighs exalting his engorged sex.

"Do you like what you see, little infanta?" he asked, and I nodded, aching now.

He dropped onto the bed. His fingers were everywhere, probing with exquisite sophistication, kindling even more heat, until just as I began to shudder and I heard my own throaty gasps, he spooned my legs on his shoulders and thrust into me.

The pain was sharp, snagging my breath. I instinctually curved upward to meet his plunge. We melded together, our hands gripping, our mouths devouring, until his entire body arched to spill his seed, and he breathed in my ear: "Now, my Juana, now we are one."

. . .

SEVEN

Two days later, we were wed again in the cathedral, our union witnessed by enough nobles and prelates to satisfy even Doña Ana's exacting standards.

Another grand feast ensued. At the height of the revelry, Philip seized me by the hand and hauled me laughing through the palace to my apartments. He locked the door and threw me onto the carpet, ripping at my clothes. From the carpet, we graduated to the bed, where he displayed me on linen sheets strewn with lavender, his hands and mouth seeming to be all over me at once. Guided by his moans and whispers, I strove to show him that I was a fast learner, finding pleasure not only in what he did to me but also in giving him what he desired.

Later in our disheveled bed, with the sheets tangled about me, I looked up at the coffered ceiling and found myself recalling the day I'd first beheld the grandeur of the Moors' vanquished world. I had felt then as I felt now, full of exultation and belief in the miraculous.

I turned to Philip. He lay with his arm across his brow. "What is it?" he murmured. He reached out to pull me closer, his eyelids drooping as he struggled against sleep.

"I want to tell you about Spain," I whispered.

He smiled lazily. "Then do. Tell me everything."

And so I did, weaving in the darkened room the colors and shapes of my land. I relived the march on Granada, my mother at the head of her armies in a soldier's breastplate, her silver cross aloft. I heard again the whoosh of catapults, my father's defiant laughter as he strode through the ranks. I stood before the ocean, watching Colón depart in the galleons my mother had purchased with her jewels; rode in procession to Toledo to witness the return of Colón with his cages of exotic birds and natives from an unknown world. I danced in the *sala;* quarreled and made up with my sisters; followed the bats as they gathered in the sunset; and beheld the Alhambra as I'd last seen it, leonine and silent. When I finished, I hugged my knees, tears brimming in my eyes.

Philip lay so quiet beside me I thought he'd fallen asleep. I leaned to him. His eyes were open, muted. "Felipe," I said softly in my native tongue. "What is it? You look so sad."

He sighed. "I was thinking about my family. Or what passes for my family." He did not look at me. "My mother died when I was a babe. My father loved her so much he could not bear her loss or, apparently, the charge of raising his own children. He sent me here and my sister to France as a future bride for King Charles. Charles eventually repudiated Margaret, but by the time she and I reunited, we had both grown up. We never knew each other as children."

I couldn't imagine it. The most time I'd spent apart from my parents had been summers in Granada, and even then my sisters were with me. My mother had overseen every aspect of our upbringing; she'd selected our tutors, corrected our workbooks, and arranged our schedules. Overpowering as her presence had been, I'd never stopped to consider that I had been fortunate, as royal children were often sent away to their own households to be reared by others.

"And your father?" I ventured. "Did he visit you?"

His smile was cold. "My father prefers Vienna, from where he can rule his mighty empire. He visited once a year. He reviewed my expenses, inquired as to my education, and then he left. Once, I begged him to stay. I was just a boy and I held on to his stirrup. 'This is your place,' he told me from his horse. 'I do not want to see you cry like a girl. We are princes, and princes must learn to be alone. We must not want or need anyone. We must never show our weakness.'"

The cruelty of this reminded me of what my mother had said to me in Arévalo. As little as I knew about the man beside me, we had this much in common: we had both felt the iron shackle of duty, forever marking us as different from the rest of the world.

"I've heard similar words," I said quietly. "They are a hard lesson indeed."

He shrugged. "Not for me. I learned there were few things I could not do without, including my father. Until I turned twelve." Warmth entered his voice. "That was when Besançon entered my service. My father appointed him as my spiritual adviser. He taught me everything I needed to know about being a prince. I was fourteen when I was deemed old enough to take charge of Flanders in my father's name, and the first thing I did was petition Rome for a dispensation to make Besançon my chancellor. Though he oversees his archbishopric, his primary duty is to serve me."

I'd never heard of such an unusual arrangement for a man of such rank. "My mother has a trusted adviser that is somewhat like him," I said. "Archbishop Cisneros. He's head of the See of Toledo, the greatest in Castile. But he only advises my mother on religious matters."

"Yes, I've heard of him." Philip's voice lowered to mock severity, his hands curled at his face like claws. "They say he is so pious, he hunts down heretics wherever they might hide and wears sandals year-round, no matter the weather."

I chuckled at his uncanny imitation and nestled beside him. He kissed my brow. "Time to sleep, little infanta. Tomorrow we rise early to escort Margaret to Antwerp and her ship for Spain, and on to Brussels. After that, I'll take you on a tour of our future empire." He ruffled my hair, kissing me again before he turned away. Soon thereafter, his breath deepened in sleep.

Lifting myself on my elbows, I gazed at his profile.

In the rush of emotions that had overtaken me since my arrival in Flanders, I'd not given thought to the fact that he was just seventeen, a man by royal standards, yes, and already a ruler, but scarcely adult in body or mind. I traced the width of his shoulder, recalling my anger when I'd first learned of my betrothal, my railing against my fate. I'd blamed Philip for separating me from Spain, longed to flee the loveless responsibility I thought marriage to him would entail.

My misgivings seemed so distant now, like the tantrum of a naïve, frightened child. Philip and I were destined for each other. I would be more than a wife to him, more than a mere vessel for his seed. We were both young; we had our entire lives ahead. We would learn together how to rule with benevolence and wisdom. We would bequeath a heritage of power and fortune to our children and retire to grow old together, basking in our memories. And when our bones turned to dust in a marble tomb, our blood would continue to rule after us, until the world ceased to exist.

I curled against him. He murmured, unconsciously adjusting to accommodate me, his hand bringing mine to his chest. My fingers spread over his heart, seeking its strong, steady beat.

I closed my eyes and succumbed to dreams.

. . .

WE BADE MARGARET A FOND FAREWELL AT ANTWERP, WHERE SHE embarked on her trip to Spain. We then proceeded on to Brussels—a dense and scenic city situated in the north of Flanders. The countryside was enchanting, lush as a garden, but I was astonished by how small Philip's duchy was, squeezed like a biscuit between northern France and the immense sprawl of the Germanic principalities. It took weeks to travel from Granada to Toledo, while we were barely in the saddle four days before we reached the bustling capital of Flanders. To me, it seemed the entire realm could have fit in a tiny corner of Castile, with room to spare. Perhaps this was why I saw so few signs of poverty or expanses of uninhabited stony land. Here, it was as if everyone had a purpose, and a place.

In the extravagantly decorated apartments of Philip's ducal palace, I set up my first household. Or I tried to, for I soon found myself quite overwhelmed.

Philip's court was like a city; never had I seen so many people. In Castile my mother's court was designed for efficiency and economy. The demands of the Reconquest had reduced us to the essentials, as we had to be ready to move at a moment's notice. In Flanders it seemed the only impetus to move was when our own stench drove us to it; moreover, the Flemish reveled in ostentatious display, augmenting their comforts with a ceaseless drive for wealth. And where better to make one's fortune than at court? Thus, hundreds crammed into that luxurious sprawl—bishops and prelates, nobles and their retinues, ambassadors, envoys, and secretaries, the ubiquitous courtiers and hangers-on, and countless servants and menials.

And women; so many women. Wives and daughters, mistresses, noble ladies, and courtesans—all angling for the limited power accorded to our sex, all determined to make my acquaintance and earn my favor. Their dress was garish, and they wore too much paint; they preened and flirted without shame and sowed intrigue like churchmen.

Gathering in the galleries in the afternoons, they shared banter about current and past lovers, discussed trends in headwear, and dabbled in politics. They seemed to know everything that was going on in every court in Europe, who was doing what to whom. I heard of the struggles in England, where my sister Catalina was destined to go, of the horrific thirty-year civil war that had decimated the English nobility and given rise to the newly founded Tudor dynasty under Henry VII. I learned of the treacheries of the French and their quest to dominate Italy, of the corrupt Valois and their legacy of avaricious kings. I couldn't help but find it all irresistible. Like a fly into their web I was drawn, for I was the principal lady of the court, the archduchess; and through flattery and compliments they engaged me in conversational peccadilloes while plying me with questions.

I discovered that, for them, Spain was a distant and exotic land, shrouded in superstition and the darkness of the Moorish domination, and that my mother was revered as a warrior queen. They wanted to know everything about the fall of Granada, the voyages of Cristobal Colón, and whether it was true that the caliphs had kept their wives immured, beheading any man who dared so much as glimpse at them. They gasped at my tales of the eunuchs set to guard over the harem, of the day I'd seen Boabdil brought low, and in return they showed me how to disguise the olive tint of my skin with powder and convinced me I'd look splendid in their daring fashions.

Of course, this could only lead to one thing.

A month or so after my arrival in Brussels, as I stood one afternoon with my ladies in my rooms, trying on the latest in a series of new gowns I'd ordered in anticipation of my upcoming tour of the Habsburg territories, Doña Ana burst in.

"I'll not stand by and abide this insolence another moment. Look at you! That bodice is fit only for a woman of ill repute, and your hair should be in a snood, as befits a matron, not hanging loose under that useless confection."

"It's a French hood," I said tersely. I'd hoped to keep my duenna and other matrons occupied with the mundane details of my household, entrusting my intimate needs to others. I should have known she'd not stay mum for long, and suppressed my irritation that she dared create this uproar before the bevy of Flemish ladies overseen by Madame de Halewin.

"Is this what we've come to, an infanta who exalts the dress of Spain's mortal foe?"

I clenched my teeth. I was rapidly reaching my limit when it came to her recriminations.

"Doña Ana, it's but a headdress," I heard Beatriz say, trying to defuse the situation.

"'But a headdress,' she says!" Doña Ana turned to Madame de Halewin. The Flemish matron stood spare as a winter branch, a pincushion dangling on a chain from her waist. "You, madame," my duenna accused. "You've caused nothing but trouble, turning Her Highness's head with these extravagances! She is a princess of Spain. She has no need of such gowns."

Madame de Halewin did not so much as raise her voice. "Her Highness told me she had nothing suitable for court occasions, as much of her trousseau sank with that ship. I simply advised her that as the archduchess, she must appear at all times befitting her rank."

"Yes, and set yourself to fashioning a wardrobe for a common harlot!" Doña Ana spun back to me. "You should have sent word to Castile. Her Majesty would not want a foreign woman to dress you."

My voice hardened. "Perhaps not, but I will still have a new wardrobe." I turned back to where my women waited, holding the sections of a lovely canary velvet gown.

"Begin," I ordered. The women hastened to dress me in the underskirt and bodice slashed with gold tissue. They attached the lynx-trimmed sleeves, fastened the stays that held girdle and bodice in place, cinching my waist into a narrow triangle. I stared defiantly into the glass, hiding my discomfort with the low, square neckline that exposed my breasts almost to my nipples.

Doña Ana exploded. "This is a scandal! When has an infanta of Spain ever selected her own wardrobe, much less pranced about in such brazen apparel?"

She had gone too far. I whirled about. "Enough. I'll not be spoken to as if I were a child!"

Doña Ana's mouth hung open. Before she could find her voice, Madame de Halewin moved to me. "I believe this sleeve should be raised at the shoulder," she murmured.

About us, the Flemish girls looked from Doña Ana to Madame de Halewin and back to me. Beatriz went to Doña Ana. "Señora, let us take a walk. You look pale."

"Yes," I added pointedly, "go with Beatriz." I waved a preemptory hand.

Doña Ana trudged out. As the door closed, I distinctly heard her say: "She'll not get away with this. I'll write to Spain this very afternoon, so help me God."

Madame de Halewin waved aside the whispering girls. "You too. Get to work. Her Highness's bedchamber needs cleansing."

I studied my reflection. Doña Ana would not spoil this for me. The gown might be indecent according to Spanish standards, but it was more luxurious than anything I'd owned. And I had a lovely bosom; everyone said so. Why shouldn't I display it to my advantage? Veils and high-collared robes would not go over well with the Habsburg court.

Madame de Halewin met my gaze. With uncanny prescience, she said, "I cannot help but notice your duenna's outbursts have become more frequent." She let out a sigh. "Your Highness has shown remarkable restraint, considering she acts as though you're incapable of making your own decisions. What will she do when you embark on your tour with His Highness, I wonder? The Habsburg territories are large. Germany, Austria, Holland: the trip could take months."

The intimation in her words cut deep, as did the thought of Doña Ana blighting what in effect would be my official presentation by Philip to our future subjects. As Madame knelt to check my hem, I suddenly realized I couldn't stomach another confrontation with my duenna.

"Madame, I was thinking I might relieve my matrons for a time of their responsibilities, at least until I return from my trip. What would you advise?"

She inclined her head. "I think it's a wise idea. Poor dears, the change in climate alone for women of their age can be quite upsetting." She pinned up my skirt to adjust it. "Perhaps your matrons might be transferred to their own quarters while Your Highness is away?"

In the mirror, I thought I saw her smile. "Your Highness needn't concern yourself with the details. Once you depart, there'll be sufficient room in the palace to accommodate them."

"In truth?" I said. "It seems everywhere I look there are hordes of people. I've even heard that our less fortunate courtiers sleep with the hounds in the rushes."

"Nevertheless, there are quarters we can designate."

I considered. If proper accommodations could indeed be found, it seemed the perfect solution and would allow my duenna and me a much-needed respite from each other. I was fond of Doña Ana, in the end. How could I not be? She'd helped raise us. I just didn't want her interfering in what I regarded as my purview, nor did I want her ranting at me night and day while I sought to make a suitable impression.

"And you can assure me they'll be well cared for?" I asked.

"Absolutely. We'll pay for their maintenance out of your own privy purse."

I reflected a few more moments, while she busied herself with my dress. At length, I said, "See to it. No doubt, we'll all appreciate the change." I laughed, albeit a little nervously. "All of us, that is, save Doña Ana."

EIGHT

...

A furious quarrel ensued when Doña Ana was informed neither she nor any of my Spanish matrons would accompany me. She threatened to take the next ship back to Spain and I retaliated by offering her paid passage. I refused to see her after that, celebrating the New Year festivities of 1497 with Philip in grand style before we departed on the first league of our trip.

While on the road, we received word that Margaret and my brother, Juan, had wed in Spain, to great fanfare. Sad news accompanied this missive; in the midst of the nuptial festivities, my grandmother passed away quietly in Arévalo.

I felt a profound, unexpected grief. I hadn't forgotten my visit with her, and one night in bed I almost confessed to Philip, longing to unburden myself of the secret I carried. But I did not. Something warned me he wouldn't understand. He had lived most of his life without family. He would surely judge my mother as a hard and cold ruler, much like his father was. And so I hid behind a brittle smile, while in my mind remembering my grandmother's haunting eyes and her whisper, *Why are you afraid . . . ?*

My preoccupation faded as our trip progressed and Philip strived to show me off to his people. In every township we entered, jubilant crowds rushed out to greet us. Elaborate welcomes were staged, and lord mayors presented us with gilded keys and proclamations. The land also began to reveal itself to me, its fields dotted with tulips and painted cities bright as newly minted coins. Shining rivers crisscrossed vales where the game was so abundant Philip told me one hardly needed to draw one's bow, and swaths of forest entranced the eye.

Still, I didn't see anything to compare with the sheer breadth of Spain's magnificence, no austere plateaus that plunged into fertile valleys, no endlessly changing skies. In Flanders everything seemed new, a fitting accompaniment to my new life; and soon I was tossing coins from my purse to the crowds with a largesse that would have been unknown in my country, reveling in the anonymous faces gazing up at me as if I were a goddess.

...

IN LATE APRIL WE WENT TO THE HABSBURG KINGDOM OF AUSTRIA for a weeklong visit with Philip's father, the emperor Maximilian. I was curious to meet my exalted father-in-law, ruler of half the civilized world and inheritor of the coveted crown of Holy Emperor. I found him a staid man of robust health and little humor. His palace was magnificent, filled with aspiring scholars and artists seeking his favor; and evidence of his wealth was everywhere. As a welcoming gift, he gave me a necklace of emeralds so heavy it hurt to wear it, and we dined with him and his second wife, the Italian-born empress, on gold plate so encrusted with gems I could scarcely pick it up. I couldn't help but think of how my mother had pawned her jewels and melted her plate to finance her wars, and how to this day she had her gowns mended and remended while she painstakingly saved up the coin she needed to reclaim her jewelry from the moneylenders.

I attended my first (and my last) bear bait at the Austrian court, held in honor of our visit. I'd heard of this peculiar custom, but nothing could have prepared me for the pitiful roars of that proud black beast chained to a stake in a pit, surrounded by yelling courtiers as mastiffs took turns tearing it apart. The bear managed to gore and disembowel three of the savage dogs before it in turn was taken down; by then, I was faint from the stench of blood and entrails, and sickened by the court's apparent delight in the suffering of these creatures. I rose to excuse myself, followed by my equally green-faced ladies; Philip barely paid me mind, flushed from his shouting and keen on winning the bets he'd laid with his men. As I staggered from the tiers with my hand pressed to my mouth, desperate for fresh air, I heard Maximilian drawl, "I'd never heard of a Spaniard lacking for spleen when it came to slaughter."

I almost retorted that spleen or not, he'd never see such barbarity exercised in Spain. Then I recalled Cisneros's burnings of heretics and clamped my jaw. Nevertheless, I vowed to never again witness such gleeful torture.

I also saw firsthand the tension between Philip and his father, confirming everything my husband had told me about their estrangement. Though they resembled each other physically, they spoke on the most formal of terms, without a single gesture of affection between them. When the time came for us to leave, even their farewell was carefully rehearsed and utterly lacking in any warmth.

After that, Philip and I were obliged to separate. It would be our first time apart since our wedding. He would continue on to the official gathering of his Estates-General, a governing body composed of officials from the Imperial states, while I returned to Brussels. I wanted to stay with him, but he assured me I'd be bored to tears and he wouldn't have a moment to spare. "Not to mention that your presence would be too tempting a distraction," he added, with a wink.

So my entourage and I returned to our palace. The afternoon following my arrival I took to the gallery, eager to tell all those ladies who hadn't accompanied me about my adventures, for I must admit, I'd enjoyed being the center of attention and was loath to relinquish the role.

I was so engrossed in my own splendor I almost failed to mark the timid girl who crept tentatively toward me, a chambermaid or servant girl, with downcast eyes. "Your Highness, I beg your leave," I heard her utter. I turned with a ready smile. During the tour, many such girls had made their way to me, hoping for a piece of ribbon from my hair or section of lace from my cuff, as though any article that had touched my person were a talisman.

Madame de Halewin stepped between us. "Her Highness doesn't wish to be disturbed. Off with you, girl!"

I held up a hand, moving around Madame to the now-cowering figure. She was just a child, one of the thousands who prepared our food, mended our linens, dusted our belongings, and swept out our hearths. I had been taught by my mother's example to always show kindness to those who served me, as justness, not pride, was the hallmark of royalty.

"Come, child," I said, "what is it?"

The girl reached into her apron pocket and withdrew a scrap of paper. "Your matrons send you this," she murmured, and she stepped back hurriedly.

I frowned, glanced at the paper. The writing was cramped, in faded ink, but the words were unmistakable: *Somos prisoneras.* We are prisoners.

"What is this?" I asked the girl. "Where did it come from? Speak up."

Beatriz and Soraya came up beside me. An uncomfortable tightness formed in my chest when the girl whispered, "It is from a lady named Doña Francisca. She asked me to bring this to Your Highness. She begged me. She also bid me tell you, Doña Ana is ill."

It was all I needed to hear. I motioned. "Beatriz, Soraya, come with me. We'll visit my matrons in their quarters." I stopped Madame de Halewin with a single glance. "Alone."

STANDING AT THE BOTTOM of a staircase in a dilapidated quarter of the palace, I gazed about in horror.

My matrons' quarters, if such they could be called, consisted of a wine cellar, the moldering walls windowless, the broken stone floor strewn with straw. I wouldn't have stabled a mule here, I thought, and I felt ill when I saw the pallets and threadbare blankets, the mess of cinders in the center, where my women had resorted to burning kindling for heat.

I gestured to Beatriz, who rewarded the girl with a purse of coins and sent her scampering off, her good deed done and financial situation considerably improved.

My four matrons stood clustered together, clad in layers of soiled clothing, all bearing the sallow look of invalids. The odium in their sunken eyes made me want to flee back up the stairs. I had signed vouchers for their upkeep before I left with Philip on tour. I believed I had seen to their welfare. How had this happened? How long had they been here, like this?

I moved to the pallet where Doña Ana lay and dropped to my knees. "Doña Ana," I whispered. "Doña Ana, it is I, your Juana. I am here."

My duenna's eyes opened, glazed with fever. *"Mi niña,"* she croaked. "Oh, my child, you must summon a priest. I am dying."

"No, no. You are not dying." I removed my shawl, tucked it about her.

"It's only your tertian fever, as you used to get in Castile. The moment we went to Granada, you always improved."

"I'll have no such relief here," she murmured.

I lifted an enraged gaze to Doña Francisca de Ayala, who stood like an accusing specter before me. "How did this occur? Why was no word sent to me of these deplorable conditions?"

She met my gaze. "We tried, Your Highness. We were denied access to you."

"Denied?" My voiced edged up a notch. "By whom? Tell me at once!"

"My lord Besançon. We were told by his secretary that you authorized our transfer, and should we find reason for complaint we could take our leave for Spain." She gave me a mirthless smile. "I suppose he expected us to walk there."

"That is impossible." My gaze flew to Beatriz. "I paid out of my own purse for your expenses. I was told you would be well cared for."

Doña Francisca reached into her frayed cloak pocket and withdrew a bunch of crinkled papers, tied with a string. She dropped it in front of me. "Here are our letters to you. Every day, for weeks, we wrote. Each one was returned. Then one night, they came and locked us in. It was only by chance we found a way out."

I reached out with a trembling hand to the papers. "Chance . . . ?" I echoed.

"Yes. Once we realized no help would come, we grew desperate and implored that serving girl who brought us our daily meal. She took pity on us, agreed to carry our message to you in person after you arrived—if my lord Besançon didn't come with you, of course. We are fortunate he did not. Otherwise you might have found five corpses."

Besançon was with Philip. He'd traveled with us throughout Flanders before retiring to one of his houses. I had mostly ignored his corpulent waving presence. Yet in all that time he had known my matrons were left here to subsist on one solitary meal, which was less than allotted to any stable boy or scullery maid.

Blind rage surfaced in me. I had let this happen, yes, but I had done so in ignorance. I could never have conceived of such treachery. In that moment, my dislike for my husband's premier adviser, for the man Philip regarded as his only true father, turned to hatred.

I would see him brought low, I vowed. I stood, my fingers closing about the packet of letters. "Soraya," I said, "please, attend to Doña Ana and help Doña Francisca and our other matrons pack up their belongings. I'll send word as to where they should go. Beatriz, come with me. I've urgent business to attend to."

I SUMMONED MADAME DE HALEWIN. "You dare tell me you knew nothing of this? How is that possible? Did you not tell me to my face that my matrons would lack for nothing?"

To her credit, Madame looked upset. Pallid and trembling, she said, "Your Highness, I swear it to you, I conveyed your order. I told them you would pay from your own purse. I . . ."

"Yes? You what, madame? Speak up!"

"I knew nothing!" She lowered her eyes. I thought she might drop in a swoon at my feet. She feared the worst, as well she should. I could see her dismissed this very hour to the same quarters my matrons were about to vacate, and had half a mind to do just that. "Your Highness, my lord Besançon said he would attend to your matrons' arrangements. He gave his express command that he was to be apprised of everything that transpired in your household."

"Yes, I've been told as much," I replied. "I also understand my lord the archbishop has taken to reviewing my correspondence, before I have a chance to. I plan to address this matter as soon as my husband returns. In the meantime, I shall personally review my finances, and see how this disaster occurred." I gave her a hard stare. "Now, madame."

She rushed out, returning minutes later with a leather register I'd never seen, and an anxious avian-looking gentleman I'd likewise never met, though evidently he was responsible for the register's contents. Bowing low, he introduced himself as Monsieur my treasurer and began to pedantically explain the process whereby money entered and left my privy purse, while Madame stood by, wringing a section of her gown. Listening to the poor man's panting explanation, staring at the cramped formulas, I hoped I did not betray the fact that they could be robbing me blind and I'd never know it. As learned as I was, the intricacies of managing my own finances had not formed part of my educational curriculum.

"My matrons have suffered unspeakable privation," I finally interrupted, with deliberate severity. "I hardly see why you simply didn't use the monies I allotted for their maintenance."

"Monies, Your Highness?" he repeated, blinking at me as though I were some strange being whose language he did not fully comprehend. "I am aware of no such monies."

"How can you not be aware? I signed the vouchers myself before I left with my husband."

"I am aware of the vouchers, yes." He flipped through the register's pages, paused at an entry. He pointed. "See here: I submitted them for approval to my lord the archbishop's secretary. But none were for the maintenance of your matrons. Indeed, I was told that as Your Highness had dismissed them from service, they must return to Spain."

I slammed shut the register, barely missing his fingers. "Who told you that?"

He recoiled, as if he expected me to strike him. "His Eminence the archbishop's secretary."

"Is that so?" My tone could have congealed honey. "Well, I am the archduchess of Flanders, and I've no recollection of giving such orders. A simple rest is all I requested for my matrons—rest and a suite of rooms where they could properly be attended. It would appear my lord Besançon needs reminding that he does not rule here."

The treasurer grabbed his register and bolted. Madame gave me a tearful look. "I fear Your Highness does not understand. I beg you, do not confront him. He is greatly respected both by the court and His Highness your lord husband. To go against him would risk his worst enmity."

I regarded her in stark silence. Somewhere inside me, her warning struck a chord, but I chose to ignore it. I would not allow Besançon to dominate my household or my decisions.

"I thank you for your advice, madame. And I do not hold you responsible. You may go."

Curtsying swiftly, she left me.

BY THE TIME NIGHT had fallen, I'd had my matrons transferred to rooms I saw prepared for them and retired to my own chambers. The next day I made the decision to send them to Spain before Philip returned with Besançon. After the humiliation my matrons had endured, they would never see Flanders as anything other than a place of torment, and in truth, I didn't want to suffer their eternal reproach. I couldn't let Doña Ana leave, not as ill as she was, but the others were hale enough to weather the trip. Once again, I summoned Madame and my treasurer and entrusted them with the arrangements. By the following week, my matrons were on their way to Antwerp and a specially provisioned ship. So too was my letter to Philip by courier, apprising him of the situation I had encountered. Let Besançon deal with that, I thought smugly.

I appointed a physician to watch over my duenna and visited her every day. To my relief she began to improve under his ministrations, eating her fill and even complaining that she did not understand anything of what the elderly doctor said to her.

"Though he understood me well enough when I slapped his hand after he tried to examine my chest," she declared. "The nerve! As if I'd let him put his hand anywhere near my bosom."

I chuckled under my breath. She was on the mend by the time Philip came home.

But he did not come to see me immediately; he'd arrived late the night before, I was told upon awakening, and I dressed at once to go to his apartments. I found him seated in his still-shuttered bedchamber, clad in his soiled riding gear, a half-emptied decanter of wine at his side.

I paused on the threshold. "Philip?"

He did not look at me. He poured a goblet, quaffed it in a single gulp, and poured again.

I went to him. "Philip, what is it? What has happened?"

He looked exhausted, bruised shadows encircling his eyes. Before I could touch him, he flinched and rose to stride to the other side of the room.

"Not now," he muttered. "I'm in no mood."

I went still. "I only wish to welcome you home and speak with you about—"

"I know what you want." He lifted icy eyes to me. "I would rather you did not. I've had a trying enough time as it is without having more cares laid upon me."

"Cares?" I was so taken aback I scarcely knew what to say. I almost let loose my tongue, informing him that I too had had my own share of cares while he'd been gone. I held back. I sensed it would be wiser to simply sit and try to discover the reason for his chagrin.

I went to a chair. "I apologize if you think I'm here to berate you. It's not my intention, I assure you." I paused. The schooled look in his eyes seemed to bore right through me. He didn't look anything like the man I'd left only a few weeks before. "Philip, what has happened?"

His rigid shoulders abruptly slumped. "Everything," he said in a low voice. "I am nothing. I am less than nothing."

"You are not nothing," I said. "You are everything to me."

"Then perhaps you should sit on my esteemed Estates-General." He went back to the decanter. I reached out, took hold of his hand with the goblet. He did not say a word as I removed it from his fingers. I rose, looked into his muted eyes.

"Did they try you so?" I asked. I wouldn't have been surprised. My father had raged often enough about the Castilian Cortes and its refusal to grant one thing or another. I'd heard him with my mother and she always managed to soothe him out of his temper with the same moderate reminder: "We rule by their sanctioned approval, as appointed sovereigns. Without their wisdom, we would be like tyrants or prey to the nobles' ambitions." I wondered if Philip suffered the same, if as archduke he too must submit on occasion to those common-born officials who looked to his realm's well-being first and disdained the exigencies he faced as a ruler.

"Try me?" He shook his head. "They do far more than try me. They humiliate me." He lifted his gaze to mine. Anger sparked in his bloodshot eyes. "I am archduke in name alone, given lip service while my father orders all behind the scenes." He paused. "I'll never have what I desire."

The helplessness in his voice roused every protective instinct in me. He looked like a desolate boy standing there, his matted hair hanging about his pale face. I took his chin in my hands. "What do you desire, my love? Tell me and I will give it to you."

They were the words of a young wife seeking to console her husband, of a woman who cannot bear to see her lover in pain. I had no idea what I could give him that I hadn't already, but in that moment I would have walked to the ends of the earth to get it.

"I want . . ." He swallowed. "I want my freedom. I asked the Estates to declare me archduke in my own right, to release me from my vassal obligations to my father so I can assume the rule of Flanders in name as well as deed. I told them I will turn nineteen soon, of age to rule alone, and that I had spent these past years proving myself."

"And they refused you?" I said. I was bewildered. I thought he was the ruler of Flanders. I thought he and Besançon oversaw the duchy. My mother had said as much: she had told me Philip had ruled here since his childhood.

He turned away from me. "They said until my father grants me legal maturity, I must abide by his decisions. I asked, why did they make a mockery of me by obliging me to attend their session when I had no authority to affect its outcome? They replied that my father wished it so. He said it was how I would learn the proper way to rule." His voice hardened. "The proper way! Blessed Christ, I've lived my entire life under his shadow. I'm but a pretty prince in his cage, without power or prestige, playing with toys given to me on loan."

So he was not sovereign. He held his title through his father, but nothing he had was truly his. It was the first time reality had intruded on our idyllic world and I failed in my innocence to recognize the darkness it could engender. All I wanted was to see him smile again.

"Are you disappointed in me?" I heard him say.

"No," I replied softly.

He looked over his shoulder at me. "Even though you know that I am my father's puppet?"

"You are not a puppet. I don't care about titles, Philip. We are happy, aren't we? We don't need anything more."

He gave a mirthless chuckle. "Perhaps you don't, but I do. I was born to rule. I inherited my lands through my late mother and am a Habsburg same as my father, damn his miserly soul. I deserve my crown. He has no right to keep it from me until he thinks I am worthy of it."

"Philip, a crown isn't all it seems. My parents have crowns and what has it brought them? My mother dedicates her every waking hour to Spain, while my father spends months on end traveling about the realm and arresting or threatening the plotting *grandes,* because otherwise they might think him weak and seek to revolt. It is not an easy existence."

"Perhaps." He turned back to me, held out his hand. "Come here."

I went to him slowly. He took me in his arms. "Forgive me. It's not your fault. But I wish to make my mark in the world. I can't be my father's undeclared heir forever."

I looked into his eyes. "You will make your mark. One day, he will die. You will inherit his mantle. You will rule everything he does, and more. And I, my love—I will be at your side."

He nodded, grazed my cheek with his fingertip. "Yes, of course. One day." He smiled vaguely. "I know you too have had a bad time of it. I got your letter and I promise to speak with Besançon the moment he returns. I summoned him to help me at the Estates, before I realized I could accomplish nothing. I thought his presence might sway them to my side. He's still there, flogging the dead horse. But I'm sure he did not deliberately intend your matrons to be quartered thus. There must have been a misunderstanding somewhere."

I bit my lip. I didn't say what I knew in my heart: the archbishop had acted with deliberate malice. I suspected he sought to separate me from my Spanish allegiances, to make me more firmly Philip's wife. I didn't like him any more than before, but for the moment I would let the matter go. I couldn't do anything while he was at the Estates-General, and my matrons were gone.

But I knew now that Besançon was not my friend.

· · ·

A WEEK LATER, PHILIP AND I DINED ALONE IN MY APARTMENTS. We'd gone hunting for a few days with a minimum of servants to a nearby wood. I did not enjoy the trapping of rabbits or stalking of boar and deer, but the time spent in his element, doing something he excelled at, returned Philip to his ebullient self. Our nights were long and passionate, charged by the lack of ceremony surrounding us. I was sad to leave, in truth. I found I preferred the rustic simplicity to the opulence of our life at court.

We were feasting on one of his catches, a roast quail in plum sauce, when Beatriz burst in. "Your Highnesses, forgive my intrusion, but a courier has come. He says he brings urgent news."

Philip pushed back his chair and stood. "No, stay here," he told me as I started to rise. "Let me see him first. It might be nothing. Finish your supper. I'll be back as soon as I can."

I nodded, looking at Beatriz. The moment he left, she said, "The news is from Spain."

"Spain?" My napkin slipped from my lap as I came to my feet. "Are you certain?"

She nodded. "I heard the courier tell His Highness's chamberlain that he'd ridden all day and night from Antwerp, where he'd been hired to convey the letter by a messenger from Spain."

"I must speak with him, then," I said, even as I wondered where Philip might have gone to meet him. Then the chamber door opened. I took one look at Philip's face and stepped back.

He said, "My love, the letter is from my sister, Margaret. Your brother, Juan . . . He died two weeks ago."

I opened my mouth in immediate protest but my voice failed me. I didn't feel myself move yet somehow I reached out a hand to grasp the back of my chair, as if for dear life.

"No one expected it," Philip said. "He fell ill with a fever shortly after his nuptials. Margaret says he didn't appear too sick at first, but within a few hours the fever rose. She grew frantic and sent word to your parents. By the time your father arrived, it was too late. Juan died in his arms."

I stared in stunned incredulity; behind me Beatriz gasped.

In my mind, I saw Juan as he rode with my father at the fall of Granada, remembered how he asked me to tell Margaret about him. We'd never been close, not as a brother and sister should be. As my parents' heir, his lot was far heavier than mine. Yet we shared holidays, winter walks in Zaragoza's lime-scented gardens, a few enchanted summers in Granada. He had his entire life ahead of him. He was supposed to become the first Castilian-Aragonese king of our united Spain, with Margaret and a parcel of children at his side.

He had been only nineteen years old.

Philip reached out. I pressed a hand to my mouth. A choked sob escaped me. I closed my eyes as he held me close, hearing Beatriz's quiet weeping.

It did not cross my mind that Juan's death had brought me one step closer to the throne.

NINE

...

The year 1497 faded away. According to the Castilian customs of mourning, I had to remain sequestered for a month. Though not yet fully recovered (indeed, she would never fully recover again), Doña Ana insisted on resuming charge of my household. I welcomed her, for in my time of grief I needed her familiar presence. I thought that I could find comfort in the age-old rituals of mourning but it soon became interminable. It wasn't long before I let Philip in to sup with me and play cards, chafing as any young woman against the hours of prayer and unbecoming black I had to don.

Philip hated seeing me in black. He said I looked like a raven and tore the ugly veiled hood from my head. He tousled my hair, murmured he missed having me in the hall at his side and, after a few goblets of wine, he invariably turned amorous, his lips at my throat as he whispered of his longing. Doña Ana warned me I must refuse his advances until my mourning came to an end, but his need proved so feverish, his touch so pleading, I had to surrender. I hardly saw the sin in seeking solace in the flesh God had given us, and the way Philip swept me up in his arms, barely removing his clothes before plunging into me, was a balm no amount of candles or litanies could provide. I decided grief must not interrupt our life anymore, custom or not. Though Doña Ana glowered, before the month was out I returned to the court, my time of seclusion over.

...

ONE MORNING IN EARLY MAY OF 1498, I AWOKE TO NAUSEA THAT sent me hurtling out of bed. Before I could reach my privy closet, I doubled over and was sick on the carpet. With my head pounding and body drenched in sweat, I returned to bed and curled up.

I must have slept again, for I didn't hear the bedchamber door open until Beatriz said briskly, "Good morning, Your Highness. It's past ten. I trust you slept well?"

The odors of the fresh-baked herb bread and warm goat cheese coming from the breakfast tray she carried hit me like a blow from a mace. I retched, leaning over the side of the bed. My stomach heaved but I had nothing to expel. Groaning, I righted myself onto my pillows.

Beatriz set down the tray and rushed to my side. "Your Highness is ill! Oh, how many times have I asked you not to indulge in such large suppers? It is bad for the digestion."

"You sound like Doña Ana," I muttered. "Besides, it's not that."

"Then the wine. That new French claret you drank last night. I knew it smelled sour."

"Beatriz, it is not the wine." I looked at her. "I think . . . I mean, I believe I could be . . ."

Her eyes snapped wide. "Blessed Mary, are you saying . . . ?"

"Yes. I think I'm with child." Even as I spoke the words aloud, warmth suffused me. I could be carrying a son, Philip's son, his heir. How wonderful it would be, and how fitting a tribute to my brother's memory. If so, I vowed I would call him Juan.

"Saints be praised!" Beatriz hugged me and quickly drew back. "But you mustn't exert yourself. Look at you, with nothing on but your shift. You'll catch your death!" She swooped to the clothespress for a robe. "We'll find you the best midwives and the freshest herbs: I've heard chamomile can do wonders. Doña Ana will know what to do. Stay here while I go fetch her."

I had to laugh at the sight of my usually levelheaded lady acting so flustered. "Beatriz, you're making my head spin. Stop for a moment. I don't want you setting the entire palace to talk."

She halted, regarding me closely, as was her wont, for we'd become like sisters, confidants who sometimes could read each other's thoughts. "You haven't told him," she said.

"No, I haven't." I stood gingerly and took the robe from her hands. "I might be mistaken. Or not, I could miscarry. I just want to be sure."

"First of all," she said, pulling my hair out from under the robe's collar and fastening the agate clasps at my waist, "you are not mistaken. Women know these things. And, second, why on earth would you miscarry? You are young. At your age, Her Majesty your mother gave birth—"

"With the ease of a mare," I interrupted. "Yes, I've heard of how my mother would take to the childbed and then mount her horse again to go on crusade, all within the hour. It doesn't mean I share her fortitude. Remember, she also suffered several miscarriages."

"That was later, when she was older, and under great strain." She wagged a finger in my face. "Now, no more talk of losing this child! You must take care, but you are no lily-livered Flemish girl. And you must tell His Highness." She gave me an impish grin. "He did, after all, share in some of the effort. Shall I send him word?"

"No. Let me go. I want to tell him in person."

PHILIP SWUNG ME ABOUT until I feared I'd be sick again. "A son! I'm going to have a son!"

I laughed. "We won't know until it's born," but of course he was beyond listening. He seized me again. "I'll proclaim the news this very hour. Let everyone rejoice! His Highness and Her Highness of Flanders are having a son!"

He could be like an exuberant boy at times, irresistible in his enthusiasm. And as he brought my mouth to his, I began to understand how much having a child would mean to us.

. . .

PHILIP HAD MY PREGNANCY PROCLAIMED THROUGHOUT FLANDERS and appointed a veritable army of physicians, apothecaries, and midwives to oversee my every whim. We traveled to the lovely city of Lierre, where the doctors deemed the air more salutary to a woman in my delicate state. The return to the spacious palace by the river where Philip and I had met, coupled with the advent of spring and sudden cessation of my nausea, proved an excellent choice. Seated in the rose bower with my embroidery forgotten in my lap, I idled for hours, contemplating the masses of tulips and marigolds that filled the gardens all the way to the Néthe's silvery banks. I'd never seen such a profuse display since Granada. It was as though the rich soil of Flanders heaved up her beauty to entertain me. And I was fulfilled.

. . .

IN LATE APRIL, BESANÇON RETURNED TO COURT.

I had not forgiven him for the situation with my matrons but a comfortable languor came over me as a result of my pregnancy, and I was relieved when the archbishop came to offer me his congratulations and then proceeded to closet himself with Philip and their council to discuss business affairs. I refrained from asking any questions when Philip emerged at dusk from these protracted meetings to dine with me. He seemed tired and preoccupied; I did not want to tax him further. However, I started to feel a prickle of doubt, until one night when I went to his apartments dressed in my damask and jewels for our evening repast and found him waiting there with Besançon at his side.

"I thought we might dine alone tonight," I said, with a frosty glance at the archbishop.

A nerve twitched in Philip's cheek. "We will," he said. "But first, please sit, my love. My lord Besançon and I have something we wish to discuss with you."

The archbishop bowed, his broad face flushed, his bulk swathed in expensive carnelian satin. A jeweled cross hung at his chest; his hands flashed with rings. Whatever labors he'd undertaken on Philip's behalf had clearly not affected his disposition.

"Your Highness," he said, "such a pleasure. I trust you are in good health?" He spoke with exaggerated deference, but I caught the furtive look he exchanged with Philip. Had my husband brought us together to make amends? I sincerely hoped not.

"I'm in excellent health, my lord." I raised my hand to caress Philip's where it rested on my shoulder. I thought I would enjoy a show of humility from the archbishop.

"That is good." He took a seat opposite mine. Servitors entered with a decanter of small beer, a watery ale favored by the Flemish. "For the physicians assure us you carry a son."

The admission that he'd consulted with my doctors sent a bolt of cold reality through me.

"Well, regardless of its sex, we'll love this child all the same." I looked at Philip.

He said quickly, "Yes, of course. It is, after all, our first; we will no doubt have others." He gave a chuckle that sounded strained to my ears. "Her Highness and I are still young."

"Indeed," I added. "And as our first child, we'll naturally wish to oversee its upbringing."

Besançon's gaze narrowed. He was no more taken in by me than I was by him. This oily man had raised Philip, for better or worse; he'd made my husband into the man he was. He clearly did not welcome the intimation that I'd want a say in how my child was reared, indeed that I merited any consideration beyond that of complacent wife.

I made certain my stare did not waver. "I trust we won't have any misunderstandings in this matter as we did in the one concerning my matrons, my lord?"

He visibly reddened. "Your Highness, that was most unfortunate. I assure you, I—"

I waved a hand. "It is done. Pray, think no more of it." My tone made it clear that even if I chose to forgive, I would never forget.

He inclined his head. "Your Highness is most gracious." He raised his basilisk stare to Philip. "Your Highness, perhaps we might attend now to the business at hand?"

"Yes," I said, "by all means, let us attend." I gave Philip my full attention.

He gulped his goblet, then without preamble declared, "My lord and I have been discussing of late the situation in Spain. In view of the fact that your parents no longer have a male heir, we believe that I could be granted precedence in the succession. In exchange, we will support your father's claim in Naples against the French."

I went still. I didn't like the sound of this. "But my sister Isabella is my parents' heir now."

"Your sister may be heiress of Castile," Besançon clipped, "but Salic Law prevails in Aragón. Your father's Cortes will never recognize a woman as heir."

I clenched my teeth. Damn him. I should have known he'd come back to court after that debacle in the Estates-General and fill Philip's head with his grandiose ideas! I regretted having forgone giving him a full reprimand earlier, for it seemed he would repay me in false coin.

"Aragón recognized my mother," I said at length. "Why not my sister?"

"Her Majesty Queen Isabel's title as queen of Aragón is nominal, a formality set forth by your parents' marriage treaty. Aragón retains its right of succession."

I stared at him for a long moment, outraged that he'd dare lecture me on Spain as if I were an uninformed pupil. I would have to tread with caution. Despite the alleged informality of our gathering, I realized we had entered a potential battleground.

"You know much of our arrangements in Spain, it seems. Surely you also must know my sister Isabella has wed the new prince of Portugal. If anyone should be named infante, it is he."

"Not necessarily. Portugal has too much power already; its claims in the New World alone rival Spain's. If your sister's new husband is named infante, he'll yoke Spain to Portugal upon your parents' deaths and rule through your sister." Besançon sighed. "His Highness your brother's death is a tragedy, but it can be mitigated through Spain's alliance with us. After all, His Highness is your husband; you stand next in line to the throne and are already with child, while your sister remains barren. Our proposal will be a blessing to your parents in their time of grief."

My alarm increased. I'd never seen myself as second in line to anything, much less the Spanish throne. My brother had always been the one who would rule, and his sons after him. Though my sisters and I had an exemplary education, for my mother did not believe a woman should be refused the advantages of literacy, our ultimate purpose was the role of queen consorts to our royal husbands. We'd been trained to be erudite but not overly so, conversant on many subjects but experts on none, to be decorous and accomplished and always discreet.

None of us was trained to rule.

I glanced at Philip. He gave me a cautious smile. "We're thinking of the future of Spain, Juana. Your parents have not been long on their thrones. You yourself told me of all the troubles they face. Your brother's loss could incite unrest among the nobles; and should Aragón refuse to acknowledge your sister as the new heir, who knows what may ensue?"

I knotted my hands over my belly. I couldn't yet feel my child, but I wished I could. I needed a reminder of the recent happiness I'd felt and which this conversation had vanquished like a finger snuffing out a candlewick.

As if on cue, Besançon stood. "I will go now, with Your Highness's leave."

Philip nodded; I did not look at the archbishop as he waddled out. The moment I heard the door shut, I raised my eyes to Philip. He regarded me for a moment. Then he sank to his knees before my chair and took my hands in his.

"There is a very real threat from France. No one knows what Louis intends, but both Besançon and I heard rumors while at the Estates that he seeks a more aggressive stance over Naples than his predecessor. Spain and France are longtime foes: I hardly need tell you what a war between them could mean to your parents—and to us."

I nodded, frightened now. My father had warned me about Louis. He'd told me the new king of France lacked scruple or conscience. My parents' treasuries were bankrupt; a conflict with a nation as large and rich as France would bring disaster upon my native land, only recently united under my parents' rule and still seeking its foothold amid the established powers of Europe.

"Do you think . . . ?" I paused, then swallowed. "Do you think he'll declare war?"

"I don't know. If he does, he'll not warn of it beforehand. But if I am named into the succession he may think before he acts. He won't want us and your parents allied against him." Philip sat back on his heels. "Besançon wants to send an envoy to Castile to present my proposal to your mother. I would like you to add a letter, explaining that you support my endeavors."

I started. "A letter?" I let out a tight laugh. "You do not know my mother. My brother is scarcely cold in his grave. She'll find the timing of this most ill advised."

"Your brother has been dead nearly six months. Your mother is a queen; she'll understand."

I saw Besançon's hand in this, manipulating Philip into thinking such a scheme was possible.

"Be that as it may," I said carefully, "I still think she'll take it as an insult. You are not of Spanish blood. How can she name you into the succession, even if she wanted to? Both her and my father's Cortes would refuse."

He frowned. "This isn't about legislation: it's about my royal rights."

I resisted an impatient sigh. "Philip, in Spain the Cortes represents the nobility and the people's interests. It must first invest a sovereign before he can legally claim the throne; it's a formality, yes, but it's always held that Spain must have a Spanish-born king."

"Are we to be dictated to by warlords and merchants, then?" he muttered. "I'm not asking to be king," he added, with a forced smile. "I just want my name entered in the succession as a safeguard and the title of infante. After we have our son, he can assume this right. He shares both our bloods. He can inherit, yes?"

"Philip, our child isn't even born yet. I might bear a daughter."

"You won't." He leaned to me. "Will you write the letter? I need your help."

What else could I do? If he was going to present his proposition regardless, an accompanying letter from me might ease the effrontery of it, perhaps smooth the way toward a compromise.

He kissed my cheek. "Now, I won't have you worrying about this. Write the letter and leave the rest to Besançon. Remember, you have our son to take care of."

His conviction troubled me only a little less than the announcement that he'd relegate our policies to the archbishop. I couldn't help but fear we were in for a rude surprise. I knew my mother. She would not rest until Castile *and* Aragón invested Isabella as heir. And she'd not take kindly to any proposal that suggested otherwise, regardless of its goal.

After we dined together, I returned to my rooms, wondering how to explain my dilemma in a letter. I owed Philip my loyalty as his wife and he wished to extend his support. My mother had instructed me—indeed, commanded me—to uphold Spain's interests above all else, but she never explained that sometimes these situations were not as clear as they looked. Still, as I sat before my desk with a blank page and quill, I could imagine my parents' anxiety over Louis of France's ambition, their crushing grief over Juan. Philip was right: everything they had fought for hung in the balance. Without a male heir, Castile and Aragón could be torn apart, fall prey to the avarice of the nobility. Maybe my father and mother had already thought ahead; maybe they would welcome Philip's proposal. And if I did bear a son, as so many believed, he'd have my blood. My parents' legacy would live on through him.

I sighed, glancing at my belly. I took up my quill.

Inking the sharpened tip, I began to write.

...

SUMMER SLIPPED TOWARD FALL, AND I OCCUPIED MYSELF WITH preparations for my child's birth. The chamber selected for me would be lavish, the bed upholstered in the finest cloth, the tapestry hangings woven especially in Bruges for the occasion. In my apartments, I spent hours inspecting fabric samples sent by all the burghers eager to curry my patronage with their wares.

"That peach satin." I pointed to the sample Beatriz held up. "It would lighten the chamber curtains, don't you think, seeing as the windows must remain shuttered." I scowled. "It all seems most primitive. Why must I give birth like a bear in a cave?"

Beatriz rolled her eyes in sympathy and reached over to extract a green velvet sample from the pile at her feet. "What about this one? It would look lovely with the amber satin coverlet."

I nodded. "Yes. We'll ask for ten yards, and—" I glanced up, hearing noise in the antechamber. The door opened. Besançon strode in, his satin robes billowing.

"Leave us," he told Beatriz. "I wish to speak with Her Highness alone."

Beatriz looked at me. I nodded.

I could not believe he had dared to barge into my rooms unannounced. We'd never been alone before; seeing him now in all his fulsome glory made me want to rebuke him for everything he had done. I did not, because I expected Philip to follow; when my husband failed to appear, I said coldly, "Yes, my lord? What is the meaning of this intrusion?"

He returned my stare in absolute silence. I could tell he was angry; his already florid cheeks were even redder, making him look like an over-baked boar. "We've received Her Majesty your mother's answer to our proposal," he said. He reached into his pocket and withdrew a folded parchment. He dropped it into my lap. "I suggest Your Highness read it and see the high esteem in which Her Majesty holds us."

I did not touch the paper. I could guess its contents. "Perhaps you should tell me," I replied, "seeing as you've apparently come here to that purpose."

"Very well. She advises that as His Highness your husband has no legal rights in Spain, she can only assume we've suffered an unfortunate lapse in judgment. She orders us to respect the decision of her Cortes to declare your sister Isabella's child as her heir."

I sat upright. "Isabella's child? My sister is pregnant?"

"She is. Seven months, in fact. Her midwives have assured your parents the child is male. He will be named heir to Castile and Aragón. A clever twist, is it not? Your sister's babe will be king not only of Spain but also of Portugal. No yoking of the great realm to its neighbor now—no, it's to be the other way around. I believe Her Majesty has set herself to building an empire."

My hands closed over the letter. I clenched my teeth against the retort that he was not fit to wipe Her Majesty's riding boots.

I heard him say, "Your Highness doesn't seem surprised."

I met his stare. "Of course, I am. I had no idea Isabella was pregnant."

"But you're relieved. You never wanted His Highness to be heir; you made that quite clear."

"And you, my lord, should have a care," I replied, "for you forget with whom you speak." I braced my hands on my chair arms and came to my feet. "If that is all, please tell my husband I wish to see him."

Besançon regarded me. "His Highness is most aggrieved by this matter and has gone riding."

Despite my effort to remain calm, my voice edged. "Then you will send word to wherever he is that I too am aggrieved but am not to blame. I did not tell my mother to refuse this proposal, nor was it I who had the idea to set it before her."

"Ah, yes," he said, to my disbelief. "And yet Your Highness is Spain come to Flanders and therefore must understand that in refusing us this request, Spain has insulted Flanders."

"Us?" I took an angry step to him. "There is no 'us,' my lord, except for my husband and I. And I did not insult him. I would never insult him as you insulted me, and him, by treating my matrons as you did."

His eyes were like shards of ice. "You forget I chose you. His Highness could have wed elsewhere had I deigned it so."

I trembled from head to toe, longing to fling the paper in my hand at his face. "The moment my husband returns, I will tell him of your presumption. You are not so well favored that he'd take your side over mine. Lest *you* forget, my lord, I am to bear his child and heir, not you."

He bowed, went to the door. He paused, looked over his fleshy shoulder. "I suggest you reconsider testing His Highness's patience," he lilted, as if we'd just had an argument over the starching of my linens. "He is not accustomed to having his actions questioned by anyone, much less his wife and her mother. He might take it amiss that in your zeal to defend Spain, you apparently disregard the fact that he too is a ruler, with his own realm to consider."

I breathed, "You will not get away with this. You have my word as an infanta of Castile."

He inclined his head. "We offered to assist Spain in her time of difficulty. Seeing as that wasn't good enough, so be it. Flanders has been forced to choose, and choose we will."

Before I could react to this implicit threat, he opened my apartment door. "I wish you a pleasant evening," he said, and he walked out.

My teeth cut into my lip. I unfolded my mother's letter. I forced myself to read it, every word, and it was as though she stood in the room with me, her presence like immutable stone. It read just as I'd supposed— a matriarchal chastisement of a prince who had overstepped his bounds. Her high-handed treatment made me want to tear the letter to shreds, even as I knew she only did what Besançon had goaded her to.

Beatriz came in, her pallor showing she'd overheard everything. "*Princesa,* can I help?"

I nodded. "Yes. Go and see if you can find out when Philip is scheduled to return."

She slipped out. Folding the letter into precise squares, I set it on my desk and went to the window. Outside, the day had started to fade, the ebbing sun casting gold over the Néthe and the hedges and flower beds of the gardens. I was not so naïve as to think Philip would not hear first from Besançon that we'd had an altercation, but he would still come to me. He would come and I would ask him to send that odious man away. I could not live under the same roof with him anymore. He had to go, for the health of our unborn child, if nothing else.

Beatriz returned to tell me Philip had indeed gone out riding but had taken only a small entourage and was expected back by nightfall. Throughout the rest of the evening, as my women endeavored to distract me, I waited. Soraya and Beatriz served my supper, but I picked at the food, looking at the door every time I heard footsteps in the corridor. I sent Beatriz back out; she reported on her return that Philip had just arrived and gone to his apartments.

"He must be changing his clothes," I said. I took up my neglected embroidery and set myself to work, anticipating his arrival. The mechanical clock on my mantel chimed each hour with excruciating slowness. By midnight, I realized he had no intention of seeing me tonight. It was the first time we hadn't spent an evening together while in the same palace, and as my women snuffed out the candles and retired to their pallets I paced my bedchamber, my mind awhirl.

I began to imagine the worst, Besançon's words tumbling over and over in my head. The choice he'd mentioned could only mean Philip would turn to France. He'd forge an alliance with Spain's enemy to spite my parents and bend them to his will, causing me no end of trouble.

My hands bunched into fists. I had to put an end to this before it went any further. I would go to Philip. I would not have our love tainted anymore by Besançon's wiles.

I slipped into a robe and low-heeled slippers. Doña Ana slept in a separate room, and as I tiptoed past my ladies in the antechamber I motioned to my ever-attentive Beatriz to stay put.

On fleet feet, I moved through the darkened palace, encountering only the occasional stray hound, dozing courtier in an alcove, and the night sentries.

At the door to his antechamber, I paused. In the small watching-room, the candles were doused, the fire ebbing. The page who usually slept here, ready to attend to whatever Philip might need in the middle of the night, was nowhere in sight.

I was relieved. Let Philip express his frustrations while I listened patiently, knowing there were no ready ears in the antechamber, recording every word. I had no doubt that I would win. The archbishop, for all his guile, was no match for a visibly pregnant and anxious wife.

His bedchamber door was ajar and I saw flickering candles within. I felt a rush of pity. He too was awake, probably unable to sleep, distressed as I was, uncertain as to—

I heard a burst of muffled laughter. I glanced over my shoulder. Was the page here after all, entertaining some guest in the corner? Another burst of laughter rang out, immediately followed by an unmistakable voice. "Be quiet, wench. You'll wake the entire palace."

I froze where I stood. The moment fractured about me. My hand poised over the door's latch; without knowing what I was about to do, I pushed it open on its oiled hinges.

His bed sat directly before me, the silver and blue brocade curtains pulled back. I had a fleeting impression of rumpled white sheets before my gaze dropped to the floor. Clothing littered the trampled rushes. I stared at a woman's overturned white satin shoe. All sound faded. I lifted my gaze, slowly, in mounting horrified disbelief, my entire body turned to ice.

The candelabra on the sideboard tossed his shadow onto the wainscoting, slashing light across bare skin. Fleshy thighs poked out at either side of his hips, lifted in midair, the red-nailed toes curling upward. I saw the supple muscles of his buttocks flexing, his spine tensing under his back as he increased his pace, plunging into the creature beneath him.

Sound rushed back to me in a sickening deluge. I heard groans, whimpers, the slapping of skin against skin, and a woman's voice saying over and over, *"Oui, mon coeur, oui, oui, oui . . ."*

Philip arched, released a husky groan I knew well, then shuddered and collapsed. The white thighs beneath his splendid body splayed onto the mattress. He rolled over, a hand at his brow, his mouth curved in a satiated smile. The woman, half-submerged within the pillows piled against the bed's headboard, gave a laugh, her large, blue-veined breasts jiggling as she pushed tangled flaxen tresses from her face and sat upright.

Her eyes flew at me. She let out a small high-pitched gasp. *"Mon Dieu!"*

Philip chuckled. "What now? Didn't you get enough, you greedy slut?" and he looked about. I looked straight at him, at his still-hard and wet sex. Tears burned in the corners of my eyes.

"Oh my God," I whispered, and I turned blindly back into the ante-chamber.

Behind me, there was commotion, Philip's brusque order: "Get out!" Bare feet hit the floor. I pressed a fist to my mouth, fighting back a wail of pain and sorrow as I saw the woman creep past me, gown and undergar-ments and white shoes clutched against her.

I did not know who she was. I might have passed her a hundred times in the gallery or in the hall and never know she'd bedded my hus-band.

Then I heard Philip come up behind me. I whirled about. He'd tossed on a scarlet robe. "My infanta, I . . ." He looked chastened, like a boy caught misbehaving.

"How—how could you?" I heard myself say, the plaintive, distraught tone foreign to my ears. "How could you do this to me?"

"I didn't mean to hurt you," he muttered. He did not try to touch me, his hands awkward at his sides. I wondered if his fingers smelled of her. "It was a bit of sport. It means nothing."

"Nothing?" I whispered. My tears broke free. "You call it nothing, when you betrayed me?"

"Betrayed you?" For a moment, he seemed bewildered. "What, be-cause of her? I told you, she's nothing. A pastime. I've had a dozen just like—" He stopped, his eyes widening.

"You've done this before?" I echoed, and a sob thickened my voice.

"No, no." He made a sudden move, his hand coming up as if to soothe me. I flinched, recoiled. "I swear, not since our marriage," he said hastily. "Please, Juana, I promise you."

I wanted to believe him. The betrayal I felt was so unbearable, so un-thinkable, I wanted only for it to go away, for his touch to make me forget the searing memory of him pumping his seed into another.

But I didn't, because I knew I could never forget. Something precious and irreparable had broken inside me.

"I must go," I said, and I started to the door, moving like a woman underwater.

He caught my arm, not hard, but enough to pull me back. "Where are you going?" he said, and I saw a flicker of impatience in his gaze.

"Away." I pulled from his grip. "Anywhere but here."

"What? This is ridiculous! All husbands do it, Juana. When their wife is with child, they seek comfort elsewhere. It hardly matters."

I felt my heart turn over. He was a stranger. I had made a terrible mistake. I had married a man I did not know. An intense rage came over me. "Is that what Besançon told you," I said through my teeth, "that it doesn't matter? That you may do as you please because I'm with child? Well, it does matter! It matters to me! I am your wife. And I loved you!"

"I was angry," he flung back. "God's death, I was angry and hurt. Your mother insulted me. She denied me my right as your husband and chastised me as if I were a snot-nosed brat. I didn't mean for you to find out. Had you stayed in your rooms, you'd never have known."

"Yes," I whispered, "you're right. I would never have known. And you would never have told me." I turned away again, to the door.

He said, "Juana, come back. Please, let us talk about this. You're being unreasonable."

I moved into the corridor. I paused, looking around as if I had never seen this place before. He stood silhouetted by the open doorway, the candlelight behind him. I could not see his face.

I broke into a desperate run. I didn't know where I headed, only that once I reached my chambers, I must have looked a fright, my hair disheveled, my bare feet soiled from the passageways, my slippers discarded somewhere behind me.

Beatriz and my other women were awake, waiting. They gaped when they saw me.

"Start packing," I cried. "We are leaving. Now."

TEN

...

I took my ladies back to Brussels. I would not confess to anyone, not even to my beloved Beatriz, even as my pain and humiliation and anger ate at me like a canker. I ordered the startled staff in Brussels to ready my rooms, and though they were only half-done cleansing the palace from our previous stay, without fresh rushes on the floors or laundered carpets, tapestries or linens, the stinking slop piles not yet carted away, I ensconced myself in my apartments and acted as if I had an entire court about me.

Not once in two full weeks did Philip's name cross my lips.

At first, I made up wild plans to depart for Spain as soon as my child was born, return home to the Alhambra to raise him as a Spanish prince. I wept more tears than I care to recount when I thought of never seeing Philip again, but then like an injured person fingers their wound, I made myself recall that scene in his bedroom and feel again the terrible disbelief. I didn't know if he had done it before or if he would do it again, but he had shattered my trust in him and as the days passed I began to wonder if everything we'd felt, everything we'd shared, the passion and laughter, the dancing and sleepless nights, had been an illusion.

I'd always known infidelity was an unfortunate but common part of marriage. My father adored my mother yet had had mistresses. My mother never raised protest, at least not publicly. In fact, when one mistress bore him a son, and another a daughter named Joanna, she had both children brought to court to be reared as befitted their rank. The mistresses were also found suitable husbands, once my father's interest waned. But how had Queen Isabel felt when she first discovered this rupture in what she believed was the perfect union? Had she wept, railed at my father in private? Or had she displayed only equanimity, burying her pain deep within? If so, I knew I should do the same, if only because, like her, I had no other choice. Philip was my spouse; I had no say in how he chose to behave. I should consider myself fortunate he was young, comely, and that he cared for me. Other princesses contented themselves with far less.

And still, I couldn't accept it. The fact that he'd bedded another woman hurt me less than the realization that he hadn't cared to deny himself. He'd thought of his own satisfaction rather than our love, squandering it the moment a difficulty came our way. It felt careless, callous, the act of a vengeful boy, and I feared I might never find the resignation I needed to forgive him.

Then one afternoon, as I prepared to take my daily walk in the gardens, Beatriz rushed in. "Your Highness, the archduchess Margaret is here! She insists that you receive her."

I went still. "Here? Why? I thought she . . ." My voice faded. The door opened and Philip's sister swept in, clad head-to-toe in black, her hands outstretched. *"Ma chérie."*

She smothered me in her embrace, then drew back to regard me with a searching look. I saw at once, she knew. She had returned home from Spain and seen Philip. He'd told her of our estrangement and now she was here, to make amends. But why was she still in mourning?

I said quietly, "You wear black."

"Yes." Margaret lowered her eyes.

"But the six months of mourning for my brother are done."

She whispered, "Oh, my dear, it's as I feared. You don't know. You haven't been told."

I met her eyes. The chamber started to keel. "Told what?" I heard myself say.

She did not speak. A tear slid down her cheek.

"Dear God," I said, "what is it? Is it Philip? Has something happened to him?"

"No, my brother is well. He waits downstairs. He didn't know if you would see him."

I stiffened. "Philip is here?"

She took me by the arm. "I am not here for him. My dear, your sister Isabella . . . I am so sorry. She is dead."

I heard her words in utter silence. Then I said, "No. That is impossible."

"I know it must come as a shock," said Margaret. "Her pregnancy went so well, almost perfect. No one expected the birth to be so hard on her. Your mother sent word, asking Philip to spare you the news until after your own child's birth. But when I got to Lierre after that infernally long sea voyage and he told me what happened, I insisted we must come to you at once. I didn't want you to be alone, in case you learned the dreadful news elsewhere."

My breath evaporated from my lungs. I did not feel myself move as memories crashed over me. I saw Isabella in her widow's garb, mourning her dead prince; her disapproval when Catalina and I escaped into the Alhambra's gardens; and I remembered her words on the day I left Spain. She'd said we would never see each other again in this life. How had she known?

I buried my face in my hands. "God, it cannot be. Not again. Not my poor sister."

Margaret moved to embrace me when a quiet voice said, "My infanta."

I looked up. He stood in the doorway, his cap in hand. He looked pale, thin. "I have your mother's letter," he said. "I'm afraid it's true. Isabella is gone."

From my bedchamber door, Doña Ana let out an anguished wail. Beatriz guided my bereaved duenna away. Philip approached me. I met his eyes. "My sister's child, is it . . . ?"

"He is. A boy christened Miguel. But the birth nearly killed him too. Your mother has taken him to Granada in the hope his health will improve."

"Granada. Yes, the air is pure there. Granada will heal him."

I felt Philip take my hand. I was so cold. I wondered if I would ever feel warm again. He said softly, "Please, forgive me," and the pain resurfaced, sharp as a blade.

I pulled back. "I can't. Not now. Please, go. You've done your duty. Let me grieve in peace."

His mouth tightened. "Juana, how long will you let this come between us?"

"I don't know," I whispered, and I walked into my bedchamber without a backward glance, closing the door on his frozen figure, Margaret helpless at his side.

I turned the key. Then I sat on the bed beside Doña Ana. Beatriz and Soraya flanked us like silent sentinels as I put my arms about my poor duenna and let myself weep.

· · ·

I WENT INTO SECLUSION FOR THE OFFICIAL PERIOD OF MOURNING for my sister; this time I did not deviate from the prescribed protocol. Directly afterward, I entered confinement for childbirth in early November of 1498. After surprisingly few hours of labor, I gave birth to a girl, who was later christened Eleanor. The midwives and physicians hastened to alleviate what they perceived as my disappointment with the declaration that my apparent facility for childbirth indicated I would in time bear a son. I nodded, hiding my covert pleasure. In bearing a daughter and not the prince he had craved, I'd thwarted Besançon's ambitions.

Philip demonstrated only joy in the squealing infant. My official presentation to the applauding court after my churching and release from confinement concealed the stalemate that had developed between us. We shared the same palace, attended the hall to dine together, but after our public duties were done, I went alone to my rooms and bolted my door. Though he tried various times to implore me to reason, I would not listen to him. I was hurt and confused; I had never expected Philip to want another woman, much less bed her, and I didn't know what to do next. I should have been the happiest woman in the world, with a new baby and a husband who, in the eyes of the world, was the perfect prince, but I had never felt more wretched or alone.

Following the New Year's festivities of 1499, Margaret came to my apartments. Her father, the emperor, had betrothed her to the Duke of Savoy, an elderly lord with rich holdings, and she had been summoned to

Vienna to meet her new bridegroom. I liked my sister-in-law. She was a lively, intelligent woman who'd survived my brother's death and now faced another arranged marriage with equanimity; and upon hearing her news, I gave her a brittle smile.

"I'll miss you," I said.

She set hands on hips. "I'm leaving next week, though I hardly see how I can with matters as they are. Exactly how much longer do you intend to go on punishing yourself? My brother is despondent. He barely eats or sleeps. And neither do you, by the looks of it."

"He betrayed me," I retorted. "Why should he be despondent?"

She sighed. "*Ma chérie,* if every wife locked her door to her husband when she caught him with his hose down, there'd not be another legitimate child born in this world."

I knew she spoke the truth. After much reflection and tears, I knew it was a wife's lot, and yet I couldn't resign myself. I didn't want to be one of those women who turned the other cheek when her husband strayed. I didn't want to become my mother.

"I've tried to forgive him," I said haltingly. "God only knows how much." I paused, meeting Margaret's gaze. "Should I pretend it never happened? Is that what you advise?"

"No. He knows what he's done." She stepped to me. "But you love him, and he loves you. Believe me, pride makes for a very poor bedmate. At least, let him come to you. Give him the opportunity to atone for his mistake."

"How can he atone? How can I know it won't happen again?"

"You can't." She sighed. "My dear, you are still so young in matters of the heart. You do not understand that men are more imperfect than we are, for all their bluster that we are the weaker sex. Who knows why a man strays? But I know this much: he never meant to hurt you. He's simply even more of a child than you, a boy forced to grow up too soon. And when boys feel rejected or betrayed, they lash out, often at those they love the most."

"I did not betray him! I did not deny him the title he sought."

"I know. All his life Philip has been taught that his overriding duty is to seek his aggrandizement as a prince and when a Habsburg is wronged he must take his vengeance."

"I understand that. But he is a man now, and Besançon does him no favors. He relies too much on that man." I resisted the urge to add that I knew Besançon had orchestrated this fissure in my marriage, that he had put Philip up to it, perhaps even selected the woman. That day we confronted each other, he had warned me. He as much as declared I should not aim above his power over Philip, and then he went and made sure I understood my limitations.

"That may be," said Margaret. "But you are his wife, not Besançon's. You must find it in yourself to forgive him, because you are the stronger one." She took my hands in hers. "You've no idea how much I prayed that he would find a wife like you, to give him the happiness and care he so desperately needs. My brother lives in a hard world. To survive, he's learned to close off his heart. But with time and patience, you can make him see the error in his ways."

How could I resist such a plea? I couldn't imagine the years stretching ahead devoid of the companionship, the love and unity I'd thought I had found. I was nineteen. I had my entire life to live. And I wanted to share it with the man I had wed.

"I will speak to him, if you want me to," she added, and I nodded, hugging her close.

"I am sorry that I've only given you more burdens to carry," I murmured.

"Ah, *chérie*," she replied, "what is a sister-in-law for? Were it not for the burdens of others, my own might be too great."

We kissed each other's cheeks, and she left to pack for her trip to Austria.

Alone in my chamber, I let something dark and painful untangle in my heart. It unraveled slowly, barb by barb, and I at last allowed myself the forgiveness I had denied us both.

. . .

EIGHT DAYS LATER, AFTER MARGARET'S FAREWELL BANQUET, PHILIP came to me. I was sitting at my gilded dressing table as Beatriz removed my jewels. When I saw his reflection in the mirror, a silhouette in white, I raised my hand. My women melted from the room.

He hovered in the archway, as though afraid to cross the threshold. I drew a breath.

"You may come in."

He moved into the room. He looked as handsome as the day we'd first met, the sapphires in his doublet catching the candlelight, vying in vain with the intense blue of his eyes, his shoulder-length hair streaked with white gold from riding under the sun without a cap.

I looked up into his eyes. "Why?" I asked.

He frowned. "What?"

"Why? Why did you do it?"

He lowered his eyes. "I told you, I was angry. Besançon showed me your mother's letter and it was as if I were with my father again, being told I wasn't worthy."

"I see." I looked down for a moment. I understood, as much I didn't like it. He had been refused his sovereign independence by his own Estates-General only then to be rejected by my parents. Though he'd never had any right to ask it of them, he had not intended to offend, nor could he admit as I did that his favored lord chancellor, Besançon, had led him astray.

"My infanta," he said softly, and he looked at me with a sorrow that cut to my core. "I've never asked for forgiveness from anyone before. But I am asking it from you now."

My throat knotted. "I—I want to. But you must promise me something."

"Anything."

"Never again. Promise me, you'll never do it again."

"I promise," he said, and I could not control myself any longer. I reached out to him, and he was suddenly in my arms, crushing me to him, as if he'd been starved of sustenance. He peeled off my clothes and swept me to the bed, my hair entwined in his fingers, my arms about him as by the light of the candle on the dressing table he tore off his own clothes. I reveled in the interplay of flame and shadow across the muscular body I knew so well and had missed so much.

Afterward, I traced his lips. He drew me close, coiling our legs and arms. A sudden chill ran through me. I turned to him, searching. His eyes had already closed in sleep.

...

I WAS OVERJOYED WHEN A FEW MONTHS LATER I REALIZED I HAD conceived again. Philip moved us back to Lierre and its canals and timber-framed houses; he threw lavish feasts, bought me jewels, gowns, and perfumes. This time, we would be blessed. This time, he declared, I would bear a son.

In early September, he departed for another convening of his Estates-General. This time, he went well armed, having spent weeks beforehand with Besançon drawing up legal arguments and statutes that proved he had reached his maturity. He took the archbishop with him, which was just as well. Though I hadn't told Philip about our confrontation that awful day, Besançon knew by my frigid stance he'd do best to keep to his proper place. Seeing as I was again with child, he did.

I remained in my comfortable apartments to nurture the babe in my womb, with my little girl, Eleanor, at my side. As with my first pregnancy, I suffered only a few weeks of the wretched nausea that prostrated other women and soon grew bored of sitting around all day. My midwives bled me, gathered around the basin to gauge my humors. They announced every sign indicated I carried a son, and I should indeed engage in some mild exercise to fortify his growth.

So I walked in the galleries, selected fabrics for my birthing chamber, and spent hours with Eleanor, who was a lovely, inquisitive babe. I also wrote to my sister Catalina, who recently celebrated her fourteenth birthday, telling her all my news and begging word of her. She wrote back a lengthy letter that startled me with its maturity, relating that Castile had suffered a terrible winter but that our little nephew the infante was improving and my sister Maria had wed the widowed Manuel of Portugal. Catalina added she was due to set sail for England soon and had begun exchanging personal letters with her betrothed, Prince Arthur. She thought him a noble and sincere prince, who seemed eager to meet her in person.

Remembering my anxieties when I learned I must leave Spain, I sent a reassuring letter in return and enclosed a gold bracelet as a gift.

Be brave, mi pequeñita, I told her. *You will soon find that marriage is a blessed state.*

. . .

IN FEBRUARY OF 1500, AS AN EARLY AND UNEXPECTED SNOW
drifted over Brussels, where we'd come to stay after the New Year and
where I delayed entering my confinement, dreading the weeks of seclusion waiting for my child to be born, Beatriz awoke me with news of
Philip's return after five months of toil with his Estates-General. I had received several letters from him in the interim, each relating that he was
closer than he'd ever been to gaining his autonomy as a prince. Ignoring
Doña Ana's objection that I was far too close to my time to risk leaving
my chambers, I rose from bed, clapping my hands. My ladies trudged
sleepily into the room.

"My toilette articles," I said. "Fetch them. And my new gown with the
extra panel as well."

An hour later, they stepped back to allow me a full view of myself in
the mirror.

I could not believe it at first. I stared in awe at my rose-tinted cheeks,
their angularity rounded by extra weight. My eyes shone bright, my cur-
vaceous figure accentuated by the gown's cut, the bodice pushing up my
full breasts, the overskirt with its extra waist panel draping in a swirling
column over my belly to my feet. I gasped, my hands dropping to my
stomach as my child suddenly kicked. Beatriz came behind me, clasped
my ruby pendant about my throat. "Your Highness has never looked
more beautiful," she said.

I nodded, voiceless.

I rarely paused to mark the passage of time, but somewhere between
Eleanor's birth and this pregnancy, I had shed the last traces of my adoles-
cence. The lanky infanta who worried about her height was gone; in her
place stood a disarming woman—the woman I would be for the rest of
my life.

"Am I?" I said, turning about. "Am I truly beautiful?"

"You are," said Beatriz. My women nodded. Doña Ana harrumphed.

"And you think he'll want to see me, like this? So . . . big?"

Beatriz laughed. "His Highness is a man, is he not? Every man wants
to see his wife big with child." She held out her hand. "Come. He awaits
you in the hall."

The great hall flared with light from the sconces. Smoke gathered in the painted eaves. Trestle tables strewn with used linen and silverware had been pulled aside, to clear the floor for dancing. Wine casks sat piled against the walls, testament to the anticipated hours of carousing in celebration of the archduke's arrival.

I halted at the top of the staircase. Music rang out, kettledrums thumping alongside the piping of rebecs. On the floor couples danced. I watched a woman laugh as her companion nuzzled her throat, and heard Doña Ana say, "You cannot mean to go down there in your state. You should have gone into confinement weeks ago. You are a woman with child."

"And a wife who will see her husband. If you do not approve, you can return to my rooms."

I did not wait for her response. She knew better, in any event, to try and stop me. Taking up my skirts, I walked down the stairs with perfect poise, focused on the dais, where Philip, Besançon, and several others sat. The archbishop's platter was piled high with roasted carcasses, his fat ringed fingers dripping sauce as he dug into a baked goose. He shouted between mouthfuls to the others, who were engaged in a rousing discussion. Philip reclined on his throne, legs propped on the table, his red brocade doublet unlaced, exposing his linen chemise. He held a goblet. Though his cheeks were flushed, he appeared sober.

Suddenly, one of his men leapt onto the table, his arms flung wide. He illustrated something to the laughing gentlemen, but when he spun about and caught sight of me coming toward him, he stopped in midaction, like a mime. The men followed his astonished stare. From the minstrel's gallery above the hall, the musicians ceased playing. The silence turned thick; the courtiers on the floor drew back. They whispered among themselves, marveling at my appearance. Even Besançon, usually oblivious to everything around him when filling his stomach, ceased shoving sauced brains into his mouth, gazing at me in slack-jawed disbelief.

I stopped before the dais, my belly jutting forth like an orb. Philip stood, adjusting his disheveled doublet, raking hands through his tawny hair. As he neared, I glimpsed the telltale flame in his eyes, familiar from our first days of marriage, when he'd been unable to contain himself and would drag me from wherever we happened to be to take me into the nearest chamber. Only this time, his lust intermingled with awe, as if he could not decide whether to prostrate himself before me or take me then and there.

He lifted my hand to his lips. "Wife, did you know purple velvet is reserved for empresses?"

My heart leapt. "Are you . . . ?"

He nodded, his mouth widening in a brilliant smile. "I am. You see before you the acknowledged prince of Flanders and official Habsburg heir. My father gave in finally. The Estates-General agreed I have reached my maturity and can rule my realm free of interference."

I shifted closer, my belly grazing his groin. "Then I am the happiest future empress in the world," I breathed. "But more important, I am the happiest mother of your future son."

His smile deepened, taking up the heat between us, all the more enticing because it had been months since we bedded together. He looked past me to where my ladies stood. "Your duenna will have my head if I let you stay. She already thinks I'm to blame for your brazen ways."

I shrugged. "Let her think what she likes. I've come to dance. And dance, I will."

"Dance?" He laughed. "If my eyes do not deceive me, you could give birth at any moment."

I laughed too, a soft, wicked laugh that brought his eyes back to mine. "Be that as it may, I shall dance tonight to celebrate my husband's return. You may do me the honor if you wish or perhaps I can find someone else to oblige me."

"You're mad," he said, even as he lifted his hand to the gallery. After a discordant tuning of strings, the musicians resumed their playing.

I sighed, "A pavane," and held out my hand to Philip. We stepped forward, shoulders and heads erect. The courtiers hastened to join us.

The music filled me. I forgot my aching spine, the stitch in my side, the weight of my stomach. Twirling about, I entered the adagio, laughing when he suddenly kissed my breast. The men and women separated to join hands with others, swaggering down the hall's length. Turning to the left, ignoring the curtsy to the bow, Philip and I found each other again, and those not participating in the dance gathered at the sides of the hall to clap.

The dancing grew more energetic, the women plucking up their skirts to expose shifting ankles. In an exuberant rush, I yanked off my coif and tossed it aside, eliciting delighted applause as my hair tumbled loose. Hands cocked on hips, I stood with the ladies, batting my eyes as Philip and the gentlemen kicked up their legs like zealous stags.

The hall grew stifling with the heat of bodies in motion. No one realized at first that as I stood clapping, the pain inside my womb began to build—slowly, mercilessly, gripping my innards until I gasped aloud. I tried to ignore it, but then another pang came, and another, until I doubled over, my knees buckling underneath me.

Beatriz ran to me. "The child," I told her breathlessly. "I can feel it!" She signaled the others, who rushed to surround me and lead me from the floor.

"I am tired," I called out, thinking Philip might follow. "It's nothing, honest. I just need to rest." I glanced over my shoulder to see him smiling at me, hemmed in by a wall of dancing courtiers. As I stood propped between my women at the foot of the staircase, I waved back and laughed between my clenched teeth.

"How many pains?" Doña Ana barked. "How close are they?"

"I'm not counting. I think—" I groaned. "Oh, no."

Pale pink water gushed from under my dress, spattering my satin shoes. Without hesitation, Doña Ana flung her stout arm about my waist. "We must get you to your chamber at once."

Slung between my duenna and Beatriz, I staggered up the stairs. By the time I reached the landing and began hastening down the corridor, I was fighting with all my will to contain the babe struggling to free itself from my womb. My water slowed to a trickle; there was a momentary lull in the pangs. I quickened my step into the gallery connected to my apartments.

Only a little more to go.

I felt the first warm blood seep down my thigh. A cry escaped me— "Dear God, it's started!"—and I faltered, the gallery seeming to stretch to infinity. I could go no farther. Flinging open the nearest door, I rushed into a privy and kicked aside the straw rushes. I started to crouch.

"No, not here!" cried Doña Ana.

"It's either here or out there," I snapped.

Without ado, Beatriz shoved her tight sleeves to her elbows and helped me to the floor, propping my legs on the privy stool. The little room stank of urine and feces, but fortunately the worst of the night's offenders had not yet made their drunken way here. My duenna stood aghast. Then I let out a high-pitched moan and she got down on her hands and knees to thrust her head under my skirts. "Like a pig in filth," I heard her mutter. "What will Her Majesty say when she hears of this?" Her fingers probed. "Someone fetch the cloths and my herb chest. Now!"

Footsteps fled.

I started to laugh at the absurdity of it all until a pain unlike any I had experienced suffocated my mirth. Doña Ana emerged from under my skirts, her hood askew. "I can see the child's head. Push, *mi niña*. Push as if your life depended on it."

"Push?" I shrieked. "I can't! It'll break me in two!"

"It will break you if you don't," she said, with steel in her voice. "Do it. *Ahora!*"

I braced myself, clutching the edge of the stool with one hand, the other digging into Beatriz as she knelt beside me. Hauling breath through my teeth, I pushed with all my strength.

Doña Ana thrust again under my gown, which was now hiked past my waist. "Almost there. Push one more time. Yes, that's it. Let nature do its work."

Soraya returned with the swaddling cloths and herb chest. I screamed, feeling an enormous obstacle prying me open. The pain was searing, all-encompassing; just as I thought I could take no more of it, something slipped loose and a vast, wet relief swept through me.

"The child," gasped Doña Ana. "Quick! Give me the scissors!"

Soraya jerked forward. A lumpy mass gushed from between my legs. In swift succession, I watched Doña Ana grab hold of a small, bloody body, nip with the scissors, and swat with her free hand. As a wail ruptured the silence, I collapsed against Beatriz. I wanted to ask if the child was healthy, if it was a boy, but my mouth was tinder-dry. Doña Ana took a vial from her coffer and rubbed the wailing infant in marigold ointment, then started swaddling it in the linen cloths.

An urgent clamor approached the privy. "My child," I whispered. "Give it to me."

I forced myself to sit up. Doña Ana set the babe in my arms. She hadn't finished the dressing, but the babe ceased crying when it felt me, and as I glanced at it, a thrill surged inside me.

I looked up to see Philip peering in, his eyes wide at the sight of the sweat-soaked women and me, spread-eagled in my bloodied finery.

I reached up, extending the child to him. "Behold your son."

And as he gazed through his tears at our boy in his arms, I laughed aloud, in triumph.

1500—1504

ARCHDUCHESS

...

BEHOLD HOW WONDERFUL AND JOYOUS

IT IS, WHEN KINGS AND PRINCES

LIVE IN HARMONY.

—ANONYMOUS

ELEVEN

...

I turned twenty-one in 1500, an age when most women of my rank have begun to settle into the rest of their lives. I had given birth to a healthy daughter and a son and had endured some of the trials every marriage undergoes. I could now look forward to a time of maturity and satisfaction, content in the rearing of my children and my role as patroness of my adopted realm.

I had the examples of countless predecessors to advise me: charity and the benefice of abbeys and convents, of the poor and the fallen, were the purview of privileged women like me. My education had prepared me since childhood for these tasks. My sisters and I had been taught that our power must be confined by our gender, that we would not rule but rather care for our husbands and their subjects in a manner that was neither obtrusive nor compromising. We would plant gardens, not monuments; we would leave echoes, not legends.

No one ever expected us to become anything other than what we were.

...

GHENT WAS A MARVELOUS CITY, ONE OF MY FAVORITES IN FLANders. With its steepled houses and their multicolored eaves, its stone bridges arching over the canal, bustling mercantile areas and majestic Gothic spires, it epitomized the enthusiastic Flemish spirit. The climate was rarely harsh (indeed, I never ceased to marvel at Flanders's temperate seasons, especially compared with the tempestuousness of Castile) and our palace nestled like a filigree ornament amid informal gardens where spring scattered the hedges with wildflowers and tulips clustered about fountains.

Seated on a chair under a canopy, I watched my sister-in-law, Margaret, pace the gravel paths with my baby, Charles, in her arms, Eleanor teetering behind with Madame de Halewin. My two-year-old daughter was growing into a sturdy child, her Aragonese blood evident in her olive-tinted complexion and the green-amber eyes that were so like mine. In contrast, my Charles was pure Habsburg, his preternaturally solemn gaze enhanced by skin so white he could not be taken outdoors without his oversize bonnet.

Margaret called to me: "*Chérie!* This boy is an angel, so patient and quiet."

I smiled in response, fingering the gold filigree brooch Philip had given me in honor of Charles's birth, an exquisite depiction of the castles and shields of Castile lined in rubies. I was pleased to have Margaret home, if only for a short while. She had arrived from Savoy declaring she might perish of boredom in her new husband's court, where she literally had nothing to do all day than accumulate a new and ostentatious wardrobe. Today she wore a pink gown slung with so many baubles she clanked like a bishop as she handed Charles to his nursemaid and dropped onto a stool beside me, her elongated features aglow with health.

"Must you go back?" I said. "I want to keep you here with us, selfish that I am. You're so good with the children, and we need every extra pair of hands we can get."

She laughed. "You've an entire palace of servants to serve you, my dear!" She patted my hand. "I wish I could stay. My husband is a frightful old goat, but he's quite fond of me and rather rich, so what else can I do? I did tell my father this is absolutely the last marriage I'll consent to for the sake of his empire." She let out a sigh. "But I'll miss the little ones so. Children can bring such joy to one's life."

"You'll make a wonderful mother someday. Perhaps you and the duke . . . ?"

Her bray startled my ladies seated nearby. "*Ma chérie,* how charming of you! Alas, my poor duke has barely enough strength to mount his close stool, much less me."

We giggled. Then Margaret said, "I don't believe I've ever seen you so happy." She went silent for a moment. "Is everything well, then?"

"It is," I said softly.

She nodded. "Good. That is how it should be." She turned her gaze to the garden, where Eleanor was yanking Madame de Halewin toward the fountain. Margaret leapt up. "You naughty child! Stop dragging poor Madame about like a mule!" She marched off to rescue the governess, scooping Eleanor up in her arms.

Madame staggered back to the ladies. "The child has the energy of three," she panted.

Doña Ana remarked dryly, "You should sit, madame, before you drop dead of apoplexy."

I resisted a chuckle. With the birth of my children, my duenna and the governess had found a modicum of mutual accord, for even Doña Ana had had to agree that Madame's years of experience made her the perfect instructor for Eleanor.

I raised a hand to my brow, shielding the sun. It promised to be an unseasonably warm afternoon and I looked forward to a nap in the coolness of my rooms before the evening banquet. Then I caught sight of a page running toward me, dressed in our livery of black and yellow.

He came to a breathless halt and bowed low. Sweat dripped from the curls under his cap. "His Highness asks that Your Highness join him. An urgent missive has arrived from Spain."

His words flung a pall over the sun. I rose, ignoring Doña Ana's stare as I called to Margaret, "Philip is asking for me. Will you see to the children?"

TENSION LAY THICK IN the chamber. My stomach knotted when I saw Besançon seated at Philip's desk, a boulder in his satin and silly tonsure cap, his unblinking toadlike stare fixed on me as I entered the room. Philip turned from where he stood by the window, his face in shadow. He started to move to me when the archbishop burst out without warning: "We've received momentous news. The infante Miguel is dead. Your Highness is the new heiress of Castile."

I felt myself gasp but did not hear my own voice, searching Philip's expression for the confirmation I did not want to hear. He said, "I am sorry, my love. Your mother has sent word, requesting we go to Spain as soon as possible."

I found it hard to draw a full breath. "How?" I whispered. "How did my sister's son die?"

"His lungs failed him, poor soul." Besançon genuflected cursorily before lifting a sheaf of documents from the desk. "Now then, these papers must be signed and—"

Sudden fury surged in me. "My family has suffered a terrible loss. I'll sign no papers today."

He paused. One thin, fair brow arched. "Your Highness, I fear this matter cannot wait."

"Well, it must!" I rounded on him, releasing in my distraught state the venom I'd nursed toward him. "You astound me, my lord. Have you no inclination to the holy office you purport to serve? You speak of the death of an infante of Spain!"

I felt Philip's hand on my shoulder, though I had not seen him move to me. "My lord," he murmured. "Let it be."

"But Your Highness, the document . . . It must—"

"I said let it be. I will speak with her. Now go."

His jowls quivering, Besançon swept out, his robes hissing on the floor like an angry tail.

Philip put a goblet in my hand. "Drink, my love. You've gone white as a sheet."

The warm claret hit my stomach like lead. A terrible queasiness overcame me. It must be the heat, I thought faintly, the heat and shock of the news.

I set the goblet aside with a shaking hand. "What are we going to do?" I said, and I realized I spoke as if of a catastrophe, an earthquake, or terrible fire that had upended my entire world.

I was Spain's heir. When my parents died, I would be queen. Tragedy had cut a swath through my family and brought me to this unexpected, frightening place. What I had never imagined possible had come to pass. Spain now waited for me.

As if from a vast distance I heard Philip say, "We must prepare, of course. But first, we'll send Besançon to meet with your parents in person."

I pulled myself to attention. "No. Not him."

Philip's mouth tightened. "Why not? He is my chancellor."

"Because I . . . I do not trust him."

"Juana, this is no time for grievances. He is an expert in these matters: he knows best how to handle such scenarios." He held up a hand. "And don't tell me he mishandled that affair with your matrons. We need an experienced adviser, and I trust him with my life. We are the heirs of Castile and Aragón. We must present ourselves appropriately."

I marked the subtle change in him, his chest puffed out and chin erect, as if he already wore the crown of prince consort. That title Besançon had sought for him from my parents was now his, and he seemed as comfortable with it as I was not. I thought it was normal for him; he was used to being a sole heir and the center of attention, but I could scarcely believe it was happening. How could my life have turned so momentous so quickly?

The air in the room felt heavy. "I'd still prefer we send another," I said. "Or perhaps we could just go ourselves. My mother did ask for us, not Besançon."

I heard his foot tap on the floor. "Juana," he said, with a hint of impatience, "you're not thinking clearly. Such a trip can't be planned overnight. We could be gone months; we have our children to consider, my councillors, and the Estates-General to address. No, best to let Besançon pave our way; he can convey our condolences and sign any official documents, then consult with your mother and her council. He is, after all, Cisneros of Toledo's equal."

He was right, of course. We couldn't simply leave. We had a newborn son, a daughter, our households, our entire court. I started to give my reluctant consent when I realized my teeth were chattering. I felt a chill seep into my very bones. I swayed on my chair; as he moved quickly to catch me I whispered, "My women . . . call for my women."

Then blackness overcame me.

. . .

I AWOKE HOURS LATER IN MY BED, MY ENTIRE BODY ACHING AS though I'd taken a fall from a horse. At my bedside, Doña Ana wrung out and replaced the marigold-soaked cloth on my brow. Beatriz and Soraya looked on anxiously.

"Am I sick?" I asked. The mere act of speaking made me want to retch. I'd contracted some plague, I thought. The curse that claimed my brother and sister was about to claim me.

"Nothing out of the ordinary," replied Doña Ana. "You're with child again."

I stared at her. "That's not possible. I . . . I've never felt this ill before."

"Nevertheless, you are with child." She sniffed. "You have all the signs. It's hardly surprising, not when a woman will indulge herself as much as you do."

I sank into my pillows. The timing couldn't have been worse.

Doña Ana stood. "You'd best rest now while you can. When a babe acts up this early, the rest of the term is bound to be difficult."

"That isn't what I need to hear," I groused. I turned away, yanking my covers over my head.

Within moments I succumbed to sleep.

...

TWELVE

Just as Doña Ana predicted, my third pregnancy proved to be my worst. Never had I felt so wretched or exhausted. I did not bestir myself to witness Besançon's pontifical departure for Spain, his saddlebags stuffed with documents and his retinue large enough to fill a hamlet. I did not greet the envoys who came from all over Europe to seek favor with the new heirs of Spain. I took refuge in my rooms, knowing as soon as I delivered my child, all of that, and more, would be waiting for me.

On June 15, 1501, after seven agonizing hours of labor that proved a fitting end to her gestation, I gave birth to another daughter. I barely looked up from my sweat-drenched pillows as the midwives cleansed and swaddled her. I feared I might hate her after the misery she'd put me through. But when she was set in my arms and I took one look at her limpid blue eyes, everything melted away. With the golden fuzz on her still-soft and misshapen head—sure sign that like my mother in her youth, she would have hair rich as a Castilian wheat field—she was the child I had awaited, without ever knowing it.

"Isabella," I announced. "I shall call her Isabella, in honor of my mother and sister."

I shook my head when Doña Ana came to take her from me to deliver to the robust peasant woman chosen as a nursemaid. Instead, to my duenna's gasp, I unlaced my shift. The greedy nub of Isabella's mouth on my aching nipple sent pleasure rippling through me. I closed my eyes, ignoring Doña Ana's remark that such a thing had never been seen, a woman of the blood royal giving teat like a cow in a field.

Philip came to visit me while I recovered and recounted with a laugh that I was the scandal of the court, word having gotten out that I nursed my own infant. He held Isabella and complimented me on her perfection, and then he told me he had received a communiqué from Besançon, saying all was going as planned in Spain.

With the child out of my womb and my malaise subsided, the news made me sit upright. "What does he mean, 'as planned'?"

"Nothing for you to fret about," he said, and he kissed me. "Now rest. You need your strength. We have a trip to Spain to plan, remember?"

Three weeks after the birth, I still had not relinquished Isabella to Madame de Halewin and the battalion of servants waiting to earn their keep. I ordered a crib set up near my own bed, and kept her there at my side day and night.

Philip went to meet with his Estates-General, leaving me in a palace full of women and old men. Times past, I would have missed him. Not now. I had recovered my strength and my wits, and I had my own business to take care of. I sat at my desk and wrote a long missive to my mother, telling her of Isabella's birth and asking for news. I included a substantial donation for masses to be said for my late sister and her dead babe and assured my mother I was preparing to come as soon as arrangements were made.

I then had my apartments cleaned, my plate polished, all my gowns aired. I saw to Eleanor's first lessons and the weaning of Charles from his nursemaid; above all else, I attended to my Isabella. Never had I felt so protective. It was almost as though I sought to shield my child from some unseen threat, though I could not name what I feared.

We were playing together in my rooms, I dangling a gilded rattle with a tiny bell over her as she cooed and pedaled her tiny feet, when Beatriz brought me the letter.

"This just arrived with the courier from Brussels." She gave me a searching look before she swept a delighted Isabella up, taking her into the bedchamber while I went to my desk, letter in hand. Cracking the seal, I unfolded the wide, rough parchment. I recognized its grain at once; my mother's stationery lacked the silky hue of my own letter stock.

For a moment, all of my childhood trepidations came flooding back, as if the great Isabel might stride into my chamber at any moment to test my readiness to assume her throne. I had never been her favorite: I had never been her chosen successor. But as I held the letter closer to my face, I discerned the faint scent of candle smoke and a touch of lavender, and it brought sudden tears to my eyes. I looked at my mother's handwriting slanted across the page:

My dearest hija,

I trust this letter reaches you in good health. I have prayed for you every day, so that you will find succor in what is surely a woman's most exacting hour. But I knew God would see you safely delivered of your child, for you are strong of body as I once was. Never did the childbed test me as it did others. Your news that you have safely delivered a daughter christened in my honor also brings a welcome balm to my heart, for I have just sent your sister Catalina to her marriage in England, and I miss her company dearly, as she was my last child and of great comfort to me in this time of dolor.

I write to you now because I am like Jonah in the whale, fighting the insurmountable. The lord archbishop Besançon has just left us, unsatisfied, I fear. His demands for your husband's recognition as infante did not go over well with our Cortes or us. He does not seem to understand that we cannot invest Philip with the title nor grant him investiture as prince consort of these realms before we have invested you, for the succession devolves on you as our primary heir. These are perilous times, and I must therefore beg you not to delay further but rather come to us as soon as you can, with your husband and your children, if at all possible. In anticipation, I am sending my own secretary, Señor Lopez de Conchillos, to you, in whom I've entrusted my advice.

Be well, my child, and remember the grand estate to which God has called you.

Your loving madre,
Isabel the Queen

I stood, silent, the letter open like a missal in my hands. I had not read the unswerving command of the mother I'd known; I had not found the asperity of a queen who must concede her succession to a daughter she'd never been close with. Instead, she sounded tired, almost defeated. I had expected stern reminders of duty, of the need to set every other consideration aside, but I never stopped to consider she had buried a son, a daughter, and a grandson in less than two years. I couldn't imagine losing one child, much less two, and in that moment I saw her not as the invincible queen but as a vulnerable woman and mother, like me.

And Besançon! He was a snake with a tonsure, demanding all he could for Flanders while my parents faced a tomb filled with crushed hopes, an ever-fractious nobility and anxious Cortes. But I had the upper hand now. He could not wring for Philip what I, in my time, could freely give: the crown of king consort. The archbishop's time of power was fast coming to an end.

My fingers grazed the letter's splintered seal. I turned to stare into my chamber.

It was as if I awoke from a long, torpid dream. The sunlight cascading through the velvet drapery illumined the costly tapestries on my walls, woven in Brussels and depicting satyrs and rubicund maidens in arbors. My Spanish standing cup sat on my cabinet, almost hidden behind a troop of porcelain shepherdesses sent by Anne of Brittany, Louis of France's queen, as a gift in honor of the near-concurrent births of my Isabella and her own daughter, Claude of France.

I'd scarcely looked at the silly things, relegating them to the hundreds of objets d'art cluttering my suite. I'd been living so long among a plethora of paintings, statues, furnishings, and hangings that I had literally ceased to see them. Now as I stood there, surrounded by this opulence, I felt abruptly starved of air, the smell of sweet herbs sprinkled over the carpets underfoot coating my senses like soot.

In my mind, I saw Spain, immense and ever mutable, with its stark granite pinnacles and parched plateaus, its serpentine rivers and dense woodlands of pine and oak. Flanders was like an enamel gem box compared with the feral treasury of my native land, where fountains sang in mosaic patios and hills changed colors as the sun died, where chalk cities tumbled down eagle-haunted cliffs, crowned by stone castles that seemed rooted between heaven and earth. I longed for the taste of tart pomegranate, of lemons and oranges from Seville; I wanted to hear bells toll across an empty plain and see myself again in the resolute vigor of a people who never surrendered their pride. The loneliness pervading me was physical, like a voyager who has grown weary after years of wandering and now seeks the road home.

I was not afraid. I could learn to be queen. It was in my blood, the same blood that propelled my mother. She had not known everything the day she mounted the throne; yet like her, I had been called to it. Spain had bestowed upon me this crown.

My eyes opened. I called for Beatriz. She came to the door with Isabella cradled in her arms.

"My mother is sending a visitor," I told her. "We must prepare."

. . .

"YOUR HIGHNESS, I AM DELIGHTED TO SEE YOU." LOPEZ DE CON-chillos bowed over my hand. He was a middle-aged, sprite man with benevolent brown eyes and a receding hairline, clad in a wool doublet that smelled of straw. I'd known him since my childhood: he'd served my mother faithfully as her chief secretary; to him, she entrusted her most important correspondence.

I smiled, indicating the chair opposite mine. "I too am pleased to see you, my lord. It has been too long since I welcomed a fellow countryman. Please, sit."

Rain spattered the window, a pebbly murmur emphasized by my chamber's unadorned walls. In the week preceding his arrival, I'd had my apartments stripped of all excess, including the lurid tapestries, and taken equal care with my appearance, donning a modest high-necked black gown. My jewelry consisted of my wedding bands and a small crucifix; I sought to exemplify the formality of a Castilian matron and saw in Lopez's appraisal that I had succeeded.

Beatriz and Soraya slipped in with platters of stuffed olives, brown bread, cheese, and a decanter of claret. From under my lashes, I saw him nod in approval at this simple fare.

A brief silence ensued while I let him eat. Then I took a sealed envelope from my pocket. "I've written to Her Majesty. In here, she will find my solemn vow to comply with my duty."

He inclined his head and took the letter from me. "Your words will no doubt assist Her Majesty greatly in her recovery."

"Recovery?" I paused. "Is my mother ill?"

He sighed. "The doctors tell us it's not serious. Her Majesty has been ordered to rest, and it is an order she does not take well to."

I gave a faint smile. "No, she does not." I paused. "I would know everything of Besançon's visit, and what Her Majesty my mother requires of me."

"Then I suggest you brace yourself, *princesa,* for it is not an edifying tale."

My hands closed about my chair arms as he began to speak. It was much as I expected, though that didn't make it any easier to hear. Besançon had acted in Spain with his customary arrogance, demanding concessions from my parents he had no right to, including several bishoprics and benefices for himself.

Then Lopez said something that sent a chill through me. "When their Majesties rebuked him for his presumption, the archbishop replied he had the means to make them reconsider. Though he did not say the words, there can be little doubt as to what he meant." He paused, looked at me. "Is Your Highness aware that he recently met with envoys from France?"

"I was not," I said. "Is it something I should be concerned about?"

"It could be. We don't know why he chose this particular time to accept King Louis' advances, but anything having to do with the French cannot behoove Spain. Her Majesty believes Besançon might seek French support for your husband, perhaps even an alliance that will, in effect, relegate Spain to the position of a suppliant."

My voice flared at once. "Philip would not allow it! He knows Spain can never trust France."

Lopez met my outburst with silence. Then he said, "Are you quite certain, *princesa?*"

"As certain as I am of my own self. My husband isn't here to speak for himself, as he had to attend his Estates to gain their approval for us to undertake this journey, but I assure you he and I are in perfect accord. We would never ally ourselves with a realm that has invaded my father's kingdom in the past and challenges his right to Naples."

"Then, I am relieved; and so will be Her Majesty. Still, it might be wise to remain attentive. We know Besançon met with French envoys but we haven't been able to learn anything beyond that. But perhaps he'll inform His Highness, and His Highness will, in turn, tell you?"

Doubt crept over me. Besançon had played me for a fool before; and his relationship with Philip was not something I'd succeeded in affecting. If he planned something with Louis of France, I would be the last person to hear about it.

"I don't want to be dishonest with my husband," I said tentatively. "He and Besançon share a long history; the archbishop is his adviser and mentor. Philip trusts him."

"Her Majesty understands. She would not want you to do anything to cause dissension. Indeed, her primary concern is that you and His Highness reach Spain. She hopes your son, Charles, might be brought as well, so that she can see him in person."

I gave a quick nod. "I'll consult with Philip when he returns. I don't see why Charles shouldn't accompany us, though he is very young. As for this French matter . . . well, I shall see what I can discover, yes? That is all I can promise."

"Thank you, *princesa*. Her Majesty urges caution in your dealings henceforth, particularly with the archbishop. She is aware of the esteem in which he is held here and does not wish for you to make an enemy of him. Once you and your husband reach Spain and are invested by the Cortes, a more appropriate adviser for His Highness will be found."

"Yes," I said hotly. "My husband lacks impartial counsel. He's relied too long on Besançon."

"And Your Highness? Do you lack counsel?"

His perceptiveness caught me off guard. In truth, I had never had counsel besides my trusted ladies. I'd not had any need of it. But princes needed councillors, and queens relied on them.

"I would appreciate some now," I said. "I wouldn't want anything to reflect poorly on me or Spain."

Lopez smiled. "*Princesa,* trust in me and all will go well."

. . .

A FEW DAYS LATER, PHILIP RETURNED TO COURT. HE CAME BOUND-ing into my rooms, a wide smile on his face, and swept me up in his arms to nuzzle my throat. "My infanta, I missed you!"

I laughed nervously as I waved my women out and went to the side-board to pour him a goblet. As I raised the decanter, it struck me how much our marriage had come to resemble my parents', with even this token gesture between us to initiate our reunions. I also felt a stab of guilt that I could not tell him what Lopez and I had discussed.

I gave him the goblet with a smile. "I gather the Estates went well. Did they grant you everything you requested?"

"They did. They've agreed to oversee the realm while we are away and approve our expenditures. We will go to Spain in grand style." He sipped his wine, looking about the room. "You've redecorated." He paused. It was as if the room took on a sudden chill. "I understand a Spanish envoy is here. You could have written to me. I'd have come sooner to welcome him."

"Oh, it wasn't necessary," I said, fearing my deception showed like a brand on my face as I returned to my chair and the bassinet cloth I was sewing for Isabella. "He's come as part of our escort to Spain. We spoke mostly of family matters."

I smoothed the cloth. He did not say anything, looking at me with intense focus. I found myself wanting to fill the sudden silence and blurted, "And my lord Besançon? Any word of him? I assume he's arrived by now?"

I raised my gaze, saw his hand tighten about the jeweled goblet stem. His response was abrupt. "He has. He sent word that he is indisposed from the voyage but hopes to be here in a few days' time." He paced to the sideboard. "So, this envoy had nothing important to say?"

"Only that my parents expect us as soon as possible, and they'd like us to bring Charles."

He gave a tight laugh and quaffed his goblet. "I hope you told him we'll do nothing of the sort. Charles is far too young to be subjected to prolonged travel. He and the girls will stay here."

I looked up sharply. "You've already decided this? My sisters and I traveled throughout Spain in our childhoods, and none of us suffered from it."

He had started to lift the decanter; he turned about, scowling. "This is not Spain. We've a long trip ahead of us, and seeing as we must go by land through France, we—"

He went still. For a moment, I was so taken aback I didn't know what to do. Lopez's advice that I not cause dissension flitted through my head moments before I clapped the bassinet cloth aside and stood. "Through France? You cannot be serious!"

"I am. Louis has invited us to his court to meet him, his queen, and their newborn daughter. I think we should accept."

"And I think not. I'd rather swim to Spain than set foot in that land of devils."

"God's death!" He banged his goblet on the sideboard. "Would you dictate to me, wife?"

My heart leapt against my ribs. I felt myself take a step back, bumping into my chair. I was riveted by the change that came over him, his eyes like icy slits, his entire countenance darkening, twisted.

"I . . . I only meant, we cannot accept," I quavered. "We are Spain's heirs now, and France is our enemy."

"That is precisely why we must accept." He swerved back to the decanter, poured himself another goblet. He drank it down in a single gulp, reached for the decanter again. He never drank this much during the day. All of a sudden, my legs felt so weak I had to sit down.

He turned back around, regarding me. His voice softened. "Juana, you do not understand."

My heart's erratic beat slowed. Cold sweat congealed under my gown. He came toward me. He seemed himself again; I thought I must have imagined the violence I'd glimpsed in his eyes.

"No," I said, "I don't understand. I see no reason why we must go to France."

"We must go because we are Spain's future rulers and must behave accordingly. Louis extended his invitation through my Estates; he has no other motive than to seek our favor."

"The French always have a motive," I retorted, but for the first time I started to doubt my own words. I'd been so inculcated against France since childhood I'd never questioned it.

"Well, Louis' only motive now is to make sure we don't strike a pact with your parents that will set half of Europe against him. He's terrified for his safety. Your sister Catalina has married the English heir, your other sister Maria married Portugal; now you and I are heirs to Spain, not to mention that one day I stand to inherit my father's empire. I've become a threat. Louis needs my friendship, and if all goes as planned I intend to give it."

He held up a hand, cutting off my protest. "I warn you now, I'll not inherit your parents' feuds. Spain, the Habsburgs, and France—this enmity must end."

"Then let Louis first end his claim on Naples." My previous trepidation vanished in the heat of my own anger. "I know you seek to do well, but my parents will never sanction an alliance between us and the French."

"I do not make an alliance for Spain," he said. "I do it for Flanders." He paused. "Juana, we share a border with France. The same threat Aragón has faced could happen here. In order for us to leave, my Estates insist we first accept Louis' invitation. I am compelled by my duty as archduke to heed them, just as your parents must heed their Cortes."

"Then you go without me." I raised my chin. "I cannot be seen there."

He sighed. "You are my wife, the heiress of Castile. Of course, you must come. It's no dishonor to show graciousness to a fellow sovereign whose position is weaker than yours. And we'll only stay a week or two, at most."

I struggled against his logic. I did not want to see the world as he did, because it conflicted with the world I'd known all my life. I felt as though I dishonored my father, Aragón, the very foundation of Spain itself. I wished I could talk to Lopez before I made my decision, but I sensed he'd tell me what I already knew: if Besançon was behind this meeting with Louis, it would behoove us to find out what he sought to gain by it. And Philip was right: our position as Spain's heirs had eclipsed France's might. One day, we'd unite the Habsburg Empire and Spain under our rule; we would encircle France like wolves. What did I possibly have to fear?

I took a steadying breath. "Very well," I said. I retrieved my embroidery with a steady hand. "But I would like to be apprised of all future preparations for our trip."

His brow furrowed. "Why? It'll be tedious business for a woman's ears."

"No doubt, but we'll be gone a long time, as you say, and I want to oversee the plans for the children. Not to mention, it's not every day an infanta goes to France."

He guffawed. "I see. You want to have the most lavish gowns and jewels, of course, though you don't need them, my love. You could outshine Anne of Brittany in your shift." He regarded me with a lingering smile. Did he honestly see my concerns as mere vanity? Or was he playing the fool, I thought, as he bent over me, his kiss rousing an unexpected lack of physical response.

"I'll tell you everything," he murmured. "We'll also dine alone tonight, so we can enjoy a proper reunion."

I raised my lips to his, perturbed by my apathy. I had never lacked for heat with him, but then, it was a dangerous game I played.

Yet as he swaggered out to change his clothes for supper, I resolved not to falter.

. . .

THE ENSUING WEEKS PUT MY RESOLVE TO THE TEST. BESANÇON returned to court looking smug and immediately closeted himself with Philip. Lopez confirmed to me that while I'd made the right decision, I should continue to be watchful. I found the ongoing deception unnerving and reassured myself it would all probably result in a mere few days of discomfort, nothing more.

I suffered anxiety over leaving my children, especially my little Isabella, who wasn't yet six months old. I must have interviewed a hundred nursemaids before I settled on one Isabella seemed to like; fortunately, Madame de Halewin and, to my surprise, Doña Ana, reassured me they would remain to oversee the children's household. My old duenna insisted she was too old to cross the Pyrenees, adding with pointed emphasis she'd rather die here than be seen alive in France. I evaded her rebuke, comforted that my children would have her to watch over them, and dedicated myself to spending as much time as I could with Charles, Eleanor, and Isabella.

Finally, on a bright winter day in November 1501, as crowds gathered at the roadside to stare in wonder, we left Ghent. Philip led the cavalcade on his white destrier, resplendent in scarlet. I rode beside him on a dappled mare, in amber brocade that matched my eyes.

To Spain, to Spain, I sang inside. Soon, I would reunite with my parents, with the memories of my childhood and promise of my future. My eyes burned with tears of sudden joy. I could survive anything, even time in France, for soon Philip and I would be in the land of my birth.

And there, we would fulfill our destiny.

THIRTEEN

...

As soon as we crossed into France, my disquiet resurfaced. Louis had sent an entourage of noblemen and -women to welcome us, and I eyed the primped and powdered ladies with covert mistrust. That old feudal enmity between France and Spain could be felt in the air, like a storm about to burst. I was acutely aware of the fact that regardless of the stated intent, here I would be seen as an enemy, the daughter of the wily Fernando of Aragón, whose claim to Naples was a perpetual thorn in France's side.

Nevertheless, I was astonished by the sheer breadth and beauty of the landscape, with its seemingly endless vales and silken forests, its radiant skies, prosperous hamlets, and luxuriant vineyards. I had never thought any realm could equal the inviolate majesty of Spain and could not resist a thrill of involuntary excitement when I caught sight of Paris in a haze of mist.

Above the labyrinthine streets, the spire of Notre Dame spiked the fading sun. Bells pealed from every church, a deafening clangor that summoned the Parisians to swarm out and welcome us, shouting and tossing bouquets of autumn flowers until the air shimmered like copper.

We were taken to the old palace of the Louvre, where we were told Louis and his queen had traveled to the Val du Loire to prepare Château de Blois for us. In their place, the princes of Bourbon acted as hosts, and while Philip toured the city with his men, I had an unexpected visit from the count Don de Cabra, my mother's ambassador to the Tudor court, who'd heard of my stop in France and had come to see me on his way to England. I received him with some reserve, thinking he might bring my mother's rebuke of my travels here. Instead, he told me my sister Catalina had arrived in England and related her entry into London, during which

she'd shown impeccable dignity even in the face of unfamiliar surroundings and King Henry VII's brusque entry into her rooms one night to
order her to remove her veil.

"She was of course most taken aback and her duenna outraged," the
count said, "but the king insisted he must see if she was deformed in some
way before he could let her marry his heir. She graciously complied.
Naturally, then he was the one to be taken aback when he saw her beauty
and he proceeded to introduce her to his court as though she were a prized
jewel."

I recalled my own unveiling before Besançon and thought with a pang
of how bewildered Catalina must feel, alone among strangers and so far
from home.

"And her betrothed, Prince Arthur?" I asked anxiously. "Did they appear to like each other?"

The count smiled. "Ah, yes. They are like two angels. Prince Arthur is
very slim and shy, but he seemed enamored of Her Highness. So did his
younger brother, Prince Henry, who threw off his doublet during their
nuptial feast to cavort before her in his chemise and breeches like a pagan.
Those English are barbarians, uncouth and loud. They're fortunate indeed to have the infanta Catalina as their future queen. They call her
Catherine of Aragón since her marriage."

"I must write to her," I murmured, ashamed that in the upheaval of
my own life I had forgotten to mark the day of her departure. It saddened
me that I would not see her on my arrival in Spain. I wrote her a long letter that very day, entrusting it to the count, who assured me he would see
it safely to England. In it, I promised to be a sister to her no matter what
and implored her to write to me anytime, for I knew what it was like to do
our duty for our country.

The following afternoon, we left for the Loire Valley. We arrived in
Blois on the eve of December 7, under an icy rain. Through the main
gateway covered in friezes, I rode into the courtyard, drenched to my skin.
Philip had gone ahead with his entourage; the moment I dismounted, a
young woman of no more than seventeen years with sloe-black eyes and
an unattractive, pursed mouth hustled up to me, accompanied by a clutch
of stiff-faced companions.

She curtsied. "Madame Archduchess, I am Mademoiselle Germaine de Foix, niece to His Majesty King Louis. I have the honor of being your escort and lady of honor during your visit."

She spoke as though nothing could have been less appealing to her. I signaled to Beatriz and Soraya, started to inform Mlle de Foix I hardly required more attendants when she seized me by my arm and literally swept me off into the redbrick château. My women hastened to follow, but before I knew it I found myself within the palace, led down stone corridors hung with enormous tapestries, the posse of French ladies hemming me in.

They might have succeeded in bypassing the hall completely had I not spied the open double doors to my left and forcibly pulled back.

The enormous room glowed under the lit tapers of huge silver candelabra suspended on chains from a rich paneled ceiling. I stepped forth. Behind me, Mlle de Foix hissed, *"Madame, c'est le chambre du roi!"*

I fixed my gaze on the dais at the far end, where Philip stood with Besançon, their backs to me. Scores of men filled the hall—the musky smell of their damp capes and perfumes turning sour in the heat of the scented smoke rising from the braziers.

I lifted my chin and entered. They turned to stare.

In the silence, the wet dragging of my skirts across the tiled floor sounded loud as spurred boots. I heard outraged male gasps. Philip spun about, white-faced, revealing the king on a dais.

I paused. Despite his fearsome reputation, Louis XII cut an unprepossessing figure. In his early forties, having inherited his crown late in life, he had lank graying hair cut bluntly above his protruding ears, his narrow face overpowered by the hooked Valois nose. His shoulders lacked breadth, even though they were draped in cloth of silver, and his shanks were spindly in their black hose. Only his narrow metallic eyes betrayed the cunning that had made him my father's avowed foe—his eyes, and his fingers, which were thin, tapering, and spidery.

I stood still. I did not curtsy. His blood was no more royal than mine. Indeed, one might argue his was rather less.

His thin lips curved. "Madame Archduchess, welcome to France."

"Thank you, Your Majesty." I could feel the French courtiers staring, infuriated by my refusal to acknowledge their king's superiority. Philip came to me. His face was stony, his hand hard where he gripped my sleeve. "What are you doing?" he said between his teeth.

I could see in his expression and the archbishop's baleful stare that they hadn't intended to see me here at all, but I couldn't for the life of me understand why not. Was there some ancient custom in France that prohibited a woman from entering the king's presence without prior leave? It wouldn't have surprised me: France was one of the few kingdoms that still barred female succession. But I was not just any woman. I was the heiress of Castile.

"I am greeting His Majesty," I replied clearly. I even managed a smile and a brief half-curtsy. "That is why we are here, is it not?"

Philip's face turned bright red. Besançon looked fit to burst. Louis chuckled from his throne. *"Mon ami,"* he said to Philip, "your wife is as enchanting as I imagined. But she must be *très fatigue, oui?"* He returned his gaze to me. Though his smile did not waver, his eyes were like onyx. "No doubt she'd benefit from time alone with those of her own sex. She should proceed to her visit with my wife, *la reine,* and leave us bereft of her presence."

I shot a look at Philip. He avoided my stare. Visit with the queen? Resentment and suspicion surged in me. What was this? Before I could find a way to counter this obvious dismissal, I heard heels clack to me. Once again, the insufferable Mlle de Foix snatched me by the arm and steered me from the hall, past my stricken women, who it seemed were to be left in their sodden cloaks here in the passageway like penitents, with my baggage piled at their feet.

"Milady, if you please, I must attend to my women." I plucked at the viselike fingers, trying to extricate my arm without resorting to force, even as Mlle de Foix propelled me into an adjoining room. I steeled myself when I saw the walls hung with white velvet, emblazoned with the ermines of Brittany and Valois fleur-de-lis.

This time, rapacious female stares greeted me. They parted to reveal Queen Anne on an upholstered chair before a massive marble fireplace, an embroidery hoop in her hands as though this were but another afternoon to fill with pastime.

"Her Highness the archduchess of Burgundy and Flanders," Mlle de Foix announced.

Anne of Brittany looked up. She had a silk skein raveled about her fat bejeweled neck, her face as round and pasty as the white cheese for which her duchy was famous. *"Ah, mais oui. Entré."* She waved her hand, ensconced on her chair, her plump body squeezed into an ornate ivory damask gown inlaid with pearls.

I knew she was lame in one leg and assumed at first her infirmity prevented her from rising. But as the seconds passed and she sat there smiling, without even a semblance of effort on her part, it became clear that Anne of Brittany had no intention of rising at all, infirmity or no.

It was a deliberate insult. Descended from eleventh-century merchant stock that had clawed its way to respectability, her blood could not compare to mine. She might be twice queen, having had the good fortune to wed Louis' predecessor before she wed Louis, but I was of an ancient royal lineage and it was on the tip of my tongue to inform her as much. I resisted the urge, thinking it wouldn't bode well for the rest of our visit.

I gritted my teeth, started to give her the same stiff half-curtsy I'd accorded Louis. She motioned. Before I knew it, Mlle de Foix stepped to me and gripped my arm. Her fingers dug into my elbow like talons, sending a shooting pain through my shoulder and, to my horror, propelling me farther to the floor than I had intended.

The queen's smile widened. *"Mais non, madame.* We are among friends here."

I stood, quivering with rage, my fists clenched at my sides.

Anne of Brittany savored her victory for a few seconds. Then she motioned again. "They will see you to your apartments. We shall dine together later, yes?"

Mlle de Foix and her ladies closed in around me.

. . .

SO IT WENT FOR FOUR INTERMINABLE DAYS.

The rain turned to sleet, limiting any escape to the gardens. Trapped indoors with nothing to do, I could not even wander the palace, forced to attend the queen in her apartments and endure her four daily masses and hours of acidic appraisal, while Philip roistered with Louis and his nobles and Besançon cooked up God knew what with the French council.

By the fifth day, I was beside myself. Philip stayed away from me at night, enjoying long banquets with the men in this court where the sexes never seemed to mingle except by prior arrangement, and his absence only added to my suspicion and distress. I stormed about my lavish hated rooms, declaring I would not be further insulted, but Lopez kept advising caution, patience, though his kindly face began to look as strained as mine.

On the sixth morning of our visit, I entered Anne of Brittany's chambers to find her surrounded by her illustrious collection of ladies; a large upholstered and gilded cradle sat prominently before her like a centerpiece.

"My daughter, Claude of France," she informed me.

I stepped to the cradle. I'd wondered why this trophy of her womb, the only child she'd borne to survive infancy, hadn't been touted out before now. I reasoned it was because in this matter Anne was clearly my inferior. I'd already borne three children, one of whom was a son and heir for Philip, while she'd failed thus far to give Louis the prince he needed to succeed him. If she did not, he'd be obliged to hand over France through marriage to his daughter. Claude could never rule as queen regnant, as France prohibited a female to take the throne.

Under lace coverlets, I saw a wan face and sad big eyes, a glittering cap on the still sparsely haired head. I was wickedly pleased to discover the French princess looked half of my Isabella's weight and had none of her charms; when the little princess then screwed up her mouth in a pained grimace and let out an astonishingly loud fart, I smiled.

I turned to the queen. "Her Highness Claude sounds indisposed. You might consider adding some more fruit to her diet and less cheese."

Anne of Brittany's face turned cold. "She's had some colic. It will pass. I do hope you do not recommend fruit for your son, madame. It is known that such can affect a boy's maturity, and my lord archbishop Besançon assured me he would grow up to be a strong, healthy husband."

I froze. I could not take my eyes from her. The room went completely still, the women's stares boring into me. The queen said, "Will you not kiss your daughter-in-law, madame?"

I felt as if she'd spewed filth on me. I could scarcely turn as, with a smirk, Mlle de Foix extracted the babe from her cradle, rousing an instant burst of wailing. I touched my lips to the little head, then turned and swept from the chamber without a word.

Behind me, I heard the queen and her ladies begin to laugh.

I banged into my chambers. Lopez sat at the table penning one of his dispatches; Beatriz and Soraya looked up in alarm.

"We are deceived!" My breath came in stifled gasps. "Besançon has betrothed my son to that mewling daughter of theirs. This visit is but a ruse!"

"Your Highness, please. Calm yourself." Lopez rose hastily. "Are you sure of this?"

"Yes. The queen just told me; she practically rubbed my face in it." I felt sick. I went to the nearest chair and sat. Beatriz immediately poured me a goblet of the fresh water I insisted on having in my rooms at all times, for I disliked drinking wine in the day.

She pressed the goblet into my hand. I drank. Then I looked at Lopez. He passed his ink-stained hand over his balding pate. "Her Majesty your mother feared something of this nature," he said at length, and I could tell that while he sought to ease my distress, he was as shocked as I. "This is indeed the archbishop's doing."

"And he shall answer for it," I declared hotly. "He'll not get away with it, so help me God. I'll never agree to his devil's marriage and will tell it to Louis himself, if need be."

"Your Highness, that wouldn't be wise. The archduke your husband, he must know of this."

I went still. "You think he . . . ?" I swallowed. "He wouldn't. He would have consulted with me at the very least before he agreed."

"Yet, he must know. Arrangements for a royal betrothal do not happen overnight." He paused. "Perhaps you should speak with him directly. He surely will explain why he didn't inform you beforehand. Perhaps he feared your reaction. After all, no Spanish princess would welcome a French daughter for her son, but they are children, *princesa*, and much can occur between betrothal and marriage. It may be a political move, to bind Louis of France to peace. If so, your protest might cause undue concern and delay our departure for Spain."

I nodded. I was horrified by the thought that Philip had had a part in this. I couldn't ignore the wisdom in Lopez's words, however, and I shared his desire to leave this treacherous land as soon as possible, before some other wretched surprise was sprung on me.

"Very well," I said. "I'll speak with him. I'll send word this very hour."

HE CAME TO ME THAT AFTERNOON. I saw at once he'd heard about my encounter with the queen, and he entered my rooms with a defensive, slightly drunken swagger that made me want to throw something at him. It was evident he'd been carousing with the French court, though it was not midday, and that he had known all along about the betrothal.

He leaned to me, his breath reeking of claret. I turned from him, paced to the other side of the chamber. I'd prepared to be cool and composed. The moment he sought to kiss me, however, my anger flared. "Why did you bring me to this nest of vipers?" I asked, without preamble.

"God's teeth," he growled. "Not this again."

"Would you take me for a fool? I know very well what you and Besançon plan."

His face turned red. "And what, exactly, is that supposed to mean?"

I lifted my chin. "You would give our son to France, though it's an insult to our blood."

My declaration had its desired effect. He stared in astonishment at me. A shudder rippled through his voice. "I warn you, don't think to meddle in this matter. It's not your concern."

"It certainly is. Let Besançon wed Claude if he so wishes, but he'll not use my son."

"*Your* son? He is also my son. Blessed Christ, Besançon was right! You are a Spaniard through and through! You cannot see through that thick pride of yours that by wedding Louis' daughter, our son stands to inherit the greatest realm this world has seen. He'll sit on the thrones of Spain, the Habsburg states, and France. He'll rule an empire to rival ancient Rome."

"Yes, at Spain's expense!" I could not stop myself now. Something fierce and cold rose in me, fed by these weeks of feigned obedience and years of swallowing my hatred of the archbishop. "I will not submit to this betrothal," I said. "You will inform Louis as much, and we shall leave this accursed place. I command it."

"You command it?" he repeated, incredulously. "Who are you to command anything?"

"The heiress to Spain. Without me, this alliance means nothing."

I knew at once I had hit the mark. He looked as if he might yell. His cap crunched in his fist, and then he whirled about and strode from the room, slamming the door with such force it must have resounded throughout the château, with the result that the following morning when I entered the chapel for matins, the queen's ladies nudged each other as I passed.

I sat on my pew, stone-faced, scarcely hearing Besançon as he intoned Mass. I had realized in the middle of the night that this was Philip's and my first quarrel since his infidelity, and I blamed the archbishop all the more for it. The bell announcing the end of Mass rang and I heard the tromping of footsteps behind me. I resisted the urge to swivel in my pew; then Louis and Philip clad in ermine-collared mantles and escorted by an entourage of gentlemen filed down the aisle, past me. To the altar.

"Behold how joyous it is when kings and princes live in harmony," Besançon declared, with a beaming smile he aimed straight at me. Before my incredulous eyes, Philip and Louis embraced, took up quills, and signed their alliance on a desk balanced on the backs of two kneeling pages.

My son had been betrothed to Claude of France.

My nails dug into my palms. The men walked out, leaving Anne and her ladies to gloat. The king's confessor rang the offertory bell. Beside me, Beatriz started to fumble in her purse for the traditional coin when the odious Mlle de Foix leaned to me from the queen's pew. "Her Majesty bids me to tell Madame it is customary in France to offer alms. She sends you this."

She dropped a pouch into my lap.

Beatriz froze, no doubt fearing my explosion. Mastering the urge to whirl about and deliver a resounding slap to Mlle de Foix's smug face, I plucked the pouch off me as though it were a bug and let it fall with a clink to the floor. "Tell Her Majesty," I said in a voice I knew would carry, "that I am well aware of the custom, it being the same in my native land of Spain."

Mlle de Foix recoiled. As intended, my words reached the queen, and Anne rose and limped out with as much indignant anger as she could muster, her ladies scuttling behind.

I did not move. The chapel descended into icy silence.

"They're gone, Your Highness," Beatriz ventured. "They wait for us outside."

"Let them wait."

"But it's snowing. . . . The queen will catch cold."

"Let her freeze to death for all I care. I'll not stray behind her like a servant."

I did not rise for another full ten minutes, counting the seconds one by one. Then I genuflected, stepped over the pouch, and moved down the aisle with deliberate slowness.

On the portico, the queen and her women huddled against the biting wind. When she saw me, Anne of Brittany stepped forth, her features livid with rage.

I held up a hand, staying her in her tracks. I continued to my apartments. There, I locked the door and turned to Beatriz. "Fetch *mi atenuado,* my Spanish gown, and my jewel coffer."

That night as the court dined in the great hall, the trumpets blared and the lord chamberlain called out in a reedy, nervous voice, "Her Highness the infanta of Castile!"

Everyone went still. From his place on the dais with the king and queen, Philip's eyes widened. Beside him, Besançon went slack-jawed, food clinging to his many chins.

I moved down the stairs, clad in my traditional Spanish garb, my overskirt a rigid cone over the whalebone farthingale favored by the royal women of Castile. My mother's ruby encircled my throat; my hair tumbled loose to my waist under my velvet hood, embroidered with Aragonese black lace. Coming before the dais, I raised my chin to meet Louis' mordant gaze and Queen Anne's glower.

I gave them a cool smile. "Your Majesties of France," I said, "I am a Spaniard born and bred, and I will remain so till the day of my death." I reached into my gown pocket and removed the jewel with the arms of Castile that Philip had given me. "I give your daughter this gift, so she can remember she will have me, Juana, future queen of Spain, for a mother-in-law."

Philip gripped his throne and half-rose. Louis said softly, "Madame Infanta is bold."

I glanced at him. His smile tugged at his lips, thin as a wire. "Will you not dine with us?" he went on. "Such a shame it would be to waste such bravura on a mere entrance."

"Your Majesty," I replied, "it would be more to my shame if I stayed."

His gaze narrowed. I turned and walked out without pause, ignoring the stunned courtiers at their tables and the staring nobles, going back to my apartments, a tickle in my throat.

As soon as I closed my door, I slid to the floor before my astounded women, my farthingale billowing about me like an inverted flower. Laughter escaped me in a breathless gust.

"We might as well start packing," I said. "They'll not see me under their roof another day."

. . .

TO SPAIN, TO SPAIN.

I repeated the words in my mind as I walked into the courtyard, where servitors hastened to finish loading the last of our belongings. As I expected, Besançon had issued orders for our immediate departure, citing, to my amusement, a favorable break in the weather. Snow lashed our faces and the wind was cruel, but I did not care. I had proven my mettle, though it did not alleviate the fact that my son had just been promised to Spain's most pernicious foe.

Snowdrifts piled against the château walls. The entire court stood in unyielding formation, muffled in oiled cloaks and sodden furs.

Louis smirked at my approach. "Madame Infanta, I fear it's been too brief a visit."

"I regret Your Majesty lacks other means of entertainment," I said, in the same suave tone.

Without warning, his gloved hand gripped mine, pulling me close. "I do hope we shall see each other again soon," he whispered. I flinched, catching a lascivious glitter in his eyes.

At his side, Anne gave me a malignant glare. I had no doubt she would barricade every border and every port, if necessary, to keep me from France again. Under the circumstances, I forwent the traditional farewell kiss.

Philip steered me toward my mare, his hand like a vise on my sleeve. "You deliberately ruined this occasion," he said.

"Not as much as I would have liked," I retorted, and I pulled away to mount.

As we passed under the gatehouse, I threw back my head and laughed aloud.

FOURTEEN

. . .

Torrential storms overcame us in Navarre—that tiny, strategically momentous kingdom straddling France and Spain—obscuring the mountain pass ahead. We had to surrender our horses for return to Flanders with our less intrepid servants and officials. The rest of us would cross the mountains on sure-footed mules bred for the dangerous alpine roads, hired at an exorbitant rate from local guides.

I was used to riding a mule, it being the preferred mode of transport over the tough roads of Castile, but even I began to think we'd not survive those treacherous rivulets our guides dared call roads. Besieged by winds and snow that often blinded us to the very path we sought to traverse, we lost several servants, and their laden mules, when they tumbled over the edge to a shrieking death that echoed in the chilled air for hours afterward. Besançon and his suite of secretaries were wretched; my ladies hunched over their mounts in mute misery. Stunned out of his bad mood, Philip went white and still, his discomfort exacerbated by a bad tooth he'd developed from all the desserts and sweet wines he'd imbued in France. I took to imploring every saint I could think of, in appeal that we'd not find ourselves entombed, lost to the world until the spring when the goat herders uncovered our frozen bodies under the melting snow.

Someone heard my prayers. Tripping over the rugged paths, our hands and feet numb, our cloaks crystallized with ice, after what seemed an eternity (but was actually just four days) that glacial hell disappeared behind us.

The sky parted. Anemic sunlight stabbed from the clouds.

Midafternoon on January 26, 1502, I had my first glimpse of the Ebro

Valley's verdant expanse stretched out below us like a vision of paradise, the tiered white-edged cliffs of Aragón rising toward the immensity of a cloud-washed sky.

I drew my reins to a halt. Beside me, Philip also stopped, his throbbing jaw enveloped in a kerchief. He stared dully at the unfamiliar landscape. One of the guides cantered ahead, to bring news of our arrival.

"España," I breathed. "I am home."

. . .

HOW CAN I DESCRIBE WHAT IT FELT LIKE TO SET FOOT ON MY NA-tive soil after seven years of absence? I thought I had remembered it, the look and smell, the very feel of Spain. But in truth it seemed as strange and vivid a world to me as Flanders once had—both lush and austere in its complexity, with its broad-leaved forests and forbidding mountains, the serpentine wind of the Ebro River seeming to go on forever as we tripped into the valley to encounter a ferocious wind blowing off the Bay of Biscay.

I heard Philip mutter the first words he'd deigned to say to me since leaving France: "Damn your mulish pride. Had it not been for you, we could be gathered around a hearth right now instead of freezing our arses off like peasants." His words lacked much bite, however, muffled as they were by the bandage, his face drawn from the pain in his tooth.

I flashed back, "Yes, but here you'll be a king." My words touched a nerve, for he visibly straightened his shoulders and barked at his page to fetch him a clean cap and cape.

Beatriz and Soraya gathered beside me. Their relief at being home shone through their fatigue as we spied a company of lords with their retinue galloping toward us on stallions.

I spurred my lathered mule to them. I knew them at once, these *grandes* of Spain, high nobles familiar to me since childhood—the slim and powerful Marquis of Villena, whose holdings in eastern Castile rivaled the Crown's; and his ally, thickset, fiery-haired Count of Benavente, who liked his meat rare. I gave them an earnest nod as they dismounted and bowed before me, but reserved my smile for the tall, lean figure of the admiral Don Fadriqué, my mother's premier noble and head of our armada, who had escorted me to my betrothal in Valladolid.

His dark hair was salted with silver now, his angular temple bearing a small scar from a wound he took during the siege on Granada. His black costume gave him a stark quality, though one belied by his regard. He had dark blue eyes, almost black, deep-set and hooded—the worldly eyes of a temperate soul who did not let the exigencies of life harden him. He looked at me now with a quiet reverence that made me start in my saddle, thrusting home as nothing else had that I was no longer the doe-eyed infanta who'd left Spain years ago.

"*Señores,*" I said, with a catch in my throat, "I am glad of you. Please, welcome my husband His Highness the archduke Philip."

They bowed to Philip, who'd ridden up in his fresh apparel. To my discomfiture, he received their obeisance in silence, briefly lifting his chin, sans its bandage, before turning to Besançon, who, despite our recent privations, had already killed one mule from his weight and looked about to kill the one he currently sat astride like a mountain in his soiled robes.

"We've prepared a house for you," the admiral announced in his gravelly timbre.

"I thank you," I said. "Is there a physician nearby? My husband is not well."

"Her Majesty's own Dr. de Soto is here," said the admiral, and upon our arrival in the simple manor a half hour later, the diminutive *converso* physician who'd served my mother since her coronation examined Philip. "The gum is infected," he said, his thick brows meeting over his nose, his eyes lucid with intelligence. "I must lance it before the humors infect his blood."

On the bed, Philip lifted a shout of protest. While the admiral held him down by the shoulders and I took hold of his feet, Soto relieved my husband of his abscess with an expert prick of a red-hot needle, followed by a poppy-seed draught. Once I was certain Philip slept, I went down to the hall alone to join the lords.

Benavente and Villena sat before the hearth, drinking wine and speaking in hushed voices, their manservants standing attentively at the wall. They clearly did not expect me to appear by myself, I thought, as they rose hastily to bow, their dialogue ceasing abruptly.

The admiral steered me with his large calloused hand to a chair, bowing low as I sat.

I bade them to be at ease, finding it uncomfortable to be reverenced. My rank as heiress would take some getting used to.

"My lords, we've had a most trying journey," I started to explain. "My husband is not himself and asks that you pardon him. He is in need of rest." I paused, resisting the impulse to further excuse Philip, whose rudeness, despite his tooth, they had no doubt been discussing.

"There is no need to explain," said the admiral. I noted he did not drink nor did he sit, taking his position with abstemious care by the wall. "A winter crossing of the Pyrenees would try even the most courageous of men."

I glanced at Villena. He arched an elegant brow, a sardonic smile playing on his thin lips. I noticed he had garnished each of his small ears with a tiny red gem, his face coldly aloof as a predatory bird's, with swarthy skin and arresting sulfuric-green eyes. I knew his reputation. He was known as a ruthless *grande* of impeccable lineage, who'd caused my parents more than their share of trials when he refused to surrender his castles for requisitioning during the crusade against the Moor. My mother often spoke of him with asperity; my father detested him.

I wondered what he thought of the Habsburg prince who had come here with his Spanish wife to claim the title of prince consort.

As if sensing my thoughts, the admiral said, "You must do us the honor of sharing a meal with us," and with a hearty bray of agreement, stolid Benavente clapped his beefy hands.

Servants hustled in. The fare was simple: bread and cold ham and cheese. It tasted like heaven. I ate like a starving woman, asking between mouthfuls that food be brought up to Philip and to my rooms as well, where my ladies attended to the preparation of my chamber.

Then I asked, "What of their Majesties my parents? Do they know we are here?"

"Word was sent, yes," said Villena. "However, their Majesties were called to Sevilla to contend with a *morisco* insurrection. Those godforsaken heretics are never content. Cisneros is on his way there now; he'll deal with them as a prince of the church. He often said he should have had them all burned years ago."

The marquis waved his jeweled hand fastidiously, as if he spoke of the extermination of rats. The silent manservant behind him leaned over his chair to wipe his lips clean of crumbs. I found myself staring as the manservant then poured him a refill of wine. When Villena lifted his eyes to me, his mouth curved in a feral half-smile and I quickly looked away.

"Nevertheless," I heard the admiral say, whose appetite was apparently as spare as his person, "their Majesties sent word that they will meet you in Toledo. Welcoming festivities have been prepared, though Holy Week is only a few weeks away."

"Festivities?" I repeated. If they'd prepared festivities, they must have known long before any official word had been sent that we'd left France. Lopez had done his job well.

Villena purred, "Why, yes. It is our understanding these Flemish expect divertissements. After all, you've just been in a realm known for its joie de vivre, n'est-ce pas?"

My stomach lurched. My mother, it seemed, had indeed been fully apprised. How had she taken the news of the betrothal? What would she say to us about it?

I hoped my anxiety didn't show on my face. "How fare their Majesties my parents?"

"In excellent health and most eager to see Your Highness," interjected Benavente, before Villena could reply. The admiral, I noticed, averted his eyes.

"Indeed," I said quietly. "Then we must make haste, for I too am eager to see them."

We finished the rest of the meal in awkward silence. Villena and Benavente said their good-nights; the admiral remained, as though he sensed my need to talk. He regarded me with attentive patience, demonstrating his years of service to a busy queen, in which he'd often been made to wait. At length, he said, "Your Highness appears troubled. I would not wish to be forward, but I hope you know you can rely on me should you feel the need."

I smiled. "My mother always said that you are noble of heart."

"I am humbled by Her Majesty's favor," he said, with true humility. "She has fought with a tenacity that exceeds any man's for the good of Spain. We are blessed to have her as our queen."

I was silent. Only now did I begin to recognize how much I would have to prove myself, how heavy was the crown I would one day inherit. I turned my goblet in my hands, thinking of how much at peace this great man of action seemed to be with silence. It presented a startling, somewhat disquieting, contrast to the fripperies and swaggering of my husband's court.

"My mother," I finally ventured, "she is well, yes?"

I could not ask outright if our visit to France had upset her enough to awaken reservations about entrusting her hard-earned throne to Philip. The contemplative hesitation in the admiral's face made me think it had; he confirmed my unvoiced fear when he said, "Her Majesty has been troubled of late. The *grandes* have been acting up again, seeking their advantage as usual in her suffering. She took your brother's death particularly hard. Many say she hasn't been the same since. But she continues to do her duty for Spain. In that, she will never waver."

"Yes," I murmured. I looked into his eyes. "And she never expected this day would come."

He understood. "She did not. Yet you are still her flesh and blood."

"Has she . . . ?" I swallowed. "Has she said anything about my husband?"

"No." He glanced at my hands, twining about the goblet stem. "But others have," he added, and I drew back. "Villena," he went on. "Your Highness saw him, did you not? He is one of our most proud and troublesome of the nobles, and I fear he carries influence with many. He has been vocal about his displeasure that a Habsburg who made a peace with France will become our king consort. His Highness has much goodwill to win here, if he is to be accepted."

"He is not a bad man," I said quickly, feeling the urgent need to protect my husband from Spain's ancient aversion to foreigners, born from centuries of enduring invaders like the Moors. "He's young and he labors under less-than-exemplary guidance."

"I believe you. But he hasn't endeared himself by his actions in France. Still, there is time for him to prove himself. I, for one, will not hasten to judgment, if it's any consolation."

"It is," I whispered. For a second, tears stung the corners of my eyes. All of a sudden, I felt exhausted. I rose to my feet. "I must rest," I said. I held out my hand. "I am very grateful for your candor and kindness tonight, my lord. I promise you, it won't be forgotten."

He bowed, set his lips to my fingers. "Your Highness, I will always strive to serve you. Regardless of your husband the archduke, you are my infanta and will one day be my queen."

...

TWO DAYS LATER, AFTER PHILIP HAD RESTED AND RECOVERED HIS strength, we departed for Castile under a dreary drizzle.

"Where is that blazing Spanish sun that supposedly blinds the eye?" he muttered at my side. "Where are the lemon trees and oranges that cost a king's ransom? All I see is rock and rain."

"You're thinking of the south." I glanced anxiously behind us at the *grandes*. Thus far, Philip hadn't spoken more than a few words to them. "You'll soon see how beautiful Spain is. Nothing can compare."

He grunted. "I certainly hope so, considering the lengths you've gone to get us here."

But the last of the pain in his tooth, and his petulance, subsided as we entered Castile. Spring had come early, and the fertile *meseta* opened before us like an offering, cloaked in tender grass. The Ebro and Manzanares ran cold with melting snow; the pine and cedar forests exuded pungent scent; and harts, hares, and quail bounded from the paths. This was the Spain of renown, of grandeur and plenty; and Philip started pointing at everything, asking a thousand questions, his fascination with what he saw seeming to dissipate some of the smoldering resentment I felt toward him from Villena, who was obliged to explain to my husband the bounty of the hunting in Castile. Male topics of interest, it appeared, were universal.

In Madrid, we lodged in the old Alcázar. Holy Week was upon us and I took Philip onto the ramparts to behold the illuminated processions and chanting clergy in their hooded robes, all orchestrated to the dolorous *saeta* sung to the Virgin in her hour of grief. He beheld it in awe, as if transfixed. Then he spun to me, yanking up my skirts as he lowered me onto the walkway and stilled my startled protest with his lips. It was deemed a venal sin to make love at this most holy of times, but it had been so long since we'd been together, I could not resist and let him take me then and there under the star-spattered sky, the *saeta* punctuating his hungry thrusts.

After that, our quarrels were forgotten, my native soil rousing fervid new life in us. We took to each other with a desire not experienced since our nuptials; even as his courtiers diced desultorily in the hall, forbidden to explore the local taverns because of the religious observances, Philip and I indulged our carnality.

"I believe you Spaniards must be all a little mad," he said to me one night as we lay in our disheveled bed, after we'd beheld the Holy Friday flagellants scourging themselves in the streets. "I have never seen such a thirst for lust or suffering."

I stretched voluptuously. "We are a people of strong passions." I resisted the pang of guilt that I had given rein to those passions with complete disregard for propriety, reasoning it was better to have Philip in a good humor for our upcoming meeting with my parents.

He slid his hand up my thigh. "Yes, so I've seen." He found my sex. "Fortunately, we Flemish have less complicated needs."

I gave a husky laugh. He was too spent to do anything more for the moment, so after we tousled languidly, like cats, I rose and went to drape myself at the casement window, leaving him sprawled on the bed, already drifting to sleep.

I closed my eyes, reveling in the sensation of air on my sweat-dampened skin, inhaling the dusky scent of wild roses drifting to me from some unseen vine.

Home. It intoxicated me: the eternal skies, the lingering light, the smell of blood and flowers and earth. I had not forgotten it, none of it. My memories had been subsumed by the opulence of Flanders, by the monotony of canals and colored gardens. As I lifted my face to the sharp crescent moon, so yellow it seemed a dim sun, I marveled I could have ever found contentment in that distant realm and was overcome without warning by an aching loneliness, a deep longing for my children, and a strange disorientation, as though I no longer knew where I belonged.

I scarcely heard the pounding hooves until I saw riders gallop into the courtyard below.

My eyes snapped open. I looked down, saw a group of men dismounting from lathered horses; when one of them whipped off his cap and glanced up at the window with a sly knowing smile, I gave an involuntary gasp and leapt back.

"Felipe! Wake up!" I rushed through the chamber, throwing on a robe, grabbing up his breeches and flinging them at the bed. "Get dressed! My father is here!"

Then I flew out the door, down the staircase, and straight into his arms.

I buried my face in the coarse wool doublet, drawing in the unforgettable smell of my childhood. All doubt fled from me. I swallowed a sob of joy as he drew back a little and cupped my chin. His smile brightened his weathered features, which were deeply changed from the last time I had seen him. *"Mi madrecita,"* he murmured, "so beautiful you've become."

Tears filled my eyes.

His dark hair had thinned; lines crevassed his mouth and eyes. He seemed smaller somehow, when before he seemed to tower. Yet his smile was the same, and his body still compact with the musculature of a man more at home on a saddle than a throne.

"Your mother and I only just returned from Sevilla." He hooked his arm in mine as we went into the house. "She'll receive you tomorrow. We heard of your mountain crossing and your husband's toothache. We wanted to make sure you both were well." He paused, eyeing me. "But perhaps I intrude at this late hour?"

I felt heat rise in my cheeks. I was barefoot, wrapped in a robe, my hair a mess about my face—a fool could see that I'd not been embroidering!

"No, not at all," I said quickly. "We just retired. Philip should be down at any moment."

My father took in the Flemish courtiers sprawled by the hearth, empty wineskins at their sides. He said suddenly, "I forget foreigners do not share our penchant for late nights. Is that archbishop of your husband's about?"

"He's sleeping," I said. Fortunately, Besançon slept like the dead. Otherwise, I was sure he'd have been down here already, waddling up to my father with his oily smile. I didn't want Philip's first meeting with Papá to be marred by him.

"Good. Then let us go to your husband, where we'll have some privacy, eh?"

I nodded, hoping Philip had bestirred himself. We climbed the stairs. "Is Mamá well?" I asked. "The Marquis of Villena mentioned some trouble in Sevilla."

He scowled. "Godforsaken *moriscos*. They lie low for a few years, then, right as rain, up and revolt. Ah, but the moment Cisneros shows up and burns a few for good measure they wail for your mother. So, we had to go to Sevilla to set matters right. The incident exhausted her, of course, but she's otherwise as well as can be expected."

I paused. My concern must have shown on my face, for he chucked my chin. "Nothing to fret about, a touch of ague, is all. Now, is this your room?" Before I could stop him, he opened the door and strode in.

Philip had heeded me. He was dressed and, to my dismay, in urgent discourse with none other than Besançon. The air was heavy with the echoes of whatever intrigue they brewed; at my father's appearance, they stood as if paralyzed for a moment.

The archbishop swerved to my father and extended his hand to be kissed, as befitted a prince of the church. It made me want to order him out.

"Your Majesty," he drawled, "such an unexpected honor."

My father ignored the outstretched hand. "No doubt," he clipped. "I hardly expected to see you again either, my lord, after your last visit."

The archbishop flushed. Philip came to my father, grasped his hand like an equal, and kissed him on both cheeks. My father accepted his French greeting with a crooked smile, then snapped his fingers, without glancing at Besançon.

"My lord archbishop, I would have a word in private with my son-in-law, if you please." Philip had enough sense of the tension between them to add, "Yes, go. We'll speak later."

With a huff and swirl of his robes, Besançon stomped out.

Philip said suavely, in French, "Your Majesty must forgive me. Had I known beforehand of your arrival, I'd have prepared myself better."

My father turned to me. "He speaks no Spanish? Well, then, you must translate for us, *madrecita*. As you know, my French is appalling."

His French was actually superb, but I was relieved their conversation began amiably. I sensed tension when the subject of our French visit came up. Then my father winked at me, indicating he'd heard of my role in the affair. He refrained from questioning Philip; instead, he embraced my husband with masculine camaraderie and ordered him to get some sleep, as we must rise early to go to Toledo to meet my mother and her court.

I accompanied my father to the room his entourage had commandeered for him.

"Close the door, *madrecita*," he said. When I turned to him, I saw a nerve quiver under his left eye. That telltale twitch always acted up when he was troubled. Or angered.

"Philip must be embarrassed," I said. "He had so hoped to impress you. He had a new suit of brocade made for the occasion."

"He can wear it tomorrow." He regarded me without expression.

I said softly, "Papá, I know how displeased you must be. I take full responsibility for our actions. What happened in France should never have occurred."

"No, it shouldn't. But I do not blame you for your husband and Besançon's misdeeds."

His rebuke stung all the more for its directness, as it had in my childhood, when I had lived for his approval. "Philip will renounce this alliance," I said. "I promise you, Papá, he just needs to understand how dangerous it is for Spain. He doesn't mean us harm. He was thinking only of the benefits. And I met Louis in person; I tell you, he could talk a bird into the serpent's jaws."

My father chuckled dryly. "That sounds like a Valois all right." He went silent for a moment. "You must love Philip very much, to defend him so."

"I do," I said softly.

"And I recall you once saying he meant nothing to you. Ah, your mother is right: how quickly time passes. Here I am, an old man, while my favorite daughter is a wife and mother."

He smiled sadly, lowering his eyes. All of a sudden, it was as if all the humor and infectious joy for life had drained out of him. "I wish you could have brought your children. Isabel and I were looking forward to meeting them, especially your son, Charles."

I reached out. "Papá, I'm so sorry. For Juan and Isabella, and little Miguel—I'd do anything to have them here."

He looked up. I saw something I had never seen before: tears, in my father's eyes. "It is a terrible thing to bury one's children, Juana. I pray you never suffer the same. Now Maria is in Portugal, Catalina in England. . . ." He paused, gnawed at his inner lip. "But you are here." He straightened, drawing in a deep breath. "Yes, you are home now, where you belong."

I put my arms around him and he yielded to me, almost like a child.

FIFTEEN

...

Toledo shone like a whitewashed barnacle, its maze of houses, serpentine streets, and *morisco* palaces seeming to shine with liquid gold in the morning light. The ramparts were bedecked in silk banners of every hue; wreaths, pennants, and precious tapestries hung from wrought-iron balconies, and the toll of the cathedral bells echoed into the Tagus Valley. The people crowded on either side of the streets roared in acclaim as we rode up the winding cobblestone road and dismounted before the *casa real,* where my mother had taken residence.

With my eyes dazzled by the sunlight, far brighter than in Flanders, all I could discern of my mother when we entered the *sala mayor* was her dark figure at the foot of the dais. My father went before me, accompanied by the nobles. As Philip and I approached, the elderly Marquise de Moya and my father's bastard daughter, Joanna de Aragón, wife to the Castilian constable, sank into reverent curtsies.

My heart started to pound. Philip and I reached the appointed distance from the dais and knelt. I heard skirts rustle. A low voice said, "Welcome, my children. Rise. Let me look at you."

I stood. I went still. Had I not known she was my mother, I would not have recognized her.

The last time I'd seen her, she had been stout, a matron, still arresting but no longer youthful. I'd anticipated the toll that age and grief might take; what I hadn't expected was to see this frail figure, her cheekbones incised under ashen skin enhanced by her dark wool dress—the mourning she'd worn since my brother's death. Only her ethereal eyes were unchanged, brilliant as though her life force concentrated itself there, intent on detaining time.

"Mamá," I whispered, before I could stop myself.

She held out her hands. I was enfolded in her gaunt, lavender-scented embrace. *"Bienvenida a tu reino,"* she whispered. "Welcome to your kingdom."

. . .

A FEW DAYS LATER, AFTER A ROUND OF UNINTERRUPTED FESTIVIties, my father took Philip and his suite hawking in the fertile vales surrounding Toledo. That same afternoon, my mother sent the Marquise de Moya to me with her summons.

We had not been alone since my arrival. As I moved with the aged marquise to my mother's apartments I had a vivid reminder of the last time I'd been summoned and felt the familiar tension between my shoulder blades. Then, my mother had called me to inform me of my impending marriage; this time, I anticipated something equally challenging. She had displayed her characteristic fortitude at each of the entertainments staged to welcome us, sitting Philip at her side and engaging him in discourse. Nevertheless, her jaundiced face and uncertain gait showed how much our reception had exacted of her, and in all that time not once had she mentioned the French alliance and betrothal of my son.

I drew myself to attention when the marquise paused at the apartment entrance. She turned to me, a tiny woman now, gray as cinders. "Her Majesty will not be treated like an invalid," she said. "I tell you this so you can be forewarned. Be patient with her. She's suffered much."

I nodded, forcing a smile on my lips as I stepped into the simply furnished solar. I curtsied, feeling like a child again, my mother seated by the window, waiting. At some unseen cue, her shadowy women dispersed. I fought back a sudden sense of helplessness and took the upholstered chair opposite my mother. I was a grown woman. Whatever she had to say, I was more than able to both hear and respond to it.

Her smile was vague, her gaze traveling over my figure. "I am pleased to see childbirth has not affected your figure."

Ever to the point; I was gratified that some things remained the same. "Thank you, Mamá."

Her face tightened. She adjusted her swollen feet on her footstool. "Now we must talk."

A strange defensiveness arose in me, though I tried to keep it at bay. She was ill, and no doubt worried, I told myself. I must focus on remaining calm and attentive. There was no reason this first discourse between us should not go amicably. I was, after all, her successor. She would not want our past disagreements to mar our reunion any more than I did. But another darker part of me already braced for battle. We had never been friends, and I was not her chosen successor, not the one she'd have wanted for her throne. We had come to this place through death and loss.

She confirmed my thoughts with her next words: "This French alliance of your husband's must be repudiated before our Cortes can invest him as prince consort. Your father has had a trying time convincing Aragón's procurators that their foolish law prohibiting female succession cannot prevail over Spain's hard-earned unity. Your husband's decision to betroth your only son and his heir to the French princess can only make the situation more difficult."

"His name is Philip," I said. "My husband's name is Philip."

"I know what his name is." She paused. "I also know what he has done." Her stare pierced me to the bone. When she saw me stiffen, she sighed. "It's never been easy between us, I know. We are not, as they say, kindred spirits. But I am still your mother. I did what I thought best for you. I never stopped loving you, no matter what you may think. And I know everything, Juana."

I could not move a muscle. "Everything?"

"Yes. Such matters are rarely secret for long at any court, much less one as licentious as his. I also understand, for I endured much the same in my youth. I know how it feels to discover your husband has sought the company of other women. I know what it is like to flee from him, and to forgive him and take him back, though he has broken your heart."

It was the last thing I'd expected to hear from her, the one sordid part of my marriage I had hoped to hide and forget. The sudden intimacy between us was almost painful.

"Papá," I whispered. "You speak of his mistress, the one who bore him Joanna."

She nodded. "I do. Fidelity is always harder for a man. And your father found it very difficult to accept the differences in our ranks. As you know, by the laws of Castile, he's my king consort. He does not hold the sovereign powers I do, though I've done my utmost to exalt him as my equal. But he's always known this realm looks first to me as its queen and it has hurt him. So he went to others, common women with whom he could first and foremost be king."

"But he loves you," I said, not wanting to see this side of my father, though I knew she spoke the truth. "He's always loved you. Anyone can see that."

"It has nothing to do with love. What I doubted was his ability to live in the shadow I cast over him." She held up her hand. "But I did not ask you here to speak of my past. Time has a way of softening us; like me, your father is getting old. Your husband, on the other hand, is still young and, from what I've seen thus far, very headstrong. He is frustrated by what he perceives as his lack of status; it festers in him like a wound. What I did with Fernando, what he accepted of me, Philip may not take so easily from you."

The admonition sliced between us like a blade. I lifted a hand to my throat, my gaze fixed on my mother's face. When she leaned to me and grasped my hand, a gasp escaped me. Her fingers were bony but firm, calloused from years of riding. Only in her hands could the memory of her strength still be felt, though her touch was cold.

"Whatever pain he has caused you," she said, "whatever doubts he's engendered must be set aside. I need your strength now. Spain needs it. This realm will demand everything you can give, Juana, and much more. We must prove you are capable of ruling after my death."

The reality of what I would soon face struck me with the force of a blow. I had never been able to imagine Spain without my mother: in my mind, the two were inextricably linked, conjoined like a child to the womb. Not until this moment did I truly let the weight of the future sink in, and for a terrifying instant I wanted to flee.

"Mamá, no." I couldn't keep the quaver from my voice. "You mustn't talk like that. You are ill, is all. You will not die."

She chuckled dryly. "Oh, but I will. Why should I, a mere vessel of dust, not go where every mortal creature must? That is why time—this time we have now—is so important."

She released my hand, the force she had emanated fading. "When I heard about this matter in France, I feared the worst. When that archbishop Besançon first came here to haggle with us as though we were cloth merchants, I saw the manner of man from whom your husband received his advice. I cannot say the French alliance surprised me; any fool could see Besançon seeks to play any side he can to his advantage. But you, my daughter—you surprised me. You demonstrated a remarkable conviction and strength before the French court and upheld your royal blood. Your husband, on the other hand, showed he is fit only to govern his paltry state in Flanders. He is weak, too easily influenced. He has the character of a courtier, not a king: he doesn't seem to comprehend that before riches, before titles, vanity, or pleasure, before, if necessary, his life itself, the Crown must come first."

These were hard words to hear. They seemed to go to the very heart of the situation with a lack of emotional ambiguity that I found unsettling. "You do not know him," I said quietly. "Yes, he has his faults like anyone else, but, Mamá, he isn't a bad man."

She tilted her head. "No man is, at first. But good has a way of losing to ambition. And nothing can alter the fact that he chose to betroth his son and heir—whom we would name after you in our succession—to Louis of France's daughter. Not to mention, he lets himself be governed by Besançon, a man unworthy to wear the cloth of the church."

Her words cut deep, as she intended. Still, I did not take my eyes from hers as she added, "Yet he will one day be your king consort, as Fernando is mine. We must therefore ensure that in the final say you are the one to rule. Rule as I have, and will continue to do, until my last breath."

Her stare was riveting, inexhaustible, as if flames had been lit inside her eyes. I knew in that instant that there was something else she wanted, something only I could achieve. Beyond her chastisement of Philip, that was the real reason she had summoned me here.

"The French betrothal," I said aloud. "You want me to get him to repudiate it."

She shook her head. "Let your father and I shoulder that particular task. What I require from you is to persuade him to remain in Spain as long as is necessary. He is too foreign in his ways and in his thoughts. We must separate him from Besançon, teach him to think and act like a Spanish prince. Only then will our *grandes* and the Cortes accept him."

Her insight into my husband's character, after a week of having known him, made me wonder about myself. It had taken me years to recognize his dependence on the archbishop; and I had not paused to consider how he might be seen in my native country, how his careless gallantry, which I found so novel, might inspire contempt in the somber eyes of Castile.

"Very well," I said in a low voice. "What must I do?"

"I'll not lie to you. The road ahead is fraught with problems. Many here would rather we named your son Charles heir, with yourself as queen regent until he comes of age. The Cortes, the nobles, the people—they will not trust a foreigner for their king. For the time being, however, your father and I have delayed the convening of our Cortes and the ratification of any titles. Mind you, the delay can only be temporary. But for now it gives us an opportunity."

Her voice deepened. "The power I offer you will set you above your husband. You will be queen of Castile and Aragón; on your head will rest our joint crowns. Philip can never have your authority, and you must never give it to him. What the Cortes demand, what the nobles require, is a monarch who will be feared and respected. I spent many years courting the favor of the one and subduing the greed of the other. That is why I must know if you're willing to do what is required. If not, any effort I make to win over your husband will be meaningless."

The silence that ensued was like a sound in and of itself.

Then I said, "Do you . . . do you think I can rule as queen?"

She sighed. "You are my daughter. Of course I do."

I lowered my eyes. All of a sudden, I felt like weeping.

She said softly, "All your life since you were a child, you were my most gifted: the quickest at her studies, the most intelligent and capable, the one who rarely showed any fear. You would have gone to war against the Moors yourself if we'd let you, and yet when we triumphed only you showed compassion. Not even my poor Juan, may he rest in peace, had your strength, both of body and spirit. But you must believe it, Juana. You must believe in who you are. Only then can you become the queen I know you can be."

I looked up. I saw in her eyes that she spoke with a newfound candor. For the first time in my life, my mother showed me her heart. Spain, her most precious possession, must remain safe after her death. She had sent me away, always demanded too much, and yet now she believed in me. She believed I could be queen.

Queen of Spain.

My mind spun. I did not know what to say. She regarded me closely, without any sign that she feared my answer. I finally nodded. "Yes. I will do it. I'll do as you say."

She sank against her chair. The fire in her eyes ebbed. *"Bien,"* she murmured. "Good. Go now, *hija mia.* I am tired. We will talk later."

I rose, tears burning behind my eyes, and gently kissed her brow.

Only as I left the room did I realize that by agreeing to help my mother, I might be forced to make a terrible choice.

· · ·

IN THE FOLLOWING WEEKS, MY PARENTS SET THEMSELVES TO TAK-ing us on a tour of Castile. Besançon had been obliged to accept the offer to view some of Spain's wealthier monasteries, no doubt at my parents' instigation, and had departed with a sour moue on his face, while we left Toledo for the imposing cliff-side Alcázar in Segovia and the enchanting filigree-stone palace of Aranjuez.

My father and Philip went hunting daily with their retinues and hawks, leaving my mother and me to sit under the lime trees in the gardens with our women. To my disconcertment, my mother did not utter a word about the matters she'd first discussed with me in private; it was almost as though we'd reverted to the days of my childhood, when she'd surrounded herself with me and my sisters to share daily tasks. Her women asked me about my children and life in Flanders and listened keenly to my replies, particularly my descriptions of the luxury of the palaces and the fantastic plethora of art. I told them how much I missed my children but how they were healthy and flourishing, as evidenced by a letter recently received from Doña Ana. Then I'd glance at my mother in her upholstered chair, her perennial embroidery in her lap, and see her gaze had turned inward, as though she were thousands of leagues away. I could not tell if she was hiding her disappointment that I'd not brought my children with me or whether something deeper, more ominous troubled her. Whichever the case, my trepidation and worry only increased as the days went by without anything of import developing.

At night in our rooms, I queried Philip about his talks with my father, thinking one of them must have broached the French alliance by now. He said there had been no such discussions; indeed he seemed blissfully unaware of any tension whatsoever. Apparently he and Papá shared only a masculine joy in the hunt, and he declared his enchantment with the way our gentlemen rode with their stirrups drawn high to the saddle, *a la jinete;* the forbidding strength of our citadels and the abrupt changes from stony field to profuse forest. The land, he said, was so immense, astoundingly fertile yet underutilized; were it farmed properly, we could feed nations.

His exertions by day made him lazily amorous by night. As he slowly moved inside me, the candle at our bedside slithering our shadows over the ceiling, I took comfort that while I still failed to lure him into more serious discussion, he appeared in no hurry to leave and indeed seemed to be enjoying himself.

On the evening before we were due to return to Toledo to meet with Besançon and my family's council (for with the sightseeing at an end, the true nature of our business must rise to the fore), Philip insisted on donning a plum velvet suit slashed with cloth of gold, a garish costume compared with my parents' simple wool garments. The early summer heat had arrived: it was sweltering even within the palace, and I opted for a sedate blue gown, though Philip cajoled me into wearing the sapphires he'd given me on the occasion of Eleanor's birth, one of the few jewels besides my mother's ruby I felt I might safely bring on the trip.

When we entered the hall, we found Moorish sandalwood screens partitioning it into an intimate chamber. The established company of lords and courtiers was absent; instead, the table was set for four, though with an unexpected magnificence that made Philip's eyes widen. Solid silver urns the size of small towers stood at either side of the buffet; the lace tablecloth offered a perfect display for the wide silver platters rimmed with gems and chased gold goblets. I stole a look at my mother; she returned a serene smile. I knew at once that while she'd appeared to drift into contemplation during our afternoons in the gardens, she had noted everything I'd said. Tonight she endeavored to show off her own wealth and luxury, which meant something was about to transpire, as these treasures were usually in safekeeping in Segovia and must have been brought here for a purpose.

Servitors brought us delicate fresh-caught quail cooked in pomegranate sauce, river trout with almonds, and bowls of greens. Philip dug in with his usual appetite: he hadn't taken at first to our custom of eating steamed vegetables covered in olive oil, but soon discovered that the absence of the heavy sauces the Flemish bathed everything in enhanced the food's flavor.

As a page began filling our goblets with a rich Rioja wine, my father said, "Well, then, shall we discuss your French alliance?" and I froze in my chair.

Philip looked up, a knifed piece of quail halfway to his mouth. "What?"

"The French betrothal," said my father. His jawbone edged. "Surely, you didn't think we brought you and my daughter all this way to give over Spain to the Valois? You must repudiate it," he added bluntly. "Louis of France looks every day to stealing our possessions in Italy. This alliance undermines our credibility and delays your investment as our heirs."

My mother did not move, her eyes fixed on Philip.

"And I," said my husband coldly, "did not come all this way to be dictated to. I told you before, this alliance brings me benefit. As archduke of Flanders, I'll not go back on my word."

"Yet as the future king consort of Spain, you must," interposed my mother, as my father's face darkened. "Fernando has attempted numerous times these past weeks to advise you that your alliance with our foe will not be tolerated. Neither Cortes will invest you unless you do as we say. And I, my lord, will certainly never entrust my throne to one who cannot recognize the difference between us and that nation of liars and wolves."

Philip dropped his knife with a clang to his platter. He shot a vicious look at me. "Besançon was right," he hissed. "You'll see me to ruin!" He came to his feet, tipping his chair over. "Absolutely not," he told my mother. "I am a Habsburg, with my own duties to consider. I am not your puppet, madame, nor will I surrender sovereignty to my wife. You are no longer in any position to negotiate. If you do as I say, perhaps then I will consider reviewing the terms of my alliance with King Louis. Until then, it stands as written."

He walked out, leaving us sitting there, the liveried page with the decanter frozen in place. The roast capon I'd been eating acidified in my stomach. I started to say something, anything, to fill the dreadful hush. My mother slumped in her chair; as one of her women rushed over to attend her, ashen pallor spread across my father's face. He turned to my mother. She nodded, pressed a hand to her breast. With the help of her woman, she rose and left the hall as if the eaves had come crashing down around her. She did not look at me once.

My father did. His stare went through me. I whispered, "*Dios mio,* what just happened?"

"Your husband is a mule," he replied, "not fit to wear a yoke, much less the crowns your mother and I have defended our entire lives. But he is right. We are in no position to negotiate, not now." His voice caught. "We received terrible news a few days ago. We tried to keep it secret, in the hope we might bring your husband to reason. It seems he found out anyway, probably through one of those daily missives that damn Besançon has been sending him."

He paused. The hand he set on the table clenched into a fist. I stood. "Papá, what has happened? Please, tell me."

"Prince Arthur Tudor is dead," he said, and for a second I didn't understand what he was saying. When I did, a gasp escaped me. "Catalina's husband?"

"Yes. We've lost the English alliance. Your sister is a widow. Now we must order our court into mourning and pray we can salvage something out of this nightmare."

I was stunned silent. When I saw his left eye quiver, I felt I might be sick. "There's something else," I said. "Something you're not telling me."

My father gave a mirthless chuckle. "Oh, yes. It seems Philip of Flanders doesn't want to be invested as prince consort of Spain anymore. No, he says we must amend our succession so that when we die, he will succeed as king. Your husband, Juana, would have your throne."

—

I RETURNED TO OUR CHAMBERS, opening the door to find Philip in his shirt, his doublet yanked open and trampled on the floor. When he saw the look on my face, he quaffed his goblet and went straight to the cabinet. Grabbing the decanter, he poured wine into his cup. He started to gulp, then threw the cup aside, spraying wine from his mouth.

"Vinegar! It's turned to pure vinegar! Christ, even the wine rots in this hellish place." He strode to the casement, flung open the window. "And the heat, it's intolerable." He whirled to me. "It's as hot at midnight as it is at midday."

"I know how hot it is." I met his stare. "Summer is starting." I closed the door. "When were you going to tell me? Or were you ever going to tell me?"

He narrowed his eyes. "Don't start with me. I've had enough Spanish recriminations to last me a lifetime—every bloody hour at the hunt, every hour on the way back, every minute of every day. Always the same tiresome adage." His voice adopted a mocking severity. "'You must repudiate the French alliance. Spain will never allow it.' Well, damn your father and damn Spain. I've had enough; Besançon has had enough. It's time your parents learned I am not some stupid boy they can manipulate at will."

"I don't give a fig for Besançon," I retorted. "Weeks have gone by and not once did you say anything to me of this. I warned you they wouldn't take the French betrothal kindly but you didn't listen. And now look at us: at odds with my parents in their time of grief—"

"When have they not been in grief?" he interrupted, with a callous laugh. "Death loves their company, it seems." He tallied with his fingers. "Let's see: First, there was your sister Isabella's first husband, who broke his neck while riding. Then your brother dies after a brief union with my sister, only to be followed by Isabella herself, her baby son, and now your sister Catalina's prince. One might say the House of Trastámara and marriage are a lethal combination."

I took an angry step to him. "Do you care so little for my family that you'd mock us?"

"I speak the truth. We Habsburgs prefer not to hide behind false piety and abstention."

"*You* speak the truth?" I said, incredulous. "You plotted behind my back with Besançon to betroth our son and have deliberately deceived me this entire time. You told my parents to name you king in the succession, though you know it is beyond their power to do so, that their Cortes will never permit it. If this is Habsburg honesty, then I pray God spare us from its treachery."

He went still, his mouth twisting. I had not expected to say these words, but I found as I lifted my chin that I did not regret them. I too had had enough. Did he think I would stand by and do nothing while he flouted my parents and made mayhem with our lives?

"Treachery," he spat, "is what you and their Catholic Majesties plan!" He flung his words like weapons. "This visit to be invested by their Cortes is a lie. Your mother has no intention of making you heir, much less letting you rule when she's dead. She wants a prince she can mold as she sees fit. So she delays our investiture in the desperate hope that if we get tired or bored enough, we'll get down to business and send for our son."

I recoiled. "That—that is not true," I said, even as the intimation crawled through me.

"No? Then perhaps you can explain why between his badgering of me to throw over France, your father made a pointed inquiry about my willingness to see our son named infante?" He chuckled at my dumbstruck silence. "I thought as much. You can't explain because you know it's true; you've known from the beginning. You've been working with them all along, haven't you, though I am your husband; *I* am the one you owe your loyalty to! You think that if you wear me down enough I'll do whatever they ask. Well, no more. The last pawn in their plan to rule the world is dead in England. Who can they turn to now, eh? Who will save their precious Spain?"

I could not take my eyes from his face—a savage face I did not recognize. Somewhere deep inside me, his awful accusations took hold, like a slow-acting poison.

"Me!" He jabbed his chest with his finger. "I'm the only one they can turn to. Only I can save Spain now. My blood is their future. Let your mother pontificate till she's blue in the face. She knows how much her nobility despises your father; how they wait like ravens for her to die so they can fall on Fernando of Aragón and rip him apart. She knows they'll never suffer another woman to rule over them. Without me, everything she has fought for will be lost, ruined."

His smile turned cruel. "So, go now. Go tell her what an ungrateful knave I am. Only also tell her to watch herself. Tell her if she tries my patience, I'll leave this accursed land so quickly it will make her royal head spin. And I'll leave you with it."

He strode past me, banging open the door.

Burying my face in my hands, I began to weep.

. . .

SIXTEEN

We returned to Toledo, where my mother instituted nine days of official mourning for Prince Arthur. Funeral masses were held morning, noon, and night. We were obliged to attend each one, to show our sorrow over a black bier bearing a waxen effigy of the Tudor prince we'd never met. I did grieve, not for him, but for my sister Catalina, so far from home and all alone, a widow at seventeen years of age. I also grieved for myself, for the shattering of my hopes for this return to Spain, now turned into a cauldron of intrigue and resentment. A veil of regal pretense might drape our public lives but in private everything began to unravel, and I feared more than ever what the future might bring.

Besançon was at Philip's side constantly, whispering further defiance in his ear, and as a result war ensued with my parent and their councillors, without a single concession to relieve the tension we lived under—as my mother never ceased to remind me.

"I know your husband cares nothing for Spain," she said. "But he's not so much of a fool as he would have us believe. I've watched him and Besançon at our council sessions. I've seen how their eyes glitter whenever we discuss the New World and our many estates and patrimonies." She gave a grim smile. "Land is power. All Louis of France has offered them are empty promises and a princess who might not survive her infancy, while we offer an established realm. Perhaps this explains why the archbishop was at me only this morning, making noises that either I settle the succession once and for all or he'll recommend an immediate return to Flanders."

As always, the mention of Besançon made my anger run thick, lending me the fortitude I'd felt slipping of late. "Let Besançon threaten whatever he likes," I said. "Neither Philip nor I will leave until this matter is resolved."

"It soon will be." My mother sighed. "I'm afraid I must do as they ask and convene my Cortes. For better or worse, I will settle my succession on you as my heir and Philip as your prince consort—but only as prince consort, nothing more. Your father will do the same in Aragón, though he'll require more time." She grimaced. "The Aragonese will be harder to convince. Yet now that we've conceded, perhaps it'll put an end to this insufferable alliance with France."

Thus it came to pass that on May 22, 1502, Philip and I knelt before the court, *grandes,* and clergy to be invested as heirs. Recently returned from his persecution of the *moriscos* in Sevilla, gaunt Cisneros of Toledo presided over the ceremony; when the time came for each of us to kiss his hand, Cisneros withdrew his fingers just as Philip leaned to it. My stomach sank; Philip reared a furious expression. Cisneros regarded him with implacable black eyes, conveying Spain's contempt as nothing else could.

. . .

OUR INVESTMENT SEEMED TO EASE MATTERS SOMEWHAT. NEITHER Philip nor Besançon had questioned the title of prince consort and we now waited for my father to pave the way with his Cortes in Aragón, with plans to travel to his capital city of Zaragoza in the fall, after the intense heat faded. For now, we sought refuge from one of the most brutal summers I could recall, a virtual inferno that charred leaves on the trees, baked the soil until it cracked, and shriveled the rivers in their beds.

After several members of the Flemish suite succumbed to an ailment brought on by ingesting contaminated water, my mother began making plans to move us back to the cooler and healthier environs of Aranjuez. Then news of another unexpected death came in a packet of letters from Flanders. Among Madame de Halewin's accounts of my children's welfare was the sad news that at sixty-seven years of age my duenna Doña Ana had succumbed to her nemesis, the tertian fever. Madame related that Eleanor had taken Doña Ana's passing particularly hard and Margaret had come to fetch her and bring her to her court at Savoy for a time.

My duenna's loss hit me with unexpected force. I was disconsolate for a time, for she had been part of my life for as long as I could remember, at

my side through my childhood rebelliousness, my youthful battles for independence and struggle to adapt to life in a foreign land. My ladies and I
pitched in together to send money for masses to be said for her soul, but I
was soon distracted from my grief when I got word that the water sickness was spreading through Toledo. Within days the populace fled to the
country. My mother commanded our immediate departure and sent word
to Ocaña, where Philip had gone on a hawking trip.

In the midst of my packing a page raced into my chambers. "Your
Highness, you must come at once! My lord archbishop Besançon is
gravely ill!"

I paused. Besançon was notorious for his penchant for too many black
olives, manchego cheese, and our famous black-foot ham: he'd suffered
more colic than a babe since our arrival in Spain. I was not about to go
rushing to his bedside to attend him.

The page added, "He's at the Marquis of Villena's townhouse. Her
Majesty's own physician has been called for. They say he might have the
water fever."

I went cold. "Beatriz, come," and we hurried through sun-bloodied
streets to Villena's *casa*.

The marquis met me in the hall. He looked dressed for court in his
crimson doublet, his hair freshly pomaded. As he spoke, I thought I saw a
smile lingering on his thin lips in their immaculate goatee. "His bowels
run black with bile. Your Highness must not go near him. Dr. de Soto attends him and word has been sent to His Highness. You can wait in the
hall, if you wish."

He led me to the hall as though he escorted me to supper. I knew he
did not care if Besançon lived or died, and I sat with Beatriz in mounting
apprehension, while his servants brought us refreshments. How had Besançon fallen ill? He had been staying here with Villena for several days.
The marquis seemed fine enough, so his water supplies couldn't be contaminated. Had Besançon eaten something fouled by the disease?

These thoughts ran through my head like rats in an attic and by the
time Philip arrived at dusk, I was in a state of nervous tension. I hurried
out to speak with him, but he shook me aside, bounding up the stairs to
Besançon's chambers, forcing me to follow.

The room was fetid, dank with heat and the stench of disease. Philip snarled at the perspiration-drenched royal physician leaning over Be-sançon's supine form. "Get out, Jew!"

Soto slipped away. I started to reach out to Philip, to keep him from the bed; he glared at me, then he stepped forth on unsteady steps. *"Mon père,"* I heard him whisper. "It's me. I am here. Your faithful son is here."

Besançon moaned, his hand fumbling blindly for Philip's. "Listen," he said in a trembling voice that made me shift toward them. "Plot . . . There is . . . plot." I could see the archbishop struggling for breath. "The king . . . You . . . must . . . go . . . Poison . . . I . . . die poisoned."

A stab of fury went through me. "Liar!"

With a strangled sound, Philip started to whirl on me. Besançon choked, arched in a contorted spasm, his eyes rolling back. A horrifying rumble in his guts preceded an eruption of foul excrement that drenched the sheets. Philip leapt back. With a hand at my mouth, gagging at the stench, I staggered to the door, calling out in a suffocated voice for Dr. de Soto.

"No! Not that monster!" Philip shouted, and he lunged at me. I had already opened the door.

Standing on the threshold was my father.

. . .

"HE IS DEAD." PAPÁ STOOD IN THE HALL ENTRANCE. HOURS HAD passed. Philip sat slumped by the hearth, an untouched goblet in his hand. I sat opposite him, Beatriz at my side.

"His servants will see to the preparation of his corpse," my father went on. "The water sickness is not contagious between people. You must drink from an infected source to get it." He paused, meeting my apprehensive gaze before returning to Philip. "In light of the accusation he made before his death, I suggest that Dr. de Soto perform an autopsy."

Philip's goblet clattered to the floor. He uncoiled from the stool, heedless to the wine spreading under his feet. "You tell that Christ killer to keep his filthy hands off him." His face was haggard in the flickering firelight. "Leave us alone. I want . . . I want to say goodbye."

He walked from the hall. I looked again at my father. I tried to feel remorse for the archbishop, but all I could feel was astonishment at the swift turn of events and a secret relief that I no longer had to contend with him or his domineering influence over Philip. I did not want to explore my un-willing doubt, though his death had come at a convenient time, on the very heels of our pending investment in Aragón.

My thoughts must have shown on my face. My father said quietly, "He was wild with fever and pain. The water sickness does that to a man. Go back to your mother now and proceed to Aranjuez. There is nothing you can do. I'll stay here with your husband."

I didn't have the heart to question him. As Beatriz and I went back through the streets with an escort of Villena's men, I decided Besançon had been as treacherous on his deathbed as he'd ever been in life, sowing suspicion up to the very end.

In my stripped apartments, where my coffers and chests awaited con-veyance to Aranjuez, I fell fully dressed onto my bed and at once into a deep but troubled sleep. I awakened what was hours, but seemed only minutes, later to the sound of my bedchamber door clicking open.

I clutched the crucifix at my throat, half-expecting to find Besançon's reproachful shade at my bedside. I peered into the gloom past my bed curtains to see Philip standing there with his arms limp at his sides. I rose cautiously, thinking he must be in terrible pain, as much as I had been when I first learned of Doña Ana's death.

Then he said in a low icy voice, "Did you know they would do this to him?"

I met his gaze. The blues of his eyes looked black, rimmed in red from weeping. I shook my head. "Philip, he was delirious. He did not know what he was saying."

"I should have known you'd say that. You're just like them, cut from the same cloth. You always hated him. You're probably glad he's dead. But I know what I heard, and I tell you he was poisoned. And what's more, I know why."

"Why?" I whispered, though there was nothing in the world I wanted less to hear. The room had begun to pitch under my feet. I couldn't take any more of this, I thought faintly. It was too much discord, too much heat, too much of everything. I felt trapped inside a living hell, stepping backward like a cornered animal as he came at me.

"Because he was my friend, and I trusted him above all others. They knew how much he meant to me and they killed him to hurt me! To hurt me and get him out of the way."

"They . . . ?" I felt my mouth move, but I couldn't hear my voice. A rumbling sound built inside my head, like the roar of black waters crashing against rocks.

"Yes. *They*. Their Catholic Majesties of Spain! Your beloved parents! They killed my Besançon. And by God, madame"—he thrust his face at me—"I *will* have my revenge."

My lips parted in horrified protest. The darkness inside roared up to engulf me.

With a groan, my knees gave way and I crumpled to the floor.

* * *

I OPENED BLEARY EYES. SORAYA AND BEATRIZ STOOD AT MY BED. I ached all over. I tried to ask how long I'd been here and what ailed me, but nothing would come out. My mouth felt sewn shut.

"Ssh. Don't speak." My mother reached into a basin, wet my parched lips with a liquid that tasted like sorrel. "You'll recover soon. A slight fever and exhaustion, Soto says, nothing to worry about. You've been abed a few days."

My last hour of awareness flashed past me. My gasp ripped my raw throat. "Ph . . . Phi . . . ?"

"Your husband is fine." My mother leaned close, her gaunt face gleaming. "Praise be, he's agreed to renounce the French alliance. Your father has taken him to Zaragoza to convene the Aragonese Cortes. You will join them as soon as you're recovered."

I felt her hand clasp mine. "There is more good news, *hija mia*. You are with child."

* * *

MY RECOVERY WAS NOT QUICK. THE REASON FOR MY FEVER RE-mained a mystery, though Dr. de Soto believed it was an anxiety provoked by my pregnancy. I rather thought it an anxiety provoked by the events of the past months, but I submitted in any event to his prescription of plenty of rest and moderate exercise. He opposed any travel; and much as I longed to escape the sweltering heat for the north, I couldn't bear the thought of being jounced about in a litter, though we did make the move to Aranjuez. In addition, my mother had me sign an official document that conveyed my agreement to Aragón's investment of me as heir. She sent it via courier to Zaragoza, assuring me I needn't be there in person for what, in essence, was a formality.

In Aranjuez, I finally recognized the apathy that grayed my days and wondered if this new child would cause me as much trouble as my little Isabella had. But my mother was so overjoyed I kept my reservations to myself. I would bear a child conceived on Spanish soil; I must show her only my gratitude and happiness.

So I put on a brave face, attended night and day by my women and my mother, with whom I discovered an unexpected concord. Relieved for a time of the political exigencies that had besotted both of us since my arrival, we took enjoyment in writing letters together to my widowed sister, Catalina, in England and Maria in Portugal, in embroidering and walks in the gardens, and quiet suppers where we dismissed the servants and served each other instead.

At midnight, after my mother retired, I would take to the ramparts, my hair blowing loose as I contemplated the vast grassland plain stretching north, a sliver of moon hanging in the mauve sky, crisscrossed by the pirouetting of bats, which had so entranced me as a child in Granada.

There was no need for court dress, for witty conversation or scintillating airs. I reveled in the freedom of not needing to impress anyone, in the absence of Philip's impatience with me and my country. Standing at the farthest edge of the battlement walkway, I gazed toward the Tagus Valley and let the dry night breeze pass over me like a stranger's caress.

For the first time since my return to Spain, I was at peace with myself.

My belly started to swell with the new life inside me. Time passed as if it had no meaning, until one afternoon I awoke after a long nap to discover it was near the end of November and five full months had gone by since Philip and my father had left for Aragón.

A biting, snow-flecked wind raked its nails on the palace. Winter had come early. From my solar overlooking the keep, I heard the clatter of hooves and went to the window to see a small group of men dismount. I searched their ranks. Each wore a dark oiled cloak and shapeless sodden cap. But as they moved to the south staircase I recognized my father at their head.

I knew at once that Philip was not among them.

I spun to Beatriz. "Fetch my cloak. My father is here. I would see him."

Beatriz draped the thick wool over my shoulders. "Should I send word to Her Majesty?"

My mother had retired for the afternoon to rest. She would want to speak with my father, of course, but for a reason I couldn't explain I did not want her to know of his arrival quite yet. I wanted to hear Papá's news first, whatever it might be.

I shook my head. "Let her rest. She's been writing letters to every monarch in Europe and fighting with that horrid English ambassador over Catalina's dowry. Papá will see her later."

I crossed the freezing keep to the staircase and climbed to the second level. I did not knock; I simply opened my father's study door and walked in, as I had a thousand times as a child. A group of lords stood at the hearth, warming their hands. They all looked up. I recognized among them the burly constable, husband to my father's bastard Joanna. He had a terrible scar that sliced down his face, sealing his right eye shut. He was an ugly man, reputed to have a taste for bloodshed. During the Reconquest, I'd heard he hung Moorish heads he had decapitated from his saddle. Now, he fixed his ferocious Cyclopian gaze on me before lowering his massive head.

Then he stepped aside, revealing my father.

My voice sounded strained to my ears. "Papá, welcome home." I self-consciously pulled my cloak closer about me, feeling the men's eyes on the bulge of my belly.

My father motioned the men out. My heart pounded suddenly in my chest. Something was wrong. I could feel it. I looked at him. "Papá, where is Philip?"

He indicated a chair. "Sit, *madrecita*. I've something to tell you."

I let my cloak fall open. "I prefer to stand. Just tell me."

"I don't know how to begin. Your husband, he . . . he is gone."

I did not move. A vast hollow opened inside me. I saw his beautiful body lanced by thieves' arrows on the road or crushed by a stallion in a freak accident.

"Where . . . ?" I whispered. "Where is his corpse?"

My father's brow knit. "Corpse? He's not dead. He's in France, or so I suppose. At least, that's where he said he was going."

Not dead. Philip was not dead. Why, then, did I feel as though he was?

"He went to France? But that's not possible. He didn't write to me. He never said a word."

My father made an irritated sound and paced to the hearth, retrieving his goblet from the mantel. "Yes, well, he wouldn't have now, would he? Not after everything that has gone between us concerning that goddamn alliance."

"Mamá told me he had repudiated it. She said you were going to Aragón for his investiture."

"We were." My father eyed me over the goblet rim. "But then that fool said he had to speak with Louis. Apparently, what he had to say couldn't wait."

I frowned. I was starting to feel weak, as if the floor were shifting under my feet. I moved to a chair and sat. "I don't understand," I said. "Why would he need to speak with Louis?"

"Didn't your mother tell you?" My father paused, taking in my expression. "I should have guessed. The child. She wrote to say you've had a bad time of it. She must have thought to spare you for as long as she could."

"I don't need anyone to spare me," I replied, more harshly than I intended. I paused, took a few moments to compose myself. "Exactly how long has Philip been gone?"

He met my gaze. "Close to a month now."

"A month! But why? What happened?"

My father chuckled dryly. "What didn't happen should be the question. First, that spider Louis decided to declare war on us over Naples. He dared send an envoy to threaten me that if we do not withdraw my claim he'll dispatch an army to kick me out. Naturally, I had to respond. I petitioned my Cortes for men and arms, as no Frenchman is going to tell me what to do. As for your husband, he decided that by his honor he couldn't stand by and watch us threaten France, though it's his good friend Louis who's doing all the threatening. So he abandoned me and my Cortes in midsession, insisting he had to cross the mountains before winter set in."

I felt as if I couldn't draw a full breath. "He . . . he went alone?"

"No, he took his gentlemen with him. I tell you he made quite an impression on my procurators—though not the one I intended. I rather doubt they'll ever invest him now, the idiot."

I took a slow, deep breath. I did not want my rage, my horrified disbelief, to get the best of me. "Is he coming back?" I asked.

"I have no idea. Nor do I really care. He's been nothing but a thorn in our side since he came here. If he wants to scrape and bow to Louis, then let him. I'm done trying to convince him that France will devour him and his little duchy whole."

"Why didn't you stop him?" I stood, unable to contain my anger anymore. "He's my husband and prince consort. He's already been invested by Castile. What am I supposed to do now? Follow him across the Pyrenees in the dead of winter?"

"God's death, what would you have me do? Put him in shackles? I told him his duty lay with us now. I listed all the reasons why it was inadvisable, insane even, to risk going to France. But he wouldn't listen. No, he had to prove his manhood. He said he alone would persuade Louis of Valois away from this war. I've had donkeys with more sense! As if Louis would ever heed anyone over the chance to do me wrong."

I stared at him. Philip had said he was going to *help* Spain? I sensed something false, just beyond my comprehension. All these months I'd been here with my mother, what had gone on in Aragón? The feeling gnawed inside me; when I caught sight of that quiver under my father's left eye, I couldn't fight the doubt that engulfed me. I moved slowly to the hearth, my mind racing.

I stared into the flames. "He knows I am with child."

"He knows. Your mother wrote to tell us the news. He thought it best if you didn't travel until after the birth. It was the only thing we agreed on, I can assure you."

"But he left no word? No letter?"

"No."

It was here. The deceit. I could almost reach out and touch it. "And all because of this war over Naples, a war he has nothing to do with?"

"As I said, he thinks he can talk sense into Louis." My father spat air out of the side of his mouth. "Pfah! Your mother might actually buy his excuse, but I know he went because he hopes to keep his feet in opposing camps, conniving Habsburg that he is. He has no intention of giving up his French alliance if he can help it."

I had the sensation of a world spinning fast out of control. My father set his hand on my shoulder. "It is not your fault, *madrecita*. Your husband will do as he pleases. But we'll care for you, and after you've borne this child we'll see what's to be done. No use in worrying now, eh?"

But there was every reason. For I had no idea where I belonged anymore.

SEVENTEEN

...

On March 10, 1503, as Castile shed its icy shroud, I took to my bed and after only a few hours of labor gave birth to a son. I named him Fernando, in my father's honor, and to my mother's delight he was pronounced of sound body and mind. Shortly thereafter, I moved with my household to La Mota in central Castile. My mother had to return to Toledo to attend to the upheaval in her Cortes caused by Philip's abrupt departure, and I had no desire to lodge in the city with the memories of my fights with Philip and Besançon's death.

I dispatched a letter to Naples, where Papá had gone to fight the French. In the midst of his war (which he described as "a nasty skirmish" in his usual offhanded fashion), he sent me a ruby ring and his regrets that he could not be here to see his new grandson and namesake. *You have fulfilled my most earnest hopes,* madrecita, he wrote, *and I'll soon have these Frenchmen fleeing like curs. I suggest you write to your husband and tell him the good news.*

I could imagine his ironic smile as he penned these last words. The truth of the matter was that I had written to Philip, several times in fact. I had not received a single reply. I knew he'd arrived in France because my mother's ambassador in Paris informed us as much, but whatever business he concluded with King Louis had not stopped the struggle over Naples. Madame de Halewin also continued to send regular communiqués about the children, but from my husband I had not heard a word since his departure seven months ago.

It was as though to him, I had ceased to exist.

I avoided my worst fear that he had abandoned me and focused instead on my new son. Fernandito, as we called him, was a beautiful child

even in his infancy, with soft brown hair and my amber-hued eyes, the
delicate bones under his plump features a sure sign of his Aragonese
blood. I knew he would grow to resemble my father's side of the family
and found special comfort in holding him close, nuzzling the sweet crev-
ices of his plump neck, and relishing the feel of his greedy mouth on my
breast. He gurgled and cooed and laughed with delight far more than he
fretted. He was as docile as my Charles had been at his birth, yet unlike
Charles, curious about the world around him, his wide eyes and perfect
little mouth fixed in a perpetual O of wonder that mesmerized all of us.

The effect he had on my mother was miraculous. She shed her mourn-
fulness like an old skin, reverting to her old self again, with even a faint
blush to her cheeks and vigor to her step, as if all her pains had vanished.
She was not that ill, I saw with relief. Rather, her recent losses and concerns over Spain had made her so. But now she had a new grandson, and
I patiently suffered her obsessive worry over the child's health and
scrutiny of his household. She wanted more attendants to serve him. I reminded her that he cared nothing for how many pages ringed his crib. I
did give in to her insistence that he have his own physician, however. My
sister Isabella's son had been hale only to later sicken and die. Death had
stalked my family for years, scything through our brightest hopes, and I
decided that Fernandito must have the best of care. On one point, however, I was adamant. I must nurse him. I would not surrender him to the
established protocol, which set forth that a newborn prince should be delivered to a wet nurse and appointed guardians.

Throughout the spring and summer, my mother came and went from
La Mota at regular intervals, keeping me apprised of the Cortes delibera-
tions. I would have to make my own way back to Flanders if Philip did
not call for me soon, but she replied that my presence in Spain was required, at least until their session concluded. I reluctantly agreed. I had
my babe to consider and the truth was, I couldn't embark on a voyage
while he was still so young. I therefore informed the procurators via a
formal document that I would remain at their disposal and set myself to
fashioning a home within La Mota's thick fortified walls.

Despite my lifelong aversion to fortresses, the old castle proved a perfect residence in which to weather another fiery summer. Situated on the

high plains of Castile and overlooking vast fields of wheat, its ramparts and curtain wall kept the place cool, and the twisting lengths of corridor and cramped staircases soon became familiar to me. Here time slipped away as I attended to my son and banal daily chores, interrupted only by my mother's visits and sojourns to the nearby township of Medina del Campo, where Beatriz and I haggled like fishwives at the trade market over imported bolts of Venetian silk brocade. We paid too much despite our attempts to outsmart the crafty merchants and returned to La Mota content as sparrows with twine for our nest, promptly setting ourselves to fashioning new gowns.

Yet such distractions grew less fulfilling as autumn neared. My mother sent word that her Cortes had concluded and she'd come to me as soon as she packed up her household in Toledo. I began to brood. I'd been in Spain for close on two years and I still hadn't received a reply to my innumerable letters to Philip. It was as if my past had become an illusion, the life of someone else. I worried that my other children would forget me, grow up reared by others, that my husband and I had become strangers to each other. I wasn't one to nurture old hurts. I wanted my marriage back, a marriage that despite its troubles had been one of passion and gaiety.

I began to prowl the ramparts as the days shortened and the long crimson twilights of summer were swallowed by the sudden fall of autumn dusk. As I stared toward the horizon, I could not imagine spending another winter in Spain. The ache in my heart, which I had kept subdued through love for my little son and duty for my country, could no longer be denied. The Cortes had adjourned; they had not, in the end, called for me. Whatever decisions they had reached had not required my presence. What did I wait for? Why did I still linger?

In my heart, I knew the time had come for me to leave. My son was still a babe, but I could go by sea. It was a shorter route. A well-equipped galleon would protect us. As I descended the staircase to my rooms, I felt a sudden sadness. I would miss Spain. I had no idea what to expect when I reached home, considering Philip's and my estrangement.

But I had to go, regardless. Sitting at my desk, I wrote to my mother in Toledo.

. . .

A WEEK LATER, MY CHAMBER DOOR OPENED AND ARCHBISHOP Cisneros walked in.

We'd had only the most cursory of contact. He'd been away dealing with the Moorish insurrection when I first arrived, and after he made his antipathy for my husband clear during our investiture, I steered clear of him. It proved easy enough. He did not live at court but rather in his diocese in Toledo, where he attended my mother and her Cortes as Castile's premier prelate.

His sudden appearance here, in La Mota, brought my women and me to a standstill.

He seemed like a cadaver of a man, his hard black stare severe as a fanatic's. My ladies paused in midmotion, arms filled with linens, sections of my gowns, and other items. We'd taken advantage of the dreary afternoon and Fernandito's nap to sort through my belongings, choosing what I would take and what I would leave behind, as a royal household, however well controlled, invariably accumulates more than one expects.

He stepped forth, clad in his trademark brown wool cloak and habit, his horny feet bare in their sandals. He took us in with a piercing glance. "May I ask what Your Highness is doing?"

I lifted my chin. I could sense he had an instinctual aversion to women. Indeed, that he and my mother had found a way to work together testified more to her sagacity and determination than his, and I did not appreciate his intrusion or his accusatory tone. Still, I owed him my respect for his rank, even if he clearly did not think of me as his future queen.

"What I am doing is sorting through my things," I told him. "I've accumulated more than a galleon can hold and I assume that given the state of the treasury, Her Majesty my mother won't wish to furnish me with an armada to take me home."

With a lift of his hand, Cisneros motioned my women out. I clenched my jaw, resisting the urge to remind him of who I was. Beatriz gave me a worried glance as she closed the door.

The archbishop and I faced each other. I felt his fury at once, rising between us like a wall.

"Begging Your Highness's pardon," he said, "your decision to leave is most sudden."

"I hardly see why," I replied. "I have my children and my husband waiting for me. I can hardly remain here indefinitely."

"Oh?" His thin, bloodless lips tightened. "And what about Your Highness's duty to Spain? Or is that not as important to you as your own pleasure?"

I met his unblinking stare. I determined not to show how much it unnerved me, for thus did I imagine he looked upon the pleading heretics he condemned to the fire. "My duty here is done," I said carefully. "I love Spain with all my heart and will return to claim my throne when the time comes. But, my lord, that time is far into the future. My mother, God save her, is well and has many years ahead of her. And I have a home in Flanders to attend to."

One wiry black eyebrow arched. "Few share your belief that anyone in Flanders is waiting for you, with all due respect. Indeed, we find this show of devotion somewhat surprising."

"Surprising?" I echoed, and I forced myself to sound nonchalant. "I don't see why. Philip and I are bound by holy matrimony. I should think that you of all people would respect said vows." I paused. "I wrote to Her Majesty my mother, conveying my decision. Are you here at her command? Or are you in the habit of opening *and* reading her private correspondence?"

The ghost of a smile touched his mouth. "Her Majesty has asked that I speak with you. She read your letter but has been tried of late, both with the adjourning of her Cortes and ongoing struggle of securing this kingdom. Your Highness's decision only added to her distress."

I felt a prickle of foreboding. "I am sorry if I have caused her distress, but she must have known that this day would come. And seeing I prefer to travel by ship, it'll require advance preparation."

"And you would take a babe to sea with you?"

I went still. "He is my child."

He eyed me. "Of course," he said at length. "Nevertheless, Your Highness cannot simply set off to Flanders at a moment's notice. We are at war with France. Think of King Louis' delight should he capture you and a prince of Spain on the high seas. A fine ransom you both would fetch. He might even demand we cede Naples in exchange for your freedom."

Had my mother sent him here to berate me? Why, if she was so concerned, had she not come herself? She had never shied away from chastising me in the past.

I drew myself to full height. "I hardly think I'm in any danger from the French. How would Louis even know of my departure unless we informed him of it?" I looked him in the eye. "Besides, that is not the reason you are here, is it, my lord? Speak plainly. Why has my mother sent you rather than come herself?"

His reply was cool. "Her Majesty has several hundred petitions approved by the Cortes to oversee, not to mention her own duties as monarch. She asked that I inform Your Highness that much to her regret, your presence is still required in Spain. Your husband the archduke's desertion in Aragón and subsequent escape to France occasioned graver concerns than we anticipated. Though the Cortes has ended for the year, you must be available in case you're called upon when the members reconvene."

I faltered. I did not like the sound of this. "What could possibly be so important that it would require my presence for another year?"

Cisneros bowed his head. That gesture of lowly ignorance made me start to tremble. "I am but a servant, Your Highness. Her Majesty will come as soon as possible to meet with you in person. I will, of course, convey any concerns you may have to her."

I clasped my hands, fighting back the sudden urge to bolt from the room. "I will compose a letter," I managed to say, and the quiet in my voice surprised me, for I felt as though I stepped across cracking ice. I even conjured up a smile. "Now, my lord, you must be tired. Let me see to your rooms. How long do you plan on staying?" I started to move to the door.

He stepped in front of me with fluid menace. "That will not be necessary. I shall be here only a short while, and my retainers and I are accustomed to shifting for ourselves."

"Retainers?" I said. Underneath me, the ice broke.

"Yes. There's been some unrest. The harvest has not been good and the winter promises to be a hard one. We've heard rumors of an insurrection in Medina del Campo and thought it best to increase your guard here." His smile was cold. "A precaution, nothing more. You needn't trouble yourself. You've much to do and His Highness the infante to care for. You'll hardly notice the intrusion."

I plunged without warning into swift black water. Retainers, he had brought retainers. He was increasing my guard. I had just been to Medina del Campo a few days ago. I had seen a prosperous town, with inhabitants who swarmed the trade fair in eagerness to share their affluence. I'd seen no signs of hardship or any insurrection.

He turned to the door.

"How long?" I asked, and I couldn't control the quiver in my voice. "How long did Her Majesty say she would be in coming to me?"

"Not long." He looked over his shoulder at me. "Your Highness must be patient. Even a sovereign queen must abide by her laws and elected representatives, which in Spain are the Cortes and the council. Sometimes she has no choice but to obey, though she wears the crown."

A chill spread through me. He bowed his head again, opened the door and left. As I heard his footsteps fade away, I reached with a trembling hand for the back of a chair.

EIGHTEEN

...

Cisneros departed two days later as abruptly as he had appeared. But his company of sixty-odd retainers stayed, turning my congenial household overnight into a barracks. Cloistered in my rooms with my son's cradle (for I feared a nefarious scheme to perhaps kidnap him away from me), my ladies and I adopted the defensiveness of women under siege.

The subsequent arrival of my mother's secretary, Lopez, did not relieve my fears. He seemed happy to see me, as always, and while a little more bald and careworn, just as he had done when in Flanders he tried to ease my strain and answer all my questions. He reassured me my mother was well, but she'd had a difficult time with her Cortes, and there was no word yet from my husband. Though he spoke with conviction, I detected a new flicker of wariness in his tone. My mother had personally sent him to serve me, he added, and he set himself to his secretarial role, penning my letters and faithfully dispatching them by courier. I know he did because I always received the same impassive reply: Patience. I must have patience. Her Majesty would be with me as soon as she could. Until then, there was nothing to be done. Winter was upon us and I couldn't travel now. I must wait until spring. If I was in want of anything, I need only request it. Certainly, La Mota must be provisioned for what promised to be a long, bitter season.

None of these replies were in my mother's hand, though each carried her seal, and as the days came and went, my suspicions spiraled to a near-feverish pitch. I wasn't under lock and key; I was free to come and go, as were my women. Yet lest there be any doubt as to where matters stood, the archbishop's retainers guarded the barbican and main portcullis day and night. There was no way I could leave without first going through them.

Every day, I took to the ramparts. Wrapped in a mantle, I stood for hours, looking up to the darkening sky where snow-laden clouds converged and lone hawks circled with remorseless deliberation, seeking their prey in the tall grasses below, before winter finally set in.

I felt a pit opening inside me, terrible and all-consuming. I wanted to believe something else had happened, a diplomatic mishap that required my mother's full attention. Such matters had been kept from me in the past: I'd not been told at first about the death of Catalina's husband or of the outbreak of the war in Naples. Though it infuriated me that she still felt I must be spared the realities of this world like a child, it didn't mean she lied to me. I told myself this over and over, because I couldn't bear the thought that she delayed and delayed until she could delay no more.

I gripped the stone merlon before me.

Dear God, what if Philip had been right? I'd placed all my trust in my mother. I defended her, even schemed for her, rousing my own husband's mistrust and enmity. Philip believed she and my father had murdered Besançon. What if they had? God knew, she was capable of it. When it came to defending Spain, she was capable of anything. Philip had said she would never let me rule, that she'd lured us here because she wanted to get her hands on our son Charles, a prince she could mold into a king worthy to succeed her. That we had not brought Charles had been a blow to her plans, but now I'd given her another son, another chance.

I spun away from the empty plain laid out before me, pacing to the ramparts over the barbican that looked out over the main road. I was going mad. It was not possible. She was my mother. She would never do such a thing to me. But my fear still unfurled like a map in my head, a map of lies and deceit. I was in La Mota, an impregnable fortress. What had first seemed a logical choice, a castle in central Castile, from where I might travel to several cities or ports, now felt like a trap. Did my mother want me isolated? Did she seek to stop me from returning to Philip? He had shown himself unalterable and had thrown her plans into disarray. Her Cortes might recognize him as my prince consort, but he could never stake a claim without me. He would not be king if I did not become queen.

She and her procurators could pass a legislative amendment barring Philip from the succession and making Fernandito heir instead, a Spanish-born prince of the Trastámara and Habsburg bloods, reared in Castile by his grandmother. Through him, she could continue to rule even after her death. Through him, Spain would be kept safe from the depredations of France.

But first, I must be dealt with. I had to be disposed of, sacrificed for the good of the realm, like my grandmother before me.

Sometimes, even a queen must act against her heart if she is to survive.

I let out a strangled gasp. I saw it now, as clear as if it had already occurred, Cisneros and his men stealing away my child and locking me away in this citadel. My father was in Naples, fighting a war that could drag out for months. By the time he returned, it would be done. My mother would hand him the new succession, with a grandson to follow him in Aragón, not a daughter whose husband had caused him no end of trouble. He might argue, even try to defend me, but in the end she'd win. She always won. Without Castile to protect Aragón, he couldn't survive. The Castilian nobles would rend him apart if Louis of France didn't get to him first.

I pressed a hand to my mouth, my panic rising to smother my very breath. I almost didn't see the figure on horseback riding hard toward the castle. When I did, I threw myself at the ramparts. Something inside me shifted. I dashed down the narrow staircase into the castle corridor. I moved with determination, past closed doors and empty galleries, making my way through the hall and out into the keep.

The retainers had gathered in groups around braziers, sharing the heat and the furtive passing of a wineskin. The rider entered through the portcullis. Visible puffs of hot breath wafted from his nostrils as he dismounted. A young man, with a satchel slung across his shoulders: our weekly courier, who conveyed our correspondence. This would be one of his final visits, if not the last. When snow began to fall, the roads would become impassable.

I had only this one chance.

Lopez and other members of my household had gone into Medina del Campo to fetch supplies. They could be gone several more hours or return any minute. Throwing back my cowl, I came before the startled youth, who was handing over his horse to a groom. When he saw me, he made a low, awkward bow. "Your Highness, I—I bring missives for Secretary Lopez."

The retainers idling in the keep paid us no mind. It was too cold, the days too short. The monotony of their routine had lessened their vigilance and they were accustomed to seeing me about at odd hours, for I often took long walks about the castle, restless as a lioness.

I smiled at the youth. With his tousled fair hair under his cap and his wind-burned cheeks, I estimated he was no more than sixteen or seventeen, the minor son of some minor courtier, entrusted with the time-consuming, wearying task of conveying his betters' letters.

"Lopez isn't here at the moment," I said. "Have you come very far?"

"From Toledo." He gave me a shy smile.

"Then you must be tired. Come, I'll have the kitchen prepare you some food." I forced out a laugh. "What was your master thinking to send you out on a day like this?"

"My lord Cisneros doesn't inquire as to my preference, Your Highness." He grinned at me now. I espied his covert, inept glance over me. It wasn't every day a boy like him got to see an infanta up close, and his admiration was plain.

But all I thought of at that moment was the name of his master. He served Cisneros. My letters, the reams of letters I'd sent to my mother. Had they all gone to Cisneros?

"Yes, I've heard my lord the archbishop can be a hard taskmaster." I leaned to him, with a mischievous air. "Let me take your missives to Lopez's study." I extended my hand, wishing I had some coin to sweeten the offer.

His moment's hesitation felt like an eternity. He looked away, his hand on the leather strap of his satchel. He murmured, "I was instructed to give them only to Secretary Lopez, Your Highness. My lord Cisneros was very clear."

"Ah, but he didn't think you'd meet your infanta, did he?" I heard myself say, and I marveled at the lightness in my voice, when all I felt was a roaring inside. "It'll be our secret. Secretary Lopez won't know who left the letters, only that they came. I'll put them just as you give them to me on his desk." I kept my hand outstretched. I almost moaned in relief when after another moment's pause he reached into the satchel, bringing out a packet wrapped in oily waterproofed leather, secured with Cisneros's seal on the cord.

I saw him off into the castle and his reward in the kitchens. Tucking the packet under my cloak, I made my way to Lopez's study, a small room overlooking the keep. Beatriz was in my rooms with Fernandito; my other servants were about their business.

I moved to the desk. It was neat and orderly, like Lopez himself. I held the packet in my hand. Then I retrieved the dagger on the desk and ripped under the cord, breaking the seal. Papers scattered. My hands were trembling as I started to look through them.

Receipts for provisions, payment vouchers for the retainers, approved lists of supplies—there was nothing here but the commonplace day-to-day documents of a royal household, all embossed with the crest of the See of Toledo, indicating receipt by Cisneros's officers.

I fumbled over them again, returned to the large open square of oiled leather, probing it with my fingers. Then I felt parchment. Sliding my nail under the secret pocket on the underside of the leather packet, I extracted a folded paper. It too was sealed. I cracked the wax, my heart beating faster as I scanned meticulous handwriting. Isolated phrases jumped at me.

Her Highness must not be told. Her Majesty cannot be disturbed.

The words swam. I had to lean against the desk to focus. More of the same: I must not be told. Something about a codicil, the utmost need for secrecy.

Then I saw a name that froze my blood: *Su Alteza Principe Felipe.*

Philip.

I fixed my eyes on the letter.

His Highness Prince Philip has sent word again by courier, demanding to know why Her Highness has not left Spain or sent any word to him. He believes she is being held under duress and threatens intervention should we fail to comply with his requests. Given his recent transactions in France, we would do Spain a grave injustice if we did not take his threats seriously. It is therefore imperative that Her Highness be kept unaware until the proper time. Her Majesty's illness is such that she

*worries without cease, and while you have been entrusted to carry out
her orders to the letter, as her premier prelate I command that henceforth no correspondence of any sort is to be allowed Her Highness. It
would not serve Her Majesty at this late hour if Her Highness were to
take some lunacy into her head before the proper time. Only once Her
Majesty has decided can you . . .*

Inside me, something tenuous held together until now by the sheer
force of my will snapped. I felt it and was powerless to stop it. It rose in
me like a molten wave. Philip *had* written. He had asked for me. I had
been right. All this time, the delays: it was all part of a trap to keep me a
prisoner. My mother had manipulated me as she had since I was a child.
Now she had me exactly where she wanted me, alone and defenseless.

As I stood there, I saw Arévalo in my mind, the shuttered walls and
forgotten loom in the corner, the hulking bed and my grandmother's
haunted gaze, begging for release. She must have felt like this on the day
she finally realized the confines of Arévalo were to be her entire existence,
when she finally understood who was responsible for her confinement.

Now it was my turn. I was to be my mother's captive and this castle
my cage.

Lunging from behind the desk, the letter crushed in my fist, I raced
down the corridor to my apartments. As I came crashing through the
door, Beatriz let out a frightened yelp, rising from her stool by the hearth,
where she'd been mending a petticoat. She took one look at my face and
shooed Fernandito's nurse into the antechamber, where my son's little
nursery had been set up.

"*Mi princesa,*" she said, coming toward me. "What is it? What has
happened?"

I brandished the letter in the air. "This is what has happened! She lied
to me, Beatriz. My own mother lied to me! She never meant to let me return to Flanders. She seeks to keep me here forever, a prisoner. This letter from Cisneros proves it!"

Beatriz regarded the paper as though it might turn into flame. "Where
did you find it?"

"From the courier! I should have known. Philip warned me; he said the only thing that mattered to my mother was her kingdom. God in heaven, I should have listened to him, followed him across the mountains. I should have heeded his warning when I had the chance!"

I thrust Cisneros's letter into my gown pocket. "How could she? How could my own mother plot against me after everything I've done for her? And Philip—he's asked for me. All this time she's kept us apart and let us believe that neither cared for the other. She has a heart of stone. No mother would do this to her child."

Beatriz reached out to me. "My lady, please, there must be some other explanation. Her Majesty would never do this. It's too cruel. And she has been ill."

My eyes brimmed with tears. I brushed them away angrily. "Why should I believe anything they say anymore? I never spoke directly with her doctors. The old marquise told me my mother was close to death when I first arrived and look at her: she's been traveling around Castile as she always has. No, there is no other explanation. She wants to lock me up in here to keep me from my husband and save Castile. She wants my son to be her heir!"

Beatriz had gone white. "What will we do?" she whispered.

I stared at her. A fraught silence fell. What could I do, with Cisneros's men at my gates and my life reduced to these four thick walls?

I whirled to a coffer, threw open its lid. "We must leave at once!" Dragging it to my dressing table I pushed my hairbrushes and vials of lotion and perfume into it, to a shattering of glass.

"I'm done with it," I cried, taking savage pleasure in hauling down the bed curtains, throwing them into the coffer, and marching past Beatriz to the side table to grab my candlesticks. "I'm done trying to please her! She won't take my freedom. I won't let her!"

I whirled back to Beatriz, who stood still. "Stop looking at me as if I've lost my mind! Help me, for pity's sake. Go get my child ready. He must come with us!"

She jerked forward toward the nursery, where my babe had started to cry. I strode to the clothes pegs, taking down my gowns and capes. I tossed them into the coffer. I was at my bed, ripping at the fur coverlets, when as if from across an abyss, I heard approaching footsteps.

I halted. At the doorway of the nursery, Beatriz likewise froze.

I shifted from the bed. I had no weapon to defend myself with. The door opened. Soraya sauntered in with Lopez, just returned from the trip to town to purchase supplies. Lopez carried the box of candles I'd requested.

My breath hissed through my teeth. Soraya flattened against the wall as I stalked up to Lopez. "I trusted you. I thought you were my friend. And you lied to me. You deceived me. You plot with my mother and Cisneros against me."

He stammered, "Your Highness, what—what is the matter?"

I ripped out the letter. "Here is the matter, my lord: this letter from Cisneros the courier just brought. Would you deny you've been doing his will against me all this time?"

The color drained from his face. The box of candles fell from his hand. "I—I do not understand. What does this letter say?"

I stared at him. "Here. Take it. Read it, though you know very well what it says!"

Lopez unfurled the crumpled parchment. Beads of sweat dotted his forehead as he looked at me. "I swear to Your Highness, I do not know what this means."

"You don't?" I let out a shrill laugh. "Do you or do you not serve my lord Cisneros?"

He drew himself erect, a small, trembling man. I thought in that instant I could push him to the floor and stomp on him and he'd not fight back. "I serve Her Majesty," he said. "I can see how this might appear but I assure you neither I nor Her Majesty plots against you. The archbishop has exceeded his authority. I will return word and tell him so myself."

"Will you?" I took a step to him, saw him flinch. "Then why are you sweating like a pig?"

"You—you misunderstand." His voice rose. "You distress yourself to no purpose." He reached out a hand to me, as he had when we'd met together in Flanders.

Why are you afraid?

In that moment before his hand closed on my shoulder, I heard locks clang shut in my mind. I pushed him aside with enough force to send him tumbling to the floor. I fled the room.

"Your Highness!" I heard him cry. But I was already running down the corridor, flying down the staircase into the hall, pausing only to kick off my shoes and gain speed as I dashed through the double doors into the keep.

Mules loaded with supplies from Medina del Campo stood tethered to rungs in the wall. When I burst into the courtyard, they shied, whinnying. Tugging at their reins, the muleteer tried to control the frightened animals, the servants unloading the supplies pausing to stare at me as if the very demons of hell nipped at my heels.

The portcullis had been raised, the drawbridge lowered. My chest burned as I sprinted forth. The retainers manning the drawbridge leapt to either side of the pulleys controlling the portcullis, releasing its brakes. A drizzle drifted from the dark sky, turning the flagstones slick. I slid, cried out as I fell onto the hard stone flags. It knocked the breath out of me. Gasping, I struggled upright, feeling a trickle of blood seep down my forehead.

The portcullis dropped on its oiled chains. From behind me, I heard Lopez yell, "Your Highness, no!" and I let out a thwarted roar as I skidded to a halt, barely missing the huge teeth of the portcullis as it slammed down. Another second, and it would have impaled me.

I screamed at the retainers. "Open it! I command you to open it! Open it now!"

Lopez came panting up behind me. I turned, blood dripping in my eye. I glared. "Tell them to open this gate now before I tear it down about your miserable head."

He regarded me in horrified disbelief. "Your Highness, this is a scandal. Please, come with me. There is no need for this."

"I am not your prisoner. Open this gate, I say. *Open it!*"

Behind him, I saw my women rushing out of the castle, Beatriz with my discarded mantle, Soraya my shoes. Even from the distance I could discern their distress when they saw me at the portcullis. Guards stepped forth, barring their passage. I heard Beatriz lift her voice in outraged protest: "Her Highness is barefoot and without her cloak!"

I had not been wrong. They meant to keep me here.

I wiped at the blood on my face, heedless to its smearing across my cheek. "Would you take me by force?" I said to Lopez. "Bind me with ropes as if I were a criminal?"

"Your Highness has lost all reason," he whispered. "This behavior, it—it is madness."

Mad. It was the first time that word was linked to my name. I did not care. In truth, I was mad. Mad with sorrow and the pain of betrayal. Mad with rage and grief and fear.

"You may think me mad," I said, flinging the words in Lopez's face. "But I am still an infanta of Castile and heiress of this realm. Set guards on me, and by God you will pay for it."

I watched him struggle to decide. He glanced at the retainers, then back at me. He pulled his shoulders to his neck and without another word trudged back to the castle. He did not look back.

I did not move as night fell and the drizzle turned into the first winter snow.

. . .

NINETEEN

A vigil was set up in the keep. I heard voices, the lighting of fires, footsteps. By dusk, I had to retreat into a thatched pen near the portcullis, where we kept goats. The poor creatures bleated and cowered, sensing my desperation. But they emitted warmth in that small hovel and I knew I couldn't survive the night outside in my gown and bare feet. Beatriz was allowed to bring me a platter of food, my cloak, and a brazier. I wrapped myself in the former and huddled over the latter, as wolves howled beyond the castle walls and the goats curled together.

"My lady," Beatriz implored. "I beg you, come inside. You'll catch your death."

"No. Go see to my son. I'll not return to that prison. If I do, they'll never let me out again."

Beatriz kept up her pleas until a retainer obliged her to leave. The following afternoon, as I dozed fitfully, always with an eye to the entrance lest they come and attempt to drag me out, I heard the slap of sandals. There was only one person I knew who wore sandals in winter.

I stiffened, crouching within my cloak.

A hooded head thrust through the hut entrance. Cisneros yanked back his cowl to show his enraged jaundiced face. "Your Highness, come out of there this instant."

"Open the gate," I replied, "and I will do so."

"That is impossible. Her Majesty has ordered that you not leave this castle."

"Then here I shall remain."

"This is an outrage! The entire castle and most of Medina del Campo by now say Your Highness has lost her wits. You are creating a scandal. Come out at once!"

"I care not a whit for what anyone says. And you are no one to tell me what I should or should not do. I am the infanta and heiress of Castile. You are but a servant."

He pulled back. My entire body quickened when I heard him bark to someone unseen outside, "We have no choice. We must take her out by force if need be."

I heard Lopez murmur, "My lord, I beg your pardon, but I came to La Mota at Her Majesty's command. I cannot sanction any act that may harm Her Highness. I fear you must summon Her Majesty."

"And I tell you, Her Majesty is too ill," Cisneros hissed, in a voice that made the hair on my neck stand on end. "She cannot move from Madrigal. You will do as I say!"

"No," said Lopez, and the resolution in his voice caused me to inch to the hut entrance. "My lord, it was your letter that caused this upset. I did not understand its contents and do not understand you now. Her Majesty instructed me to keep Her Highness comfortable and safe until she could be sent for. Unless I receive word to the contrary from Her Majesty herself, I cannot comply. Find another man, if you must."

My entire world came to a halt. I could tell he spoke the truth. He did not know what Cisneros meant. And my mother was ill. She lay in Madrigal, less than an hour away. I knew then she must be close to death, for otherwise she would have sent for me. Cisneros must have waylaid her missives, usurping her power while she lay unaware and intimidating Lopez into keeping me here, away from her.

I made myself rise, pull the cloak about me, and emerge with as much dignity as I could. I must have presented a terrible sight—my hair matted, disheveled about my sleepless face, my feet filthy, dried blood caked on my temple and cheek. I faced Cisneros and Lopez with my chin raised and declared, "My lord Lopez, prepare an escort. I will go to Madrigal. At once."

Lopez bowed and hastened away.

I turned to the archbishop. His face contorted with rage. "If I discover you've played my mother false, you can be sure that premier prelate or not you'll have cause to regret it."

As I walked past him to the castle I felt his stare like fangs in my back. But I knew this time he would not dare stop me.

I ARRIVED AT THE PALACE of Madrigal as a glassy sun without warmth slid behind the glacial bank of clouds, turning the sky into a dull gray shield.

No word had gone ahead of my arrival. I rode out of La Mota with only Lopez and two retainers. My women had instructions to shut themselves in my room with my child and await my return.

As we clattered into the empty courtyard of my mother's favorite palace, the place of her birth, it looked deserted. But the sound of our horses' hooves on the cobblestones alerted grooms and pages, who rushed out in obvious astonishment. Moments later, I was striding down wood-paneled corridors to my mother's apartments, past awestruck sentries and women who dropped to the floor in hasty curtsies.

I wore a wool gown, my face scrubbed clean and my hair coiled at my nape.

The marquise, so stooped and gray she resembled a twist of cinders, met me at the entrance. She took in my appearance with a judicious sweep of her eyes and motioned to the women seated like guards at the doors of the bedchamber. My heart cracked in my chest when she then took my arm—she who was my mother's most intimate lady, who had known me since birth yet had never willingly touched a person of royal blood without leave.

"I assume your delay in coming and that look in your eye means a grievous wrong has been done," she said. "It can be sorted out later. For now, Her Majesty need only know that which can ease her passage to God." Her fingers, so twig-thin they looked as if they might snap at any moment, gripped me with surprising strength. "Do you understand me, *princesa?*"

I nodded, set my other hand on hers. She released me. The women at the doors rose and opened them. I walked through.

The curtains at the embrasure were drawn back, letting in colorless light. The room was smothering, braziers in every corner, a haze of herb-laced smoke drifting below the eaves. I did not see my mother anywhere, not at the upholstered chair by her desk near the embrasure nor at the empty throne on its small dais. It took me a few seconds to realize with a pained jolt that she lay in the bed before me. I moved to it.

She lay against mounded pillows, her eyes closed. I gazed on her translucent pallor, under which bluish veins and the very structure of her bones could be traced. A linen cap covered her scalp; her features seemed oddly childlike. It took a moment to realize she had no eyebrows. I had never noticed before. She must have had them plucked in her youth; those thin lines I was accustomed to seeing arched in disapproval were, in fact, painted. Her hands rested on her chest. These too I stared at, the fingers long and thin now, without any rings save the ruby signet of Castile, which hung loosely on her right finger. I hadn't realized how beautiful her hands were, how elegant and marble-smooth, as if made to hold a scepter.

The hands of a queen. My hands.

How could I not have seen it?

"Mamá?" I whispered. I watched her struggle to awaken; her emaciated breast quickening, her brow furrowed and eyelids fluttering.

Then her eyes opened and I drowned in their ethereal blue, glazed over with the effects of the opiate draught.

"Juana? *Hija mia,* is that you? Why have you taken so long? Where have you been?"

I dropped onto the stool at her bedside, took her cold hand in mine. It was frail, almost brittle, as if it might crumble like an autumn flower in my fingers.

"Forgive me, Mamá. I did not know you were ill. No one . . . no one told me."

She shook her head with trademark indignation, though the denial was heartbreaking now, a futile attempt to refute her own mortality. "This cursed ague. I adjourned the Cortes and planned to visit you as soon as I closed down my household in Toledo, but I felt so poorly that my Moya insisted I take to my bed for a few days." She gave a hollow chuckle. "And here I am. I would not be separated so long from you and my grandson, so I finally told them to bring me here, by litter." She paused, staring at me. "What has happened to you? Tell me."

I averted my eyes. "It is nothing," I murmured. It was clear to me Cisneros had set himself to keeping us apart, for his own unscrupulous reasons, but I would not trouble her further. Later, I would deal with the archbishop, for like Besançon before him I now knew him for an enemy.

"I know it is not," she said, and the iron in her voice brought my eyes back to hers. "Cisneros argued before the Cortes that you are not fit to rule. He says that together, you and Philip will bring Spain to ruin. I was most displeased with him and told him so before my procurators."

Her hand tightened in mine. She fixed her gaze on me. "He was wrong. I know it. I know you can rule. You are my daughter. With a loyal council and the Cortes at your side, you can rule as well as I and perhaps even better. It is not a mystery, this business of wearing a crown, for all we pretend it is. Rather, it is a matter of devotion and hard labor."

I did not hold back my tears. I let them fall. I let myself feel the incredible, unexpected grief that swept away a lifetime of misunderstanding, of mistrust and the struggle to assert myself against this woman who cast such an inexorable shadow over me. Isabel of Castile had been a stranger to me for most of my life, but in that moment I understood her. We were joined as queen and successor, mother and daughter; by blood and suffering and strength.

It was a gift more precious than any crown she could bequeath.

"Go." She motioned to the desk. "Bring me the document there."

I rose. The document lay on her faded, ink-stained leather blotter, adorned with ribbons and strings of seals. From behind me she said, "We've little time, my child. Do not dawdle."

With a smile I turned to her, document in hand. "Mamá, can't this wait until later?"

"No. It is your future, Juana. You must hear what it contains. I must have your consent."

I returned to her. She took the vellum, regarded it in silence for a long moment. Then she said: "This codicil makes provision for Castile after my death."

I went still. I knew she had not ordered my detainment in La Mota, but it had been Cisneros's doing, part of his plan to keep me isolated until her death. Was this codicil the reason why?

"Mamá, is it Philip?" I asked softly.

She grimaced. "God save me, I wanted to secure you an annulment. I petitioned Rome, went against everything I believed. But there are no grounds. This codicil is the only thing I have to protect you from him."

"Protect me?" The room abruptly darkened, as if a passing cloud muted the sky outside. "Dear God," I whispered, "what has he done?"

"What hasn't he done? Not only did he flee to France in the midst of his investment by Aragón's Cortes, but he lied to us about his motive. He made no attempt to persuade Louis away from his attack on Naples. Instead, he reaffirmed your son Charles's betrothal to Louis' daughter and sent word that unless you return to him, he'll send for you with a French-paid army. He also demanded your father forsake his claim to Naples before it is too late. In short, he deceived us. He told us he went to France to set matters right, but instead he sat at Louis' feet like a dog."

My hands clenched in my lap. I wished I could pretend I didn't believe it. But I did believe it. It had been there, all the time: his arrogance and lust for power, his weakness and thwarted rage. He had played a treacherous game even as my mother lay dying, my father fought a bloody war in Naples and I struggled for my place in a world he'd torn apart. This was the man he was. This was the husband I was bound to.

"He's been in France, all this time?" I finally said.

"Yes." The compassion in her eyes sundered me. "Juana, you will never change him. This is why I must know if you are still willing to assume my throne and all it entails upon my death."

I met her stare. I had no hesitation. "I am."

"*Bien.*" She sighed. I had to fight back an overwhelming sense of loss, knowing I would soon face the world alone. I couldn't imagine Spain without her.

I poured a goblet from the decanter by the bed, held it to her mouth. Her hand as it clasped mine quivered with the effort of holding herself upright. She fell against the pillows with a stifled gasp, lines of pain taut about her mouth.

"Only you, Lopez, and your father will know of this codicil. It shall be kept secret until after my death. We must not let word of it get to Philip. Already, some of the *grandes* look to their own ambitions. They will seek their advantage the moment I am gone." Her voice lowered; as I leaned close, her gaze flickered to the closed chamber door. I went cold. She now lived in fear—fear of her own court, of her high nobles and Cisneros. She knew the wolves she'd spent years subjugating had begun to gnaw at their tethers.

"This codicil to my last will and testament grants you my crown of queen regnant," she went on, "with the succession devolving to your sons in order of their birth. Your husband will never rule in Spain. He will hold no lands or revenue of his own accord; he'll not be granted the title of king consort without your consent nor pass it on to progeny not of your blood. Like you, he'll be bound to the Cortes for his coronation. Your father will see to the same in his Cortes in Aragón when the time comes. Thus shall we bind him."

I did not move as I absorbed this mortal blow dealt to the man I had loved and defended, the prince who in the end had failed Spain.

"And your father," she added, "will be given the governorship of Castile until you claim your throne. He will hold the realm for you and ensure Spain stays in Spanish hands."

Her grip tightened. She was breathless now, betraying the return of her pain. "Remember the Cortes, Juana: they are your ally. Only they can approve a monarch's right to rule. Keep them on your side and they will see you through."

"Yes, Mamá." I bit my lip, her hand squeezing mine as if she might impart the last of her ebbing strength to me.

"I wish it were different," she whispered. "I wish I had more time to stop him. But all I have is this codicil. This codicil and your father. I pray God, they will be enough."

I looked at our clasped hands. Then I said in a low voice that came from my very soul, "I will stop him if need be, Mamá. I will fight for Spain."

She went limp. She dropped my hand. "I . . . I must rest now. I am so tired."

I sat anchored at her side, as night crept over the palace.

. . .

WINTER EBBED INTO SPRING AND STILL MY MOTHER LIVED. MY women had brought my son and my possessions to Medina del Campo. There in that intimate palace with its arched inner patio and intricately carved windows we installed ourselves, our every hour scheduled around her. Cisneros stayed away; a host of royal physicians hovered, ever hopeful. Only my mother's most trusted Dr. de Soto dared to tell me she suffered from a malignant growth in her stomach. The growth had begun to affect her other organs, and he warned we would not see another recovery as the one she'd staged upon my arrival in Spain and the birth of my son. Knowing this, I could only stand in awe of her spirit, which had shrugged aside even death's manacle for a time.

I believed only Fernandito's presence and the desire to see my father again kept her alive. Every afternoon when I brought my son to her apartments, she insisted on rising from bed to sit on her chair, a wraith muffled in fur as she dangled his rattle and he made his first clumsy attempts to crawl. The sight of him softened her waxen countenance; she'd hold him in her frail arms and he would gaze at her in reverent silence, as if he knew who she was.

It was then that I decided to leave Fernandito with her. The danger of travel aside, whatever awaited me in Flanders was not something I would subject a babe to. He would be safe here.

I then wrote to my father in Naples. My mother had demanded absolute silence as far as he was concerned; she knew from experience the fickle nature of war and did not want him racing home when a victory could be at hand. I finally broke my promise and informed him of her condition, telling him he must find a way to make haste. I would not have a chance to see him and I didn't want her left alone for too long. I also left orders with her household and guards that under no circumstances was Cisneros to be allowed near her.

On April 11, 1504, my possessions were loaded onto my ship in the northern port of Laredo. We made the trip to the rugged coast of Cantabria in stages, allowing the people to see us and dispel the rumor spreading through Spain that the great Isabel was dead. Now the wind blew strong, returning me to the day when I had first bid my family farewell.

Nothing was the same.

The ship that would convey me to Flanders was sturdy but small, without gilded standards; and of the hundreds who attended my last departure only my mother on her chair, the admiral, the elderly Marquise de Moya, and my women Beatriz and Soraya stood on the dock. My son had been left behind in Madrigal under the care of his household servants.

Involuntarily, my gaze went to the empty space where my brother and sisters had stood. They were all gone now, the children for whom my mother had held such hopes, scheming and sacrificing for the day when we would lift Spain to eminence from our thrones, arranging our lives as she arranged her own, with precision and an utter disregard for the vagaries of fate.

I went to kneel before her. She could no longer stand. I smiled as I gazed into eyes glassy from the narcotic draught she now relied on. She never took enough to induce oblivion; she wanted to remain alert, but her nights had become a purgatory and Dr. de Soto had increased the dose, so she might gain a few hours' rest.

I hugged her close. Under the padded gown, which she wore to disguise the wasting of her flesh, I felt bone. "Mamá," I said, in a voice only she could hear, "I love you."

I felt her emotion overtake her as with a trembling hand she tucked the stray hairs back under my hood. "I have always asked so much of you," she said. "Be strong. Remember who you are." She embraced me. In my ear, she breathed, "I love you too, *hija mía*. I always loved you."

I could not see through my haze of tears. I clung to her as I might cling to a rock in a raging torrent. "I will come back. I promise you."

The admiral shifted to us. "Your Majesty, Your Highness, I fear the tide will not wait."

Her fingers gripped mine. Then she let go. The emptiness she left seemed vast as the sea that awaited me. She motioned to the admiral. "My lord, please see Her Highness safely out."

The admiral offered me his arm. I looked up into his beautiful, sad eyes and terror gripped me, just as it had all those years ago. I could not feel my own legs as I moved with him to the rowboat that would convey me and my two women to the ship docked at the bay's opening.

I clutched the admiral's arm. "Will you keep my son safe, my lord?"

He said softly, "Your Highness, I'll guard him with my life. Do not fear."

I nodded, glanced again over my shoulder. My mother looked so small, indistinct now on her chair. The admiral helped me down the water steps and into the rowboat.

"Thank you, my lord," I whispered. "You will take care of her?"

He bowed low. "I will remain at her side, *princesa*, and be here when you return. May God protect you." He kissed my hand. Before he drew back, he lifted his eyes to me and I saw in their depths a stalwart resolve that gave me strength.

I nodded and turned away.

The rowers took up their oars. We crested the waves. The figures on the dock receded, grew smaller, more distant, until they eventually faded from view.

1504–1505

HEIRESS

. . .

DEL ARBOL CAÍDO,
TODOS HACEN LEÑA.
(FROM THE FALLEN TREE,
ALL MAKE WOOD.)

—POPULAR SAYING

TWENTY

...

The moonlit sky dipped into the sea, submerging a thousand stars. On deck, I stared into the endless darkness, mustering the courage I knew I would require.

Soon I would reunite with Philip and everything that had come between us. I had to stay steadfast, knowing I fought for the good of Spain and my sons. I did not know what awaited me; I did not know who the man who had forsaken me in Spain had become.

I held out very little hope.

When a footstep came behind me I looked around. Beatriz and I stood together in silence. I finally whispered, "I am afraid," and it felt as though the entire world shuddered. She took my hand in hers. "I know, *princesa.*"

On the seventh day, we arrived in Flanders.

...

RAIN AND MIST OBSCURED THE QUAY AND FLAT MEADOWS. AN ENtourage waited for me, swathed in oiled cloaks. I didn't recognize anyone, pondering them when a strange, elegantly dressed figure emerged.

He was only a little taller than a dwarf, an odd, sallow-skinned man, his features overpowered by a jutting chin tipped with a goatee. Cinderblack eyes gleamed above a hooked nose; his mouth was a wide gash with uneven teeth. Yet when he spoke his voice was disarmingly melodious, his words in perfect Castilian. "Your Highness, it is my honor to welcome you home."

I regarded him warily. "Have we met, my lord?"

He inclined his head. "I've not yet had the privilege. I am Don Juan Manuel, Spanish ambassador to the Habsburg court. I previously had the

honor of serving Her Majesty your mother at the Imperial court of Vienna. His Highness the archduke sent me to escort you."

I vaguely recalled his family name. "Your aunt, she is my sister
Catalina's duenna?"

"Yes, my aunt Doña Elvira currently resides with the infanta Catalina
in England." He gave me an obsequious smile. "Your Highness honors us
with her recollection."

I had no use for flattery, not in this dreary downpour after weeks at
sea. I looked past him to the litter and horses. Standards hung sodden,
held by pages in sopping livery. Only a few officials and this envoy to welcome me: a pauper's reception. It spoke volumes.

"Where is my husband?" I said.

Don Manuel sighed, "Ah, but of course. Your Highness could not
have heard. You were at sea when word came to us of a peace settlement
between France and Spain."

"Oh?" I wasn't sure of his loyalties and decided the less I revealed the
better. "What has this to do with my husband?"

He bowed. "*Princesa,* if you would accompany me to your litter, I
shall explain. You will be proud of His Highness, most proud."

I caught Beatriz's eye and had to suppress unexpected laughter. This
was absurd. Here I was in day-old soiled clothing, weary to the bone,
having left my child and a dying mother behind, and he honestly thought
I'd take pride in Philip's dubious accomplishments?

"I'm certain I will," I managed to murmur.

WRAPPED IN FUR AGAINST the chill, I listened in silence as Don
Manuel relayed how Philip had apparently single-handedly negotiated a
break in the hostilities over Naples. It wasn't clear to me if my father or
Louis had sued first for peace, but whichever the case, Philip had gone
once again to Paris. It had happened suddenly, Don Manuel said, though
of course a courier had been dispatched at once to him as soon as word
came that I was on my way.

I did not comment. Reassuring as I found the news of a peace, I'd still
arrived to uncertainty. And I had learned that anything Philip did in the
political arena was rarely what it seemed.

We reached Ghent by nightfall. The florid palace looked dark, shuttered, a few lone torches illuminating its gilded facade. Everyone in residence, Don Manuel told me, had retired. No one had been certain when my ship might dock, and my children were always put to bed directly after supper, to "aid their digestion."

"We can of course wake them if you like," he added.

"No, let them sleep." I pulled my cloak tighter about me. The palace reminded me of a filigree ornament in comparison to the stark edifices of Spain. An overpowering feeling of emptiness came over me, as though this realm of gardens and laughter, where I'd given birth to my children and known such fleeting happiness, were a conjuror's illusion.

Together with Beatriz and Soraya, I entered a home I no longer recognized.

...

I AWOKE TO SUNLIGHT SEEPING THROUGH DAMASK CURTAINS. Lifting myself on my elbows, I stared in momentary bewilderment at my surroundings. Then I slid from the bed to pad barefoot to the window, pulling back the heavy drapes.

The gardens below me were drenched in morning light, the colors of the roses so profligate it hurt my eyes. I turned back to the room. A night's sleep had done little to soothe my discomfort. Everything still looked strange, garish, overblown. Had I ever felt comfortable in these rooms?

Beatriz entered with my breakfast. Moments later Madame de Halewin appeared, svelte as ever in ash-gray, silvery white threading her immaculate coif. She curtsied, expressing all the appropriate sentiments required for my return and for the loss of Doña Ana, whose body had been sent to Spain for entombment.

I had to bite back a rush of tears. I would have done anything at that moment now to have my duenna's abrasive presence at my side.

"Is there anything Your Highness requires of me?" said Madame, as if we had only the most formal of acquaintance.

"There is. I wish to see my children. Bring them once I have bathed and dressed."

I disposed of a wardrobe replete with gowns, cloaks, hoods, sleeves, and shoes; before my departure for Spain I'd ordered everything I did not take with me packed into sandalwood chests scented with lavender, in anticipation of my return. The court attire that had traveled with me was by now hopelessly soiled; yet when Beatriz asked if I wanted her to fetch a few of my stored gowns (for the wardrobe was kept in a different part of the palace), I shook my head. I chose instead one of the black brocade dresses we'd made from the Venetian cloth.

Don Manuel accompanied Madame de Halewin and the children. In the cold light of day he seemed an unlikely choice for a Spanish envoy. During his time at the emperor's court, he'd adopted a continental mode of dress, with costly satin and abbreviated slashed breeches, and rings on every finger. In a manner, he reminded me of the Marquis of Villena, and yet he had served Spain for many years, his family one of noble descent. I couldn't think of a single reason to dislike him, and still there was something about him that reminded me of rank meat.

Ignoring his platitudes, I turned to my children.

Three perfect strangers stood before me. I knew my three-year-old Isabella at once, for her blue eyes and the shy, curious smile that touched her lips when I beckoned. After she submitted self-consciously to my embrace, she held on to my hand, inspecting the ruby ring my father had sent me in honor of little Fernando's birth.

"You have a brother in Spain," I said, encompassing my other children with my smile. "He hopes to meet you soon. I had to leave him. He is too young for a long voyage." I paused, motioned to my eldest daughter. "Eleanor, my dear, come closer."

Eleanor took a wary step forward. At six, she was tall for her age, thin and somber-faced, her curtsy executed with stilted precision. I was about to ask if she remembered me when she said abruptly, "Is Tante Margaret coming to visit?" making it clear that in my absence she had bonded with her aunt, with whom she'd spent many months in Savoy.

"No," I said quietly. "Not that I am aware of."

If my eldest daughter was disconcerting, my eldest son proved even more so, his anemic gaze uncanny, his disinterest in me, indeed in anyone save his head tutor, Bishop Utrecht, all too apparent. Like Eleanor, Charles responded to my questions in polite monosyllables, though he did at one point ask if I'd brought him a gift. Taken aback by his request, I plucked the ruby ring from my finger. "Your grandfather in Spain gave me this." I watched him eye the gem in expert appraisal before he tucked it into his doublet. He bowed, thanking me with an indifference that made me cringe.

"Did Grandfather send me anything?" Isabella piped. I nodded. "A pair of pearl earrings. I'll get them for you later." I pulled her close, reveling in her squirm. She alone of my children showed any sign of warmth.

It was not the reunion I'd envisioned and I set myself to investigating their circumstances. I found everything in order, albeit regimented by the inflexible rules of how royal children ought to be raised. Eleanor disposed of her own household of ladies, overseen by the ever-efficient Madame de Halewin. And I could see she had an educational schedule of impressive breadth, proof of the influence my erudite sister-in-law had over her upbringing. Not even my sisters and I had enjoyed such a demanding array of studies, yet Eleanor seemed content, her sole complaint that Tante Margaret lived so far away. I promised her we would have Margaret visit us soon, quelling the sting of resentment that in a mere two years I should find myself a suppliant for my eldest daughter's affection. I could hardly accuse Margaret of caring *too* well for her.

Utrecht informed me Charles had a "delicate constitution," which apparently justified the army of officials surrounding him. I did not like the isolation my son dwelled under; the grueling daily lessons and protocol that did not allow him to go to the privy without three attendants. Recalling how my brother, Juan, had loved to ride and shoot with the bow, indeed how all of us had relished being outdoors, I suggested Charles should engage in activities normal for every child. The bishop retorted that His Highness would be taught all the requisite physical skills once he reached the proper age. Surely, I did not wish for my only son to be injured while swinging a sword or riding some unruly beast?

"He is not my only son," I said, a lump in my throat. I turned away, though not before I issued the command that henceforth all three of my children must enjoy at least two hours of fresh air every day, free of books and responsibilities.

As the days wore on and I waited for word of Philip's return, I tried to adapt to the monotony of life in Flanders. I joined my children in the gardens when the weather permitted, sewed and read and wrote letters, ate informally with my women. All along, a quiet dread built inside of me.

Then Don Manuel came to inform me that Philip was due back in May. On the morning before his scheduled arrival, I awoke early and summoned Beatriz. "Help me select a gown, and have Soraya fetch my pearls from my wardrobe. I would greet him like a queen."

Beatriz brought me a crimson gown cut in the Spanish fashion. As I sat before the mirror while she brushed out my hair and started to coil it into a coiffure, Soraya entered. There was a pause. Beatriz barked, "Stop dragging your feet. Her Highness wants her jewels today, not next week."

I watched Soraya's unsteady reflection in the tarnished glass as she came to my side. Her hands were empty; her eyes averted. "*Princesa,* there is nothing there."

"What do you mean?" said Beatriz impatiently. "Of course they're there, you stupid girl! I put them in the vault myself before we left for Spain."

Soraya dipped into her pocket, brought out the set of keys. "I looked." She met my gaze. "*Princesa,*" she repeated. "There is nothing there."

"Impossible!" snapped Beatriz. I stood, an evil prickle creeping down my spine. "Beatriz, go fetch Madame de Halewin. Tell her to meet me in my wardrobe." Throwing a short cloak over my gown, I marched with my hair half-dressed toward the wing where my clothes were kept, ignoring the startled servants in the corridors.

I couldn't stop my gasp when I entered my private closet. We had left a room filled with neatly packed coffers and chests of personal belongings; what lay before me now was pure wreckage, the coffers strewn haphazardly about the chamber, their painted lids flung open, clothing crumpled on the floor beside them. I saw at once that all I had left was informal wear, my older dresses and day gowns. When I spotted one of the light linen dresses from my summers in the Alhambra, I felt hot color rise in my cheeks. I went straight to the panel in the wall and clicked the lever. Soraya had not relocked it. As I opened the hinged door onto the hollow compartment cleverly fitted into the wainscoting, I knew she had not lied.

My jewel caskets had been ransacked, as well.

Behind me, Madame de Halewin said, "Your Highness sent for me?"

I turned. Her expression was impassive, as though she beheld an organized royal closet and not the blatant evidence of thievery.

"Who has been in this room?"

To her credit, she had the presence of mind to pause. I was reminded in a flash of my first weeks in Flanders, when she so assiduously guided me into sending Doña Ana and my matrons away. I had forgiven and forgotten, kept her in my employ because of her qualities as a governess and lifelong service at court. Now I regarded her as though she were an avowed foe.

"I have no idea," she finally said, and she clamped her lips in a thin line.

I took a step to her. "You have no idea? My personal jewelry is missing, including many gifts from His Highness. My coffers have been opened and searched, my best court gowns taken. I find it hard to believe, madame, that you do not know how this occurred."

She started to inch back over the threshold. In a flash, Beatriz barred her way.

"You'll not leave this room until you tell me the truth," I informed Madame. I took pleasure in watching her always-pale face turn a sickly shade of white. "Should you persist in your silence, I will dismiss you from Eleanor's household and from this court."

That hit a nerve, perhaps the only one she had. She was not young. She had devoted her life to service, first as a governess to Margaret and now to my daughter. She had no family, no life other than this one. I could almost see the calculations scrabbling through her mind, the weights and counterweights to my threat, the consideration that I truly did not hold the power to see her banished without Philip's consent, as she was, in the final say, answerable only to him.

But I was not to be trifled with, and after a long moment in which our gazes locked, she drew herself erect. "I will deny I said anything if questioned, but His Highness allowed a lady into this room." Her voice was mechanical, as if she recited the evening menu. "His Highness told her you were in Spain and might never return, so why should your belongings go to waste? He said there were gowns and jewels aplenty, and pretty things should be displayed on pretty women. She came in with him and took what she fancied."

Behind Madame, Beatriz went still as a pillar.

"Who is this lady?" I whispered.

"A Frenchwoman, from the court of France; she came and went with

His Highness. That is all I know." Madame raised her chin. "The princess Eleanor awaits me. Will that be all?"

I lifted a hand. She curtsied and swept past Beatriz. I saw in my lady's stunned expression what she did not say aloud. I turned my eyes to the room, taking in the destruction, the callous disregard and utter violation of my privacy.

Then I turned and walked out.

TWENTY-ONE

...

I awaited him clad in crimson, my figure displayed to perfection, down to the alabaster nudity of my hands and throat. About me, my women sewed, though Beatriz barely glanced at her embroidery hoop and Soraya looked as if she might lunge to her feet at any moment. I had my daughters with me, as well, Eleanor stiff in the window seat, while Isabella turned the gilt-edged pages of my book of hours. I would have had Charles with me too, only Utrecht had insisted my son had a slight cold and must stay in his apartments for the day.

When the distant blare of trumpets came, Madame de Halewin stood. "His Highness is here. We must go into the courtyard to greet him."

"No." I did not look up from my sewing. "Let him come here to greet us."

"But Your Highness, it is customary—"

"I said no. You will sit, madame. Now."

Madame de Halewin dropped back onto the chair.

I stabbed my needle through my embroidery hoop, my every sense attuned to the hallway beyond my door. When at last I heard his approach, I set my task aside and looked up.

The door burst open. In strode my husband, flushed from his vigorous ride. He wore no cap. His hair tumbled like spun gold to his shoulders, streaked with sunlight. I had forgotten in my fury that he had a commanding presence, though my practiced eye noted he'd grown heavier, his cheeks ruddier and coarser than I recalled. I consciously drew a breath, reminding myself that regardless of his physical attributes, he was still the man who had forsaken me in Spain. Yet when I saw the unfeigned surprise in his expression I felt a rush of mortifying desire.

How could I still lust for a man who was so unworthy of me?

I submitted to his hot kiss. "My infanta," he breathed as if we'd been separated only a few hours. "Did you miss me?"

"As much as you missed me," I replied, and the chill in my tone pleased me. I could feel every pair of eyes in the room watching as he went to an astoundingly blushing Eleanor and greeted her—"So pretty and tall you've grown, my dear"—and then to Isabella, who cooed in delight when he handed her a beribboned feather he produced as if by magic from within his doublet. "This is from a white owl my falcon took down in France. Put it in your blue velvet bonnet, *ma petite reine*."

I found myself momentarily speechless. It was plain to me that our daughters adored him, though he'd arguably been more absent from their lives than I. But of course they would. What girl would not adore such a father? It did not make him any less a liar or adulterer.

He spun to where I sat like an effigy amid my women. When he clapped his hands, it sounded as though a storm broke overhead. "Out! I would spend time alone with my wife."

I saw Eleanor's annoyed glance as Madame led her and Isabella out. My Flemish ladies scampered into the antechamber, my two Spanish women following with heavy steps.

After two years of strife and separation, Philip and I were alone.

I did not shift from my chair as he went to the cabinet to pour a goblet of wine. He quaffed it. It was not until I saw him reach again for the decanter that I realized he was only feigning nonchalance. His hand trembled as he raised the goblet to his lips. When he turned with a disingenuous smile, I knew that he had every intention of pretending nothing was amiss.

I wanted to throw myself at his throat. Instead, I said, "How was your trip to France?"

His smile slipped. "Didn't Don Manuel tell you? I went to negotiate a peace settlement." He chuckled uncomfortably. "It's not as easy as you might think, getting two kings to agree, but I think we made progress." He took in my stare, turned heel to cross the room, away from me. "Blessed Christ," I heard him mutter, "I've been riding all day through mud and mire. I'm in no mood for an inquisition."

I folded my hands in my lap. "Yes, I heard about your travels, though not by you." And then my accusation came, almost as if by its own volition: "Your mistress must have kept you busy indeed, that you couldn't find the time to tell me of your negotiations with Louis or indeed remain here in Flanders to welcome me home."

He went still. "Mistress? I've no idea what you refer to."

"Come now, my lord." I forced out a curt laugh. "I find it poor taste indeed that you'd let your French whore pilfer my belongings while I gave birth to our son."

His eyes narrowed. "And I see nothing has changed. For a year and a half, you remained in that accursed land of yours. Now you return with your proud airs and your reproaches. Where is this son you gave birth to, eh? How do I know he even lives?"

I came to my feet. "He lives! I left him with my mother. He—he's too young to travel."

"You lying bitch," he breathed. "You left him there so she can use him against me. She got what she wanted, what you and she schemed for. You've shown where your loyalty lies."

I felt a sense of devastating loss. I needn't do this. I could win him back to me, as I had before. I didn't have to wreck whatever remnants of affection remained between us. We could still find happiness; we could still be who we were. It took all my effort to remember that I deluded myself, that though he might negate it, in fact everything had changed. I now fought for a greater cause than our marriage.

"My loyalty lies with the country we will inherit," I said, "the country you seem intent on casting into ruin to suit your pride. Are you so blinded by hatred you cannot see the truth?" My voice shook, despite my attempt to control it. "Louis doesn't care about you. He seeks only to work through you so he can destroy my father."

"Your father," he spat, "is nothing more than a cowardly murderer, who poisoned Besançon! If I had to strike a deal with Lucifer himself to destroy him, I would do it!"

I should have known then that I had lost him. The venomous suspicion he nursed for Spain and my parents had poisoned his mind as surely as he believed my father had poisoned Besançon. And yet I heard myself say in a voice as icily contemptuous as my mother's, "I've no doubt you'd lick Louis' boots if he ordered you. But I, my lord, will not. Spain is not Flanders."

He threw his goblet aside. Sudden fear bolted through me. Not until that moment did I realize how vulnerable I was: a woman alone, his wife, practically his property, to do with as he pleased.

He stepped so close I felt his breath like a furnace on my brow. "If this is how you feel, then you have my leave to return to your beloved Spain and veil your mother's deathbed, Madame Infanta. I'll be there soon enough to claim my throne."

My throne.

I raised my chin. "You forget I am Spain's heir. Without me, you will claim nothing."

His eyes turned to slits. Without warning he struck me with his open hand, hard enough to send me sprawling backward against my desk, its contents flying. I grappled for something to protect myself with as he lunged over me, his hands about my throat. "You will never rule Spain," he hissed. "When the day comes, I *will* take the throne—I, and no other!"

I flung up my arm, my jeweled letter opener in my fist. I raked the blade down his cheek. A bloody ribbon appeared. He hit me again; as the room reeled in a sickening haze around me, he gripped my wrists, twisting as he yanked me up and around. I started to shout for help when he hurled me facedown upon the desk.

My jaw slammed against the leather blotter; I tasted blood. A strangled scream clawed at my throat as he kicked apart my legs, forcing both my wrists behind me in a vise while with his other hand he heaved up my skirts. Brocade and the stiff horsehair padding of my underskirts smothered me. He tore at my stockings. I fought him, my wrists burning in his grip. He clouted me on the side of my temple. My ears rang. I kicked back desperately, slamming my feet as hard as I could against his legs. I knew with breathless horror what he intended.

There was a sudden silence. Then I heard him rip at his codpiece. Searing pain stabbed through me as he thrust himself inside. He pounded into me, banging me against the desk, turning an act we'd indulged in so many times with joy and passion into a brutal obscenity. I went limp, my body becoming a piece of flesh I could not feel.

He spent himself, his breathing harsh in my ear. "Castile is mine, do you hear me? Mine! And when the time comes, you will hand it over to me. You will give it to me without protest. If you don't, if you dare try to stop me, I'll do this to you every night. You'll carry my children one after the other until you die like a spitted cow."

I slid to the floor. He struck me once more, then turned and stalked out, crashing open the door on my appalled women.

As they rushed in, the scream I had held in erupted from me in a primal wail.

· · ·

I WAS SEQUESTERED IN MY ROOMS, MY BODY SO BRUISED AND blackened I could barely leave my bed. At first I could not even speak, my jaw and right eye were so swollen shut. Despite my feeble protests, Beatriz insisted on summoning the court physician; he examined me with discomfited tentativeness, muttered that nothing seemed broken, and prescribed a rosemary poultice before he hurried out.

Nothing broken.

By the fifth day, I could walk without cramping and was able to eat more than the simple broths my women painstakingly prepared for me. They'd created a haven of my apartments, a cocoon of feminine solicitude where they conspired to keep the world outside at bay. They brought my little Isabella to see me after she raised a fuss that she missed her mamá, but I saw in her frightened gaze and gently uttered "Does it hurt?" that she sensed something was terribly wrong. Holding back my tears, I reassured her that Mamá was just a little sick and she must wait for me to get better so I could come to her.

When Beatriz informed me that Philip had announced he would leave tomorrow on a hunting excursion, I ordered her to see me dressed and accompany me to the gallery. I had not been out of my rooms in weeks; as I entered the gallery in my black brocade Spanish gown, the veil of my coif drawn over my face to hide my bruises, idling courtiers stopped and stared, so taken aback they forgot to offer their obeisance. I moved past them as if they didn't exist, paused at the diamond-paned bay window overlooking the inner palace courtyard.

A light rain fell like satin, turning the brick walls a moist red and exalting the loud colors of the company below. No one would see me, even if they thought to glance up. In my unrelieved black I was a shadow. I saw my husband and his group of mincing favorites mount their horses. Don Manuel was with them, a toad in gaudy green velvet on a pony, his rings flashing dully on his gauntlets. Professional falconers rode behind with a cart carrying a week's supply of foodstuffs. It seemed my husband was going to the same lodge where he'd taken me once, years before.

I saw only four women. I ignored three of them; they were obviously professional courtesans in their garish low-cut dresses and ceruse lathered on their faces.

The fourth, however, I marked. She sat on a palfrey, her wealth of fair hair coiled about her face and threaded with the distinctive blue-gray of my pearls. Even from where I stood, I saw she was pretty but not remarkably so—a French doll with her pale complexion and rubicund lips. My husband brought his horse close to her; my breath caught when he reached out to tuck her trailing cloak over her palfrey's hindquarters, exposing her full breast in a gray velvet bodice I recognized as one of mine. His gloved hand caressed her; she arched her throat and laughed.

On her bodice, I espied a gold brooch with the arms of Castile—the very brooch I had given to Louis and Anne of Brittany in France, as a mocking gift for their daughter.

A black flame pulsed in the core of my being. I turned away, returned to my rooms.

There I waited. I did not go to the gardens or visit my children. I did not venture outside my doors. Each day seemed an eternity; each night a lifetime as I felt myself succumb to something so terrifying and insatiable I wondered that no one else could see it.

This time there would be no forgiveness.

. . .

THE NIGHT OF PHILIP'S RETURN I ENTERED THE HALL ALONE. Beatriz had begged me to let her go with me as she helped me dress. My choice of the same crimson gown that I had been violated in alerted her that whatever I planned, it couldn't be good. But I ordered her and Soraya to stay behind. I also wore my hair loose and disdained all jewels. The bruises on my face had faded to faint yellowish discolorations; these were decoration enough.

Only a few astonished murmurs from those closest to the hall entrance greeted my appearance. No doubt everyone at court had heard by now of the altercation in my apartments and my seclusion, but I had deliberately come late. The tables were already drawn back for the dancing and everyone fast on their way to complete drunkenness. On the dais Philip's chair was empty; at his left side, where Besançon had once sat, was Don Manuel. He looked up and froze, his protuberant black eyes bulging even more. He rose and started to scamper down the steps, shoving at the courtiers barring his way as if the floor under his little feet had taken flame.

I followed his intended direction to where my husband stood. Philip was flushed, a goblet in his hand as he guffawed with his men. Not too far away, seated in demure but prominent placement before the long, magnificent tapestries lining the hall, was the woman. Tonight, she wore an opalescent gown that had also belonged to me, altered to fit her larger bosom. Her hair—in truth, I thought, her only claim to beauty—fell in a contrived cascade of spun gold to her waist. She sat surrounded by ladies of questionable virtue, my pearls now coiled about her throat. As she gestured with her plump hands, I saw her gaze turn again and again to Philip.

Once again on her breast, she displayed my brooch.

I surveyed her from where I stood. Then I walked straight toward her, carving a path through the courtiers on the floor, smelling their rank sweat and musk but scarcely hearing their shrieking laughter and clang of goblets. As I neared her, I caught sight of Don Manuel breaking free from an inebriated lord who'd latched onto his sleeve to gabble in his ear. He was now rushing as fast as he could to Philip, his hands wagging in comical desperation. It made me want to laugh. He could have shouted to the eaves. With the music and other noises of carousing no one would hear him until it was too late.

I halted before her. She stood, her face blanching. Her lips were painted with carmine but not enough to disguise a small ugly sore at the corner of her mouth. The ladies around her gasped and drew back. It gratified me that I still commanded a level of respect.

"You wear something that does not belong to you," I said.

She gaped at me. "Your Highness?"

"That brooch, it is mine. So are the gown and pearls. You will return them to me. Now."

"Now?" Her voice was unpleasant, a shrill squawk, though perhaps this was due to her astonishment at my request.

"Yes." I took a step closer. "Or would you rather I took them from you, madame?"

Her eyes widened. Then her mouth pursed in a knot and she spat: "I'll do no such thing. These are a gift from His—"

I didn't let her finish. I lunged at her and grabbed hold of the brooch, tearing it with an audible rip of silk from her bodice. She screamed, tumbling backward over her chair in a flurry of skirts. I grabbed hold of her by the hair, seeking the pearls. A clump of hair tore out in my hand. I looked at it, looked down at her. She was on her knees, scrambling to get away. I leaned over and seized another fistful of her hair, yanking her back. She fell face up, her white-stockinged legs splayed, her mouth letting out an incessant hysterical noise.

I gripped the pearls and twisted. Her scream became a choked cry as the pearls snarled about her neck. Then the clasp gave way and I held them in a tangled length, adorned with errant gold wisps of hair. A thrill went through me when I saw the bruise blooming about her throat. She threw her arms over her head, gasping as if she couldn't get enough air. None of the ladies who only moments before had been fawning on her moved. They stood open-mouthed, aghast, like painted petrified statues.

I heard thunderous footsteps charge behind me. I turned to stare into Philip's bloodshot eyes. At his side, Don Manuel glared at me like a troll in a children's fable.

"Never again," I said to him. "I will die before I do anything you want again."

He bellowed, "Guards!" and the yeomen behind him pushed past the now-silent, horrified ranks of staring courtiers. "Take her. Lock her in her rooms. She is insane!"

I wrapped the pearls about my wrist as the guards surrounded me.

. . .

TWO WEEKS LATER, WORD CAME TO FLANDERS. MY MOTHER WAS DEAD.

TWENTY-TWO

...

"*Princesa? Princesa,* they are here. They await you in your presence chamber."

I knelt on the prie-dieu. I had not spoken in days. I had not cried or crumbled into a heap. When Beatriz with tears in her eyes handed me my father's letter, a brief but tender missive that promised to send further news through an embassy, I went into my bedchamber and closed the door. There in the darkness I prayed for my mother's soul to rise far from this world.

"Go, Mamá," I whispered. "Do not look back."

The guards posted outside my apartment doors were dismissed, the illusion of my liberty restored. Then Philip came to see me. Though news of my mother's death had plunged much of Europe into mourning, for she'd earned the respect of her fellow sovereigns if nothing else, he staggered in half-flown with wine. I lay rigid in bed, hearing his lurch across the dark room, Beatriz's gasp as he kicked her awake on her truckle bed and ordered her out, followed by the shedding of his clothes and fumbling under the covers.

When I felt his hands on my thighs, pushing my nightshift up and parting my legs, it was all I could do not to scream in rage and revulsion. I loathed his touch now, the very smell and feel of him, when once he'd been all I ever wanted. I could not stop him, though. He would hurt me again if I tried to resist and I'd not give him the satisfaction. He came night after night, and I shut my eyes, fleeing my body as he thrust inside me. After he spent himself, he sauntered out proudly and I rose from bed to scrub myself with a cloth, wishing Doña Ana were still with me, for she'd have known the secret herb lore that could prevent conception.

His nocturnal visits were intentional, of course. I had no doubt Don Manuel had advised him to it. They wanted me with child. That way, I'd be more vulnerable to whatever they planned for me. Indeed, Don Manuel had the temerity to visit me by day, ostensibly to inquire if I needed anything during this time of grief, while eyeing me for a telltale pallor or sign of queasiness.

I ignored his blandishments, staring past him to the wall. Though the guards might be gone, the prison remained, and it was more effective than any locked door.

Already, I knew I had conceived.

Day after day I rose at dawn, forced myself to swallow the breakfast Beatriz brought, and went to the prie-dieu, where I remained until dusk, motionless and alone.

In those hours of solitude, I relived my past. I saw again that innocent girl entranced by the bats and recalled how my mother had seemed a near-divine being, so aloof I could never offer her something as fallible as love. I traveled again to Flanders, France, and back to Spain. I stood on the docks of Laredo and felt the reconciliation of a final farewell. I did not shed a single tear.

Beatriz now stepped to me. "*Princesa,* they bring news of His Majesty your father."

Papá.

I turned to her. "Is it my father's embassy?"

She nodded. "His Highness met with them before he departed for a meeting with his Estates. One of them was granted permission to see you. The others returned to Spain." She paused. "It is Lopez. Will you receive him?"

Lopez: my mother's secretary, whom I'd last seen at La Mota. Why was he here?

I rose on stiff legs. As I passed my mirror, I avoided the shiver in the glass. I went out into my main chamber and sat on my upholstered chair. I pulled my veil over my face. The curtains at the windows were drawn, filling the room with shadows.

Lopez entered, accompanied by Don Manuel. My chest tightened when I saw how old my mother's devoted secretary had grown, his spine bowed as if by some inner grief. Recalling my harsh words to him in

Spain, I gave a tentative nod. I did not want my past behavior to ruin our dealings now, not in front of Don Manuel.

"My lord," I said to Lopez, "a terrible hour brings you here, but I am glad of you."

He inclined his head. "Your Majesty," he said and a jolt went through me. "Your Majesty, I offer you my sincere condolences."

I swallowed, glanced at Don Manuel. He stared at me, a smug smile lurking just behind his thick lips. This creature of my husband's was enjoying the farce.

"Please," I said softly, "you mustn't address me thus. I am still your princess, as I've not yet been sworn in by the Cortes and thus cannot receive the reverence given to my late mother."

This, I noted in satisfaction, wiped the smile off that gloating toad's face.

"Forgive me," Lopez said. "I've no desire to further distress you, *princesa*."

I experienced a sense of abrupt peril. "You do not. As difficult as my mother's loss is, I've every intention of fulfilling my duties. I understand you bring word of my father?"

"Yes, of course." Lopez reached into his doublet and withdrew a small velvet box. At that instant, I remembered my mother had entrusted Lopez with her codicil. This must be why my father had sent him. Papá knew he would not betray me.

Lopez knelt at my feet and lifted the box. "Your Highness, the Cortes of Toledo and His Majesty King Fernando order me to present you with the official signet ring of Castile. They ask that you make haste to Spain so you can be invested and crowned as sovereign queen."

His declaration rang out with hollow impact. I took the box from him, opened it to find the chipped ruby ring that I had last seen on my mother's hand. My throat closed. I could not move for what seemed an eternity, staring at that dull stone with its faded insignia of a castle and crown: the symbols of Castile, which had not left my mother's hand since the day of her coronation. Slowly I removed it from the box and slipped it onto my right index finger, with it was said the vein ran straight to the heart.

I lifted my eyes to Don Manuel. He had not moved from his stance a short distance away from us, as if he sought to afford me a semblance of respectful privacy. His face was shuttered, unreadable. I had my mother's ring. My father had summoned me. What would he do now? What would he tell Philip to do?

I returned to Lopez. His tired brown eyes remained fixed on me. There was something else he needed to say, something he dared not speak aloud.

"I do not wish to tire you," he added. "I came only to present Your Highness with the ring and to say that if you have any needs I might serve, I am entirely at your disposal."

The slight emphasis he placed on the word *needs* went unnoticed by Don Manuel, it seemed. The ambassador had looked down and was now regarding his cuticles in obvious boredom. It relieved me to note that in his arrogant urbanity he clearly didn't think this elderly secretary and his archaic ceremony posed any real threat.

I said carefully, "I would like to dictate some letters to my mother's servants, seeing as they served her for years and share in my grief."

"It would be my honor," Lopez replied. He turned to Don Manuel. "Her Highness has need of my secretarial services, señor. Does that meet with your approval?"

I saw Don Manuel hesitate, his eyes shifting from Lopez to me. He could hardly tell my expression under my veil but I hoped what he did see was a pathetic sight: a woman who had only recently been locked in her rooms without anyone of import to succor her. Treacherous turncoat that he was, he was also a Spaniard. He had to feign some modicum of respect for me, at least in the secretary's presence. After all, I was, on paper at least, his queen.

I took advantage of his momentary indecision to motion to Beatriz, who stood waiting in a corner. "My lady can serve you refreshments in the antechamber if you care to wait, señor. I'm afraid these letters could take some time."

Don Manuel stared hard at me. Then, with a glare, he gave a curt bow and retreated into the antechamber. As soon as Beatriz closed the door on him, I said to Lopez, "The ambassador cannot be trusted. He is entirely my husband's creature."

He looked over his shoulder and moved close to me. "I am aware of it.

He's been plotting without cease since your mother's death to raise your husband above you."

I stared at him. "Above me?"

"Yes. His Highness is calling himself the new king of Castile and heir apparent to Aragón."

My stomach clenched. "I see. And what does my father have to say about it?"

"His Majesty is very perturbed. He's doing his utmost to protect your throne."

"But my mother made him governor of Castile. Whatever my husband may choose to call himself, without my and the Cortes' approval surely Philip is nothing in Spain."

"Alas, not all is as it should be." He paused, eyeing me. I could see he had not forgotten my fury at La Mota. "Your Highness, I must ask that you remain calm. My news . . . it is disturbing."

My hands knotted in my lap. "Go on."

In a low voice he told me of the days following my departure from Spain, in which my mother had returned to Madrigal with my son. She feared for my safety, Lopez said, and her anxiety aggravated her condition. As she made her painstaking preparations for death, stipulating that her corpse be entombed in the cathedral in Granada, site of her greatest triumph, she received a letter from Philip and Don Manuel relating everything that had transpired since my return to Flanders, including my attack on my husband's whore and imprisonment in my rooms.

"They claimed Your Highness was very ill and had gone so far beyond reason it was doubtful whether you'd ever be fit enough to rule. They asked Her Majesty to alter the succession in favor of Charles, in whose stead His Highness could govern until your son comes of age. As you can imagine, their letter greatly aggrieved Her Majesty."

I had suspected this. From the moment I met him, I had sensed corruption in Don Manuel. With his expert knowledge of court intrigue, coupled with a lifelong courtier's ambitions, he had divined the weakness in my husband's character and stepped neatly into a dead man's shoes. Still, that he had so callously and maliciously contrived to disturb my mother's final days made my blood run cold with rage.

"Did . . . did she believe them?" I heard myself ask.

"No. But she wasn't the only one to receive their letter. Don Manuel had copies sent to the Cortes and select high members of the nobility, including the Marquis of Villena, who hardly needs an excuse to commit treachery. He demanded audience with Her Majesty to discuss an alternate succession but Her Majesty refused him. By then, she was near death."

He paused. When I did not speak, he went on.

"After Her Majesty's death, His Majesty had to assume her burden. He deliberated long before choosing a course. Villena continued to demand an audience, but His Majesty, like Her Majesty before him, knew well who had advised your husband to this act. King Fernando bears the ambassador no love. Don Manuel has never been exemplary: indeed, he was instrumental years ago in thwarting Aragón's request of help from the emperor against the French and has a reputation for venality. But at length His Majesty came to the conclusion that he must allow the *grandes* to vent their concerns. Never for an instant did he believe they had any grounds, but the matter begged a solution and he could think of no other."

I remained absolutely silent for a long moment. Then I said quietly, "Are you telling me the Cortes and high nobles of Castile believe . . . I am insane?" As I spoke, I thought of the admiral. Had he heard these lies? The thought made a hollow of my chest.

"I fear so," Lopez told me. "You must understand that King Fernando had no other option. The situation in Spain verges on catastrophic. Don Manuel has sent his sycophants throughout Castile to bribe the nobles, many of whom are defecting to your husband's cause because he promises to restore the lands and privileges they were deprived of years ago by their Majesties. Some of these same *grandes* have gone even further and sent a petition to the Cortes asking that your father be ordered to abandon all further rights in Castile."

I clenched my hands about my chair arms, as if to anchor myself in place. "It was my mother's will that my father govern in my place until I claim my throne. He is her husband!"

"It stands to reason that if Your Highness is unfit to rule, then Her Majesty's appointments are also under question. And in truth, His

Majesty has no legal rights to the position he held as Her Majesty's consort. With her death, he is but king of Aragón."

I struggled to remain seated. My mother's words returned to me, haunting in their assessment of the man who had become my enemy: *His lack of status festers in him like a wound. What I did with Fernando, what he accepted of me, Philip may not take so easily from you.*

"They want to destroy my father," I said aloud. "Don Manuel and Philip will use the noblity's hatred of Papá against him to win the throne."

"Yes," said Lopez, "but there's something neither His Highness nor Don Manuel anticipates—Her Majesty's codicil. God rest her soul, she feared something like this might occur and she prepared a codicil she appended to her will. In it, she states that until the Cortes invest you as queen the archduke Philip has no claim to any title or revenue in Spain. Should Your Highness decide for whatever reason that you do not wish to rule, it is your father, King Fernando, not the archduke your husband, who will assume the throne as regent until Charles comes of age. His Majesty could use this codicil, should the need arise."

My heart thundered in my ears. She had done it. My mother had guarded my path to the throne. She would not see her own flesh and blood or the inviolate lineage of her succession cast aside. I had something with which to fight: something to fight for.

"And Papá can present her codicil to the Cortes," I asked, "before Philip . . . ?" All of a sudden my composure deserted me. I couldn't find the breath to voice the dreaded words aloud.

Lopez nodded. "He can. For now, he has merely persuaded the Cortes that you may suffer a temporary ailment brought on by grief at Her Majesty's loss. It in turn has agreed to uphold his regency until your true state can be ascertained. That is why I am here. Officially, I bring your summons but I am also under orders to convey you to Spain as soon as possible."

I went still. As if he read the trepidation on my face, he said softly, "The past is past, *princesa*. Her Majesty believed you capable of being queen. I would never presume to question her wisdom. But your husband is another matter. In him, I fear you have made a mortal enemy."

I said in a whisper, "I know."

He glanced over his shoulder again. "Her Majesty ensured your husband could never legally usurp your throne. Only through your voluntary abdication can the succession devolve to your sons. But we still face tremendous obstacles, foremost of which is getting you to Spain. I must leave now, before Don Manuel becomes suspicious. But I'll return tomorrow, with your leave, to discuss our plan. For have no fear, I have a plan."

It was as if we'd never been at odds. A devoted servant to his last breath, Lopez would defend me even if I were truly insane, for thus had Isabel of Castile ordained. Even from her tomb, my mother continued to wield her power.

I came to my feet. "My lord, you have my leave. Indeed, I am in your debt."

He bowed. "*Princesa,* the debt is all mine, for you allow me to serve."

As soon as he left, Beatriz came in. "Don Manuel left. He muttered something about an old secretary and a madwoman not being able to do any harm. How I loathe that man!" She went still. "My lady, what is it? You're white as a ghost."

I turned to her. "He will not have Castile," I said. "Never, while I live."

I had never meant anything as much as I did those words.

...

TWENTY-THREE

*L*opez came the next day as promised. I hadn't slept thinking Don Manuel might detain him but it seemed the ambassador had decided Lopez and I were as impotent as he hoped.

Beatriz dressed my hair and applied discreet cosmetics to conceal the shadows under my eyes and add color to my cheeks. Instead of mourning, I donned a sedate blue velvet gown—a wise choice, I noted, as Lopez's face brightened the moment I entered the room.

"Beatriz, stand outside the door," I ordered, and I turned to him. "I'm prepared to do whatever is necessary. Given the circumstances, I think it best if I confirm my father's regency until I can reach Spain."

"I couldn't suggest a wiser course." He drew me to the desk, his voice low. "We must be careful. Don Manuel suspects something. He questioned me for over an hour about the true significance of your having Her Majesty's ring and how long I planned on staying. I told him the ring was symbolic and that I would see you today to say my farewell. We must make haste."

Taking quill and ink and a fresh sheet of parchment, we composed my official reply to the Cortes' summons, reaffirming my commitment to my throne and bestowing upon my father the power to maintain his role of governor until I could arrive, by arms if necessary. *Under no circumstance is Philip of Flanders to style himself as anything other than prince consort*, he wrote, *nor is any* grande *or other high prelate or official in service to the Crown to grant him any such privileges without Her Majesty's official consent, on pain of her worst displeasure.*

Then I signed the letter: *I, Juana the Queen.*

"Once King Fernando presents this to the Cortes," Lopez said, "it'll drive a stake in Don Manuel and your husband's bribery and claims that you are insane. They'll have no other choice but to bring you to Spain. And once you're there, we'll do whatever is required to defend you."

I looked down at the paper. He was waiting to sand it to dry the excess ink.

"Whatever is required," I said. A shiver went through me. "Do you think it'll come to that?"

"I pray not," he said. "Nevertheless, Your Highness must prepare. It seems to me His Highness your husband is as determined to take what you are determined not to give."

"Yes," I said. I motioned. The sand was dusted, blown off; the wax cone melted over a candle flame and dripped onto the folded edge.

Lopez said, "The seal, Your Highness. Only the seal can make it official."

I started. Then I pressed my signet ring into the wax. It took on the faint imprint; as it hardened, I realized it was my first official act as my mother's successor.

And a declaration of war against my husband.

Lopez concealed the document in his satchel containing my letters of condolence. I'd written to the Marquise de Moya and other members of my mother's entourage in the hope such a pile of sealed letters would dissuade all but the most assiduous of spying eyes.

Lopez bowed over my hand. He may have looked old and frail when he first came to me, but I now saw the spry intelligence that had made him one of my mother's most trusted confidants. "I will go straight to Antwerp," he said, "and book passage on the first ship for Spain. By next month at the latest, I'll have delivered your letter to your father. He will take it before the Cortes, who will see by your own hand and my testimony that these rumors concerning your inability to rule are unfounded. You will be summoned to Castile. And there, you will triumph."

"Godspeed," I whispered. I reached over and embraced him. "I will wait for you."

...

I SAT WITH MY WOMEN, MADAME DE HALEWIN, AND MY DAUGHTERS, Eleanor and Isabella.

My nerves were worn paper thin, my nights a purgatory as I paced my room. I despised the endless hours, the pretense and feigned submission. I knew I must behave as though I were reconciled to my lot, that nothing could alert Don Manuel of my plans. It must take him by surprise; he and Philip must find themselves with no other solution than to take me home. I forced myself not to contemplate more than that. I did not delude myself that the road ahead would be easy, but at least I would be in Spain, where my father and those nobles who still revered my mother could support me.

Still, I lived in daily fear that I would soon be unable to conceal my pregnancy. I'd told only Beatriz, knowing that if it was discovered it could be used as a reason for delay. I had to depart for Spain before I began to show. And I must leave my other children behind.

The very thought horrified me. I didn't know when I might see them again, but after hours of whispered debate in my rooms with Beatriz I came to the conclusion that I could not subject them to whatever strife awaited me in Spain. Lopez had hinted it might come to war between Philip and me. I knew from firsthand experience the toll war could have on a child's life and I would not have my children suffer it. I reluctantly wrote to my sister-in-law, Margaret, requesting she welcome Charles and the girls for a spring visit. Margaret was overjoyed in her reply, asking if I would accompany them. Though she must have known of Philip's and my situation, she chose to turn a blind eye and I returned word that I would, as soon as I settled my affairs. Even if Margaret would never openly defy her brother, I knew that at least with her my children would be safe. She would not let them become embroiled in our battles.

I turned to look at my children now, fighting back the sharp pain and fear I had for them.

With her errant gold curls and curious blue gaze, Isabella was at that precocious age when children relish in annoyances. She delighted in yanking off Eleanor's headdresses, cackling with impish glee as Eleanor stomped her foot and cried she was no better than a changeling. She was at this very moment tugging at the threads hanging from Eleanor's embroidery hoop, ruining my eldest daughter's concentration.

I clicked my tongue. "Isabella, *hija mia*, can't you see your sister's trying to sew?" I patted my lap. "Come here. Let me tell you a story of Spain."

Isabella promptly left Eleanor. She adored stories and would sit wide-eyed for hours as I spun tales of the crusades against the Moors and my parents' struggle to unite Spain. Initially devised to pass the time, these stories had developed into my secret weapon. I might leave them for a very long time, but I wanted my daughter to know she had Spanish blood in her veins. Charles and Eleanor were older, reared to be Habsburgs, but Isabella was still young enough to be influenced. I hoped I could instill in her a memory that would counter any accusations about me she later might be subjected to.

I hoisted her onto my lap—"Uff! How big you're getting!"—and smoothed her ringlets. "Shall I tell you about Queen Urraca?"

Isabella shook her head. "No. Tell me about Bebidal."

"Bo-ab-dil," I corrected. "His name was Boabdil, and he was the last sultan of—"

Raised voices in the corridors cut off my voice. I glanced at the door, rising from my chair when I heard footsteps marching toward us. My gaze fled to Beatriz. I clutched Isabella close. The apartment door crashed open.

Guards tromped in, led by Don Manuel. With an ugly twist of a smile, he announced, "Don Lopez has been arrested in Antwerp as a spy."

For a second I could only stare at him. Beside me, Soraya and Beatriz clenched their embroidery to their chests like shields.

"He . . . he is no spy," I managed to say, my voice splitting along the seam as I realized my letter to the Cortes, which Lopez had carried, had not reached Spain.

"Oh?" Don Manuel cocked his oversize head. "He had Your Highness's own letters on him, which he attempted to bring on board a ship. There were official notifications there that he had no authority to convey."

I felt doom crash down around me. I lifted my chin. "I gave him the authority. It is you who should be arrested, my lord, for daring to lay hands on a servant of your queen."

At this, Madame de Halewin rose and took my pale-faced Eleanor by the hand. I tightened my arms about Isabella.

"Your Highness," said the governess in an impassive voice, "let me have the child. It is not fitting to subject her to this disgraceful situation."

Isabella cried, "No! I want to stay with Mamá!"

Don Manuel barked, "Give Madame the child. And all of you, out! Now!"

I released Isabella to Madame de Halewin, my hands turning to ice. Madame de Halewin hustled my daughters out. As Isabella's terrified cries faded, that dark flame that had set me upon Philip's whore flared and I had to dig my nails into my palms to stop from throwing myself like a shrieking devil at Don Manuel.

"You have no right!" I hissed. "No right!"

"I have every right," he retorted, though he inched back into the phalanx of guards behind him. "I am here by order of His Highness the archduke. He commands that you have no further congress with anyone until his return." He pointed at Beatriz and Soraya. "They must go."

Beatriz said through her teeth, "Over your dead body," and as she took a furious step from my side, Don Manuel cried out in high-pitched panic, "Seize her! Seize her!"

Two guards shifted forth, knocking over a gilded table. It toppled to the floor. Soraya grabbed up a vase. I whispered, "Soraya, no. Go with Beatriz. Do as they say."

The guards took hold of my women and pulled them struggling from the room.

Scarlet seared my veins. Whirling to the hearth, I snatched up a poker. I advanced on Don Manuel, fully intending to bring it down on his head. A guard's gauntleted hand shot out and gripped my wrist. The poker clattered to the floor.

"I hope we won't need to restrain Your Highness," said Don Manuel, though he sounded far more frightened than menacing. Indeed, he looked like a deformed child in his overblown garb, hemmed in by our palace corps.

I whispered, "By God, I'll have your head for this."

His face twitched. He said, "I only fulfill my orders." He motioned to the guards, already scampering to the door on his high-heeled shoes. "Let us go."

"Yes," I taunted. "Go. Run like a cur, now that you've terrorized a roomful of women."

The door shut. From where I stood, I heard the guards ordered into place.

The walls closed in around me.

...

PHILIP ROARED IN A WEEK LATER, BARGING INTO MY ROOMS SMELL-
ing of horse sweat and wine. "What? Do you take me for an idiot? Did
you think I wouldn't find out your silly game?"

I looked up from my chair. "How nice of you to come home. Perhaps
now you can see fit to release me. Or would you have it said you mistreat
the mother of your unborn child?"

I deliberately flung out the words because I had no other choice. I had
not been allowed fresh clothes, to bathe myself, nor to have my women
attend me. My chamber pot in the corner was full and reeking, as were
several of the vases. My meals, shoved in through the guarded door on a
tray, moldered. The entire suite smelled like a sewer.

He paused. His narrow eyes raked over me. He looked almost fat, I
thought, satiated on roast and good wine from time spent conniving with
his Estates and God knew how many whores, his once-jutting but shapely
chin nested in a florid roll of flesh. The beard he'd attempted to grow
didn't do much to distinguish him; its sparse coverage only enhanced the
girth of his face.

How had I ever found him desirable?

He paused. "You're with child?"

"It will happen when a man forces himself on his wife," I replied. "If
I had disposed of the means, I'd have torn it from my womb with my bare
hands."

"You must be mad to say such things," he said, with a snort.

I took hold of the armrests, hauling myself to my feet. The room
reeled about me. I had been sitting so long I felt light-headed but I forced
myself to laugh out loud.

"Yes, I must be mad. Mad to have ever loved you, to have thought you
had a shred of honor in that treacherous Habsburg body of yours. Mad to
have believed all the lies you told me, over and over again. Mad to have
ever thought you could love anyone but yourself."

I paused, gave him a smile that showed teeth. "But I am not so mad as
to relinquish my crown. You can lie, betray me, keep me a prisoner for the
rest of my days, but while I live you'll never have Castile. I'll see you dead
before you ever sit on my throne."

He didn't move an inch; then he suddenly leaned close, looming over me. "Do you realize what you've done, you stupid woman? You just handed Castile to your father." He curled his meaty fist in my face. "You will write to the Cortes. You will tell the assembly you have no intention of depriving me of my legal rights."

I met his eyes. "I think not."

Without turning away, he bellowed, "Ambassador!"

To my disgust, Don Manuel tripped in. I gave him a withering look. Behind him, an obviously nervous secretary hastily set a parchment on my desk. Taking me by the arm, Philip brought me to it. "You will sign it or I'll have Lopez served to my hounds. In pieces."

"You'd not dare," I scoffed. I ran my eyes over the tight lines of writing on the parchment, official lines, no doubt promulgating my ruin. Fear knifed through me.

Philip said to Don Manuel, "Tell her."

The ambassador stepped forth. "Your Highness, Don Lopez is in prison. He is accused of espionage and treason. He's also become grievously ill since his . . . questioning. I fear if he does not receive medical attention soon, he may die."

I ignored him, lifting my stare to Philip. "What have you done?"

"Only what that miserable spy deserved. Let's see: First, he was put on the rack and stretched until his bones snapped. But he was too strong. Or is it stubborn? I never can tell with you people. Then he was introduced to an ingenious instrument called the Boot, developed by your own Holy Inquisition, I might add. That loosened his tongue well enough."

"You—you tortured him? But he is my servant!"

"Your women are next," Philip added. "Your beloved Beatriz and Soraya." He sighed. "A pity it would be. As it is, they won't last long. Their cell can barely contain them and the rats."

I wished I weren't with child. I wished I were a man and could run him through with a sword. Because in that instant, I knew he would not hesitate to torture and kill a thousand women if he had to. His hunger for my crown, for power, had swept all other considerations aside.

Nothing mattered, not if it got in the way of his ambition. I was not the one who was mad here. He was. Mad with power and his own overwhelming self-importance.

I looked at the paper, willing my eyes to focus. I felt bathed in ice. It was addressed to the Cortes. I skipped the usual salutation, seeking the meat. When I found it, it took my breath away.

> *Yet since I know it is said in Spain that I am mad, I must be allowed to speak in my defense, though I cannot help but wonder how such false witness is borne against me, for those who spread these rumors do so not against me but also against the Crown of Spain itself. I therefore command you make known to all who wish me ill that nothing save death could induce me to deprive my husband of his rightful governance over Castile, which I shall entrust to him upon my arrival in our kingdom.*

> *Given in Brussels in the month*
> *of May of the year 1505,*
> *I, Juana the Queen*

I looked up at Don Manuel. "Your work, I presume?"

"Just sign it," growled my husband. "We've no time for questions."

"Indeed?" I savored the moment, turning from his smoldering gaze and returning to my chair. "It seems that I, on the other hand, have all the time in the world. You sent a letter before to my mother and the Cortes, claiming I was mad. Now you want me to say I am not. You'd best make up your minds, for in the meantime my father rules as regent in my name until I say otherwise."

Rage suffused Philip's face. Don Manuel wagged his hand at me. "Your Highness makes a grave mistake. Your father held his title in Castile through your mother, who is now deceased. He therefore has no further right to it, and not even the Cortes can prevail over popular sentiment. Fernando of Aragón was never liked. He'll not rule in your name much longer."

"What do you know of my father?" I retorted. "You're not fit to clean his boots! He'll crush you under his heel like the miserable toad you are and I'll applaud him when he does."

I caught the flicker of fear in his protruding eyes, contradicting his next words: "Your Highness, most *grandes* of importance have either sent a missive or representative swearing allegiance to His Highness. If you hope to ever assume your throne, you should think first before you refuse us this simple request."

I met his eyes. My fists clenched in my lap. Double-talk: the art of the ambassador. Two could play this game. "Very well. But in return, I too have a few requests."

"You are in no position to barter!" Philip slammed his hand on the table.

I gave him a frigid smile. "I am the queen of Castile. Without my signature on that letter, you cannot order a single mule in Spain."

Don Manuel murmured, "It is true, Your Highness. We are running out of time."

Philip glared at me. "What do you want?"

"My women. You will also free Lopez and send him back to Spain. And no guards; I am to bear your child. I'll not be a prisoner. If you do these things, I will sign your letter."

The light leached from his eyes. Had we been alone, he wouldn't have hesitated to beat me into submission. But we weren't alone. He'd brought Don Manuel and his by now agitated secretary to bear witness to my "voluntary" signing. He would not want it bantered about that he had coerced me by force.

"Fine," he snarled. "Now sign."

I stood. "Don Manuel, you heard my husband. I pray you remind him of his promises." I went to the desk, inked a quill, and scrawled my signature.

Philip stalked out, Don Manuel and the secretary scurrying behind. Only then did I grasp at the desk's edge. I felt my knees give way. For the first time, I felt the child in my womb quicken with a sharp kick. I took it as a sign.

I had won a victory, bought at a terrible price, yes, but a victory nevertheless.

And thus, step by step, would I win the war.

...

THE DAYS THREADED WITHOUT END. THE GUARDS WERE REMOVED; once again the palace was open to me. But I did not leave my chambers, knowing that the moment my letter reached Spain it would prompt those few who might have remained loyal to my father to declare for Philip. He promised riches, titles. I had said I would make him king. Only the very brave or foolish would continue to support my father now. I prayed Papá could still convince the Cortes that my letter must have been obtained by force, for I'd never willingly deprive him of the defense of my kingdom.

On September 15, 1505, I took to my bed and bore my fifth child, a daughter Philip ordered christened Mary in honor of his late mother. Immediately after the birth he departed again, leaving me under Don Manuel's guard and the care of my few loyal women.

My new babe was healthy, with the Habsburg skin and a shock of wiry red hair. But I did not enjoy her for long. Soon after the birth I fell ill for the first time with that often-lethal ailment of new mothers—milk fever. The doctors expressed immediate consternation and advised Don Manuel to lift any restrictions imposed on me. Don Manuel agreed, though not before he first sent Mary and her wet nurse off to Savoy, to join my other children with their tante Margaret.

From my sickbed, I summoned preternatural strength to pen another letter to Margaret, which Beatriz entrusted to the wet nurse. In it, I implored her to remember my children were innocents and mustn't be used. I entrusted them to her care until I could be reunited with them.

The fever came close to killing me. As soon as my letter was sent, I succumbed to a fiery hell. Later, Beatriz told me of her and Soraya's constant vigil at my side, watching helplessly as I thrashed for days, delirious and inchoate. Not until late October did I recover sufficiently to leave my bed; not until November did I have enough strength to venture into the gardens to partake of the fresh wintry air.

Only one thing gave me satisfaction: his anxious inquiries and daily visits proved that the mere thought of my demise provoked heart-stopping terror in Don Manuel. My death would be a disaster for him and Philip. Without me, they had nothing. By law, my father could set my son on the throne and rule in his name as regent. The dream of a Habsburg Spain, which had torn apart our lives, would be over before it had even begun.

I had no intention of dying. The doctors might pronounce my survival miraculous, but I knew my time had not come. With my fur-lined cowl over my head and my hands in a muff, I sat in the garden for hours, watching darkness overcome the leaden sky, my shadow freezing on the hard ground. Snow fluttered in the air. I hoped it would bury Flanders in a glacial tomb.

It was here that Don Manuel came to me. Beatriz stood, a flush to her cheeks. She hated him even more than I did. I motioned her to step aside and regarded him coolly as he bowed low, almost upsetting the huge beaver skin hat on his head. He was all deference, indicating something of import had taken place. "Your Highness, I bring good news. Our letter reached Castile and the summons from the Cortes has come. We'll depart for Spain as soon as arrangements are made."

I absorbed this news without a word. He bowed again, hand on the hat, then pulled his thick cape about his little person and hurried away.

I looked at Beatriz. Around us the snow gathered strength, blurring the outlines of the shrouded fruit trees and topiary cut in the shape of rampant beasts.

For the first time in our years together, my devoted lady and friend did not notice my disquiet. She embraced me. "Finally, *princesa,* we are going home!"

Home.

"Yes," I said softly. "So it begins."

QUEEN

...

FOR SHE WAS A WOMAN MADE TO BEAR
ALL THINGS IN THIS WORLD,
WITHOUT FAILURE OF HEART OR COURAGE.

—ANONYMOUS CHRONICLER

TWENTY-FOUR

. . .

I stood before Brandenburg Bay, which churned like an enormous cauldron, lacerated by the high winds and causing our fleet of top-heavy galleons to bob in the water like gilded corks. It was the start of the winter storm season; not even the hardiest of fishermen would dare brave a trip by sea at a time like this. But winter's fury meant nothing to my husband—not if it came between him and his ultimate ambition.

I smiled.

After dispatching my letter, Philip had had no choice but to reach accord with my father, after which he ordered a flurry of preparations to rival the intensity of the winter storms. Now he strode about like a king anointed, shouting orders left and right with Don Manuel scampering at his heels, and leaving me to mull over this unexpected turn of events. I wished I had Lopez here with me, to help me unravel the tangled skeins whereby I found myself bound for Spain.

Of course, I already knew Philip had no intention of honoring any accord he had with my father or indeed anyone else. He'd break it as soon as he could, had in fact already broken it, at least in his mind. If not, why gather his entire guard and corps of German mercenaries? Why this arsenal of crossbows, swords, and lances and this fleet of seventy-odd ships? There could be no other explanation. My husband prepared for war.

So did I. Only I didn't need a single soldier to initiate it.

Philip strode to me. He wore topaz brocade shot with gold, his cloak lined in marten. He'd been exercising tirelessly for weeks, tilting at the joust, practicing his archery and swordplay, losing the excess weight and regaining that muscled frame that now seemed to block out everything around me.

"It is time." He glanced peremptorily at my women. "They'll have to travel with the others of our suite. There's no room on the flagship."

"Beatriz and Soraya go where I go," I replied. "They can sleep in my cabin. I am forced to leave my children behind. Surely, you don't expect me to make any more sacrifices?"

He stared at me. I met his eyes, ice against ice. Though I still felt the remnants of sorrow that our youthful love had degenerated into this dangerous game of wills, there was really nothing left in my heart for him. I looked on him as I might a stranger.

"Do as you will," he said. "Only be quick about it, or I'll leave you behind." He strode away. I followed at a leisurely pace, boarding the rowboat that would bring us to our galleon, providing it didn't roll over and drown us first.

Night closed in, obscuring the shore.

I did not look back. I had already decided I would never again return to Flanders.

...

ON THE THIRD DAY, AS WE ROUNDED THE COAST OF BRITTANY, A bird dropped out of the sky and fell at my feet. I looked down at the panting, feathered body, about to kneel when I saw a nearby sailor genuflect fervently. "No, Your Highness, don't touch it. It is an omen!"

I chuckled. "Nonsense. It's a poor sparrow that's lost its way." I scooped up the creature as it feebly beat its wings. One wing was crooked. Wondering if it was broken, I looked about for Beatriz.

The sailor watched me with terrified eyes. "I beg Your Highness to toss it into the sea. Please, for the love of God. It will blight our voyage."

I laughed and went to my cabin, where I set the sparrow on my berth. After dipping a goblet into the barrel of fresh water outside, I fed it droplets with my fingers, crooning as if to a child. I wrapped my shawl about it, lulled it to sleep in this makeshift nest as twilight fell and the sea's murmur sang with the creaking of the ship and whoosh of sails.

Beatriz came to tell me that everyone on board was talking about a winged beast that had come to curse the ship. I motioned at the tiny bundle. "Here's your winged beast: a simple, tired sparrow. Now, go fetch me a cup of hot broth. I'll feed it until it's strong enough to fly again." As I spoke, I felt unexpected warmth in my chest.

Perhaps my heart wasn't as dead as I'd thought, after all.

...

THE FOLLOWING NIGHT, THE STORM HIT. THE SKY TO THE WEST turned a dark crimson, awash in tattered burgundy-black clouds. A menacing darkness overcame the fleet, whipping the sea into savage heights and consuming everything in its path like a gigantic maw.

In our cabin, my women and I raced to clear the floor, stacking the table and chairs at the far corner and shoving my chests against them. I stored the bleating sparrow in a perforated coffer where I kept my pittance of jewels, nestling it safely inside.

Outside, the wind howled, flinging down icy rain. The ship began to career as if it were on wheels, its rolling motion growing increasingly violent as the sea heaved. Huddled with my women, I listened to the crashing of mountainous waves up and over deck railings, the desperate clamor of the crew as they fought to save us from destruction.

Then came a piercing splintering sound, followed by panicked yelling. Instants later, the galleon started to keel. Soraya keened while Beatriz began whispering prayers to every saint she could think of. I, in turn, began to get a feel for the motion, which was a little like riding a wild stallion. It was an exhilarating, completely unexpected sensation. I felt alive. Alive and free.

The ship groaned upright. I gave a sudden giggle. Drowned with the husband I'd come to loathe and his foppish suite: what an epigraph it would make!

"Come," I said to my ladies. "We shall go outside."

"Outside?" repeated Beatriz, as though I'd declared I would throw myself from the prow.

"Yes." Supporting myself with hands against the wall, I moved toward the door. Despite the dire situation, Beatriz was not about to forgo her responsibility. She came after me with a cloak, sickly green as she was. When I wrenched open the door, the wind leapt at us like a feral pet. Braced against the high tower railing, I gazed on pandemonium below, the Flemish nobles racing about in hysterics in their sopping finery while deckhands struggled to secure the cracked mast and keep the galleon afloat.

I spotted Don Manuel, a drenched monkey in his soaking brown velvets. Philip was at his side, his figure grotesquely misshapen. What on earth . . . ? I peered. A burst of laughter tore from my lips. My husband wore an inflated leather sack! Even from where I stood, I could discern bold red words splashed in ink across his chest: *El rey Don Felipe.*

I tossed back my head, laughing uproariously. *El rey!* The king! So in case he fell overboard and managed to float ashore, he'd not be mistaken for a common sailor. It was so ridiculous I would not have believed it had I not seen it for myself.

Beatriz cried out, "We must pray for safe passage to the nearest port!"

"That would be England," I said. "But not to fret. I've never heard of a king who drowned."

I must confess that had we sunk that day, I would have gone down a happy woman.

. . .

BATTERED AND WITH SEVERAL SHIPS LOST, WE LANDED ON THE coast of Essex, where the local gentry made haste to accommodate us, surrendering for our use a small manor. Word was sent to King Henry VII. Two days later, I awoke to find that my husband, Don Manuel, and the majority of the Flemish suite had gone, leaving me behind with my few servants.

"Gone?" I said furiously to Philip's sneezing chamberlain, who, like most of the Flemish, had caught a nasty ague. "Where did they go? Tell me this instant!"

The chamberlain was in no position to deny me. He had seen my bravura on board during the storm and probably believed I was indeed as mad as Philip claimed. "To court," he muttered miserably. "Word came from His Majesty of England that he would receive them."

"Receive us, you mean," I retorted and I stormed back to my rooms. With the fleet dry-docked for repairs, it could be days, weeks even, before we were ready to set sail again and I was not about to sit here twiddling my thumbs while Philip and Don Manuel created God knew what mischief with the Tudor. I was the queen of Spain and my sister Catalina had lived in England for several years, having been betrothed anew to her late husband's brother, Prince Henry. Her position here would make ignoring me quite difficult. I was eager to see my sister again after so many years, and wasn't going to let the chance pass me by.

While my women set themselves to countering the pervasive damp by lighting braziers all around the room we shared and countering the boredom by airing any gowns they could salvage from my waterlogged coffers, I set the sparrow in a cage by the window and sat at the table to write a letter. When I was done, I handed it to Soraya, along with a few gold coins. "Find someone to deliver this to court." I looked at Beatriz as Soraya hurried out. "Either they send an escort or I'll go to them. It's their choice."

Three days later, a missive came. I expected an official invitation; instead, to my surprise, it was from my sister, just a few lines, but enough to raise the hair on my nape.

"What does she say?" Beatriz asked anxiously, Soraya looking on.

"She wants me to come to Windsor Castle in secret," I said. "Tomorrow night."

. . .

A SLASH OF LIGHTNING ILLUMINED THE STONE PILE OF WIND-sor Castle, perched atop a forested hill like a massive toadstool.

The messenger who'd brought Catalina's letter guided us on our horses into a cobblestone courtyard. After we dismounted, we were led into the castle proper, traversing several galleries before the messenger paused at a brass-studded door. Within, we found a spacious chamber furnished with oak chairs, a table, various painted coffers, and an upholstered bench before the hearth. The hearth was huge, built right into the wall, the snapping fire in its depth casting more gloom than light. I glimpsed another door in the far wainscoting, leading into what I assumed were the bedchamber and privy. A velvet curtain glittering with embroidered stars partially covered an embrasure. This was a privileged person's suite.

I turned to ask the messenger if my sister would meet us here. But he had vanished, closing the door and leaving Beatriz and me alone.

I unclasped my cloak. "I can't believe we actually made it here without being noticed," I said uneasily as I moved to the hearth. "Surely, if nothing else, Philip set someone to watch me. Maybe the letter was a ruse, to get me here without ceremony, though I can't imagine why."

"Neither can I—" said Beatriz, and then she let out a gasp.

I turned. And froze.

A figure stepped from behind the curtain into the light—a small woman, dressed in a gown without rustle or sheen, her coiffed head bowed. I understood Beatriz's reaction. The woman bore an uncanny resemblance to my mother, down to the glimmer of gold hair under her hood.

As I struggled for my voice, the woman dropped into a curtsy.

"*Su Majestad,*" she uttered. She lifted her face. In the muted glow of the hearth, ethereal blue eyes shone at me like a forgotten memory.

With a muffled cry, I went and embraced her, kissing my sister's cheeks, her mouth and nose, my tears overflowing. When I finally drew back, I found myself staring straight into Catalina's somber gaze.

"They know you are here," she said, glancing to the door. "My messenger is one of the few trusted servants I have left. Unfortunately, we've little time."

"They?" I stared. I could not reconcile this staid, stalwart woman with the pretty laughing child I had last seen in Spain.

"His Grace King Henry and your husband," she said. "The archduke told the king you'd taken ill from the voyage, but then your letter came and no one knew what to do. I found out and discovered where you were lodged. I feared you might not come."

"I see," I said, though I seethed. Of course Philip had told Henry Tudor I was ill. He'd do anything he could to keep me away from this court, which meant he was up to no good.

Catalina went on, "If they ask, you must tell them you decided to come on your own. Don't let them know I wrote to you, whatever you do. I have so few confidants these days. I wouldn't want those who serve me to come under suspicion for relaying news not meant for my ears."

I nodded. There were sunken circles about her eyes, thin lines at the corners of her pale mouth. She was not yet twenty-three and she looked twice her age. What had happened to her?

"Catalina," I said, reaching for her hands, "you speak as if you were in danger. Why?"

She looked away. I brought her to the bench before the hearth. Without my needing to tell her a word, Beatriz went to stand vigil at the door.

Catalina let go of my hand; I saw in the light that her fingers were reddened, chafed by chilblains. I knew then that wherever she lived, this was not her room. Her gown too looked threadbare. It was evident she did not thrive in England. Indeed, her hands were those of a common charwoman, not the cherished future queen of the Tudor heir.

I bit back my fury. "You must tell me who has done this to you."

"The king." Her voice was low, hesitant. "He has forbidden me from coming to court, but I disobeyed him." She raised her eyes to mine. "I had to. You are the only one who can help me."

"But I don't understand, *pequeñita*. Are you not betrothed to Prince Henry? Why would he forbid you from coming to court?"

Her smile was unrevealing. I thought with a pang that she had our mother's smile, gracious, yet remote. She reached into her gown pocket, withdrew a paper. "Mamá wrote this to me before she died. Perhaps you should read it. It will explain my circumstances better than I can."

For a moment, I could not move. The entire room seemed to darken at its edges, crouch in around me. I took the letter, shifted so that the firelight fell on the page.

The parchment was worn, indicating Catalina had been carrying it with her. Undated, lacking salutation and seal, my mother's painfully familiar handwriting raced across the page without interruption, a fervent outpouring of her thoughts engraved in fading ink.

I breathed deep.

I write to you on the eve of my death; and my desire to go unto God is marred only by my concern for those I must leave behind. You cannot know, being so far away, how much I suffer for you in this trying time. You must be strong, hija mia, *stronger than you've ever been. The dispensation has finally been sent from Rome and should reach England by the time you receive this letter. You can rejoice in knowing that His Holiness has decreed the affinity between you and Prince Henry valid,*

as your marriage to Arthur was never consummated. Only the most evil
of men would dare dispute your maidenhood now. I cannot be here to
protect you, but God is with you always, and justice shall prevail. I
pray that you will have no further need for succor, but should it come to
pass that the dispensation is not sufficient, you must rely on Juana. I
shall write to her as I write to you, asking her to use her power as queen
of Castile to coerce the Tudor, if necessary, into honoring your be-
trothal. I know she loves you dearly and will not forsake you. As for
myself, I carry you in my heart always, and from that glorious place
where we all must go, I shall watch over you and guide you with my
spirit.

> *Your devoted mother,*
> *Isabel*

The letter crinkled in my trembling hands. I looked at Catalina. "I
never received it," I whispered. "I never received her letter."

"It must have gotten lost. Mine took nearly two months after her death
to arrive."

"It was not lost." I checked my sudden fury. I had to focus on Catalina
now. Time enough there would be to exact revenge on that miscreant
Don Manuel, who had kept my mother's last letter from me. "Tell me why
the king refuses to honor your betrothal to the prince. I must know everything if I am to help you."

In a flat voice, she said, "You remember Prince Arthur died a fortnight
after our marriage? Well, during my widowhood, King Henry's queen,
Elizabeth, brought me to live at court. She was very kind, and when my
period of mourning ended she suggested Prince Henry and I be betrothed. His Grace agreed. He wrote to Mamá, and she initiated negotiations to obtain a dispensation from Rome, as Henry is my brother-in-law.
I swore before witnesses that Arthur and I never consummated our marriage, and no one thought we would be denied."

She paused. Her hands bunched in her lap, just as they had in times of
frustration in the classroom, when she couldn't master a particularly trying lesson. Like me, she did not suffer failure gladly. "Then Queen Elizabeth died in childbed. His Grace was beside himself with grief, as were we

all, for she was a gracious and loving woman. Still, His Grace assured me that his council would ratify my and Henry's betrothal, as that had been his wife's last desire."

A brief smile illumined Catalina's drawn face. "I cannot tell you how happy it made me, even in my mourning for the queen. Henry and I had grown fond of one another in a way Arthur and I never did, and I began to prepare for when the marriage would take place."

"And then what happened?" I asked, dreading her reply.

"Mamá died." She stated it without visible emotion, though I knew she must have felt a deep pain inside. "Overnight, the king sent me to live in a dower manor by the Thames. He reduced my allowance to such an extent, I did not have money to support my household, and many of my servants deserted me. I had to pawn my plate for food. I wrote to His Grace every day to remonstrate, but he replied that he was not responsible for my predicament. If I was in such dire need, he advised I ask Papá for money. I was but a guest in England, he said, and not his ward. Then he—"

Her voice caught. "He told me the pope had sent word that my marriage to Henry would be incestuous, as I had been wed to his brother. I repeated that on my honor, I am a virgin. Arthur and I never consummated our marriage, but he refuses to believe me. Since that time, I've learned that Rome did issue the dispensation, and the king lied because he seeks another bride for Henry. He has left me to fend for myself. My duenna, Doña Manuel, insisted I write to you, but when I heard you had left Flanders for Spain, I decided to wait. I did write to Papá, however. He never replied." She searched my face. "He is not ill, is he?"

"No. Not that I'm aware of." My own voice throbbed. I wanted to tear down this castle with my bare hands. My beautiful sister, a princess of Spain in the prime of her youth, forced to endure penury and humiliation at the hands of an upstart Tudor, whose lineage was bastard-sprung. And Philip had been roistering with him for days now, while I'd been left unaware. I now understood why he had snuck away, why no summons for my presence had been issued. No one wanted Catalina and me to meet. No one wanted me to discover the outrageous neglect she had been subjected to.

I came to my feet. "Beatriz!" My lady came to us. "Tell the man out-side to prepare our mounts." I held out my hand to Catalina. "Come, *pequeñita*. We are leaving."

My sister rose. A frown creased her brow. "Leaving? I think you've misunderstood. When I said I needed your help, I did not mean I wished to leave."

I paused. "Not leave? But why on earth would you stay? You're not beholden to anything here. You are an infanta of Spain; I am Spain's queen. You can come home with me."

"And do what? Live at court as your spinster sister? Take holy vows and enter a convent? Or perhaps wed the first noble who takes pity on me? I've been married once before and widowed. I am not a thirteen-year-old girl with a host of suitors outside my door, Juana. You know that as well as I. At my age, you had already borne your husband a child. Be-sides, I *am* beholden; I am betrothed to Prince Henry. Through no fault of mine, doubts have been cast on my honor. I must not concede defeat. You read Mamá's letter. God has a plan for me. He wants me to be queen of England."

"God may want it," I told her, "but I can do nothing for you here. I've no power until I reach Spain and am invested by the Cortes. Don't you see? I . . . I too am fighting for my life."

The words were out before I could take them back. I saw her expres-sion falter, knew at once that despite her isolation from this court, she had heard something of my plight. Then she leaned close. "There *is* some-thing you can do. Your husband and the king negotiate a treaty. His Grace would betroth Henry to another princess, perhaps one of your own daughters. You could refuse, offer him something else in exchange for honoring my betrothal."

Her eyes and voice were fervid as she grasped my hands. In that in-stant, she terrified me. She was like our mother, once her mind was made up—immovable, impermeable, a rock against which the entire world might break and not make a difference.

"His Grace is not well," she said, with a gleam in her eyes. "He coughs up blood and tires easily. All I need is time. Henry loves me. I know he does. And once he becomes king, he will make me his queen."

"Oh no, Catalina." I looked down at our entwined fingers and felt a void open between us. "It is *you* who loves him, beyond reason. I can see it in your eyes. You love him with all your heart and soul, and such a love can only destroy you, as it almost destroyed me."

I saw her flinch. I reached up, cupped her chin in my hand. "Look at me. I too have loved as you love this prince. And in the end, he has betrayed me. You must forget this Henry. Come with me now, before it is too late."

She was silent. Then she said, "No."

It was then we heard voices in the corridor. Catalina whirled to the bench, grabbing up her discarded letter. She fled to the door in the wainscoting. There she paused for a moment, looking at me. Our eyes met. She slipped out, as if she had never been with me at all.

I fought back a crushing wave of sorrow and rage, motioning Beatriz to the door; moments later, a group of lords strode in, accompanied by grooms carrying torches. The fiery flood of light hurt my eyes. I did not have to be told that the stooped, gaunt figure in the sable robe, standing in the center of the staring men, was Henry VII of England.

Beside him stood my husband.

· · ·

I DID NOT SEE CATALINA AGAIN AND SOMEHOW MANAGED TO RE-frain from asking, recalling how frightened she had been that our visit would be discovered. I suspected the king knew, however, even as he expressed surprise at my arrival, though I understood I would have been sent for eventually, as the suite had been prepared for me. He held festivities in my honor, accorded me the courtesy of a fellow sovereign. I had an immediate dislike of him for what he'd done to my sister and our subsequent encounters only confirmed my impression.

Seated beside him on the royal dais, I felt his flint-gray eyes appraising me as if I were on display, his bronchial guffaw underscored by the lurid undertone of a man who has slept alone too long. The shuffling of his bony fingers reminded me of insect wings. He retched frequently, dribbling blood-flecked saliva onto his napkin. Whether his illness was mortal or not, I could not tell. If it were, he might endure for years before it killed him. Lung rot was unpredictable, and he was the kind of king who'd cling to his last gasping breath. When he introduced me to his heir, the young prince whom Catalina refused to leave, I understood why.

Startlingly tall, with the face of a cherub and body of a god, the king's sixteen-year-old namesake was impeccably courteous, engaging me in brief conversation before he excused himself. I noticed the swagger of his broad shoulders and long muscular legs as he walked away and the way his father scowled and averted his eyes. The king couldn't bear to see such a magnificent counterpart to his own decay.

"He'll make a strapping husband one day," Henry VII chuckled, leaning so close to me I smelled his rotting teeth. It was his first allusion to the fact that he knew my sister and I had met.

I gave him a vague smile, anticipating the snare I knew he and Philip would spring.

. . .

IT CAME WITHIN THE WEEK.

Philip walked into my rooms and set before me the draft of a new treaty between him and the Tudor. It required only my signature. I read it thoroughly before I lifted my eyes. "No."

His mouth twisted. "What do you mean, no? It's an excellent arrangement. In exchange for these few concessions, we will have English support in Spain. What could you object to?"

I pushed the treaty aside. "Everything. First, why do we need English support in Spain? We just signed an accord with my father. Second, these concessions consist of three different marriage alliances, one between our son Charles and the king's youngest daughter, Mary; another between your sister Margaret and the king himself; and last, but not least, one between his heir and our Eleanor."

"Yes? And? They're good matches, all of them."

I wanted to spit in his face. Instead, I stared him in the eye. He drew back, unnerved by my visible contempt, which at certain moments could reduce the violence and hatred between us to the insignificance of a domestic squabble.

"You may do as you please with your sister, though I doubt Margaret will appreciate it. But when it comes to our children, I have a say in who they shall wed. And"—I raised my voice, overriding his protest—"as far as Prince Henry is concerned, lest you have forgotten, he is already betrothed to my sister."

He flushed red, rapped his knuckles on the table. "I asked for your signature only to spare you that mulish pride of yours. With or without your consent, I *will* have this treaty."

"Then do so. Sign your life away. In the meantime, I leave this very day for Essex and our ships." I strode to the door, startling Don Manuel and the Flemish nobles, who skulked in the corridor with the dogs. "My lords, send word to His Grace the king of England that Her Majesty the queen of Castile wishes to bid him farewell. At once."

. . .

I RODE BACK TO ESSEX IN A RAGING STORM, MY THOUGHTS TURbulent as the gusting winds.

Once again in that damp manor, I waited three weeks until Philip's return, his attendants laden with coffers of baubles given to him by the Tudor. I would have departed for Spain long since had the ship's crew obeyed me. As it stood, I wished I'd taken to the sea in a rowboat when Philip returned carrying that treasure trove of gifts and plate from Henry VII, and the English Order of the Garter about his neck.

"Pity you missed the ceremony," he said. "I was the toast of the court. Archduke of Flanders, King of Castile, and Knight of the Garter."

I refrained from comment, forced to share supper with him in the hall. When Don Manuel tried to converse with me—as Philip had the supreme bad taste of seating the ambassador at our board as if he were of equal rank—I rebuffed him. Not until I got back to my chambers did I give in to my nausea, revolted by the bland English fare and the events that had preceded it.

That night, Philip banged at my door. I'd thought he might. I had seen the drunken glitter in his eyes and anticipated the price of barring my door against him. Beatriz sat wide-eyed on her pallet with Soraya as I stood silently listening to him yell, "Open the door! Open it, you Castilian bitch!" He slammed his fists and booted feet against the door, no doubt rousing the entire manor with his belligerence.

In the end I unlocked it because in his current state he was capable of ordering his men to break it down. As my women hurried out he whirled on me with his fist raised. "Don't you ever lock your door on me again!"

His eyes were red slits. He'd drunk more than his weight of the heavy ale the English preferred. Glancing at the large hand poised above me (for he had put on weight guzzling Henry Tudor's victuals), I said, "If you strike me, not only will I lock my door, but you will never so much as look on me again."

He snorted, lowered his hand. "As if you could ever stop me."

I refrained from reminding him I just had, turning back to the bed as he fumbled at his codpiece. I knew why he was here. Get her with child again, the gnome had said. Get her with child so she'll be more malleable in Spain.

I lay back, lifted my nightgown. I would not enter Spain bruised and battered. Better to let him have his way. "Ah, Juana," he slurred. "You still want me, don't you? You still want your Felipe in you." He couldn't get his codpiece off. He was too inebriated to untie the stays. He had to pull his sex out the side and pump it to hardness in his fist.

I wondered if despite everything, I might feel something, if a last ember of our flown passion might somehow smolder and ignite. But all I felt was greasy fingers, the unbearable heaviness of his flesh as he pushed inside. It was grotesque, a travesty. I considered whether I could induce myself to vomit on him as he bucked and heaved.

In only seconds he gasped and rolled off me. He fell asleep at once, snoring with his mouth ajar, his breath rank with ale. Slipping from bed, I went to a chair by the window.

I sat, staring into the blustery darkness.

I remained there all the night, not moving, not thinking, as his seed filled my womb.

At dawn, I opened the sparrow's cage and released it into the gray English sky.

TWENTY-FIVE

...

There was something indescribable about coming home. As the rugged white cliffs and coves of Galicia's northern coast reared in the distance, the green headlands crowned by the Torre de Hércules, I felt released like my sparrow from the confines of an incomprehensible existence.

Fishing boats sent from the port city of La Coruña sidled up to the galleon. I enjoyed the fishermen's wide eyes and gaping mouths when the captain of the fleet yelled out in broken Spanish that he conveyed their Majesties the king and queen of Castile. I did not care that he cited Philip first. The astonished elation of my countrymen as they rowed furiously back to shore was more than enough to appease me.

I was in Spain. And La Coruña at the northeastern edge of my realm, with its steep fertile vales and granite towns populated by an industrious, taciturn people loyal to Castile, would be the first to welcome me.

"Miserable, isn't it?" Philip had stepped beside me. "I had hoped to land anywhere but here."

I did not look at him. "Yes, I know where you'd prefer to land: in Laredo, where the *grandes* you have bribed await you with their vassals. Fortunately, your fear of drowning has outweighed your determination to betray my father."

He chuckled. "Such a spitfire you are, my infanta." He gripped my arm. "But I suggest you exercise control over that sharp tongue, unless you want to arrive in your precious Spain wearing my bridle and reins."

I pulled away. I hadn't yet told him our coupling a month ago had borne fruit and had no intention of doing so until it became absolutely necessary. As before, he would seek to use it as an excuse to confine me again and I needed every moment of freedom I had.

"I must change." I pushed past him. "I want to be seen as befits my rank."

"Why bother? All you ever wear these days is black!" He released a cruel laugh.

I continued to my cabin. He wouldn't have reason to laugh much longer.

...

THE ENTIRE CITY TURNED OUT TO RECEIVE US, THE WOMEN AND children carrying hastily picked bouquets of early spring flowers, the men in their Sunday finest. Our arrival was completely unexpected and the town officials wrung their hands as they tried to make the best of it. They were overjoyed, of course, but they wished they'd had more time to prepare, fearing I would find their reception frugal, lacking in the grandeur I deserved.

I smiled, shook my head. I cared nothing for fanfare. Let my subjects welcome me and I was well satisfied.

Philip tapped his foot, understanding little of what I said, as he'd never bothered to fully master Spanish. He required Don Manuel to stand on a footstool and breathlessly translate into French, and the words *my subjects* made my husband glower. Throwing up his head and puffing out his chest, he interrupted my conversation with the officials (a breach of etiquette that would not endear him to anyone) and we set out on foot to the cathedral, where we were scheduled to receive the keys to the city before retiring to the Dominican monastery that had been selected for our lodgings.

As we proceeded down the flagged streets, preceded by the clerics and lord mayor, the people pressed at either side of the cordoned path went silent, staring in awe at the contrived splendor of the Flemish ranks. Philip had donned flamboyant violet and his ducal coronet. He seemed a giant, big and fair and foreign; and he'd ordered his men to likewise wear their most sumptuous cloth—a stark contrast to my black velvet gown and veiled beguine Spanish hood, my hair concealed under its curved shape.

The streets grew narrower, a labyrinth of old houses leaning like weary trees into each other, flowered balconies snuffing out the light. It was blessedly clean. Unlike Flanders, France, and England, here people did not toss the contents of their chamber pots out their windows but rather used designated heaps outside the city. The repetitive clacking of boot heels and clanking of scabbards against jeweled belts resounded. All of a sudden from some unseen balcony overhead a lone voice cried: "*Viva nuestra reina Doña Juana, hija de Isabel!* Long live our queen Juana, daughter of Isabel!"

Philip looked up furiously. Youths in the crowd lifted their voices, followed by husbands and grandfathers, daughters, widows, and mothers, until it seemed the entire city echoed the same cry: "*Viva Doña Juana! Viva nuestra reina!* Long live our queen!"

I paused in disbelief. I had already noticed how these hardened coastal folk, these strangers I'd come to rule, stared at me. I'd wondered if they disliked the severity of my dress, if they sensed the perceptible chasm between Philip and me. Had they heard of my struggles in Flanders? Were they aware of my previous visit and Philip's subsequent desertion? Had these simple fishermen, goatherders, and tanners been told of the battle between us over my throne?

Had they heard I was mad?

I couldn't tell by looking nor did I wish to stare. But those faces that blended into a single, questioning visage now separated into glimpses of individuals who cheered me with heartrending sincerity. I saw a flushed man with shining green eyes waving his cap; a prematurely weathered woman with a wide open smile, clutching a baby to her breast and leading a little girl by the hand; a couple with tears on their faces as they reverentially inclined their heads. I felt their inherent respect for their monarch, but more than that I felt their love, a love they had given my mother for bringing the kingdom together and providing them with years of peaceful prosperity, and it was so uncomplicated, so encompassing it replenished me.

Instinctively, I drew up my veil. The revelation of my countenance brought a cluster of widows in perpetual mourning to their knees. One of them raised a gnarled hand and said, "*Que Su Majestad disfrute de mucha vida y triunfé!* May Your Majesty live long and triumph!"

Ignoring Philip's hissing protest, I moved to those kneeling widows, scions of Spanish culture, women who bought bread every morning in the marketplace and sat in their doorways every afternoon to gossip about the living and remember the departed. I was about to bid them to rise when a stooped figure broke through them to where I stood—an impoverished woman with a tattered shawl flapping from concave shoulders.

She peered at me with lucid black eyes.

"Get that hag away!" I heard Philip bark. He strode to me, his hand closing about my arm like a vise. I stayed the guards with a look. I smiled at the lined face. "*Sí*, señora?" I asked softly.

I thought she wanted to be touched for the scrofula or needed alms. But she did not speak to me. Turning to Philip, she intoned, "You may come as a proud prince today, young Habsburg. But you shall travel many more roads in Castile in death than you ever will in life."

Silence fell. She turned back to me, gave me a sad, knowing smile that froze me where I stood. Then she shuffled away and was swallowed by the crowd.

I looked at Philip. He was white about the mouth. As the procession resumed its pace, he muttered, "If I ever see that witch again, I'll order her skewered."

At the portals of the church, we halted. The traditional ceremony would now ensue, and I steeled myself, for my next actions would either secure me popular acclaim or sever forever that still-fragile bond.

The governor of Galicia stepped forth to present the symbolic keys to the city, reciting the ancient oath that required Philip and me to swear to uphold the statutes of the Galician province. Philip nodded impatiently, as this time he was truly lost, seeing as Don Manuel was not at his side but relegated now to his appropriate place at the end of the line.

My turn came. "No," I said, and I made sure it carried into the crowd. "I cannot swear."

The governor started. "No, *Su Majestad*? But it is the custom. Have we displeased you in some way that you will not uphold the oath?"

"What is he saying?" Philip said through his teeth.

I ignored him. "No, you haven't displeased nor have any of these good people. But to swear the oath is to declare myself your anointed sovereign, which I am not until the Cortes invest me as such. Therefore, any oath sworn here today would be invalid."

Astonishment rippled through the crowd. I sensed at once it wasn't dismay but pride. Just as I'd hoped, my refusal was interpreted as a sign of respect for the long-established traditions of Castile, a declaration that like my mother before me I would rule with dignity and honor. I had to stop myself from giving my now-flushed and enraged husband a triumphant smile, for if he hadn't understood the words, he comprehended their intention clearly enough.

Philip hissed, "I don't know what you're up to, but whatever it is you will stop it now!"

I turned to the mayor. "I am weary, señor. I think I will hear Mass later. Pray, take me to my lodgings." Motioning to my women, I turned and walked away, leaving Philip standing there among his overdressed minions.

The battle had begun.

. . .

TWENTY-SIX

Following my public refusal to swear the oath, Don Manuel and Philip found themselves in a quandary, unsure as to how to proceed and unable to order me confined lest it be said I was being treated cruelly for no apparent reason. All of La Coruña had seen that I looked, and acted, quite sane; and so every night we held court as though nothing were amiss, though I could see in Philip's dark frown and Don Manuel's frenetic whisperings in his ear that they were not going to concede defeat. When the first of the Castilian nobles began to arrive with their vassals and retainers, it became clear that if I had chosen to make my stance as my mother's legal heir and queen proprietress with words, they would make theirs with muscle.

Lopez had warned me during his visit that the *grandes* sought their own benefit. I was therefore not surprised that those who came sought to reap the rewards of my husband's and Don Manuel's largesse. Still, their presence obliged Philip to seat me at his side, where I bestowed each one with a gracious smile, particularly when the Marquis of Villena, who'd greeted us at the border during our first trip to Spain and now actively campaigned against my father in Castile, arrived with his ally, red-haired and ruddy-faced Benavente. I found it hard to believe that less than three years ago I had dined with these same gentlemen after crossing the Pyrenees. I also noted Benavente seemed discomfited when I asked pointedly for news of my son the infante Fernando, whom I had left in my mother's care. He mumbled the child was well and had been removed to Aragón by my father, following my mother's death.

Villena, elegantly serpentine as ever, just smiled.

Don Manuel hastily translated for Philip. At the mention of our son, whom he hadn't met, he sat upright from his insouciant slouch and barked in garbled Spanish, "Then the king of Aragón has done me a grave insult, for the infante is not his son!"

I kept quiet, as did Villena and Benavente. I was relieved my son was safe. Though it meant I might not see him for some time, for my father had no doubt ordered him moved to Aragón for his safety, at least Philip could not try to use him as a weapon. He knew the succession devised by my mother cited our sons as heirs after me; it wouldn't serve his interests to have a Spanish-born prince in my father's keeping and his outburst revealed as much.

The admiral did not make an appearance. When I asked of him, Villena replied he'd not been at court since he accompanied my mother's coffin to her tomb in Granada. Whether or not his grief had kept him away, the admiral's absence made clear his position. Nevertheless, those who were here, crowding our lodgings and depleting our supplies, precipitated Don Manuel and Philip's decision to order our departure.

Thus it came to pass that two weeks later I emerged from my chambers with Beatriz and Soraya at my side, into a sun-drenched courtyard where the lords of Spain and my husband's army waited. I took care to hide my consternation as I confronted the lords on their stallions, surrounded by their men. I felt a near-overwhelming fury at their impudence. That they had dared flout my parents' edict that no nobleman could assemble his retainers to arms without prior leave proved they now felt themselves above the law.

Beatriz whispered, "Look at them, the traitors. Have they no shame?"

I did look. In fact, I did not take my gaze from them. This display of their might was not only for my benefit but also for Philip's, had he been wise enough to recognize it. The *grandes* as much as declared aloud that they held no power higher than their own, anticipating that hour when they could reclaim their feudal rights and plunge us into lawlessness and chaos.

All of a sudden, I saw someone I had not expected. He sat slightly apart from Villena and Benavente, a massive broad-shouldered man astride a dappled Arabian that seemed almost too small to hold him. He wore a hooded cape, and before he could look away I glimpsed the scar sealing his right eye shut. It was my father's son-in-law the constable, husband to my bastard half sister, Joanna, the last man I thought to see. Why had he not presented himself formally? And what was he doing here, hiding among the ranks like a common criminal? Had my father sent him to watch over me? Did Philip or Don Manuel even know he was here?

A quick glance at my husband told me he did not. But the constable knew I had seen him, and he returned my stare without any visible reaction before that unsettling single eye dropped to the loose drapery of my cloak, as if he could divine my secret.

I turned away from him and went to the mare awaiting me. Soraya and Beatriz loaded our valises onto a cart. Mounting his destrier, Philip raised his hand.

The vast retinue surged onto the road.

I glanced over my shoulder. Philip's army stretched far behind like a serpent of steel, the nobles with their men augmenting the ranks. I had not seen such a massive assembly since my parents had taken to the crusade against the Moors. I fought back a stab of crippling fear as I turned resolutely back to the road. I could not let this show of power intimidate me.

Soon I would reach Castile, where I would reunite with my father and make my stand.

. . .

THOUGH IT WAS ONLY MIDSPRING, THE HEAT WAS INTENSE. EVERY day, the sun mounted into a cloudless sky and bleached the very land of its color. As we crossed the rugged *cordillera* that separated the Galician provinces from Castile, the fallow vales of the north surrendered to arid escarpments where stunted pines barely took root and hawks circled endlessly with their eerie cries. If it was this hot here, Castile would be an inferno, I thought with a grim smile. Such heat had not sat well with the Flemish the last time we were in Spain. Traveling under such arduous conditions could only rouse dissension.

I was right. Within days, fracas erupted between Don Manuel and our proud lords, none of whom appreciated the upstart ambassador who clung to Philip like a jealous lapdog and barred their passage to him as if he were already a king anointed. During his time abroad amid the excessive protocol of the Imperial and French courts, Don Manuel had clearly forgotten that in Spain our nobles were equally proud of their blood and accustomed to approaching their sovereign without undue ceremony. His assiduous protection of Philip's person, and Philip's willingness to let him act as a personal adviser and guard, did not endear the ambassador to the lords, several of whom were overheard threatening to put a dagger in Don Manuel's gut.

One evening as my women and I spread dried lavender on the carpeted floor of my tent to keep our environs free of louses, we heard shouting coming from Philip's encampment. I sent Beatriz to investigate. She returned with a broad smile.

"The Marquis of Villena is furious with Don Manuel. It seems that in exchange for his support, the marquis was promised restoration of a castle in the south, which their Majesties took from him during the Reconquest. But now Don Manuel claims there can be no disbursement of castles or lands until His Highness is invested as king by the Cortes and claims the royal treasury." She smiled. "*Princesa,* I thought Villena would draw his sword then and there, and cut Don Manuel in two. And Benavente is an ogre! He grabbed Don Manuel by the shirt and shook him until the ambassador screamed. The archduke your husband had to intervene and hand Villena a gold goblet from his own table and Benavente a platter."

"So," I remarked. "My husband is giving away his own plate now. *Bien.* Let them steal from each other. The more discord there is, the better it will go for us."

I settled in. I could afford to wait. The primitive conditions, which the Flemish had already begun to complain about, did not perturb me. Riding all day under the relentless sun in a fog of dust kicked up by thousands of hooves; pitching camp at dusk; sleeping in tents; eating dried foods and boiling water to drink were activities I'd grown immune to during my parents' years of crusade against the Moors. Concealing my pregnancy for another month or so would prove a challenge, yes, but I took comfort in the fact that Philip and Don Manuel faced far greater ones.

The Galician peasants, for one, almost proved their undoing. Don Manuel had contracted them to convey the train of carts laden with weapons, finery, and other gear. One night, the Galicians unhitched their oxen while we slept, and vanished. The Flemish guard took the Galicians' place but not before a pitched volley of recriminations was launched between them and the nobles' retainers, who, with customary arrogance, refused to help at all with the carts.

Then, as we entered the first of León's provinces, food supplies became unavailable, or available only at an exorbitant cost. I silently exulted as I watched Philip's fury mount. He'd begun to see the other side of this realm he so coveted, the insular suspicion of all foreigners and greed for their money. Fit to burst, he railed at the *grandes,* ordering them to deal with their obstinate people, thus alienating himself even further, for who else but a Habsburg would think of ordering Spanish blue bloods about as if they were lackeys?

In the town of Santabria, Philip called for a halt. We had reached the edge of Castile after weeks of travel and Philip declared he needed to rest. He commandeered the nearest *casa;* I was given an upstairs chamber with my women.

That evening as I stood in a brass tub in my shift while Beatriz rinsed the road's grime and dust off me, the door banged open and Philip strode in. I didn't bother to cover myself with my arms; it was too late. He took one look at my thickened figure and said triumphantly, "I knew it! You *are* with child, just as Don Manuel thought. You will dine with me this evening so I can announce the good news."

"Dine with you?" I stepped out of the tub, took a robe from Soraya. "I think not. I am very tired and in no mood for company."

"You'll do it anyway. I need everyone to see you're not being held against your will."

The moment the words were out, I saw he regretted them. He hadn't intended for me to know that now that we stood on the threshold of my kingdom, he was unsure of his reception. It explained why he (or rather Don Manuel) had elected to have us stop in this miserable town rather than proceed straight into Castile. Who knew what reception awaited them?

I regarded him with detachment, noting the pulsing vein at his temple, the coarseness of his sunburned skin that betrayed his increased penchant for liquor. Philip did not fare well under these conditions; for all his outward impressions he was a pampered man, bred for halls and hunting excursions, not taxing ordeals over mountains in the blazing heat.

"Oh," I finally said, with deliberate asperity. "In that case, of course I shall dine with you. We wouldn't want my father to think I'm misused."

Philip scowled. He stabbed a finger at Beatriz. "See to it she's there."

THE HOUSE WAS A SIMPLE timber-framed affair, the central hall used to stable beasts as well as people during the harsh winter months. It was hardly the setting for a court dinner, yet true to form Don Manuel sought to shore up my husband's princely status by ordering the musty tapestries unpacked and hung on the walls, the gold plate set on the scarred table, and the minions dressed in their finery. They made a marked contrast to the Spanish nobles, none of whom had found a particular need to refresh themselves after the hard day's ride and sat in their soiled doublets and dusty boots, markedly apart from the Flemish.

I entered clad in my azure velvet, my hair loose and my mother's ruby at my throat. The nobles rose in unison and bowed. I took the empty seat beside Philip. Had my deportment so far sown a seed of doubt? Were the nobles beginning to question their willingness to throw in their lot with Philip and his slavish adviser? I found myself searching their faces in turn, pausing on Villena, who arched a manicured brow and gave me his usual implacable smile. I had seen during our travels that while he could be as vain as any Flemish when it came to his appearance, he had the tireless constitution of a true Spanish lord, born to the saddle.

Burly Benavente sat at his side; I did not see the massive constable anywhere. Had I not trusted myself, I would have thought I'd imagined glimpsing him in the courtyard so many weeks ago.

Servitors set platters of fresh cheese, sautéed fowl, and roasted meats before the assembly. As we ate, Philip said without looking at me: "You might like to know that your father has finally dignified himself to send word. He wishes us to make haste to Toledo so we can be invested by the Cortes. He has your son with him."

My heart quickened. I kept my stare fixed ahead.

"What?" Philip added. "Have you nothing to say? I would have thought you'd be overjoyed to know your darling Papá and Spanish child have asked for you."

I felt like an animal that senses but cannot see the steel snare hidden under its feet.

"Don't you want to know our reply?" He brought his hand under the table, gripping my thigh. "I've sent word we'll indeed make haste and command him to meet us in Castile, where we will assume our throne and he will formerly relinquish any further rights to our kingdom."

I tasted blood where my teeth cut the inside of my lip. I should have known. He had found a way to use my own stance against me. How long had Don Manuel sat up at night, worrying the problem in his brain with the tenacity of a rat? They would see my father disposed of and appear to give me my title to appease the Cortes and any others who might balk at contesting my mother's will, but I would never rule.

I suspected Philip wanted me to explode, to take up my goblet and fling it at him in shrieking rage. It would serve him well if I displayed my deranged family blood. I would not oblige him. No matter what it cost, I would see this meal through to its cold completion.

His fingers dug into my flesh. With my smile like frost on my lips, I said in a low voice, "My father will never agree. He'll never let you steal what does not belong to you."

"We'll see about that." He released me, took up his goblet, and stood. "My lords," he called out, bringing immediate silence to the *sala*. "I propose a toast." He lifted his goblet. "A toast to my wife the queen, who carries my child."

The Flemish burst into fervent applause. The nobles sat still. I couldn't focus on their expressions, but I knew some must view this development with pleasure. A pregnant queen would be so much easier to contend with; if everything went in their favor, Philip would rout my father and I would oblige them by dying while giving birth, as so many women did. Then they'd have the Habsburg fool in their hands and all of Castile at their disposal.

"Come now," I heard Philip chide, "is this any way to greet such news? Rise, my lords, rise! A child is a blessed event. Let us drink to its health and to Her Highness my wife's, of course."

The sound of chairs scraping on the plank floor abraded my ears. The lords stood, the sputtering flames of the wall sconces capturing the sparkle of their raised goblets.

Philip waved his hand. "Thank you, my lords. Her Highness, as you must understand, is weary after our travels." He motioned to the guards stationed nearby. "Please, escort Her Highness to her rooms. We mustn't keep her from her proper rest."

I lifted my chin and came to my feet. As I walked between the guards, a prisoner once more, I could not avoid glancing at Villena.

To my disquiet, the look he returned was almost pitying.

AS SOON AS I REACHED my chambers, I allowed myself to vent my rage. "He sent word to my father that we wish to see him in Castile!" I spun to Beatriz. "I must get word to Papá. It's a trap!"

"His Majesty won't agree," she said. "Surely he of all people knows what your husband is capable of."

"Yes," I said quickly, "yes, he saw who Philip was when we were last in Spain. And I didn't see the constable at the table tonight. He's left, I'm sure of it. Maybe he went to report to my father." I paused. "But what will he say? The *grandes* will all testify that I am traveling with them. None seems to care that I cannot use the privy without Philip or Don Manuel's leave."

"His Majesty will still know," Beatriz persisted. She glanced at Soraya. "In La Coruña, you declared you would not endorse a single act until the Cortes invested you. This alone proves that your husband forces you to his bidding. His Majesty will smell the rat."

I nodded, moved in tense silence to my window. It was too far to jump, even if I weren't with child. The drop from the balcony would break my legs, if it didn't kill me outright. And now the guards were back, outside my door. My fists bunched. "I should have left. I should have taken horse and fled the moment I had the chance."

"When?" said Beatriz. "How? Your Highness, we are prisoners here as surely as we were in Flanders. There is not a soul who will help us."

"There must be a way." I looked to the table where Soraya had set out my brushes and hand mirror. "Do we still have those writing materials from England?"

Soraya went at once to one of the valises, retrieved the sheaf of parchment, ink, and quills we had hidden there under my linens. "What are you thinking?" said Beatriz.

I took a moment to gather my thoughts. "If you're right and Papá has heard something of my plight, he still might not know I am determined to fight my husband for the throne. I must warn him that under no circumstances can he consent to leaving Castile." I paused. "The question is, how do I get a letter out? We can't bribe someone. It's too dangerous."

Silence descended. Then Soraya said softly, "I'll do it."

I looked at her in surprise. She regarded me with resolute dark eyes, her narrow shoulders poised with a confidence I'd not seen her display before.

Beatriz let out a nervous chuckle. "You? You're a Moor, practically a slave. You can't possibly go off alone with Her Highness's letter, even if they were stupid enough to allow it."

"I'm not a slave, though," said Soraya. "I'm a *converso*. We are in Spain. There are hundreds like me, among the retainers and the guards and serving women. Who'll notice one more or less? I'll hide the letter on my person, steal a mule, and slip away when no one's looking." She looked at me; it was one of the longest speeches I'd ever heard her make, and her impeccable Spanish and astute assessments were almost hypnotic.

"I've been listening to the *grandes* as I come and go from the kitchens," she added. "They don't even see me. But, I see them. I listen. Many say they do not know what to do now. I overheard that fat count say His Majesty waits in Segovia, in the Alcázar with the treasury. Segovia isn't far, a week's ride at most. I can make it there."

"Remember Lopez," I told her quietly. "They tortured him, and he was a member of my mother's household. If they catch you, I dare not imagine what they will do."

"I survived the fall of Granada," she replied, as if that said it all.

Beatriz nodded. "Much as I hate to admit, it's not a bad plan." She directed her next words at Soraya. "You mustn't falter. You must leave first thing tomorrow, before everyone is awake. After you deliver the letter, don't rush back to tell us the good news. If you do, God only knows where we'll all end up. Do you understand? Stay away until you know it is safe."

She nodded. "Yes. I promise."

I reached out and embraced her. She had been my constant companion since childhood, and we both knew we might never see each other again.

—

BEFORE DAWN, SHE LEFT with my letter hidden under her skirts.

The hours passed like eternity. When night finally fell, Beatriz and I hugged each other close. "She did it," I breathed. "She is on her way. May God watch over her."

"May God watch over us all," said Beatriz.

...

TWENTY-SEVEN

Three suspense-laden days passed. On the fourth, clamoring voices and the discordant clanging of steel roused us. German mercenaries in their full mail, large as barbicans and holding pikes, came into my room to announce our immediate departure. Beatriz and I scarcely had an hour to throw my belongings into the coffers and pack our valises before we were being escorted into the courtyard, where the thunder of Philip's army gathered.

No one said anything. Surrounded by guards, we were led amid that cacophony of men into Castile and the Count of Benavente's native city. Upon our arrival, Philip lodged me in a suite of chambers in the *casa real*, with sentries posted day and night at my door.

Trapped in these luxurious apartments, I knew something terrible had occurred. Beatriz reported there was much murmuring among the nobles, but she could not discover anything concrete. I feared for my brave Soraya, of whom we hadn't heard anything at all.

On June 28, my worst fears were confirmed.

Philip arrived in my rooms accompanied by Don Manuel, the Marquis of Villena, and Count Benavente. In his mellifluous voice, which wrapped about the words of the document in his hand as if they were the lyrics of a chanson, Don Manuel recited aloud:

"It is hereby announced that Her Grace Queen Juana, our much-beloved consort, does not wish to take part in any governmental or administrative affairs or be informed of them. Should she wish to participate, it would lead to the upheaval of our kingdom, owing to her malady. To avert said evil, we advise our father-in-law King Fernando to renounce his regency and leave Castile at once, for should he or anyone in

his support interfere further in the assumption of our throne, we will condemn such as a treasonable offense, punishable by imprisonment or death.

"Signed on this twenty-seventh day of June 1506, by His Highness
Philip, archduke of Flanders and king of Castile."

Don Manuel rolled up the scroll and extended it to me. "A copy for
Your Grace's records. You will see the majority of the *grandes* have added
their signatures."

I clutched my shawl about my shoulders, my other hand at my belly. I
was alone. Beatriz had gone to fetch my afternoon meal. "Do you have
my or my father's signature?" I asked. "Because if you do not, bring it before the Cortes and it will mean nothing."

"Your father knows not to defy me," Philip snapped. "He has no one
to help him anymore save for his nobles in Aragón and they'll not risk
themselves for his sake. And my army is big enough to crush him and
his measly kingdom to a pulp, if I so choose. You best pray he leaves
Segovia for Aragón forthwith before I take him to task. In the meantime,
tomorrow we will hold a bullfight to celebrate. You are excused from
attendance—though I expect you to honor my elevation to the throne at
a special gathering of the Cortes next month in Valladolid."

He stalked out, Don Manuel scuttling behind. Villena and Benavente
stayed. The count averted his eyes as I met their gaze; for once in his life,
Villena had the wherewithal not to smile.

I raised my chin. To my surprise, my voice scarcely trembled. "I'd be
careful if I were you, my lords. As you have just seen, my husband holds
nothing sacrosanct. I wonder what he'll do when the time comes to reward you?"

"We'll take your words under advisement," Villena replied, and with
a low bow he left. Benavente looked at me; I saw fear in his gaze. He was a
man of simple appetites, who preferred an uncomplicated life and had always left his decisions to his ally, the marquis.

"Your Highness," he mumbled, "I . . . I do not wish to see you come
to harm."

Before I could reply, Beatriz rushed in with a covered platter in hand.
She took one look at Benavente and barked, "Traitor! Have you no
shame? She is your queen and with child! You will pay for all you do to
her, so help me God!"

"I did not want to do this!" he burst out. He turned beseeching eyes to me. "Your Highness, I swear to you, were it up to me I would never see you so defamed."

I whispered. "Tell Villena your concerns. The marquis has much to lose should my husband fail. And so, it seems, do you."

He bowed hastily and left. As the door closed on him, I reached blindly for the bedpost.

Beatriz set the platter down and came to my side. "What did those villains say to you? Come, you must get into bed this instant. You are pale as death."

"There's no time for that." I forced myself upright. "I've run out of options. Philip will call the Cortes to session next month. But my father is still in Segovia. I need you more than I ever have before. I must escape."

BY DUSK, WE WORKED out a plan. Beatriz sat on the bed, absorbing my instructions.

"They must believe you. They must think the shock of this news has put my health and that of my unborn babe at risk. Tell them unless I'm allowed some exercise, I will surely sicken. Tell them a ride in the park will do me good. Cry, beg; throw yourself at their feet. Do whatever you must to convince them. Ask them where can I possibly go, a woman with child? Appeal to Villena and Benavente; if there's any honor left in their miserable souls, they'll persuade Don Manuel. They don't want my death on their hands."

She nodded tremulously. "*Princesa*, I'll do what I can. But why won't you let me come with you? It would be safer if we went together."

"I already told you why. They could refuse us. You must use the occasion to pretend to clean my rooms. Our leaving together will rouse suspicion. We have this one chance. We cannot fail." I leaned to her, placed my hands on her shoulders, and stared into her dark eyes—eyes I could remember winking at me so long ago, on the day of my betrothal by proxy. She had been with me from the beginning. I feared our separation almost as much as she did.

I forced out a laugh. "Don't look so worried. I'll probably get there before you! Remember, as soon as you hear the alarm that I am gone, you too must make haste. And don't let them catch you whatever you do. I need you with me in Segovia."

. . .

I COULDN'T BELIEVE SUCH A SIMPLE PLAN HAD WORKED. YET HERE I was, astride a chestnut mare, riding out into the park with Benavente and Villena at my side.

I lifted my face to the sun's heat, reveling in the oppressive air around us. The park's tender spring lawns were charred, the gnarled oaks and olive trees interspersed amid flowering dog roses, the only plants to thrive in summer. Their brilliant reds and mauves mesmerized me. They looked painted on a brittle canvas, too bright to be real.

From behind us I discerned the distant cries of *"Olé!"* coming from the bullring, where matadors dueled with the fifty bulls Philip had ordered killed. As I hoped, the entire city flocked to the spectacle, and during the ride into the park the only souls we'd seen were the sullen sentries manning the gates. They barely glanced at us, too put out to be missing the festivities and free wine to pay us any mind.

Benavente cleared his throat. "Your Highness, may I have your leave?"

I gave him a nod. "By all means, my lord."

"We want you to know that we . . ." He glanced uneasily at Villena. "I mean, the marquis and I, we do not condone His Highness's actions necessarily. But he ordered we accompany him to witness his declaration and we're hardly in a position to refuse."

"Yes, my husband can be a persuasive man," I said. "No one knows that better than I."

"That he is," interjected Villena tersely. "He threatened to imprison us if we didn't comply. But there is still the Cortes to contend with. His Highness requires its support to make himself king here and anyone can see Your Highness is with child. Women in your state are naturally prone to melancholia. It does not mean you are unfit to rule, now, does it?"

"Indeed." I scanned the area ahead. Beatriz had told me that when she went to plead my case, Villena had mentioned that an old Roman wall enclosed this park and therefore a ride would be safe enough. Impatient to get to the bullring and flaunt his success, Don Manuel agreed. As we passed through the city gates, I had noticed with trepidation that the wall did indeed look stout, but now I began to see that here, near the confluence of the Elsa River, it had been neglected, and in one or two places, almost dilapidated. Could I jump it? Or would I end up shattering my mare's legs and my own neck in the process?

Benavente was running on at the mouth, eager to purge himself now that he had found me willing to listen. "Of course if the Cortes deems it lawful that the archduke rule as sole sovereign, we must oblige. But we don't bear Your Highness any ill will. We never did."

"Naturally," I said. Did they think me a fool? They'd see me locked away if they thought they could get away with it. But my words to them the day before had clearly taken root: he and Villena had begun to wonder whether it was wise to entrust their future to Philip and Don Manuel.

I tightened my grip on my reins as we rounded a bend in the road. I dared not look about me, lest I betray my purpose. "My lords," I said, hoping my voice didn't sound as high pitched to them as it did to me, "might we quicken our pace a little?"

"Why, yes. Yes, of course." Benavente beamed, only too happy to oblige and thus earn himself the ability to say he had done all he could to assist me in my time of need.

"Thank you, my lord." I filled my lungs with air, wound the reins about my fingers, and invoked my strength. Then I rammed my boot heels as hard as I could into the mare's sides. Startled from her insouciant trot, she leapt forward.

I did not look back. I did not even breathe as I kicked again, harder this time, and leaned close to her arched neck, my belly pressing against the saddle horn. "Run, *bonita*," I breathed into her flattened ear. "Run as fast you can. Run for your queen."

Villena's shout reached me as if from across a vast divide: "Your Highness! Your Highness, stop this instant!"

I knew one must go after me while the other raced back to the city to raise the alarm. I prayed Benavente would be the one to follow, as he was the eldest and least fit. He also rode a mare like my own, while Villena's was an Arabian gelding, bred for speed. I didn't know how fast my mare could run. Fortunately, I weighed less than during my previous pregnancies, and as if she sensed my anxiety the valiant creature increased her stride, seeming to fly toward a section of bulwark looming ahead.

A gasp tore from my throat. It was impossibly high.

I am going to die, I thought. I am going to break against that wall. But at least I die free.

Closing my eyes, I buried my face into the mare's mane. I felt myself lift upward, up and up, soaring. I tensed, braced for the bone-shattering crunch, the lethal projection onto rocky ground.

The mare landed, graceful as a dancer. My teeth cut into my lip. I looked up, saw that we had cleared the wall and now galloped over the open salt lands. Tears streamed down my face.

I had done it! I had escaped!

I braved a glance over my shoulder. My exultation died. Villena was fast behind me, having jumped the wall as well. He gesticulated furiously, his cap blown from his head, his hair billowing about his enraged features.

I jammed my heels into my mare again. The poor creature was running as fast as she could, panting now with exertion. With a stallion like Villena's, I could have flown to Segovia, but I'd been given an older horse, bred for ladies and docile rides around the park.

I had to get off the salt flats. With any luck, I could lose Villena. I spied a dense pine forest on a ridge. Pulling the mare to the left, I raced toward it.

Villena began to drop behind me, not yet out of sight, but growing more distant. I had released my grip on the reins. Feeling the bit slacken in her mouth, the mare picked up speed. The forest neared, individual pines becoming visible. There was enough foliage and undergrowth to hide in. I would stay in the forest until nightfall and start out again under the cover of darkness.

The mare plunged up the ridge, loose rocks and gravel scattering under her hooves. When we reached the top, at the edge of the forest, to my horror she came to a halt, her flanks lathered, heaving. Saliva drooled from her mouth. I'd ridden her into exhaustion.

I anxiously searched the barren flat below me. I had deviated from my original course toward the river, but my swerve must have dissuaded Villena, for he was gone. Either he'd ceased his pursuit in favor of going back for reinforcements or he sought a way to intercept me as I emerged from the forest. By now, word would be out; it would only be a matter of time before they guessed my destination. Fortunately, I had decided on a circuitous route.

I slid to the ground and led the mare into the thicket of trees, pushing down a surge of doubt. This was my land: I had been born and raised here. I would find the way.

I only knew the sun had started to fall when after having picked my way through a labyrinth of deer paths for what seemed like hours, I stumbled upon a clearing.

Below the scarlet streaked sky was an old hut, fenced by an enclosure with a few skinny goats. A stooped woman in a ragged dress hung bunches of herbs on her threshold to dry; at the sight of me, she froze. Her ageless face was carved by life, her skin brown and creased, like the leather cover of a book. My entire body throbbed. As the woman set aside her herbs and moved toward me, I had to grope at the mare's reins to keep myself from sinking to the ground. God help me, I could go no further.

"*Doña? Doña, está bien?*" The woman was thin to the point of emaciation, her eyes a watery black. She dropped her gaze to my stomach. "*Está embarazada,*" she said. "You are pregnant. Come. I'll give you a cup of goat's milk, *sí?*"

"You don't understand," I whispered. "I must reach the road that leads to the river."

Her puzzled gaze lightened. "The road. Yes, I know where it is. But it's too far. It'll be dark soon. I'll show you tomorrow. Come now. You are tired. You must rest."

She was a poor gypsy who lived in the forest, isolated from the world, deemed as heathen as the Moor. Yet she offered all she had to a passing stranger large with child, a fellow woman and outcast: shelter and a cup of milk.

With a grateful nod, I allowed her to lead me into the hut.

. . .

THE NEXT MORNING I AWOKE TO BIRDSONG, AN ACHING BACK AND buttocks, and the unfamiliar sense of peace. I reveled in it as I lay in my rumpled clothing on a pile of straw in the crude hut. I had not felt free in so long I had forgotten what it was like. Rising from the mat, running a hand through my tangled hair, I saw the woman was gone. On the table were strewn her dried herb cuttings, which she'd painstakingly shown and named for me. Mandrake, chamomile, belladonna, and rosemary, and a strange dried red berry she called *el sueño del moro,* the Moor's Sleep—the lethal and benign gathered together by an herbalist's expert hand.

"A few pinches of the Sleep in a cup of wine will vanquish all your enemies," she had said, and her dark hooded eyes glittered in the tallow light, as though she knew why I fled.

Beside the herbs, I saw she had left another cup of milk, still cool from the clay jars she set in the hut's earth floor. There was also country bread slathered with honey and some stringy ham. I devoured the fare. My mare had spent the night in the enclosure with the goats. I found her there alone. The woman must have taken her goats to graze while I slept. I must soon be on my way, but I took a moment to enjoy the sunbeams coming through the treetops, festooning the clearing in patterned gold. It seemed to me at that moment so uncomplicated an existence that I felt a pang of envy for this anonymous life.

Then the world tore apart. One moment, the birds were chattering and my face was raised to the sky; the next I heard a wail of terror cut short with lethal suddenness, and men on horses came pounding into the clearing—a troop of my husband's mercenaries, herding the frantic cluster of goats. One of the men tossed a lump at my feet as I backed away. I looked down at the bloodied mess of the gypsy woman's head and let out a horrified scream.

"There you are! God in heaven, must you ruin everything?"

Philip came cantering toward me. I spun about to race back into the hut, hearing the men dismount, laughing, and the whicker of my mare, unnerved by the smell of fresh blood. I was panting, cursing aloud, searching for a knife, an ax, anything to defend myself with, caught up in a maelstrom of terror and disbelief when I felt his gauntlet on my arm.

I yanked away. "Murderer! Monster! Don't touch me!"

He chuckled, seeming enormous in that closed space, defiling the peace that had once dwelled here. "Enough. You've had your fun, now come with me. I've no time for games."

"Games? You've killed an innocent woman!"

"She means nothing. Now come with me before I drag you out by your hair."

"You are a coward," I said. "A miserable coward who hides behind a dwarf's skirts."

"Don't call me a coward, you—you madwoman!"

He took a menacing step toward me. I paused, my fear evaporating, leaving me cold. "Would you prefer I address you as Your Majesty, like that pack of traitors you've surrounded yourself with? They hate you, you know. The moment you turn your back, they'll betray you. They'll hang you and Don Manuel from the nearest gibbet."

"SILENCE! You are the one who betrays me, time and time again. Do you think I don't know your ploys, your pathetic attempts to set your father on me?" He thrust his face at me. "I let your handmaiden go because I knew she'd never make it to Segovia, as she did not. She barely made it halfway before my men found her and let her know in no uncertain terms she had caused far more trouble than she's worth."

I gasped. Not Soraya. Not my loyal Soraya.

"I'm told she put up quite a fight," he added, with a chuckle, "but in the end she learned a lesson she'll not soon forget."

I whispered, "What—what did they do to her?"

"What she deserved. But they were merciful. She still lives. You, however, will never see her again. Nor will you ever see the son you left here to usurp my place."

"He is our son!" I screamed. "How can you speak of him as if he means nothing to you?"

His face twisted. "Because he was never mine! You made sure of that when you left him here with your mother. All he is to me now is a threat." He paused. A terrible smile fractured his face. "And now, after everything you've done to me, you think I'd let you ride off to join them? You think they'll protect you? Idiot. Your father has forsaken you. Even if your Moor had reached him, it would have done you no good. He fled from my army without so much as a fight."

"Liar." My hand stretched out behind me, to the table. "Whatever my father has done, you forced him to it. He did it to protect me!"

Philip guffawed. "You always did like to pretend the world is better than it is. But I know the truth. And I'll tell you one more thing: your father isn't in Segovia. He sent a messenger even as you hatched your plan. He's on his way to Aragón and from there will go to Naples. So this silly escapade was for nothing, unless you planned to ride all the way to Italy on that nag of yours."

My fingers closed over the herbs; as I drew my hand toward my cloak pocket, he laughed.

"Tomorrow you *will* go with me to Valladolid and show the Cortes how you honor your husband. You can go like a lady or you can resist. Only I warn you, if you choose the latter"—he grasped my wrist, yanking me close, and his savage kiss cut my mouth—"I'll bring you into the city in chains."

He let me go. I did not lift a hand to my bruised mouth. I met his eyes and said in a voice that issued from the very core of my being, "I will see you dead."

I swept past him outside and the guards awaiting me.

...

TWENTY-EIGHT

Veiled and dressed in black, I made my state entry into Valladolid, the same city that had witnessed my betrothal by proxy. The people had gathered to cheer me then; now their silence was palpable as I rode past, a woman in mourning among a thousand men, a mother without her children, a queen without her crown.

For six days I was shut in a chamber in Valladolid's *casa real,* my windows boarded up even as the city officials hung banners in preparation for the Cortes. I was forbidden the services of women, my meals brought by sentries. Every morning Philip came to me, accompanied by Don Manuel and none other than Archbishop Cisneros, who'd grown so thin he resembled a petrified tree. This powerful Castilian prelate who had known me since my childhood, who had no doubt sworn to uphold my mother's will, watched impassively as Philip harangued and threatened, demanding I sign a warrant of voluntary abdication.

"Nunca," I said. "Never!" I tore the document to shreds before his eyes, indifferent to his dire threats.

On the seventh day, my door opened. I looked up through burning sleepless eyes to find Admiral Fadriqué on the threshold. Cisneros hovered close behind, a lurid specter; I wondered how the admiral had gotten in, even as my heart leapt painfully at the sight of him.

"I told you, Her Highness is ill," I heard the archbishop say. "Your Excellency, it would be best if you let us assist you in your requests. She cannot—"

The admiral held up his long hand. Though in his late forties, he was still very lean, almost rigid in his signature unadorned black velvet, which he had worn for as long as I could remember. His features had retained the handsome angularity of his youth but wisps of silver now threaded his black mane and his thin mouth was framed by deep lines, sorrow etched in the skin around his eyes. His tender gaze gave me a burst of almost painful hope.

"It is against the law to forbid a senior member of the Cortes access to our sovereign," he said, without glancing at Cisneros. "Please, leave us. I will speak with Her Highness in private."

He closed the door on Cisneros's astounded face.

"Don Fadriqué." I came to my feet, my belly protruding. I held out my hand. "I thank God you are here. I—" My voice caught. "I feared they would never let me go this time."

He bowed low. "*Su Majestad,* I beg your forgiveness. I retired to my estates in Valencia following Her Majesty your mother's death. I was one of those who conveyed her body to Granada for entombment in the cathedral. I did not hear until recently of your predicament."

"I am glad you came," I said softly. He brought me back to my chair, his hand on my sleeve. When I sat, he said quietly, "Do you know what they say? They claim you are unfit to rule and that you wish to bestow your crown on your husband." He paused. "Is this true?"

Anger sparked in me. "My lord, you've known me all my life; you saw me as a child in my parents' court and welcomed me home when I first returned from Flanders. What do you think?"

He did not look away from me. "I believe they would impose a cruel fate on you, *princesa.*"

Tears pricked the corners of my eyes. "Yes," I said haltingly. "They would lock me away like my grandmother before me. But I swear to you, *I am not mad.*"

He went still. I held my breath. Did he detect a flicker of the wild, inchoate fear that fed on isolation? Did he understand how such a seed, with enough despair and enforced darkness, can turn into lunacy? I was fighting against its seductive embrace with every breath in my body, with every nerve and sinew; and still I knew the desperate portrait I must present, far too thin for a woman with child, unwashed and alone, as anguished as my grandmother must ever have been.

Then he said, "I believe you. And I promise you that while I am here, they'll not harm you anymore. You must trust in me. I am your servant."

I nodded, my tears brimming now, spilling down my cheeks.

"Will you tell me everything that has happened?" he said.

I whispered, "Yes."

HE STAYED WITH ME until midnight, ordering a meal brought up to us and removing the nailed shutters from the window with his own hands. After we dined, we talked again, until I had related everything that had befallen me. When he finally quit the chamber, he left me curled on my bed, knees pulled to my chest, fast asleep after weeks of torment.

I awoke ten hours later to find I'd been released. There were still guards and sentries about, but I had new clothing brought and women to attend me, though none could hold a candle to my beloved Beatriz, who had fled when I did and whom I had not seen since.

The admiral proved in those days why he had been one of my mother's most stalwart supporters. Of impeccable noble lineage, a respected peer and defender of the Crown's rights, he had risked himself by coming into the viper's lair, where the other *grandes* no doubt viewed his presence with mistrust and fear. But neither Philip nor Don Manuel dared say a word against him and he scarcely left my side, sleeping in the room next to mine with his retainers taking turns standing vigil at night in the corridors, so no one could approach without him knowing.

Every morning we met. He told me of Philip's growing penury and his frantic need to win the permission of the Cortes to take over the treasury, which was currently held in Segovia by my mother's lifetime friend the Marquise de Moya.

"He needs that coin," the admiral said. "Without it, his mercenaries and most of the nobility will abandon him. Don Manuel has exhausted their reserves in bribes and extravagances, but the old marquise, God bless her soul, has vowed to burn down the treasury itself if your husband dares set foot within ten kilometers of her city."

I smiled. "No wonder my mother loved her well. And I believe my lady Beatriz de Talavera is with her. We'd agreed to meet in Segovia when I tried to escape Benavente. The marquise will have heard from Beatriz everything my husband and Don Manuel have done."

"Indeed. The marquise will die defending that treasury, Your Highness. That is how we shall force Don Manuel and your husband into a corner. Without the treasury, they cannot proceed."

"But what about Cisneros? I do not trust him."

"Cisneros knows what we plan." He lowered his voice. "He came to me last night, after Your Highness retired. He showed me letters he's been exchanging with your father in Naples."

I started. "My—my father?"

"Yes. Cisneros is his informant. Everything that transpires here, our archbishop records in coded dispatches. He'll not impede us. He wants your husband to fail. He's ambitious and far too canny for an old churchman but to surrender Castile into Habsburg hands would be unthinkable."

The mention of my father roused sharp doubt in my heart. I looked away.

"Many a night I have pondered his reasons for leaving me when I most had need of him," I said, my voice catching. "I have tried to accept that he is no longer the invincible king of my childhood, that my mother's passing has left him vulnerable to my husband and the nobles."

"It is true," said the admiral, and I thought I heard a guarded note in his voice. "Your father has borne the hatred of Castile's nobility all his life; had he stayed and fought he would have risked not only his safety but also that of your son the infante and Aragón's as well. Without your mother to defend him anymore, he is but a minor king."

"And yet I cannot help but feel he has deserted me." I brought a hand to my throat. My voice hardened. "I've no doubt Cisneros is capable of playing a double hand, but why does he not speak out against my husband if he serves my father? He is still Castile's premier prelate."

"According to him, because His Majesty your father asked that he not disclose their plans under any circumstances, save for a direct threat on your life."

I stared at him. "What plans?"

"All he said is that His Majesty wants your husband to make an open bid for the throne."

"An open bid!" My voice rose despite myself. I paused, took a deep breath. "Why?"

"I do not know. But have no fear. Cisneros or not, Lucifer be damned, we *will* stop your husband. I swear that to you on my honor."

On the day the Cortes was to convene, he came to me before dawn. "They don't suspect a thing. They anticipate protest from me but not from you. I leave my body servant Cardoza outside to escort you." He bowed over my hand. "I must go now to take my seat in the Cortes."

"My lord," I said softly. He paused, raised his sad, beautiful eyes to mine. "I thank you with all my heart. Were it not for you, I do not know where I might be."

His sudden smile illumined weathered crinkles at the corners of his eyes, the gleam of his strong white teeth and proud line of his jaw. "You are my queen. To serve you is all I require."

I felt the touch of his lips on my hand, the rough caress of his beard on my skin. "I will await you," he murmured, so quietly I almost didn't hear him. Then he turned and left, as though he could not bear to deny the communion between us.

I rose and went to the window.

Far below, the Duero crawled past the city walls, its arid banks cracked by the sun's wrath. Only ten years ago I had stood in this same palace, a virgin bride awaiting the arrival of the admiral, who'd escorted me to my betrothal. Now I waited again, this time to declare open war on the man I had wed.

I was a queen. I could not look back. I would fight until I had nothing left to fight with.

A knock came at the door. I smoothed the folds of my stiff new gown, adjusting the extra panel at my waist. As I went to the door, my heel clacked on the floorboard under which I'd hidden the herbs taken from the gypsy's house, those herbs I had grabbed in desperation and wildly considered using on myself should Philip succeed in imprisoning me for good.

The admiral's body servant Cardoza, a burly Castilian with arms the size of beef haunches, stood on my threshold. "Is Your Highness ready?"

I smiled. "I have waited all my life for this moment."

He took me through a narrow passage connecting the *casa real* to the Alcázar and up a spiral staircase into an empty room. He clicked open a star-shaped aperture on a wood and mother-of-pearl screen partition and motioned me to it. When I peered through this peephole, I saw that the screen looked out onto the Cortes' hall, where procurators gathered on their tiers.

The speaker of the Cortes banged his staff of office three times. Silence descended. I discerned Don Manuel as he stood before the dais to read aloud Philip's declaration. The procurators murmured. Then, as my hands knotted my skirts, Philip stood, clad in violet silk, his voice reverberating against the walls:

"Noble lords, it is a dolorous burden I bring before you, one I would gladly forsake my entire fortune to remedy. But the sad fact is that my wife, Doña Juana, infanta and heir to this realm, has fallen prey to that malady that claimed her maternal grandmother. She worsens with each day, and cannot, even by all the love we bear her, possibly recover. She mustn't be made to suffer the burden of governance in her state. Rather, we must send her to dwell in a safe place, where malcontents cannot disturb her. I humbly ask that we resolve this terrible matter and then embark on the task of enthroning me as king, so I can assume the treasury of Castile and begin to guide us past the dangerous uncertainty my wife's dementia has created."

I whirled about; Cardoza detained me with a gentle hand. His eyes glimmered. "Your Highness, please. Your time will come."

In the *sala*, the admiral stood like a pillar of marble and velvet. "By the saints, never have I heard the like! Where is Her Highness to defend herself against these claims? Are we, the members of these Cortes, not to be graced by her presence this day?"

He swerved to the procurators, all of whom sat staring at the figure before them as though he were an avenging archangel. "I have met with Her Highness," he continued. "I have spoken with her at length and seen with my own eyes this alleged malady she suffers. And I tell you she is as fit as any one of us. I'll not consent to the farce proposed here today."

"We sympathize with your misgivings, my lord," drawled Philip, though I could detect the fury underscoring his feigned indifference. "But the fact remains that these very Cortes invested me as prince consort two years ago. I ask only that you recognize my claim as king apparent, given the circumstances. You needn't do anything that goes against your conscience."

The admiral retorted, "All of it goes against my conscience, by your leave. Our late queen Isabel left this realm to her daughter. No one save Doña Juana can bestow it on another person. I say no to your request, no to the disinheritance of our sovereign queen Juana of Castile!"

I wanted to applaud. The Cortes erupted, members' voices clashing, fists banging on tables, caps swept from brows and thrown to the floor, while the admiral beheld the result of our insurrection.

Cardoza murmured, "It is time." I straightened my shoulders, hearing the speaker cry out for silence as Cardoza led me to a small door that opened onto a narrow flight of steps. As I quickly descended these steps to the hall, the speaker said, "We, the members of the Cortes, have heard His Highness the archduke's and my lord admiral's requests. We will honor our past oaths to His Highness as prince consort, but"—he lifted his voice over another surge of shouting—"we must also abide by the statues that uphold Her Highness the infanta as our rightful queen. We therefore ask that she be brought before us to answer these claims, and—"

He did not have time to finish. "She is here, my lords," bellowed the admiral.

I walked into the hall, alone.

The silence that descended was so absolute that the cries of playing children could be clearly heard through the overhead windows. I did not falter as I confronted the mass of gaping faces, lifting my chin to meet Philip's horrified stare.

"My lords," I declared, and I threw all my force into my voice, so that it would carry to the very rafters, "do you recognize me as legitimate daughter and heir of Isabel, our late queen?"

The speaker stammered, "We—we do, Your Highness. Most certainly."

I raised my head a fraction higher, seeing Philip start to rise from his throne, his hands clenching the gilded armrests as if he might crush them to splinters. "Then since you recognize me," I said to the speaker, "I will answer any questions you have."

He turned to confer with the procurators beside him. There was an angry shaking of heads, fervid mutters, before the speaker returned his solemn gaze to me. "We have only one question at this time, Your Highness."

"*Adelante,* my lord."

"Does Your Highness wish to rule Castile as sovereign queen?"

I paused. The procurators, Don Manuel, and Philip were like effigies in their chairs. I spoke the words I had prayed for, in hope that one day this moment would come. "I do."

There was an audible ripple of astonishment throughout the hall. Philip hurtled from his seat. "By God, I'll not sit here and have my rights stolen away by a madwoman!"

Cisneros arched his brow; the speaker said, "Your Highness, please sit down and honor the processes of this assembly, which were established long before your birth."

Philip's shoulders hunched about his neck, his features malignant as he inched back onto his chair as if the cushions contained live coals. The speaker inclined his head, "Thank you, Your Highness." He returned to me. "Does Your Highness have any other requests of us?"

I nodded. "Yes, my lord. Since you recognize me as your lawful queen, I command you henceforth take yourselves to Toledo, where I shall be crowned according to ancient custom. I also command that the treasury in Segovia remain in the Marquise de Moya's safekeeping."

The speaker nodded. "We are overjoyed by Your Highness's apparent good health. May we have your leave to withdraw and discuss these requests with the gravity they deserve?"

"My lord," I replied, "you and these noble lords most certainly do."

Then I turned and quit the hall.

· · ·

A TENSION-LADEN DAY PASSED. PHILIP DID NOT COME TO RAGE at me, nor did Don Manuel. But in a way, I found their disregard more disturbing than their previous berating; even the admiral confessed that though the procurators met daily, there was a mysterious reticence on everyone's part to confront the beast in the room: mainly that to enforce my claim, they must in turn disavow Philip's.

On the third day after my appearance before the Cortes and another sleepless night in which I paced my rooms and felt my child quicken in my womb, the admiral arrived. I took one look at his drawn face and felt myself turn to ice.

"Plague has broken out," he said.

There was a terrible hush. Plague hadn't been an affliction I worried about in Flanders, though it struck there as surely as anywhere else. We had seemed far removed from its threat, so much so I couldn't recall it ever being an issue. In Spain, however, it was a specter I'd lived with since childhood. I remembered how my mother insisted we leave every summer for the mountains of Granada before plague season started and that dreadful summer in Toledo, when Besançon perished. Plague flared up with often catastrophic effects in Castile, especially in the crowded cities, an unstoppable scourge that decimated entire provinces in a matter of days.

I genuflected. "God save us. Is it very bad? Is this why the Cortes delays judgment?"

"Partly, yes." He let out a terse chuckle. "So far, there haven't been any cases reported in Valladolid itself, though your husband has seen the way the matter with the Cortes could go and has used the plague as an excuse to leave. It seems he harbors a terror of infection."

"Yes, ever since his adviser Archbishop Besançon died."

"Or so he'd have us believe," remarked the admiral, with uncharacteristic asperity. "In any event, the *grandes* swarm to him like wolves, hoping to squeeze favor out of his fear. The procurators prepare to flee to the country. They claim they'll reunite in Toledo once the plague dissipates." He grimaced. "There are far more cowards among them than even I suspected. I argued this morning that we must do our duty; that Castile cannot wait for them to render a judgment. But they're beyond reason. Not even old Cisneros with his harangues could detain them. I have to say this much in your husband's favor, he has the devil's own luck."

"I'm to blame for that," I said bitterly. "I told him the nobles would hang him from a gibbet when he least expected it. It's just like him to heed me now, after having ignored my advice for years." I paused, searched his face. "Where will we go?"

"Burgos," he said. He paced to my window, where he looked out toward the city, brooding.

"Burgos! But it's nowhere near Toledo! We are going backward. Burgos lies in the north."

He turned back to me. "Don Manuel wanted to order the move to

Segovia, to siege the city if need be and take the Alcázar there by force. But word has come that Segovia has become a pesthole and your husband refuses to go farther into Castile until he's assured there is no risk."

Segovia. I went cold. "If Philip is willing to backtrack north, it must be a real threat." I met the admiral's somber stare. "My lady Beatriz de Talavera hasn't sent me word. Dear God, what if she's taken ill?"

"If she's in Segovia," he replied, "the Alcázar is the safest place to be. The marquise is a tough old woman: she'll bar the gates and let nothing in or out." He paused. "I have other news. The constable has agreed to receive you in Burgos. He prepares his own house for you."

"The constable? But I saw him last in La Coruña. I thought he was with my father."

"He did not go with him to Naples. He and Cisneros have been in contact; he's been spying on your husband all this time." The admiral stepped to me. "Your Highness, the constable has retainers in Burgos. It is his city and he is in your father's camp. He may not be the most moral man I know, but he'll not condone any harm done to you under his roof."

I looked into his eyes. "What about you?" I whispered.

"I must go to Naples." He lifted his voice against my immediate protest. "I must tell your father in person of everything that has transpired. Without a definitive verdict from the Cortes, your husband could still prevail. He has Don Manuel, Villena, and the other nobles at his side. Not even the constable and I can gather enough retainers to counter those who support him. We need your father's help. If he will agree to come with his men from Aragón, then we could have a force to be reckoned with."

My father. I had sought to put him out of my mind. As long as he had my son safe, I told myself, it was all I could expect of him. And still the thought of him roused raw hope.

"I could stay here," I said. "You said there's been no plague in the city. Maybe it won't come at all. Better here than hundreds of kilometers away in Burgos."

"Your Highness, I beg you. You are with child. You cannot risk contagion. If you should die, God forbid, then your husband will indeed win everything. He will invoke your son Charles's right to the succession and Castile will fall into Habsburg hands forever. You must go to Burgos.

Your appearance before the Cortes has won you time. Your husband heeds Don Manuel's advice and Don Manuel knows they don't dare move against you now. I would not send you with them if I did not think you'd be safe."

"Safe?" I gave him a small smile. "I think I don't know the meaning of the word anymore." I felt Philip's hand as he grasped my wrist in the gypsy woman's hut; saw again the decapitated head rolling at my feet. My gaze fled for a moment to the loose floorboard before I pulled myself to attention. I had forestalled Philip's investment as king by the Cortes; with a bit of luck and some tenacity, I could stave him off indefinitely until my father arrived.

I was not powerless anymore.

"Surprise is the one asset we have," the admiral went on. "While your husband flees the plague, I'll reach Naples. His Majesty loves you and Castile. He will not let the Flemish destroy everything he and your mother built. He only left because he had no other choice. But I promise you we'll return with an army large enough to rout your husband once and for all."

He stepped closer still. I smelled the faint masculine tang of his body under his black brocade, sensed his taut strength. I looked up into his eyes. All of a sudden, desire surged in me, overwhelming in its intensity. He must have felt it, as well. He must have known that in that moment I longed for him to take me as a man takes a woman, to feel, if only one last time, the release of being in the arms of someone I could trust.

He started to lean to me, murmuring, "Your Highness, I . . ." He drew back, raised his hand tentatively. He touched my cheek. "I dare not," he whispered.

I understood. Taking that calloused, long hand in mine I lifted it to my lips.

"May God be with you," I said. "This time it is I who shall wait for you."

. . .

IN THE MUTED HEAT OF THE EVENING, WE DEPARTED VALLADO-lid. It would take almost a week to reach Burgos, and by the third grueling afternoon the Flemish were suffering the agonies of purgatory. Unaccustomed to late July in Castile, clad in their suffocating velvets and brocade, they dropped fainting from their stallions or rushed into the bushes to relieve dysenteric bowels. Philip commanded that anyone who was ill must be left behind; I realized then that whatever his ultimate intent, he was truly terrified of the plague.

Palpable foreboding added to the tension and gloom. In the lingering dusk, strange lights scattered across the violet horizon where night never fully fell, causing the Spaniards to cross themselves and mutter of bad omens. They drew apart from the Flemish, emphasizing their growing antipathy to my husband's minion.

I rode among a regiment of guards and the only servant I had—an elderly laundress named Doña Josefa who'd been part of my retinue in Valladolid. Vigorous of body and spirit, she was stone-deaf and regarded as inconsequential; she rode a donkey beside me, mending my worn gowns by night, tending the fire, and serving my meals.

It was as though I were another of the hundreds of retainers and soldiers, no one paying me any more mind than those left wallowing in their own excrement. Though I had no doubt Philip would strike at me again, for now we were at an impasse, pursued by a more implacable foe.

We reached Burgos under a damp twilight. The high walls loomed out of a thick mist that blanketed this part of northern Castile often in the evening, after days of intense heat. I could barely see my hands in front of my face as the sentries at the gate checked everyone in our train for any signs of fever or telltale buboes. Several more of the dysenteric Flemish were kept from entering the city and they lifted wailing protest as Philip turned from them to enter the fog-swathed castle on the hill. As if by tacit agreement that it would go better for all concerned if my husband and I did not share the same roof, I was taken to the Casa de Cordón, a small palace adorned with the corded knots of the constable's clan—an irony that did not escape my notice.

Here my half sister, Joanna, the constable's wife, awaited me.

My every bone ached from the hard ground on which I'd slept for the past days and the long hours of being jostled about in the saddle. I was looking forward to a hot meal, a bath, and a real bed. Instead, I had to contend with Joanna in her best sateen, bejeweled and coiffed to the hilt as if she were expecting a parade.

"My dear," she exclaimed. "Your belly is tremendous!"

I grimaced. It was true. I felt enormous in my fourth month, having lost flesh everywhere but my abdomen. She, on the other hand, remained slim as a ferret. I'd never liked her, and not because she was my father's bastard. Even in childhood she demonstrated a decided affinity for seeking her own advantage. She apprenticed in the service of a noblewoman and wed the constable, a strategic alliance that removed her from my immediate life. I felt only disdain and a faint amazement that we shared the same blood. She had made no effort whatsoever to even feign care for me, much less seek out my service when I needed help, and I tartly informed her she need only show Doña Josefa where to fetch my food and see that my linens were changed every few days and my chamber cleansed.

"But Your Highness will need attendants," she said. "You've only this old matron and—"

I cut her short. "Were it not for this old matron, I might have starved to death. As for attendants, I've learned to do without. Now, if you would kindly show me to my rooms?"

With a rigid curtsy, she took me upstairs. I took some comfort in the fact that my status must be on the rise, given her concern over my lack of servants. Or perhaps she was preoccupied with how it might look to the outside world now that I dwelled under her care, never mind that I'd spent most of my time since my return to Spain in some form of captivity.

I found the rooms a blessed refuge, with a fire in the hearth, braziers throughout, and a fresh nightdress and robe laid out on the bed for me. Dropping my soiled cloak to the floor, I started to move to a chair when I heard something rustle by the large poster bed in the corner.

I whirled about. "Who—who is there?"

A figure stepped from the shadows. *"Princesa,"* said a familiar voice, "don't you recognize me? Not even the devil himself could have stopped me from coming to you."

With a cry of joyous relief, I ran into Beatriz's embrace.

TWENTY-NINE

. . .

From my chamber I gazed toward the castle's bulwark perched above the city, its battlements punctuated by the great cathedral spire. Torches flared on its gates; as I looked at their oily light, I reflected on the three weeks that had passed since our arrival in Burgos, during which Philip had made no attempt to see me or receive any of the Burgos officials with me at his side.

But I was glad of the respite. I was overjoyed to have Beatriz with me again, having learned that none other than the admiral had gotten word to her of Philip's intent to retreat to Burgos. My devoted lady escaped plague-ridden Segovia and traversed Castile to join me; she had confronted Joanna until my half sister allowed her into the *casa*. Her courageous presence helped ease my fear that this move north might result in another attempt to lock me up. Like the admiral, she believed I would come to no further harm until my child was born.

"There are two kinds of women inviolate in Spain: an expectant mother and a recent widow," she reminded me. "Not even that snake Villena would allow anyone to touch you in your state. Besides, you declared before the entire Cortes that you wish to rule as queen. No doubt they're all gnashing their teeth, but they know they can't declare you mad again. For now they'll have to wait like everyone else—which is just as well, for time is exactly what we need."

She was right. Time would work in my favor and against Philip's. Indeed, his worries increased daily. Not only was the plague spreading with a horrifying facility, but bandits prowled every road and doomsayers incensed crowds with their calamitous predictions. Many preached against the Flemish, blaming them for the disasters that befell Castile. Many began to shout *"Flamencos fuera!* Flemish out!" whenever they caught sight of my husband with his retinue.

Within the castle, Don Manuel fared no better. Beatriz proved adept as ever at sniffing out the gossip and learned the diminutive ambassador had been threatened so repeatedly he refused to go anywhere without an armed escort. The constable told him bluntly that Burgos lacked the resources to withstand a prolonged royal stay and couldn't possibly be expected to shoulder the expense of feeding and lodging His Highness's entire foreign retinue. With their bid for the treasury thwarted, Don Manuel made frantic advances to his former master and my father-in-law the emperor for a loan but thus far His Imperial Majesty had demurred. Don Manuel was fast running out of the money he needed for bribes to keep the nobles content and fierce arguments soon broke out between him and several of the *grandes,* one of whom suggested he advise His Highness to melt the gold plate weighting his dinner table before someone did it for him.

"Never have I seen a court so on edge," added Beatriz, with a mischievous smile. "One might say His Highness and Don Manuel are the most unpopular men in Spain."

I welcomed the news. It might take the admiral and my father weeks to reach Spain. While Philip and his henchmen battled the nobles they'd have less time to focus on me. It did seem that for the next five months or so, providing I didn't go into premature labor, I would be safe.

I turned back to the chamber. Doña Josefa sat on a stool close to the hearth, adding panels to one of my new brocade gowns, while Beatriz embroidered its hem. Outraged by the threadbare remnants in my wardrobe, Beatriz didn't cease complaining until she cajoled a Burgos merchant to donate a costly (albeit limited) supply of cloth, out of which she and Doña Josefa conjured three new dresses and a cloak for me.

"There's another banquet tonight in the castle," I remarked. "The torches are lit on the gates."

Beatriz scowled. "Don Manuel may plead poverty to anyone who cares to listen, but he'll never willingly forgo his own pleasure. How he can dare call himself a Spaniard is beyond me. The plague rages throughout the realm, killing off our people and leaving our grain to molder in the fields, and he slaughters geese and oxen by the dozens so he can hold his feasts."

I chuckled. "It's all he has to offer. Either he feeds the nobles or they'll eat him."

"Let us pray the admiral brings His Majesty back soon before the *flamencos* eat Castile."

I put a finger to my lips. "Beatriz, hush. Someone's coming." We were alone. My half sister, Joanna, had made a vague excuse to absent herself this evening and I didn't bother to query her further. I could scarcely bear her falsely obsequious manner and cat-eye stare. I might have dismissed her entirely from service had I not deemed it wiser to keep her and her husband the constable on my side.

I heard the sound of footsteps outside my door. It flung open and Joanna rushed in. Her coiffed hair was disheveled; her jewels and lavish gown proof that she had indeed been feasting with the court tonight. Without warning she gasped: "Your Highness must come at once. They are bringing the archduke here from the castle! He—he has fallen gravely ill."

I STEPPED INTO EERILY quiet apartments. Philip lay in his banqueting costume on the red brocade bed, his silver tissue doublet open to his naval, exposing his fine linen chemise, drenched in sweat. This sight of him gave me pause. I despised him more than I had despised anyone in my life but he'd always been a dynamic man, always in motion. The only times I'd seen him still was when he slept, either after a night of lovemaking or drunken excess.

I saw Villena and Benavente standing in the antechamber. Joanna joined them, her face white as she clung to her grim one-eyed husband. They must have brought Philip here, but I could see in their stance they would flee as soon as I turned my back. Though the plague hadn't spread north yet, the mere whisper of it swept all semblance of loyalty aside.

A physician in a black robe bent over the bed. When he heard my approach, he turned to me. The resignation in his eyes made my heart pause. "What is wrong with him?" I asked in a thread of a voice, and I realized that despite my lack of volume I sounded perfectly calm.

He sighed. "I was told His Highness complained of some stomach pain in the afternoon and retired to his rooms to rest. He later sent word that he would attend the banquet tonight, where he collapsed. At first I thought he had drunk too much wine or that his roast had gone bad, but now that I've examined him I'm inclined to think whatever it is he's been fighting it for some time."

I looked at Philip. He was moaning in his delirium. "He's been healthy all of his life," I heard myself say. "I've never known him to have so much as a cold."

The physician motioned, "Your Highness, if you would?" I jerked forward. I smelled human waste as he parted Philip's chemise. The linen was plastered to his skin; as the physician peeled back the cloth, I covered my mouth. Philip's neck was swollen, the skin tinged with a blistery, virulent rash that seemed to spread to his chest even as I watched. Even the palms of his hands bore the blisters. He had also soiled himself, and his breeches had been removed.

"Is it . . . ?" I couldn't speak the word aloud.

He shook his head. "If it is the plague, I've never seen it manifest like this before. This swelling and discoloration are more consistent with some type of water fever."

Water fever. Besançon had contracted a water fever.

"Your Highness, I believe we should send for an expert. Such ailments are beyond my limited wisdom. I know of one in Salamanca, versed in such maladies: Dr. de Santillana."

"Yes," I whispered. "Do it. And before you go, tell them I'll need warm water and cloths."

...

I DID NOT LEAVE HIS SIDE.

Some no doubt said I was a fool for love, a woman so far gone I surrendered even the last shreds of my pride, for never was my madness more apparent than in that hour when I agreed to tend my mortal enemy, when any sane person would have walked away and let him die.

But they had never known love. They had never felt its wildfire and brimstone. Philip was my enemy, but I had loved him once. I would not let him suffer alone like a beast. I would not have it said one day to our children that I denied their father in his hour of need.

I was a queen. I knew the meaning of honor.

I removed his soiled clothing and bathed his feverish body with my own hands. It was no longer the body I remembered, taut with youth and vigor. That gorgeous sculpture of white muscle had turned flaccid, corrupted by vice and wine and his own relentless demons; but at the touch of my fingers his skin seemed to remember me and respond.

I then called for Doña Josefa and Beatriz. Together, we dressed him in a fresh linen bed gown and eased him under the covers. No one else made an appearance. Only Don Manuel expressed concern, albeit via a courier who stayed only long enough to hand me his missive. Word had gotten out of Philip's collapse and fear of the plague ran through Burgos, with many fleeing with whatever they could carry. I found it telling that even my half sister, Joanna, forsook her preoccupation with my state, promptly leaving for her country home outside the city, where the constable no doubt joined her. In less than twenty-four hours, Philip went from aspiring king to abandoned victim.

Within the *casa*, the silence was broken only by his whimpers as he fought the fever. The physician's name was Dr. Parra, a simple medic with no experience treating royalty. His pale face showed his overriding anxiety that his exalted patient might die in his care.

Beatriz kept me fed and Doña Josefa tended to the washing of linens and the fire. I often found myself alone in that room, seated on a stool by the bed, swabbing Philip's brow with rose water. It was as though a wall of glass enclosed me. I was not afraid, not even for the unborn child in my womb. I knew with a curious certainty that whatever afflicted my husband would not harm me.

On the fourth day, Dr. de Santillana arrived.

A corpulent man with fleshy jowls, he hummed over Philip. After poking and prodding his swollen glands, scrutinizing his white-coated tongue and the rings of his bloodshot irises, Santillana made an uncomfortable moue and turned away to discourse with Dr. Parra. I went across the chamber to where the doctors stood.

"Well? What is it?"

Santillana glanced past me to the bed. Philip reclined on mounded pillows, his eyes closed, his face so white it blended with the linen.

"Your Highness," said Santillana, "might we step outside?"

I wondered at the need for privacy, seeing as Philip had not regained consciousness. Still, I led the doctors into the indoor patio. Sunlight flashed off the colored paving stones and center fountain, where water trickled from the mossy spout. I blinked, adjusting my vision, which had grown accustomed to the gloom of the sick chamber.

It was a lovely day, I thought faintly.

I sat on a nearby stone bench, folding my hands in my lap, utterly serene. I must have looked it, as well, for Santillana and Parra exchanged a puzzled glance before the portly expert blew out his breath in a worried puff. "Your Highness, I don't quite know how to begin."

"Just say it. Whatever it is, I want to know."

"Well, it is not a water fever as we first thought."

"Then, what? The plague?" Water fever or plague, it didn't matter. I just needed to know if he would survive. Everything depended on it.

"No, not the plague." Santillana let out a troubled sigh. "Your Highness, I believe your husband has the pox."

"The pox?" I stared, completely taken aback. "Are you saying he has the French malady?"

"Unfortunately, I am. It is rarely seen in Spain. I myself have never treated a case of it. However, His Highness's symptoms match those described by colleagues who have."

"But you've not treated it yourself, so you can't be certain." I collected myself in the ensuing silence. For a moment, the world had spun out of control. I recalled that Philip had consorted with that French harlot, whom I assaulted in Flanders. She'd had a sore on her mouth. Had she infected him? And if so, had he given it to me? I thought he mustn't have, for surely I would have fallen ill by now or at the very least failed to conceive.

Santillana sighed. "If it is the pox, he will recover. The disease produces terrible symptoms at first and then it disappears. I'd say this is the first stage. The infection can hide for years afterward." He raised somber eyes. "Your Highness must know that I've not heard of any man, or woman, who escaped the disease's ravages. Though they may appear to completely recover and regain their strength, in the end they all go insane, though of course His Highness may have many years ahead of him, with the proper care."

A rushing sound filled my ears. Philip had the French pox. He would recover, in time. He would regain his strength. He would continue to wreak havoc for years before he went completely mad; and if I didn't appreciate the irony in this it was because I envisioned something even more horrific—a future in which I'd be disposed of and a mad king ruled Castile, rousing the *grandes* to bring chaos and ruin to the kingdom my parents had built; a future in which there would be nothing left to bequeath our sons but ashes and death.

I flashed back on a haunted room in Arévalo, heard again my mother's voice as she faced an angry, uncomprehending fifteen-year-old girl: *I couldn't risk it. My duty was to protect Castile, above all else. Castile had to come first.*

Of all the wrongs Philip had inflicted on me, none moved my hand as this one.

"Years?" I repeated, and I was surprised I sounded as calm as I had a moment ago.

"Indeed. If my diagnosis is correct, he should soon show improvement. His Highness has been sick for, how many days now?" Santillana turned to Parra; as the doctor opened his mouth to reply, a bloodcurdling call came from the bedchamber.

"*Where is everyone?*"

I turned, moved in a nightmarish haze back into the room. I came to a halt. The doctors nearly collided into me from behind. Philip sat upright, looking like a resurrected cadaver.

He fixed burning eyes on me. "I'm hungry. Get me something to eat. Now."

I HAD SOME OXTAIL BROTH brought and spooned it into his mouth as he scowled. He muttered he would never eat anything at a banquet again. At one point, his eyes caught mine and I saw his suspicious disbelief that I'd been with him throughout his ordeal. The doctors pronounced him on the mend. Santillana hastily took his leave, refusing any payment, relieved he'd diagnosed a prolonged death and not one he need attend.

I was left with Parra and an empty house that would soon fill up again once word got out that Philip was recovering. I had very little time.

I wiped the residue of broth from his lips and took the empty bowl to the tray. "There, now," I said. "If you like, I'll bring more soup later. But for now, you should rest a while, yes?"

He eyed me. "Why would you care?"

I paused, the tray in my hands. "I am your wife. Is there anything else you need?" I heard myself say as if from far away, "A warm claret, perhaps, to help you sleep?"

The moment hung between us. I was shocked by my steady grip on the tray, the impassive way I met his stare, as though I were behaving in the most normal manner imaginable. If nothing else, my very ability to project the demeanor of an efficient wife at her husband's sickbed proved how monstrously he had warped my heart.

"No? Very well. I'll be in the next room. Please do try and get some sleep."

I started for the door, my steps leaden, my heart capsizing in my chest. Then, just as I set the tray on the sideboard and reached for the latch to open it, I heard him grumble, "If that doctor you brought in doesn't forbid it, I suppose a bit of wine couldn't hurt."

I did not glance over my shoulder as I left the room.

. . .

THE RATTLE WAS AUDIBLE NOW, HIS BREATHING SO SHALLOW IT scarcely lifted his chest. For the past two days, he had shouted out inchoate words before slipping into a silence so profound it was like finality itself. The fever raged again. This time, nothing could vanquish it.

"Your Highness must rest," Parra said. I could see he too was exhausted, baffled by the abrupt turn in Philip's condition, by this new assault that churned my husband's bowels to bloody water and raised evil pustules on his flesh, as though he festered from within.

"No." I gave him a weary smile. "But I would welcome a glass of water."

He bowed his head and left me.

Philip's mouth was ajar, that awful gurgle deep in his throat reminding me of the sound stone-filled udders made when children played ball on the plaza cobblestones. I took his hand in mine. When my fingers grazed his skin, I felt the heat emanating from his pores, though the skin itself was cold, unexpectedly hard to the touch. Though he had taught me the meaning of loneliness and betrayal, I wanted him to feel he was not alone.

I would show him a compassion he had never shown me.

His forehead creased at my touch. I set the goblet I'd prepared in his hand, in which the last of the herbs melted in the warm wine. A shadow darkened his face.

"Drink," I whispered.

I forced the lethal mixture through his broken mouth. Some of it seeped down his chin. I wiped it with my sleeve. "It's almost over," I said, and I took his hand once more. "Almost over."

A few seconds later, he gasped. I felt his fingers tighten in mine, then go limp.

Everything came to a creaking halt. We were frozen in time, painted figures on a facade. The quiet pressed in around me. With the illusory weightlessness of a dream, I experienced the scarce warmth fleeing his flesh. I stared at his face. Had it not been for his stony pallor, he might have been asleep. He looked young again. Death had restored to him the lost beauty of our halcyon days: a tangle of gilded hair on his brow and his long, fair eyelashes—the envy of many women at court—resting like poised butterflies. Looking at him, I lost all sense of the past. I lost awareness of my self, of the child in me, of my heavy aching body.

And of what I had done to save my kingdom.

All I had was this moment beside my husband's corpse and, in my mind, the words of a prophecy uttered only five months ago: *You may come as a proud prince today, young Habsburg. But you shall travel many more roads in Castile in death than you ever will in life.*

THIRTY

...

My husband, the man I'd wed for politics; whom I loved for four years and hated for five; bedded countless times and wept countless tears over; borne five children and conceived a sixth; battled, plotted, and fought against: my husband was dead.

Did I mourn him? The answer is simple, and private. I had done what was required to save my realm, and his death did not turn me into a deranged, bereft widow. Our love was a ravaged memory; his corpse only confirmed it. Now I faced a choice that could free me or condemn me forever, a means of escape that could seem to prove I was indeed as mad as he had claimed.

But I had my reason, incomprehensible as it may have seemed.

...

SO I WAITED. IT DIDN'T TAKE LONG. A MERE HOUR AFTER PHILIP died, the Flemish, Cisneros and his band of clerics, and the nobles descended on the Casa de Cordón like locusts. Beatriz, Doña Josefa, and I had barely finished bathing and dressing the corpse when the lords came stampeding into the room to assume charge of the situation.

I swayed on my feet with exhaustion and didn't try to fight them. I allowed myself to be taken back to my rooms, while the Flemish wailed and Cisneros let the embalmers in, after which the body was wrapped in linen for conveyance to the monastery of Miraflores outside Burgos, where the monks would hold vigil for Philip's immortal soul. Proclamations were posted throughout Castile announcing the untimely death of Philip of Habsburg, posthumously titled "prince consort of our heiress apparent Queen Juana"—which, I suppose, glossed over the political incertitude.

As for me, I was a twenty-seven-year-old widow and six months pregnant. Outwardly, I showed no signs of distress. I donned black out of respect but otherwise was content to take my meals with my women and remain in my rooms, pondering my next move, as I knew the *grandes* did.

Overnight, the world had changed. With Philip dead, I was most definitely their queen, but I did not delude myself that I held any more power than I had when Philip was alive. Indeed, it was barely a month after his death that my half sister, Joanna, returned to the *casa* swathed head to toe in black. She immediately set herself to infiltrating my household, despite Beatriz's overt scowl. To my disgust, other noble wives followed—a veritable legion determined to barricade me behind a wall of feminine solicitude. I knew this was Cisneros's doing, part of his plot to keep me estranged. He did not want me running loose while he cajoled the nobility to the negotiating table. I tolerated the invasion for the moment because faithful Lopez, whom Philip had tortured in Flanders, had also come in haste to join my household, and Soraya showed up one day without warning, haggard and thin and bearing the marks of the whips and violations Philip's men had subjected her to, yet resolute as ever to be at my side.

As I embraced her, I wept my first tears since Philip's death.

With Soraya back in my service and Beatriz at my side night and day, I bided my time, until one afternoon when Archbishop Cisneros and the Marquis of Villena barged into my rooms.

"It is imperative we act before the situation worsens," Cisneros declaimed. He'd surged into startling life, with even a hint of sparse color to punctuate his hollow cheeks. "Castile has lacked guidance for too long. If Your Highness would read this list"—he set a paper on the crowded table before me—"you will see every appointment is in order and the lords cited therein most eager to serve as your councillors."

I faced them impassively. I'd been expecting something of this nature from him. Indeed, with Philip dead, I'd assumed it would only be a matter of time before some new alliance was forged with the *grandes*. The admiral believed Cisneros was my father's supporter and had worked secretly to undermine Philip, but I suspected I'd been right about him all along. He was no better than any noble in his lust for power. I'd made an enemy of him during my last trip, when I confronted him at La Mota. He would not be a friend to me now, not until my father showed up and put him in his proper place.

"This talk of a council is premature, my lords. I will address this, and other matters pertaining to my estate, at a more appropriate time." I couldn't resist a small smile. "Are we not, after all, still in mourning for my late husband?"

"The thirty days are past," Villena said with his suave air. "This matter concerns the very future of Castile. Surely Your Highness doesn't wish to deprive her people of proper governance at a time like this?"

"This realm has lacked for proper governance since my mother died," I said dryly. "I hardly think a few more weeks will make any difference."

His mouth worked. I could see he was doing his best to control his temper, to try and divine my reasons for delaying. When he next spoke, it was with a deceptive softness that chilled me to the bone. "My lord archbishop, the lords, and I believe Burgos is no longer an appropriate place for Your Highness. After having suffered such tragedy here, we humbly suggest you honor our offer of assistance and move your household to—"

I held up my hand, hiding with that peremptory gesture the stab of alarm that went through me. "You forget with whom you speak, my lord. I am your queen. I alone will decide when and where I shall move my household."

I watched his face turn scarlet and let the seconds pass, one by one, until I felt the air curdle like sour milk. "I must be invested and crowned," I said. "The decision of the Cortes to recognize me in Valladolid was delayed by the plague, but with my husband the archduke gone there can be no further debate as to my rightful claim. My mother willed this realm to me, and I will rule it. In the meantime, I have some requests of my own."

Cisneros's face darkened. "What requests, if you please?" he asked through his teeth.

"All appointments made by my late husband must be annulled. They were undertaken illegally, without my consent. The traitor Don Manuel and his *flamencos* are to be found and arrested. I understand they have fled into hiding, with a significant amount of gold plate and jewels stolen from my husband's apartments in the castle. I command you, my lord archbishop, as head of the church, to issue my decree and you, my lord marquis, to enforce it. Anyone who dares give shelter to or hide Don Manuel faces immediate arrest and execution."

It was my first command as queen, and Villena's reaction was predictable, his voice throbbing with barely controlled rage. "Though loved Don Manuel is not, I am no mercenary to hunt him down. Your Highness has perhaps spent too many years watching the Flemish scrape to the French."

I elected not to remind him that only a few weeks ago, he'd apparently scraped to Philip with quite the same lack of compunction. But his hypocrisy was expected. In fact, none of these so-called lords sought to support me. They might hold differing opinions as to who should ultimately rule in Castile, were probably at this very moment scheming against each other behind their backs, but on one thing they were unanimous: I must not be crowned. Either my son Fernando or, if worse came to worst, my son Charles. But not me, never me. They had lived too long under my mother's whip to abide another woman on the throne. With Philip's death, I had simply exchanged one set of enemies for another. Only this time, I had a weapon. Beatriz's advice had served me well: *There are two kinds of women inviolate in Spain: an expectant mother and a recent widow.* I was now both. I'd hoped to forestall my plan until the admiral returned with my father but I could not wait anymore. I had no idea when they might arrive. I had to act.

I lifted my chin. "Moreover, I want word dispatched to my sister-in-law the archduchess Margaret to send my daughters to me as soon as passage is safe. My son Charles, naturally, is now archduke of Flanders and will be obliged to remain there. But I gave birth to my son Fernando here in Spain and I've not yet set eyes on him. He too must be brought to me from Aragón. And you may issue my summons to the Cortes to assemble in Toledo, where I shall also see my husband's body interred in the cathedral."

They greeted my announcement with an astounded hush. I had pondered it for days, ruminating over its outcome, wondering if it would free or ensnare me. For the moment I saw I had caught them off guard. Villena's fists clenched. Cisneros considered me for a long moment before he said, "Does Your Highness wish to personally escort the archduke's catafalque?"

"It is not my wish," I replied, "but rather my duty. Or would you rather we left his remains here? It's hardly a suitable resting place for a prince of his stature."

Cisneros's gaze narrowed. No doubt, he *had* intended on leaving Philip's body here. He had let the embalmers cut it apart to send his heart and brain to Brussels in a silver casket, according to Habsburg custom. What did he care where the rest of it ended up? Under any other circumstance I too would have left him undisturbed in Miraflores, save for the fact that a queen escorting her husband's bier afforded me a shield like no other to get out of Burgos.

"It is a rather unorthodox request," said Cisneros. "Unprecedented, even."

"It's out of the question!" added Villena. "Your Highness cannot pretend to convey a corpse all the way to Toledo in the dead of winter."

"My mother's body was taken all the way to Granada in winter without undue hardship," I replied, even as I realized that Villena had guessed my purpose. He knew that not only did I seek to protect myself with Philip's coffin but the people would see me as I passed through Castile. By putting my tragedy on display, I would reap the sympathy of my subjects.

"Indeed," added Cisneros suddenly, and I caught a furtive gleam in his eyes. "And when, pray, does Your Highness wish to undertake this journey?"

"As soon as possible," I said, thinking quickly. "Have a cart collect the coffin and assemble the funeral cortege. You and the other lords must of course remain here to oversee my dictates. I don't require you for this endeavor." I paused, aiming my next words at Villena. "My lord, you and the admiral hold equal power in the Cortes, yes? Since you deem the hunting down of Spain's foes beneath you, would you do me the honor of establishing Don Fadriqué's whereabouts? We cannot convene in Toledo without him. "

"He will," interjected Cisneros, before Villena could reply. "You may trust in us, Your Highness." With a bow, he herded the marquis out like an unruly schoolchild.

As soon as they left through the front door, Beatriz came in through the back. She had listened to everything through a peephole drilled in the wainscoting. She now stood in the doorway, regarding me with troubled eyes. *"Princesa,"* she said, "what do you intend?"

"What else?" I met her stare. "Cisneros thinks I don't have ears or eyes. He thinks I don't know he only lets me undertake this journey so he can use it to spread more of his lies. Already, the legend Philip created for me grows. He would spread it far and wide, maybe all the way to Naples. With any luck, it will finally summon my father and the admiral to my side."

"Legend?" said Beatriz. "What legend?"

I smiled. "Why, that I'm mad, of course. Mad with grief. Juana the Mad."

. . .

FROM THE FROZEN FIELDS OUTSIDE BURGOS, I EMBARKED ON MY voyage to Toledo, Philip's coffin draped with its cloth of estate loaded onto a sturdy cart.

I took special delight in ordering Joanna to stay in Burgos. Besides my small retinue of pages, Lopez, and my musicians, I had an escort of sentries and Beatriz, Soraya, and Doña Josefa. At long last, I would travel through Spain with my friends, free of restraint.

My heart was so full, my hope so enormous I did not care at first that dreary fog and rain wreathed the land. We traveled along the confluence of the Duero, its yellow waters swollen by the rains. I rode a black-caparisoned mare, my women and other servitors behind me, dressed in mourning. A herald held aloft my sodden royal standard.

We were hardly an impressive congregation but word of my approach went before me, bringing emaciated peasants to the roadside to watch me pass. Some kneeled when they caught sight of me in my black mantle and veil; others genuflected and called out for alms. The misery in their faces reflected the destitution of my native land. The plague had left countless villages deserted and the harvest moldering in the fields. Makeshift crosses littered the vast plains, marking the graves of the dead. Groups of ravens cawed and scavenged, but there were no dogs to be seen and the few cattle I glimpsed looked dead on their feet.

It was as if all of Castile had become a graveyard.

I seethed. This was what Philip and his henchmen had accomplished! This was their legacy: poverty and fear and destruction. Once I reached Toledo, I vowed, I would do everything in my power to restore Spain to its former pride. Love had served me nothing; only this land had remained constant, the place of my birth, which had borne witness to my vale of tears. Like my mother before me, I would wage battle against those who plundered and defiled it. I would put an end to the strife, the feuds, the bribery, and the ruthless quest for personal enrichment.

I would prove myself a worthy successor to Isabel of Castile.

This beacon of hope sustained me. I endured the pitched tents in fields, the bedding on stony ground, the dry foods and boiled river water. I braced myself with these minor travails for the larger ones that waited ahead, for the war I'd already mapped out in my mind; but I was not prepared, had not even paused to consider, that my own body might betray me.

The pangs came upon me suddenly, as we rode across a desolate field just outside the hamlet of Torquemada. I gripped my saddle horn, wincing. It was too soon. I still had a month or so left. The child would have to wait. I was expected in Segovia, my first official stop. There, I would be in the care of my mother's friend the Marquise de Moya and would find refuge to give birth before continuing to Toledo. By then, I hoped to have word of my father and the admiral.

I felt my water break and gush from under my skirts. Beatriz heard my stifled gasp and cantered to me. Gripped by pain, I had no choice but to let her help me dismount.

Lopez raced ahead to commandeer a suitable lodging. Supported by Soraya and Beatriz, I was brought to the stranger's house destined to be my final birthing chamber.

. . .

SHE TOOK ALMOST TWO DAYS TO ARRIVE—TWO DAYS OF SUCH bloody, bone-sapping struggle that I feared she would be my death.

Never had a child of mine so tested my endurance; never had one seemed so impossible to disgorge. It was as though after making her decision to emerge early, she had changed her mind and tried to clamber back into my womb. I screamed like a demented woman, railed, and wept. And yet when she finally came in the twilight hour of the third day, she stunned me with her beauty. Covered in mucus and blood, she still glowed like alabaster lit from within.

Doña Josefa cut the cord binding us, cleansed and swaddled her; from my sweat-soaked bed I asked that she be brought to me. Soraya laid her in my aching arms while Beatriz sat and let tears slip down her weary face. My stalwart Beatriz was far more emotional than she ever let on, and I too felt my eyes moisten as I gazed upon the crying babe who, at the lightest touch of my fingertips to her lips, suddenly went silent.

She gazed up at me. I could see already that her hair was light auburn, with threads of gold, and as she tried to suck my finger, I sighed.

"Catalina," I said, freeing my heavy breast. "I shall call her Catalina."

...

THE BIRTH LEFT ME LIMP AS A WET RAG. WHILE CATALINA LUSTILY suckled at my breast, Doña Josefa and Soraya trudged through that paltry hamlet, gathering whatever fresh foods they could find, tearing live chickens from the coops of astonished peasants too overawed by the fact that their queen had just given birth in their vicinity to protest. Soraya brewed draughts and ladled out soups; Doña Josefa cooked up poultry in a thousand different ways and insisted I eat every morsel. I had lost more blood than was considered safe, yet I wouldn't hear of anyone sending to Burgos for a physician. I would live, I told them from my bed. I had given birth before.

I tarried too long. I should have gotten back on my horse, even if I had ended up dying of it. For there, in Torquemada, they found me. They'd had second thoughts; I underestimated their tenacity. Cisneros and Villena and their retainers—they crowded into town and demanded I act as a newly delivered woman should and remove myself to "a castle readied to receive me."

The moment I heard those terrifying words, I hauled myself out of bed and issued orders for departure. Only my loyal few obeyed; as I angrily waved Cisneros's protests aside and mounted my horse, I saw Villena watching from the shadows by the house, staring at me with his unsettling eyes. Did he suspect the limits to which they pushed me? Did he understand that no mortal being could endure this unremitting persecution?

I think he did.

The storm struck that night as we traversed the wide plateau. The rain fell in blinding sheets, churning the ground to mud. Finally, unable to go any farther, I ordered a halt and dismounted. I stood uncertain, my cloak slapping in the wind. Confusion and doubt waged a fierce battle inside me; my head pounded with unspoken fears. Where should I go? Where was there a refuge for me? I would never reach Segovia in this state, much less Toledo. I needed somewhere I could burrow in and hide: like a hunted animal I craved darkness and peace without high walls, without fortresses and waiting lords who sought to imprison me.

Shivering, I whirled about. I searched the night. Then I felt *him*. Watching me, reveling in my desperation. He had not left me. He was here. Waiting. Anticipating the hour of his revenge.

He was not dead.

I let out a strangled gasp, turned, and ran past the astonished pages, stumbling over the muddied hem of my skirts as I reached the cart holding the coffin. I paused, panting. I heard his laughter in my head. He taunted me. He knew what I had done. He knew I had got the best of him, that I was a murderess. Now he would drag me down into hell with him. I must not let him. I must not let him get me. I must destroy him again. Destroy him before he destroyed me.

Grabbing hold of the coffin's rungs, I began pulling it from the cart. *"Ayúdame,"* I cried at the pages and sentries who stood as if paralyzed, gaping. "Help me!"

My ladies rushed to me, Beatriz at their head. *"Princesa,"* please. Do not—"

I threw out my hand, sent one of them sprawling. Now the fury erupted, pouring from my mouth like poison. How dare they disobey me? How dare they! I was their queen! They must do what I commanded. They must never, ever, question me!

"I said help me," I roared. "Now, do you hear me? NOW!"

The sentries leapt forward to the cart's levers, sending the coffin careening onto the field. Mud sprayed as it hit the ground, splashing my skirts. I stood staring at it, afraid, half-expecting the lid to fling open and the cadaver to rear up with a leering smile.

I heard him whisper—*Mi infanta*—and I said in a shivering voice, "Open it."

The sentries backed away. Lopez and the pages crept to the coffin, hoisting open the heavy lid. They gagged, dropped it, and reeled back, arms pressed to their mouths.

For a moment, I could not move. From where I stood, I glimpsed cerements, submerged in lime. He did not sit up. He did not turn his dead-blue eyes to me, open his mouth, and accuse me of burying him alive.

I took a step forward. He lay on a dark satin lining, shrouded head to toe. Even the hands crossed over his chest were wrapped in crusty cloth. As I sought to recognize something that would confirm this . . . this thing was Philip, the odor reached me, suffocating in its intensity. I resisted the urge to cough, feeling the wind snatch my coif from my head as I inhaled the stench. Whatever the embalmers had used had failed.

He rotted before my very eyes.

"The cerements on his face," I whispered. "Take them off."

I felt all of them staring at me in horror. I looked at Lopez. He took a step back. Soraya came forth, past me. She leaned over the body and began to unravel the cerements.

The seconds passed like years. My breath lodged in my throat. Traces of flesh became visible—an ear, a nose, part of a twisted, blackened mouth. I lifted a hand. She paused.

"No . . . no more," I whispered, and she withdrew.

It was Philip. Or what they'd left of him. The surgeons who'd removed his brain and heart had butchered him. The eyes had fallen into his misshapen skull. He had no teeth. All that remained of the virile beauty I had once reveled in was his nose, still prepossessing in a face withered as an ancient's. He looked as if he'd been dead a thousand years.

There was nothing to fear. Nothing left to hate.

My rage evaporated. "Close it," I said. I returned to my horse. Doña Josefa regarded me, my baby girl cradled in her arms. Beatriz stood apart, her shawl clutched to her muddied face.

"We must go on," I said.

—

THREE DAYS LATER on that long empty road, where only the barren plain stretched about us like a painting done in ocher and black, I looked up from under my veil and saw someone riding fast toward us on a lathered black stallion.

It was the admiral.

. . .

THIRTY-ONE

"My father is here?" I looked at him in disbelief, the letter untouched in my lap.

He nodded, his weathered face subdued. He'd accompanied me to Hornillos, another small town where we commandeered a house. As overwhelmed by relief as I was to see him, his exhaustion was so plain I would have insisted he take to his bed had his news not been so important.

"We landed in Valencia a month ago," he explained. "I came as soon as I could to tell Your Highness but you had left Burgos. I had to ride back and forth until I found you."

I nodded, the letter like a stone on my thighs. I could not lift a hand to break open the seal, as if my fingers had stuck together.

I saw the admiral's gaze shift to the coffin sitting on the floor nearby like another table, its cloth of estate tattered, soiled. As a frown creased his brow, I wondered what he would think when he heard of that wild scene outside Torquemada, when I lost all control of myself and even struck Beatriz in my haste to get to my husband's corpse. He had been to Burgos, had been apprised of my decision to bring Philip's body with me to Toledo. What other lurid tales had been poured into his ears?

"I used his body," I said quietly. "He was my shield. I . . . I thought they'd not touch me if I conveyed his remains to Toledo."

Even as I spoke, I realized how bizarre my words sounded, how lacking in reason they must seem to a man like him, a *grande* who had never experienced the plight of a woman in fear for her life, the rigors of childbirth, the vulnerability of widowhood. How could he understand? How could anyone understand?

Without warning, tears filled my eyes. I bowed my head. God help me, I would not weep before this proud lord, who'd ridden all the way to Italy to bring my father to me.

He remained still, watching me. Then he did something he would otherwise never have done in all his years of service to royalty: he reached down and embraced me. I melted against him, felt his hand caress my hair.

He murmured, "Your Highness need not fear anymore. His Majesty will protect you. This struggle of yours is too much for any soul. You must trust in His Majesty now."

Hearing the faint beat of his heart under his stiff black doublet, his breastbone sharp against my ear, I whispered, "I don't know if I can ever trust anyone again."

In response, he retrieved the letter that had slipped unnoticed from my lap. He pressed it into my hand. "Read it. Your Highness will see that His Majesty has every intention of seeing you to your proper estate. He would never have left Spain if he'd known what your husband intended."

I held the letter for a moment before I finally cracked the seal and unfolded the parchment.

Madrecita,

I have learned of all that has befallen you through the admiral, and your pain causes me great sorrow. Had I known that matters would reach such a pass, I would have come sooner to assist you. Yet as you must know, I had to leave Castile because my kingdom and very life had been threatened. I send you this missive by the faithful offices of my lord the admiral and ask you not to come to Valencia, as I plan to leave on the morrow. I suggest we meet in Tortoles, where I'm assured there has been no sickness from the plague. Until then, my daughter, I pray for your good health, and trust that we'll soon be reunited in happiness. Given on this 29th day of August, 1507,

I, Fernando de Aragón

I lifted my eyes to the admiral. I felt a fragile joy I was almost too afraid to acknowledge. "He wants us to meet in Tortoles."

He smiled. "And Your Highness's answer is?"

"Yes. My answer is yes!" I threw my arms about his neck. "I will meet with my father and together we will claim my throne."

...

I LEFT HORNILLOS THE NEXT EVENING, HAVING SENT THE AD-miral ahead to Tortoles to find me the best accomodations available. Upon my arrival, I was taken to a two-story house on the edge of the town.

Beatriz, Soraya, Doña Josefa, and I went to work, opening my battered coffers that contained my plate and linens, and airing my embroidered pillows from Flanders and wool tapestries. We spread rushes mixed with lavender and thyme on the floors and sat together at night repairing my gowns. I decided on one with an ebony satin bodice inset with onyx beads for my meeting with my father but had Soraya replace the draping sleeves with fitted, crimson damask ones. And my coif needed a new veil, with some pearls to adorn it. My father always liked to see me in finery.

On the morning of his arrival, my ladies awoke me before dawn. They bathed me and dressed my hair. After they laced me into my gown, they set the coif on my head, adjusted the fall of veiling, and stepped back.

I turned to them, plucking at my skirts. "Well?"

"Your Highness looks beautiful," said Beatriz, though she made the mistake of glancing away. I strode to my dressing table, picked up my silver hand mirror. In the cracked, tarnished glass, my face swam like a reflection in murky water—so pale and gaunt, I could not contain my gasp.

"*Dios mio,*" I said. "I look as if I've been to hell itself."

"You have. There's no use pretending otherwise."

She never minced her words; with a faint smile, I set the mirror back on the dresser. "Is Catalina dressed yet? Papá will want to see her."

"Doña Josefa attends to her." Beatriz took me by the arm. "Come, let's go to the courtyard. That way, we'll be the first to see His Majesty when he approaches."

BY MIDMORNING the sun was vehement.

We took shelter in the shade of the portico, where dust clung to our gowns and perspiration stuck our petticoats to our thighs. When we finally heard muffled shouts in the distance, I sent Soraya to the gates. She peered out. "I can see them!" she cried over her shoulder to me. "Many lords ride to the house."

I moistened my parched lips. Many lords. Probably everyone who had plotted against me. In my anticipation of this moment, I hadn't paused to consider that my father might arrive with an escort. But then Cisneros must have hastened to greet him, Villena, Benavente, and the constable as well, all eager as ever to curry favor where favor could be found.

I braced myself. No matter how much it cost me, I would not let them see how much I dreaded their presence. Let them find only cold indifference; let them wonder if once I was safe on my throne they would find much to answer for.

All of a sudden, the entourage was before the gate, an impressive collection of men whose cloaks draped over their mounts' hindquarters, the bright scarlet and gold and blue of their insignias glistening with unnatural brilliance against the bone-white sky. Villena and Benavente were among them; so was the constable. I had seen him skulking in the ranks of Philip's army at Burgos, then in Burgos when Philip died. It seemed he had indeed been spying for my father.

Then I saw my father. He rode at their head on a stallion caparisoned in green velvet. My knees turned to water. I flashed on an icy-cold day on a charred field outside Granada, what seemed an eternity ago, when I'd waited on tiptoes for him in all my innocence. Then, he had ridden with his head bare and with my brother like an angel at his side. Now, his features were shadowed by his black cap, the lone jewel pinned to its brim winking in the light. He turned to speak to a man behind him.

Then he dismounted, his boots hitting the dust with an audible thump. The others followed suit. As each lord leapt from his horse, my heart beat faster and faster, until it seemed it would burst from my chest.

He turned to us. My ladies sank into curtsies. I stood immobile, staring as though he were a mirage that might vanish at any moment. He straightened his shoulders and began walking across the courtyard.

Slowly, with a composure that belied my trepidation, I moved to him.

He stopped. He removed his cap. The sunlight glinted on his balding head, his pate tanned copper by the Neapolitan sun. He'd grown a beard, its chestnut sheen liberally sprinkled with gray; he looked shorter and stouter, yet his stance was the same, achingly familiar, his legs bowed and his gloved hands on hips, his leonine head tilted.

I clutched my skirts above my ankles and broke into a run, my coif flying off unheeded.

Brightness glistened in his eyes as I came before him. His face was deeply scored.

"*Madrecita*," he said. "*Mi madrecita, al fin . . .*" He pulled me to him. "I am home," he said, as his arms closed about me. "I have come home to you."

Before I closed my eyes, I saw the admiral among the lords. He inclined his head gently.

WE SAT IN THE *SALA*, the remains of our supper on the table. The lords had departed to their separate lodgings at my father's request; after serving us, my ladies retired from sight.

Strangely, through supper we spoke only of safe things. I asked him about my son, whom he had left in safekeeping in Aragón, and of his trip ("Naples is a hellhole," he laughed, "but a rich hellhole, at that"). Our five years of separation were heavy between us, and we were both reluctant to break the illusion that we simply enjoyed a long-overdue reunion, until the time came when we could avoid it no longer.

Rising from his chair, he took up his goblet of wine and paced to the doors leading to the patio. With the fall of night, clusters of flowering jasmine had released their fragrance, and it wafted through the open doors. He closed his eyes. "Jasmine. It always reminds me of Isabel."

I sat silent. Hearing my mother's name on his lips made me hurt.

He turned back to me, shaking his head. "Forgive me. I did not mean to cause you any discomfort. I spoke without thinking."

"I know, Papá." I met his gaze. "You can speak of her, if you like."

"No," he said, with a wry laugh. "Best to speak of you, yes?" He returned to the table, set down his goblet. "I do not wish to burden you further. I want you to feel safe and I understand that won't happen overnight, not after everything you've suffered."

I gave him a smile. "I will not break, Papá. And I have questions only you can answer."

He regarded me with bemusement. "Questions?" He reached again for his goblet, drained its contents, and immediately refilled it from the decanter. He had consumed more than I recalled him drinking. Times past, he'd all but abstained save for formal occasions.

"Very well." He straightened his shoulders. "Ask your questions."

I took a breath. "Why did you leave Spain without trying to see me?" To my relief, I did not sound resentful. Not until this moment had I fully realized how bewildering his actions were to me, how much I had needed him during my struggle to survive my husband and win my throne.

He frowned. "I thought you knew. Philip forced me. He threatened to invade Aragón. I do not have the power I held with your mother. Even as regent, I still needed the *grandes'* support. And they sided completely with your husband."

"And Cisneros, did he act as your spy?"

"Yes. He kept me informed of everything that transpired, up until that Cortes session where you defied Philip. Then, for some reason he has not explained, he ceased to write."

"There's no surprise there. He tried to finish what Philip started. I think he wanted to rule Castile, perhaps through one of my sons."

"No doubt. The old vulture has certainly added a few new plumes to his roost since I saw him last, though he did come to me as soon as I arrived to explain he only sought to protect the realm. In fact, most of the nobles have begged my forgiveness."

I bristled. "It's *my* forgiveness they should seek."

He nodded, giving me a pensive look. "They assume I will seek to reclaim my regency. I've not said anything. Castile has a queen to rule it now. I have no aspirations for myself."

I absorbed these words in silence. I did not want to probe further, but knew I would never rest unless I heard the answers from him, and him alone. "I have one more thing to ask, Papá."

"Yes?"

"Did you . . . ?" My voice caught. "Did you have Besançon . . . ?"

I had no idea why I asked this. I must have sought to expunge my own heart, to scare away my fears with the thought that I was my father's daughter and had only done what was necessary. I knew that had I not acted as I did, Philip would have destroyed Spain. But there were still nights when I woke gasping, seeing again my hands as they coldly crumbled the herbs into powder and sprinkled it into the wine, watching it float like smoke for a moment before it blended with the red liquid. How else could I have known that those herbs grabbed in a moment of terror would do my bidding? How had I known that with a mere two goblets, I would be freed of Philip's tyranny forever? How else had I found the strength to kill my husband?

He stepped close to me. "Do you truly think me capable of such a deed?"

"He said he was poisoned," I replied. "I heard him tell Philip. Philip believed him."

My father's eyes turned hard. "Then your husband was almost as much a fool as that old archbishop. I don't much care either way what they believed. But in answer to your question, no, I did not poison him. Though Christ only knows if anyone deserved it, that man did."

I fought back a rush of conflicting emotions. How could I have doubted him? Had I lost so much of myself that I had ceased to trust my own father? And yet his answer unsettled me. I could never tell him the truth now. I could never confess what I had done.

It was a deed I must carry forever, to atone for on the day of my own death.

"Forgive me," I murmured, averting my eyes. "I . . . I had to ask."

He leaned to me, cupped my chin. "Besançon died by God's hands, not mine, just like your husband—which is a form of justice in and of itself, eh?"

"Yes," I said. "I suppose it is."

"Good. I could not bear it if you thought ill of me." He turned away. I thought he might pour himself more wine. Instead, with his back to me he said without warning, "I too have a question now. Do you wish to rule as queen?"

I hesitated, quelling the immediate urge to say yes, to take on my own burdens and steer the path of my destiny from this day forth. I had experienced too much to succumb to another potentially devastating mistake made in heated pride, particularly one that could cost me everything I'd fought to obtain. The truth was, not even my mother had ascended the throne alone. She had already wed my father, who helped her win Castile from her foes, and they had initiated their reign together. Spain had never had a widowed sovereign queen before.

"I do wish to rule," I finally said. "But I know many would prefer one of my sons on the throne. You ruled Castile with Mamá for years. What do you advise?"

A pensive silence followed my words. Then he laughed shortly. "I can't pretend to advise anyone. I've made too many mistakes. Besides, you've been forced into too many decisions that were not your own. You should decide now what is best for you."

"Very well, then. Then what about the codicil?"

His brow furrowed. "Codicil?"

"Yes. The one Mamá left. It stated you would rule Castile as regent until I was invested as queen. Its terms are still valid, are they not?"

He rubbed his bearded chin. "I don't know. She originally devised it because she feared your husband would seize everything for himself. Now that he's dead, I'm not sure if it applies."

"What if we altered it, then? Aragón and Castile should stay united. I could give you a premier place on my council, Papá. You needn't leave again. We could rule as father and daughter, rid Castile of the last of the Flemish, and see the Cortes summoned for my coronation."

His smile was odd, a mere curve of his lips. "Are you saying you never intend to wed again?"

"Never," I replied. "I have my children and my kingdom. I don't need anything else."

"You say that now, because you are tired. But you are young. The flesh has its needs."

"I am done with all that. There isn't a man alive I could wish for as a husband."

But as I spoke, I thought of the admiral, of his compassion and his strength, of his unswerving loyalty. It was unthinkable, of course. The *grandes* would never allow one of their own to rule over them. Yet I couldn't deny the emotions that had taken seed in me, born of the despair and torment of these last years with Philip. If I had the choice, the admiral was the man I would want. He, I would make king.

My father said, "You are aware there could be trouble? Any assumption of power on my part might make matters worse."

"How can they get any worse?" I stood, rounded the table. "For the past six years, I've been a prisoner." My voice broke. "I don't trust the nobles, Papá. I don't trust Cisneros. Each plotted against me in one way or another. Only the admiral has been steadfast; only he showed me any care. With you and him beside me, we can bring the *grandes* to task. You know them. You earned their fear during your time as king with Mamá. You can help me do it now."

"I appreciate your trust in me, *madrecita*," he said in a low voice, "but you give me too much credit. I am older now. I am not the angry young king I was when I married Isabel."

I searched his eyes. "Are you saying you can't do it, or you won't?"

He sighed—a long, drawn-out sound that seemed to carry the weight of the world. "For you, I will do it. For you, I'll deal with the *flamencos* and the noble lords of Castile who hate me as they hate little else. But I'll need your consent if they make a move against me. The last thing I want is Villena or another of those wolves coming at me with an army at his back. I cannot summon men to arms in Castile. The Cortes took that power away from me when they sided with your husband, though by your mother's codicil I was granted it in perpetuity."

"I shall restore it to you," I said firmly. "It will be my first act as queen." I felt hope. I could do this. I could be the queen my mother had wanted me to be. Castile would be mine.

He met my gaze. "Are you certain this is what you want? You have time to think it over."

"I've never been more certain. It's not what I want, Papá, but what Spain needs. Mamá made you regent until I could claim my throne. She trusted you. Why shouldn't I?"

"Very well, then. Together, we'll set Castile to rights." He kissed my lips. "And we'll start by finding you a suitable place to live, where you can recover your strength and I can ride to you at a moment's notice." He hugged me close, as he had so many times when I'd been a child. "I cannot tell you how pleased I am," I heard him say. "I dreaded the thought of leaving you again."

I closed my eyes, abruptly overcome by fatigue, all the tension and fear and doubt seeping from me. I needed to rest, to come to terms with these welcome, but abrupt, changes in my life.

"I am tired, Papá. Will you stay here tonight? I've readied a room for you."

He smiled. "I wish I could. But Cisneros is no doubt pacing his room in town at this very moment, wondering what we're talking about. I want to surprise him with the good news." He tweaked my cheek. "I'll come first thing tomorrow. I've yet to see my new granddaughter."

I laughed. "She's still a baby, but she looks just like Catalina."

"Then you named her well." He went still, looking at me as though he sought to engrave my face in his memory. "Rest well, *madrecita*," he said, and then he turned and strode out.

As I climbed the stairs to my chamber, I could barely keep my eyes open. I checked on Catalina, whom I found sprawled in her crib, Doña Josefa slumbering in a chair beside her.

My ladies waited for me. They helped me undress without speaking, sensing my need for quiet. Snuggling naked between crisp linens, in a few seconds I succumbed to sleep.

I did not wake once. And I did not dream.

THIRTY-TWO

...

My father came to me the next day. He declared himself delighted with little Catalina, who gurgled and sucked on his thumb. After she was taken away for her nap, he and I ate on the patio and strolled in the walled garden, enjoying the benevolent summer dusk.

He spoke of the many obstacles he would face in the coming months, not the least of which was persuading the nobles to join him in routing Don Manuel. I learned to my outrage that the treacherous ambassador had snuck back into Burgos and seized the castle there, installing himself like a feudal warlord with his mercenaries. Papa said the constable was already on his way there to raise his men, and he was confident others would join, for if there was one thing in which the nobles were united it was their hatred of Don Manuel.

I insisted he have Cisneros officially draw up our agreement for my signature. I had my mother's ring but didn't yet possess an official seal, so my father brought me the one she had used. I had seen that worn cylindrical stamp on my mother's desk many times, and I felt she was with me in spirit as I stamped the parchment that restored my father's powers in Castile.

In a carefully orchestrated ceremony, Villena, Benavente, and the other *grandes* who had flocked to Philip's standard came before me to beg forgiveness for the wrongs committed in my name. I had no choice but to pardon them, though I winced as Cisneros bowed low over my hand, his eyes like smoldering coals when he lifted them to me. Despite my father's assurances that the archbishop had rallied to him "like a well-trained hound," I would never trust him.

In early September my father located the perfect place for me to hold my court—a royal palace in the township Arcos, a mere two-day ride to Burgos. Winter approached and with the lords' support my father had assembled the troops he needed to fight Don Manuel. Word had already gotten out of his impending march on the city and those Flemish courtiers not beholden to Don Manuel had fled with pieces of Philip's household gold stuffed in their satchels. Several were arrested; others, however, reached port and commandeered a ship to return to Flanders.

"If we want to catch Don Manuel," my father laughed, "we'd best be about it before he too finds himself a hole to hide in."

He looked as if he'd shed years, the impending war bringing a gleam to his slanted eyes and bloom to his bronzed cheeks. He chuckled as I fumed over Don Manuel's insolence. "Chains are what he deserves," I declared, "and a dungeon to keep him in them!"

"And so it shall be," he replied. "Now set your ladies to packing. I've a surprise for you."

WE MADE THE TWO-DAY TRIP to Arcos in the blessed cool of the night. Flambeaux illumined our passage, and peasants and hamlet dwellers materialized from the shadows to witness the sight of their new queen riding beside the old king, followed by our train of nobles and clerics escorting the bier upon which rested Philip's coffin.

Women knelt in the dust; men doffed their caps. A group of children ran up to me in the middle of the road, braving the horses' hooves to thrust brittle autumn wildflowers and clumps of chamomile into my hands. *"Dios la bendiga, Su Majestad,"* they said breathlessly. "God bless Your Majesty!"

Leaning from his stallion, my father murmured, "They love you well, *madrecita,* just as they loved your mother," and I clutched those simple offerings as if they were precious jewels.

In Arcos, I found a spacious, well-equipped palace with a full staff, including, to my distaste, my half sister, Joanna. I'd hoped to have seen the last of her but couldn't very well refuse her service, given our familial blood. I accepted her rigid curtsy with as much graciousness as I could muster. Then I turned to the bowing ranks of cooks, chamberlains, stewards, and chambermaids. Not since Flanders had I disposed of so many servants.

"I'll hardly know what to do with them all," I said to my father. "My needs are simple."

"Nonsense. You're a queen now. You require a court." He pointed to an alcove. "See there. I believe there is someone who wishes to greet you."

I looked to where he pointed. Light spilled from the overhead windows, falling in shafts onto a small figure who stepped forth. I couldn't move, could not speak, as I gazed through a start of tears at my five-year-old son, the infante Fernando, whom I had last seen as a babe.

He bowed with perfect solemnity. *"Majestad,"* he intoned, *"bienvenida a Arcos."*

I felt a fluttering in my chest. I sank to my knees to look into his large, thick-lashed brown eyes. Of all my children, he most resembled my father, as if he had absorbed the physical traits of the man who had raised him.

"Fernandito," I said. "Do you know who I am?"

He glanced at my father before returning to me. *"Sí. Vos es mi madre la reina."*

I reached out and embraced him. "Yes," I whispered, "I am your mother the queen." Holding him to me, I gazed up at my father. "Thank you, Papá, from the bottom of my heart. You've brought me so much happiness."

He bowed his head. "May it always be so, *madrecita.*"

. . .

FROM MY PALACE IN ARCOS, I WAS KEPT APPRISED BY DAILY COURI-ers of the siege. My father and the *grandes* marched into Burgos to meet the constable and his forces. Surrounding the castle walls, they trapped the mercenaries in the citadel. They waited it out for a full three months before all inside capitulated without a single blade being drawn. My father promised them mercy if they swore allegiance to Spain and turned over the traitor Don Manuel, only to discover that Don Manuel had slipped out days before the surrender through an underground passage, carrying a small fortune in Philip's plate and his private jewels.

"Can you believe it?" my father said when he came to escort me to Burgos for our triumphant entrance. "That miserable frog found some old medieval passage everyone else had forgotten about. It led directly to a convent and he forced the poor sisters at dagger point to help him escape. From there, he took ship at Laredo for Vienna." He guffawed as he spoke; he found the ambassador's cowardice amusing, even as I replied tartly that justice had not been served.

"Oh, it's been served," he said. "Being exiled to your father-in-law's court will be punishment enough. From head councillor, he's reduced to stowing away to Vienna in a stolen nun's robe, to beg succor on hands and knees. Lucky for him, he has your dead husband's jewels. Otherwise, Maximilian would have his head."

"He had no right to those jewels," I countered. "And he's still a free man."

"Yes, but a ruined one. And Burgos is mine."

I didn't remark on his slip, reasoning he'd meant to say "ours." A week later, he and I rode into Burgos, to the clangor of the cathedral bells. I wore my finest gold gown and a coronet; this time, however, the populace called out, *"Viva el rey Don Fernando! Viva la reina Doña Juana!"* and I espied my father's proud grin. He must have looked this way countless times before when he'd taken a city for my mother. It pleased me to see him have the veneration and respect he deserved and to see the nobles' scowls at our reception. Let them be warned that under my rule Castile would no longer be prey to their wiles or ambitions.

At the cathedral doors, my father clasped my hand and lifted it together with his, to a resounding roar from the crowd. "And once we put matters to right here," he told me as I threw back my head and laughed, "the bells in Toledo shall ring for your coronation."

• • •

AUTUMN TURNED TO WINTER; WINTER FADED INTO SPRING. THERE was much to do in Burgos, but I left my father to wrangle with the constable and the other *grandes* while I returned to my palace and my children, where for the first time in years I could devote myself to being a mother. My Catalina approached her first year; I wanted to spend time with her and my son, and enjoy the tranquillity I'd so painstakingly earned. The sound of laughter soon pervaded the house; and with my devoted Beatriz, Soraya, and old Doña Josefa (who also seemed to shed years as she assumed charge of the children) I set myself to fashioning an intimate cocoon.

My father had shown singular care in his rearing of Fernando. My Spanish-born was quick-witted, intelligent, and studious, but not as overtly as my Charles. I spent every morning watching over his lessons, recalling how my mother's personal supervision of my and my sisters' education had ensured our academic success, but in the afternoons I insisted we go out into the gardens to partake of the fresh air.

He shared stories of his time in Aragón, where he said the mountains dwarfed anything he had seen in Castile, and how he longed one day to own his own hawk. I sent all the way to Segovia for a renowned falconer and the perfect bird, and while I privately feared the creature was far too wild for a child, it took to Fernandito like a kitten. The falconer assured me my son was a born hunter and they plunged with gusto into his hawking lessons in the wide fields outside the palace, landing us quail and other small birds for our dinner table.

Sometimes I joined them, wearing the thick-padded gauntlet on which the tethered and blinded bird perched, feeling its claws dig into the leather as it waited impatiently for me to untie it and release it into the sky. I was mesmerized as it effortlessly soared upward, seeming not to notice the frantic rustling of the creatures the falconer beat out of the bushes with a stick, and I always watched breathlessly as it swooped down with lethal precision to catch its prey. I did not like the smell of blood but I could only admire how it always delivered a sure, quick death.

I also had my private moments, in which I made peace with my past. No one seemed to know what to do with Philip's coffin. The smell alone grew so terrible I finally had to order the lid nailed shut and the coffin itself removed to a ruined chapel on the palace grounds, where it rested before the leaf-strewn altar. I had the chapel roof repaired to keep out the elements but otherwise did little else. I didn't believe anything but dead flesh remained in that box, and still I took a strange comfort in visiting the chapel in the afternoons when everyone took to their beds for the siesta, to sit by it and sometimes touch the now-tarnished handles. I even spoke to him at moments, of our son and how handsome he was, and of our girl Catalina, who was starting to resemble the best of both of us in her looks and personality. Philip had gone to a place where crowns did not matter anymore; I wanted to remember him as he'd been when we first met, beautiful and young, uncorrupted by the ambition that tore us apart.

"Rest now, my prince," I would murmur, and I leaned to the coffin to set my lips on the cold lid. The smell of death was gone now. It was as though the coffin held only memories.

And I would not hate memories.

THE ADMIRAL HAD REMAINED in Burgos with my father, but he sent letters to me detailing the events shaping Castile. He reported there had been much wrangling and threats when my father announced his and my decision to set the kingdom to rights together, with the Marquis of Villena in particular flinging down his cap in disgust and declaring he would not let himself be ruled by Aragón again. My father, the admiral reported, proved uncharacteristically mild in his rebuke, given his own past with the nobility of Castile. At his side, supporting his every move and facing down the lords with the full wrath of the church at his back, was Cisneros, who'd recently been granted a cardinal's hat at sixty-seven years of age.

I was taken aback by the announcement that Cisneros had been elevated to such prestige. My old feelings for him had not gone away, and I did not relish that he would now enjoy even greater ecclesiastical power in Castile. No one had told me beforehand the pope was considering him for a cardinalship and I wrote back to the admiral that I wished someone had seen fit to inform me as much. I assumed I would have to attend Cisneros's investiture ceremony at some point and asked that I please be told in anticipation so I could prepare. I expected a reply within a few days; to my disconcertion I heard nothing more. "I wonder why I wasn't consulted," I remarked to Beatriz one night over supper. "Did they fear I might protest elevating Cisneros to such a rank? I certainly might have, but I've no say in how Rome chooses to reward her servants."

I paid no heed to the servitors around us, ready with the decanter and clean napkin. No sooner had I vented my frustration than I forgot it and returned to my daily activities.

I wrote to my sister Catalina in England, asking for news of her and promising to help her in her struggle to wed her prince now that I was queen. I also wrote to my sister-in-law, Margaret, requesting that she prepare to send my daughters to me in the coming spring.

I hadn't heard from her at all, not even a word of condolence on Philip's passing. I knew Charles, as the new Habsburg heir, must remain in Flanders, and I suspected Margaret had assumed charge of him as well. I wondered if she had grown so attached to my children she kept silent in hope I wouldn't ask for them. If so, I feared she must relinquish my three daughters. I wanted to raise them with Catalina and Fernando, as my mother had raised us together. I didn't want my children to grow up strangers from each other, as Margaret and Philip had, and as so many royal children often did.

I was therefore preoccupied and completely unprepared when my father came barging into my chambers one afternoon, after months of absence.

"What?" he said, the hot tinge to his face betraying a hard ride in a temper. He threw off his cloak onto the nearest chair. "Have I so displeased you, you must remonstrate about me before everyone?"

My women sat with me, working on our sewing. Glancing at them, I saw my own surprise reflected in their expressions and started to wave them out.

My father laughed curtly. "Don't send them away on my account. You've complained times enough behind my back, anything you say now will come as no surprise."

I regarded him in silence as Beatriz rose with Soraya and left.

I set aside my sewing. "Papá, what is wrong? You are angry at me and I have no idea why."

"You don't?" He eyed me, his gloved hands clenched. "Are you saying you did not complain that I deliberately keep you ignorant of the state of this realm?"

"I . . . I never said that." My mouth went dry. There was a hard, cruel edge to his voice I had never heard before.

"Never?"

"No."

He spun to his cloak and reached into its folds. He removed a folded parchment, brandishing it between us with a trembling fist. "What of this, eh? Haven't you learned that everything you say or do is important? By not consulting me, you cast doubts on your very trust in my abilities!"

For an endless moment, I could not draw breath.

My letter. He had intercepted my letter.

A shadow gathered in the corners of my mind. I made myself look away from the crunched paper in his hands to meet his stare. I found a cold and inscrutable stranger looking back at me, someone I did not know.

"I didn't think I needed to consult you about my children," I said carefully. "That letter is addressed to Philip's sister, requesting news of my daughters, Eleanor, Isabella, and Mary. I haven't heard of them in over a year, and I left Mary when she was just a babe."

His jaw worked. "What do we want with another parcel of girls here?" he said, proof that he had not only intercepted but also read my correspondence. "They need households, dowries. We can't afford it. Best leave them where they are and let the Habsburgs find matches for them."

I felt an icy fear. I rose, moving past him to the window. "My daughters belong here with me," I said at length. "If we can't afford it, I'll economize. I told you I don't need so many servants, and what feeds three can feed five. If need be, my daughters can sleep in my bed."

He pawed the floor with his booted foot. "Need or not, everything comes with a price."

"So it would seem." I turned to him. "As it would also seem I suffer spies in my house. I will not have it, Papá. I don't understand what I have done to make you think you need watch my every move and intercept my private letters. Perhaps now would be a good time to tell me."

His face changed in a flash, the anger fading as if it were a mask. I did not like the chameleon swiftness of it, nor his quick conciliatory tone as he said, "*Madrecita*, forgive me. My behavior, it's inexcusable."

My voice momentarily failed me. He had not denied he set spies on me. Why? What did he fear? Something shifted between us, crumbling the trust I had believed we shared.

"I'm overwrought," he added. "I always did have a bad temper. Your mother used to chide me about it all the time." He paused. "It's those damn *grandes*. I tell you, they have no loyalty. Months I have spent in Burgos trying to bring them to reason, to no avail."

That much I understood. I knew from experience that the lords of Castile could set a saint to gnashing his teeth. "What have they done this time?" I asked quietly.

"The usual. They're threatening that if I do not honor the promises your dead husband made to them, they will find the means to make me regret it. They want everything your mother and I took from them, though they've done nothing to deserve it. They claim having helped me take Burgos deserves a reward. Your husband and that idiot Don Manuel taught them well, it seems. They now think that any time they obey me, I should give them a title or castle for it."

I nodded, returned to my chair. It was only his temper, I told myself, that infamous Aragonese cauldron my mother had patiently curbed during their years of marriage.

"They dare to threaten me!" He hit his gloved fist in his hand. "It's high time they were taught who rules over them. I'll not have them destroy this kingdom after they connived with the Habsburg behind my back. They let him throw me out but now I am back, and by God, they will do me the proper honor."

"You speak of civil war," I said.

He scowled. "More like civil slaughter. I've subdued them before. If I must I'll do it again."

"But they are members of our nobility, with seats on the Cortes. If we declare war on them, it will indeed be a violation of their rights."

"They have no rights! They scheme to no end, plot and intrigue, forgetting this is not the Spain of old. Isabel may have seen fit to placate them, but I will not." He stopped abruptly, swallowing hard. "You must understand my predicament. These *grandes* are dogs, and like dogs they must be put down for the good of Castile."

A surge of heat rose in me. I was sick of posturing and high-handedness in the name of Spain. I wanted this matter stopped before it led to further calamity.

"The last thing I desire is to begin my reign by sending an army of Spaniards against Spaniards. I agree this matter with the nobles is serious and do not disregard your frustration, Papá. But there must be another way to show them we've a higher authority in the realm now." I straightened my shoulders. "Perhaps the time has come to announce my coronation."

He stared at me. "Coronation?"

"Yes. You told me months ago, we would go to Toledo and have me invested and crowned. Why not now? It seems the perfect occasion. The high lords need to understand they have a queen. We needn't make a production out of it, just enough to entertain the people and remind the lords of their proper place. The admiral once told me Mamá always made it a point to deal with the *grandes* firmly but gently. He said that it was one of her most impressive—"

"Your mother is dead." His tone was flat. "I rule here now."

I went still. My heart felt as though it stopped in my chest. He must have seen the look on my face, the utter horror, for he came to me, tried to take my hands in his. I pulled away.

"I did not mean that," he said. "It was a figure of speech, *madrecita*, nothing more."

I let out my withheld breath. I kept my gaze on his face.

"By the saints, I'm a hard man, unused to women's sensibilities." He grimaced. "I'm just working so hard to restore this realm to some semblance of order, and every time I turn my back one of those lords tries to counter me. They're more treacherous than the Moors, I tell you. At least with the Moors you can threaten a burning to keep them in line."

"I still think we must give them one more chance to mend their ways," I heard myself say, despite the ice seeping through me. "I don't want bloodshed. It will bring Spain no good. I want us to summon the Cortes for my investiture. It is time. Then, if the *grandes* resist, we can consider harsher measures."

He nodded. "If that is what you desire." He turned abruptly to gather his cloak. He strode to the door, his hand reaching for the latch before I managed to say, "Papá."

He glanced over his shoulder at me.

"My letter," I said. "You will send it on to Savoy."

It was not a request, and I saw in the tightening of his face that he knew it. "Of course, I will. Everything will be fine, you'll see."

Yet as he left, I wondered if anything would ever be the same again.

. . .

I WAITED FOR DAYS AFTERWARD, REFRAINING FROM PRIVATE DIS-
course with anyone save my women and keeping any letters I needed to write neutral. I doubted my secretary, Lopez, had had anything to do with

the interception of my letter to Margaret, but I no longer trusted that what I sent would arrive at its intended destination.

This much was easily managed, as letters required my signature. But it proved impossible to regain the placid passage of my days. With corrosive precision, that web of suspicion that had plagued my final years with Philip returned to haunt me and I could no more escape it than I had when he'd been alive.

My bastard sister, Joanna, for one, became insupportable. She headed the gaggle of sharp-nosed women who served me in my chambers, and where before I had put up with them, relegating them to mindless chores like cleaning out my hearths and seeing to my bed linens, now I found such an insidious way about them that I could not abide to look at them. I suspected that one, if not all, acted as informants and treated them with a remote formality, as I couldn't refuse their services completely without bringing undue attention to myself.

Every night after my ladies retired, I spent the hours of moon-limned silence pacing, my doubt consuming me. The shadow unfurled its ominous wings in my mind, growing larger, more threatening, until I feared I might truly go mad this time, as I could no longer tell if what I felt was real or the delusions of a woman who'd been betrayed too many times before.

I needed confirmation and finally succumbed to what I'd struggled against ever since my father had come to me. I called for Beatriz and handed her a sealed missive.

"Find a trusted courier to get this to the admiral," I told her. "I must see him."

. . .

WE MADE ARRANGEMENTS TO MEET ON THE PLAINS IN A SECLUDED woodland, where Fernandito often went hawking. We needed cover from prying eyes and I waited until the hour of the siesta to saddle up the mare I kept stabled for my ambles about the grounds. I had taken to riding weekly for exercise, or so I told my ladies, and therefore no one thought anything untoward when I went out with Beatriz on her mule to partake of the afternoon.

A slight breeze rustled the clumps of oaks and linden; from the west drifted the brackish smell of the Duero's tributaries. Winter had bleached the plains of color, but clumps of wildflowers and startling yellow broom scrub had begun to rise with the incoming heat of summer, and I found myself gazing over the landscape with possessive tenderness.

At the woodland entrance, we dismounted and I left Beatriz with the horses while I proceeded alone under a whispering canopy of leaves.

At first, I thought he had not come. All I heard was the susurration of the breeze and the crackle of twigs underfoot. It reminded me of the time I had tried to escape Philip by taking flight over the salt flats, and I closed my eyes for a moment against the unbidden image of the anonymous gypsy woman who had died by his hand.

Then I saw him standing by his tethered horse in a sun-dappled clearing. I unwound my shawl from my head. He turned. I almost ran to him, for in the saffron light he seemed like a dark statue of hope. As he bowed over my hand, I said, "My lord, you've been missed."

"As has Your Majesty." His gentle regard was heartrending. I searched his deep-set cobalt eyes, arresting in the sculpted pallor of his face, and saw reflected there what I had feared.

"My father," I stated, and my words felt like jagged glass. "He works against me."

"Yes. I would have come sooner, but I feared he'd have me stopped or followed. When I received your missive, I took a circuitous route. He suspects me. He knows you place your trust in me, and he'd not have it so."

He paused. "I must beg your forgiveness. I made a terrible mistake in bringing him to you. When I learned of his intent, I lifted immediate protest. I told him you were not there to approve such a decision and he forbade me to see or correspond with you. He did not order my arrest because of who I am, but he and Cisneros will find a way to deprive me. They move against anyone they perceive as a threat."

"What . . . what is his intent?" I heard myself say.

He tilted his head. "Is it not why you sent for me? He came to you, did he not?"

"Yes, and he was very angry. I found out he was intercepting my letters, but then he said he was having trouble with Villena. I told him to summon the Cortes for my coronation."

He didn't speak for a long moment. Then he sighed. "Of course, that explains why he returned to Burgos in such a rage. He did not tell you he had taken a new wife."

"A wife?" I started. "My father has wed again?"

"He has. He's betrothed himself to none other than King Louis' niece, Germaine de Foix. She is on her way to Aragón as we speak."

Germaine de Foix: I recalled sloe eyes, a pursed mouth, and a sharp voice. I had met her in France; she had tried to steer me past the hall, stalked my heels throughout the visit. Why did my father seek to marry a woman born in a land he had despised and fought against all his life?

And all of a sudden it became horribly clear. A new wife, another queen in Spain.

"He wants a son," I breathed. "An heir for Aragón."

"Yes." Anger colored the admiral's voice. "You are now his heir apparent and your sons after you, but if he sires a son on Germaine, then Aragón will no longer need Castile. Rather, it could be the other way around, for with a French alliance to enforce his power over the *grandes* they'll not dare revolt if they think Louis will send in an army to defend him."

"Like Philip," I said, and my heart constricted in my chest. "He uses France to bolster his position. But my sons are also his grandsons, heirs by my mother's will." I paused, met his somber gaze. "Dear God, he would go so far just to keep them from the throne?"

"They carry Habsburg blood. He and Cisneros are determined that they can never rule here. And that is not all, my lady. When he announced his marriage to the lords, he spoke of one for you as well. It was then I lifted protest and gained his enmity."

I struggled for composure, even as I felt a scream pulse inside me. "Do you know who?"

He shook his head. "No, but whoever he is, it cannot be to your advantage. Your Highness, he sees your sons, and therefore you, as threats. If you are our queen, then your mother's succession must stand. In time, your son Charles will inherit. Your father will fight against this to his last breath; he wants to bind Castile to him now, and he has Cisneros's full approval."

I turned away, the woodland darkening all around me. "I am being punished," I heard myself say aloud. "It is my punishment for what I did."

The admiral set his hands on my shoulders, turned me back around to face him. He looked terrible in his starkness, like a doomed knight from a childhood ghost tale. And yet he had never seemed more beautiful to me than in that moment when he said, "These are the ambitions of men. They are to blame, not you. You've done no wrong."

"You do not understand," I whispered. "I killed Philip. I poisoned him."

I saw comprehension dawn in his eyes. He reached for my hands, looked into my eyes as he said passionately, "You did what any queen would have done. You had no sword or army to defend yourself with, and yet you vanquished your enemy. You are indeed Isabel of Castile's daughter. She would have done the same to save her realm. It is her legacy, alive in you."

I could not see through my tears as he raised my chin and brought his lips to mine, like a lover. "You must leave this place," he said against my breath. "Take your children and your trusted servants and make haste for Segovia. The Marquise de Moya awaits you there. I will join you once I rally my retainers. With any luck, I can convince some of the nobles to fight with us. We'll wage war on your father and win Castile for you."

I heard his words, felt them in my blood and my sinews; in that terrible moment, I knew with a sudden, deep certainty what I had to do. It had been with me all this time, the hour when I must face both my past and my future and decide my own course. I had been a pawn blown by the vagaries of fate for most of my life: an innocent girl used for a political alliance, a wife deceived and manipulated for her crown. Now, at long last, I had the strength to be the woman I had always wanted to be, the queen my mother had believed I could become.

"No," I said. I drew back. "There can be no war. I forbid it."

He went still. "If you do not declare war, he will win. You could face—"

"I know what I face. I've known it and run from it from the day I was named heir to this realm. I will not run anymore. Castile must come first. I'll not have blood spilt in my name."

"My lady." He gripped my hands again. "Your father will not stop until he has what he wants. No one can help you if you do not fight."

"Who says I will not fight?" I said, and I gave him a tender smile. "You are right: he will not stop, not unless I stop him. There isn't a place in all of Spain to shelter me. Wherever I flee he will follow. He'll endanger the lives of those who love me, including my children. And I will not risk my children, not even for my throne."

"If you want to survive, there is no other way! Please, my lady, I beg you."

"No," I said again, and I took my hands from his, leaving a hollow inside me. "Castile is my birthright, my legacy. No one and nothing will take it from me. I must look my father in the eye and show him that I am not only his daughter but also the daughter of Isabel of Castile."

I saw him hesitate, his mouth tightening. Then he dropped to his knees before me and I heard him say in a broken voice, "Your Majesty need only send for me and I shall be at your side."

I set my hands on his head, let the pain of this final loss move through me. I whispered, "Go now, my lord. Save yourself and those who rely on you."

I did not touch him again. I pulled my shawl about my head and I walked away, back through the trees to Beatriz and the horses, back to Arcos and the fate that I had decreed for myself.

Though I did not look back, I knew he still knelt there, watching me.

I RETURNED TO THE HOUSE, evading Joanna and my other women. Once I reached my room, I asked for Lopez to come with his paper and quill. Beatriz stood pale-faced at my side as I dictated my summons. I pressed my signet ring into the wax and told Lopez, "You will deliver it to him personally. Tell him I will await him here."

His mouth trembling as he held back his tears, my secretary bowed low.

I turned to Beatriz. She met my eyes and in her solemn gaze I saw she would have gone to the ends of the earth for me, if I asked it. I embraced her, holding her close.

I then stole into my daughter's room. She slept amid tousled sheets, her gold ringlets disheveled, a sheen of afternoon sweat on her brow. I had to press my hands to my mouth to stop myself from sobbing aloud. She was still so innocent, so unknowing of the world's incomprehensible cruelty. Who would tell her of me? Who would tell her the truth? What did the future hold for these children of mine, caught up in the maelstrom that was my life?

I bowed over her, inhaling her sweet scent. My lips grazed her cheeks. For her, I must do this; for her, and for Fernandito; for Charles, Eleanor, Mary, and Isabella. They too were my legacy. My blood ran in their veins as surely as Philip's. There would be time later for anguish. For now, I must protect them and give them the peace I had rarely known.

Come what may, my children must survive.

THEY ARRIVED FOUR DAYS LATER, at dawn. One minute the house seemed empty, the servants just awakening to start their daily business; the next, there was a commotion in the hall, a banging of doors and the tromping of footsteps coming up the staircase.

I had been awake most of the night. Beatriz set my coif on my head and kissed my hands. I set a hand to her cheek for a moment before I walked out into the corridor. Soraya was with Catalina and Doña Josefa with my son.

The lords stood below in the entranceway. I recognized the one-eyed constable, sulfuric Villena, and sweaty Benavente. They paused, returning my stare, and then they bowed in unison, as if it were a normal occurrence for them to be here unannounced at daybreak.

Moments later, my father entered, his riding cape flaring behind him. He looked up at me.

"Papá," I said calmly. I descended the stairs. "I've been expecting you." I leaned to him to kiss his cheek. "Shall we repair to the *sala*? You must be thirsty."

He evaded my eyes, gesturing with his hand. The lords retreated.

I led him into the hall. A bleary-eyed chambermaid hastened in with a decanter and set it on the table. I poured a goblet, turned to him. He took it, not meeting my eyes.

There is still time, I told myself. He has come with only a few of his men. I saw no guards. If he meant ill on me, he would not have come like this.

I resisted a sudden laugh.

"Hija," he finally said, and he motioned to a chair, "you should sit. I bring important news."

My heart started to pound. I made myself go sit, as I had so many times before as a child.

He stood silent, looking at me. He lifted his goblet as if to sip, then went and set it aside on the table. "I have come to you," he began, and he stopped. He cleared his throat. I found it strange that after everything I knew, everything he knew, he could seem so reluctant.

Then it came, in a sudden taut burst: "There are malcontents among us who would thwart the proper governance of this realm and plot treason. I will not tolerate it."

I gathered my strength from the pit of my stomach. I had heard this tale of malcontents too many times before. "Are you certain? Who would have reason to plot against you?"

He barked, "Are you questioning me?"

I thought suddenly of my children upstairs. If I feigned conformity, pretended to be the pliant, submissive daughter he had always thought me, if I convinced him I posed no threat, maybe he'd leave me alone for today—a day to be with Catalina and my son, a day of freedom.

Again, I felt the wild laughter rise in me and I forced myself to say, "I do not question. I just want to know why you believe anyone would plot treason."

"It is good you do not question," he said, ignoring my own question. He paced the room, his compact body emanating tension. He paused. Though I could not see his eyes, I felt them aimed at me. "What would you say if I told you a king has asked for your hand in marriage?"

Here it was. At last. I did not speak.

"Not just any king, mind you," he added, and he had the audacity to actually chuckle, "but one who enjoys great respect and prosperity."

"Is that so?" I could scarcely hear my own voice. "And who is this great king?"

"The king of England," he replied, and I went completely still. At first, I didn't believe my own ears. I almost laughed aloud then, in hysterical disgust. It was a joke. It had to be.

"Henry Tudor has asked for me?"

"He has. Apparently, he was quite taken with you during your brief visit to England. At the time, of course, any such proposal was out of the question. You were wed and he a widower. But he now says he can think of nothing else and, after much deliberation with his councillors, has decided to cast aside his mantle of widower to offer you a place at his side as his queen."

"I see." My fingers knotted in my lap. "I trust you told him it is out of the question."

His eyes narrowed. That telltale tick quivered. "Actually, I told him nothing of the sort." And he walked straight to me, so abruptly I felt my spine flatten against the chair back. He stopped, reached into his cape, and extracted an envelope. He dropped it in my lap. "From His Grace Henry VII. He writes well, for an Englishman. I suggest you read it."

I did not touch the envelope. "I have no interest in what he has to say."

My father chuckled again, only this time it was cold. "I'd not be so hasty if I were you. It could be that with some time and reflection, you'll find his proposal has its merits."

All of a sudden, I pushed back my chair and stood, the envelope falling to the floor. "I will see to some food. You are no doubt hungry after your ride here."

I was about to walk away when he said, "It would be a dual marriage."

I froze.

"Yes," he added. "He says that if you consent to marry him, he will honor your sister's betrothal to his heir, Prince Henry. Think of it. You shall be queen of England, and when your husband dies Catalina will take your place. Two infantas on the English throne; a lifelong alliance with Spain, not to mention his promise that you'll dispose of a considerable income as his royal widow and a permanent place at his son's court. Not a bad arrangement, if I do say so myself. Better than living here with your dead husband's coffin moldering in that chapel."

I whirled about. "But not better than marrying France."

His eyes widened.

"Yes," I said. "I know about Germaine de Foix. You may do as you wish with your person, Papá, but not with mine. How dare you lay before me, the queen of Castile, this degrading proposal, using my own sister, your own daughter, as bait?"

"I merely state the facts." His voice turned hard. "Here are a few more for you to consider: I need foreign support and my French alliance will provide it. So will the English one. And the *grandes* will not suffer an unwed woman to rule over them. You are queen here in name alone, and only by my good grace. Had it not been for me, they'd have done away with you years ago."

There was not a hint of compassion in his voice, not a trace of empathy. He spoke as if I were a problem to be disposed of, an inconvenience he no longer had time or patience for. Even as I cried out in silence at the destruction of my childhood illusions, of my love for this man whom I had always made so important to my life, another part of me hardened, turned to stone.

Nothing had changed as far as he was concerned. He expected me to do whatever suited him best. As he'd convinced me to leave Spain for Flanders, so would he now send me to England. Only this time, he wanted me gone so he could steal my throne.

I did not take my eyes from him. "You cannot think I would ever agree to this monstrosity."

"You have nothing else. Cisneros and I believe it is time you assumed your rightful place."

"Castile is my rightful place. Henry Tudor denied Catalina the most basic comforts; he toyed with her even as Mamá lay dying. I would never marry him. The very thought insults me."

He regarded me impassively. Then he stepped forth and picked up the envelope from the floor. "I lied. Someone else desires this marriage. Indeed, they need it." He extended it to me. "You should read this before you say anything else you'll have cause to regret."

I took it from him. The seal was cracked, but I recognized the broken castles and lion of Spain. When I unfolded the paper, I saw desperate lines scrawled there that tore at me like talons.

Mi querida hermana,

I write because you said that if you could, you would do anything in your power to help me. I find myself at the mercy of this English king, who as you know has denied me all station and proper rank at his court and treats me as though I were a disease come to his shores. Yet now, after years of denial and humiliation, he has informed me he wishes for you to be his new wife and queen and will allow Prince Henry and me to renew our betrothal if you would honor his suit. I beg you, Juana, for the love you bear me, to consider my plight. Never has an infanta of Castile fallen so low as I. But you can save me. You can come here to England and we can live together again as sisters, as we did in our childhood. You will lack for nothing, I promise, even upon the king's death. You are a widow now and Papá has conveyed you have no wish to take up the throne but would rather seek a place of respite. This you will find with me. I need you more than ever, Juana.

With all my love,
your sister, Catalina

The silence stretched into eternity. I stood holding the paper and saw my beautiful sister, reduced to such misery that she'd demean herself by playing the scheming suppliant.

And yet, I thought, I could go to England. I could say yes and this would all end. I could take my daughter, perhaps even my son, and never look back. I would wed a man who slowly drowned in his own decay, but when he died I would be a widowed queen with her life before her. I was still young; I had years ahead in which to make a new existence.

As if from very far away, I heard my father say, "You are her only hope. All you need do is sign a writ of voluntary abdication. I will rule Spain as regent until your son Charles comes of age. You can leave with a clear conscience."

Voluntary abdication.

He lied. I would never have a clear conscience. If I signed away my rights, I would sign away the very succession of Castile. Not even the Cortes would be able to stop him. He would win everything for Aragón and the son he hoped to sire on his new French queen. My sons would be forever disbarred, my struggle to save Spain cast asunder.

In my mind, I heard my mother as clearly as if she stood at my side: *Good has a way of losing to ambition.*

I looked at him. I felt as if I had never seen him before, as if he were someone who looked and sounded like my father, but whose nature was frigid and ruthless.

"Cisneros and I have spent many hours negotiating these marriages," he added. "Like me, he is dedicated to this realm. With my marriage to Germaine and yours to the Tudor, I will stifle all those who dare say that I, Fernando of Aragón, am unworthy."

I let the parchment stained with my sister's shame slip from my numb fingers. How could I have thought for a moment of turning away from my own blood?

"This is *my* kingdom," I said. "I weep for Catalina, for she has no other recourse, but I cannot help her. Not like this. I won't hear another word about it."

He lunged. For a horrifying moment, I thought he might strike me as he grabbed my arm, his eyes gone black with rage. "How dare you speak to me as if I were your lackey?" he hissed. "I rule here now, not you! And from this day forth, *you will do as I say!*"

His words fell on me like hailstones. But in that moment, I was no longer afraid. I understood now what I'd never seen before, the final terrible truth.

My father did not fight against me. He fought against a ghost.

All those years he had stood in my mother's shadow, known derisively as the Aragonese under Isabel's petticoats—he could not forget or forgive. He had bided his time, waited for the hour to claim what he believed was his, after years of bowing to my mother's throne. He had waited and watched while Philip persecuted me and did not lift a finger to stop it, not because he couldn't but because it had never been part of his plan.

It has nothing to do with love. I doubted his ability to live in the shadow I cast over him.

Now his hour had come. He would pulverize a lifetime, quench forever the invincible light that had eclipsed his own. I was but an obstacle in his path. It was my mother he sought to punish—her and everything she stood for. He had been ridiculed, insulted, humiliated. Never would he abide it again.

He released me. Under my sleeve my arm burned. "For the last time," he said in a dead-flat tone, "will you abdicate and do as I say?"

I took a step back from him. "No. I will not abandon my realm. I will not disinherit my sons. If I abdicate, everything Mamá wanted will be lost. I will not betray her."

"Then you betray me!" he shouted. "You betray your father!"

A roaring filled my ears. I could not feel my feet as I took another step back.

"It seems you are unwell," he said, and he spoke to wound, to maim, to kill. "You imagine things. These flights of fancy that have been yours since childhood have finally gotten the better of you. If you will not wed and resume a normal life, you must be mad. You must be taken somewhere safe, far from this"—he waved derisively—"this cemetery you call a home."

My hands clenched. I started to tremble. "Do as you will," I whispered. "But whatever you do to me will avail you nothing. I am still the queen. One day my son will be king. A prince of the Habsburg and Trastámara blood, he will build an empire greater than anything this world has seen. He will be everything I dreamed for Spain and more."

"You are a fool," he spat. "He will build nothing but his Habsburg interests, and when he does, *my* blood, the blood of Aragón, will be here to stop him!"

He turned heel and strode from the room.

I heard him yell out orders. I spun about, staggering against my hem. In the doorway to the *sala* was an escort of guards. I looked past them to see the constable descending the staircase with a squirming bundle tossed over his shoulder like a sack of mead.

I cried out. A slim man in scarlet stepped from among the guards. His eyes fixed on me with a raptor's intensity: the Marquis of Villena, whom my father had called a traitor.

"Your Highness," he said and he bowed, swiping off his cap to reveal that wealth of dark hair, which the years had not thinned or grayed, as if he'd made an unholy pact to preserve his youth. This man who supposedly betrayed Spain for Philip's service—he now served my father.

"Get out of my way," I said through my teeth. "Get out, by God. I command you!"

He sneered. "Your Highness should obey before I'm compelled to use harsher measures."

I threw myself at him, raking my nails across his face. As he reeled away, clutching a hand to his lacerated cheek, I saw the guards hesitate. I leapt forth. None dared lay hands on me as I broke through them to race to the stairs, my wail tearing from my throat.

Doña Josefa stood with my women at the top of the stairs, her weathered face running with tears. I whirled about to the open door. I reached it in time to see the constable and other lords mounting their steeds. My father was at the gates, his gauntleted hands yanking at his reins so that his stallion balked. Perched in front of him, clutching the saddle pommel, was my Fernandito.

He saw me. "Mamá!" he cried out. "Don't let them take me away from you!"

I opened my mouth to yell, to shriek, but all I could do was reach out in mute appeal.

My father looked at me. Then he kicked his stallion's ribs and galloped away. The lords followed. A cloud of dust floated in the empty courtyard.

Behind me, I heard the guards and Villena move in.

. . .

THIRTY-THREE

I was locked in my rooms. There, I huddled on the floor in my cloak and gown, my knees drawn to my chin. I pretended not to see or hear the odious women who entered with a guard to deliver my meals, which I left untouched. I ignored their acidic clucking that I cease my unseemly behavior. Only when I heard Joanna among them did I rear up to throw myself at her like a woman possessed, grabbing hold of the nearest platter and heaving it at her, sending its contents flying. She yelped and bolted from the room, never to return.

After that, they allowed Beatriz to come to me. In a whisper she told me Soraya and Lopez had been dismissed. The house was surrounded, the gates bolted. Fresh supplies of food were brought from the town and left outside the gates to be retrieved by one of the guards.

"And my daughter?" I asked.

"She is here. They've not harmed her. Doña Josefa was allowed to stay and attend her. But Villena watches her closely, as he watches everything, though the infanta is but a child."

I gazed at her through burning eyes. Only then did I realize my hair hung about my face in matted tangles and I smelled the rank odor of my unwashed body.

"Let me send for warm water to bathe you," Beatriz said. "Let me care for you."

I submitted to her ministrations. Dressed in a clean gown, I even ate a little and began to ponder what lay in store for me. Much as she tried, Beatriz could not get anyone to tell her anything. She said Soraya had not left Arcos, however. She'd taken residence in town and came every day to the gates to beg admittance. No one let her in. Only after Beatriz's repeated pleas for my health did Villena grant me parchment, wax, and ink, supposedly for letters—which of course he would review before sending.

I did not expect mercy from my father and I did not write to him. But I did write to my sister Catalina in England. I poured out my heart, begging her forgiveness that I couldn't assist her in her trials, but it was inconceivable for me to abandon the throne entrusted to me by our mother. Even as I gave my letter to Beatriz for dispatch, and wondered whether it would ever reach Catalina's hands, I replayed that terrible scene with my father in my mind and again asked myself why I had sealed my own doom by not accepting Henry Tudor's proposal. I even started to go to the door to call for Villena to tell him I had changed my mind.

I stopped myself. I could never do it and my father would never let me go now. Perhaps he had never intended to. Perhaps he had needed me to deny him so he could do what he wanted to do ever since he learned of Philip's death.

Weeks passed. I sent other innocuous letters, to the Marquise de Moya in Segovia and my son Charles in Flanders, but in truth I spent most of my days and endless nights writing these words, recording the events that had led me to this hour.

And I waited. One evening Beatriz brought me my dinner and told me we'd not learned anything of importance because my father had been absent from Castile, dealing with some revolt in the south. But he'd returned now, after reaching accord with the rebels.

Then she leaned to me, her eyes febrile in her weary face. "I overheard Villena tell that vixen Joanna that the admiral has sent His Majesty a letter questioning your imprisonment. He said Castile will never cease to fight for its rightful queen and His Majesty should consider well his state of grace before he commits an act that neither God nor Spain will ever forgive."

I clasped her hand. My voice faltered. "Then all is not lost."

Beatriz put her arms around me. "No matter what, I will always be with you, *mi princesa*."

They came for me that night.

Looking up through my hair, I saw figures gathered about my bed—faceless apparitions whose steel glimmered in the flicker of a handheld torch. At my side, Beatriz awoke with a frightened gasp. My gaze went to the foot of my bed. Cisneros stood there, regarding me with eyes like burning embers in his bone-white face.

"Time to rise, Your Highness."

I rose from bed. I felt numb as Beatriz divested me of my nightclothes and dressed me in a warm dark gown. As she tied the sleeves, I whispered, "Do you know where we are going?"

"No," she whispered back. I could feel her hands trembling. She searched my face, her eyes filling with tears. I took her hand for a moment as I fought back a wave of paralyzing fear.

A half hour later, I entered the frigid *sala* with Beatriz at my side. In addition to Cisneros and Villena, the assembly included a full retinue of guards.

My heart quickened. I gazed past the men to the courtyard and saw Doña Josefa on the threshold, with my daughter in a shawl in her arms. Catalina was crying, having been awoken abruptly. I immediately moved to her.

Villena snapped his fingers. A guard seized Catalina from Doña Josefa and strode off. Clutching her shawl to her face, Doña Josefa bowed her head and started to weep.

I whirled to Villena. "Where are you taking my daughter?"

"The peasant and your ladies stay here," he said. "You and the infanta will go with us."

"Stay here? But I've need of my women. They must come with—"

"There'll be others to attend you." He grasped me by the elbow, his fingers digging into the bone. "Come now, without protest."

"Get your hands off me, you traitor," I breathed.

He met my stare. He released me, motioning with a sweep of his arm. "Your litter awaits."

I glanced over my shoulder. Beatriz stood surrounded by guards. My half sister, Joanna, raised her chin. My breath froze in my throat when I saw her execute a mocking curtsy.

Not a star or wisp of moon relieved the darkness. The litter was closed, slung between four dray horses. I faltered at the sight of it, looked back at the cavalcade. When I saw guards loading Philip's coffin onto a cart under the direction of the constable, my knees threatened to buckle underneath me. He turned to look over his shoulder. Even from where I stood, that terrible scar and one searing eye riveted me. His mouth curved within his thick beard, a grimace of a smile. Like his wife, Joanna, he had always served my father.

A spectral figure stepped before me. Cisneros inclined his head. "This is not La Mota. You'll find no escape here."

"One day, you will pay for this," I told him, my voice shuddering. "You will pay for what you do. Were my mother still alive, she'd see you beheaded for this. You spit on her memory."

He flinched. "The infanta Catalina will travel with you," he said, and he turned away, his cloak swinging behind him like a leathery wing.

I mounted the litter. Within, I found my child, her eyes wide. I clutched her close to me as I heard the men mounting their horses. We moved forward with a sickening lurch.

Tar-soaked torches held by guards lit the road ahead. We clattered out of Arcos, turning south. I peered through a crack in the curtains and saw figures at the roadside, the townspeople who had come to know me during my time here. They stared sullenly. A woman raised her fist. Others followed, in a silent united gesture of defiance.

I gazed at them, the anonymous and downtrodden, who toiled the land, wed, reared and buried children, lived and died. Never had I felt closer to them than I did at that moment. Never before had I understood how much they too had suffered.

And in their midst I suddenly heard a low keening, a lament in the lost tongue of the Moors. I leaned out farther, desperately searching the shadows. I saw Soraya on the ground, at the foot of a group of women. She was on her knees, taking up handfuls of dirt and pouring it over her head. She raised her dirt-streaked face. We looked straight at each other.

A guard rode up swiftly and yanked the curtains closed. But not before I heard someone cry, "*Dios bendiga y cuide a Su Majestad!* God bless and succor Your Majesty!"

They knew. My people knew what was being done to me.

I had become one of them. One day they would rise to avenge this treachery.

After that, the guard rode by the litter at all times. It seemed as if we traveled for years. Unable to look out, I cradled Catalina in my arms, singing lullabies to lull her to sleep. Her smell filled my senses, bringing me a calm I might otherwise have lost forever. I still had my child; and I held her so close, a last comfort in my fractured existence, that she awoke. Her sea-green eyes opened. She gazed at me with an intensity that made me want to weep.

"Mamá, where are we going?"

I smiled through my tears. "Home," I whispered. "We are going home, *hija mia*."

Toward dawn, I reached out to ease back the curtains. The guard had not left but he did not stop me this time. My eyes strained past him and the other mounted sentries, past the rising, rocky escarpments I recognized immediately as the domain of the Duero, in Castile.

In the hem of the dying night, owls hunted. I stared at their swooping shapes, entranced for a moment by their grace. I *was* home, I thought suddenly. At long last, I had returned to the land of my birth, the place where my life started.

I did not look at the stark outline of the fortress looming ahead, its battlements limned in blood by the sunrise. I did not see the portcullis hanging over me like a maw of teeth, nor did I heed the creaking of its massive chains as it was lowered back into place.

It clanged shut with a finality that echoed throughout Castile, over the whitewashed villages and arid plains, past my desolate *casa* in Arcos and the haunted parapets of La Mota, through the streets of Toledo and walls of Burgos, until it reached an empty hall where a king sat alone on his throne, his hands folded before his pensive face.

Here, it faded into silence.

TORDESILLAS,
1554

It has taken me a thousand midnights to reach this hour.

My hand aches now from writing, my heart from remembering. Yet I have done my duty as a queen. I have not looked away from the truth; I have not embellished or lied away the past in order to make my present less bitter. Rather, I have trod once more that long, unexpected path that brought me to this place, reliving every mistake, every tear, and every delight; I have looked upon and touched, wept over and hated, all the faces of those I loved.

Strangers surround me now. No one is left to me—no one save him, whose body has turned to dust in the battered old coffin, which rests in this castle's chapel. Sometimes they take me there to visit. I sit at his side and reach out my gnarled hand to caress the scarred wood bier. I am not ashamed to talk to him. I have long since forgiven him, and myself. It all seems so meaningless now. We are all we have left, and we can do each other no further harm.

Like him, I will soon go to a place where thrones mean nothing.

But not yet. There is still one more place I must go. I need only close my eyes to see it: the horizon dressed in violet and chased silver clouds, the wind's keening fading into a jasmine-scented breeze. At my feet, spring gardens of mosaic and lace. White quartz paths twine past fountains, and ripe pomegranate saturates the air. I can feel droplets of water on my skin and speckles of mimosa, and the chanting of slaves in the keep entices me to dance. It is so close I can touch it, a vermilion sprawl on the hill, where gilded gates open to welcome me.

And in the sky above, the bats have returned.

AFTERWORD

...

Following her imprisonment in Tordesillas in 1509, Juana's father, Fernando of Aragón, ruled Spain until his death in 1516. His final years were plagued by paranoia and the ceaseless intrigues of the *grandes*. He never sired a son on Germaine de Foix, though he resorted to many folk remedies believed to increase virility, including drinking distilled bull's testicles. He became an unwelcome wanderer in the land he once ruled in triumph with Isabel; he never expressed remorse for the enormity of the wrong he had committed against his daughter.

Upon his death, Spain passed in its entirety to seventeen-year-old Charles of Habsburg, who'd been groomed since childhood by his aunt the archduchess Margaret to inherit his paternal grandfather's empire. Known as Charles V of Spain and I of Germany, he entrusted the governance of Spain to his regent, Cardinal Cisneros, who oversaw the nation with an iron hand until his death at the venerable age of eighty-one. Charles then traveled to Spain, where negotiations with the Castilian Cortes proved difficult until he agreed to learn Castilian, appoint no foreigners, and respect the rights of his mother, Queen Juana. The Cortes paid homage to him in Valladolid in 1518. In 1519, he was crowned before the Cortes of Aragón.

Regardless of his promises, Charles favored his Flemish and Austrian courtiers over their Castilian counterparts, and the heavy taxations he imposed on the Spanish people to finance his wars abroad eventually drove the people to rebellion. The most tragic of their attempts to throw off the Habsburg yoke was the Comuneros Revolt of 1520. The Comuneros initially sought to restore their captive queen to her throne; alas, their poor organization and training, coupled with Charles V's immense manpower, put a swift end to them. More than three hundred Spaniards were executed for treason. Some, nevertheless, reached Tordesillas, and for a brief spell a bewildered Juana was released. She had no idea her father had died or that her son now held her throne. By the time she managed to absorb the monumental changes that had occurred since she'd been locked away, it was too late.

She never left the precincts of Tordesillas again.

Following his subjugation of the Comuneros, Charles came to Spain and visited his mother. What Juana said privately to her son after more than twenty years of separation remains unrecorded, but he must have known her refusal to surrender her rights as queen had given him Spain. Nevertheless, by Castilian law he would not be fully recognized as king until her death, and he did not release her.

Prematurely aged by his obligations, Charles V abdicated in 1555. He retired to a monastery in Avila, Spain, where he spent his final years in seclusion, obsessed with clocks. He died in 1558. He bequeathed Spain, the Netherlands, Naples, and Spain's New World territories to his son, Philip II. Raised in Spain, Philip became the country's first official king: he ruled over a united realm and elevated it to preeminence and power. His influence would last into the seventeenth century; under him Spain entered the apex of her Golden Age, mirroring the thriving of the arts under Elizabeth I in England. Philip's era was one of undoubted savage religious persecution, of slavery and the destruction of Native populations throughout the Americas; it also gave birth to Cervantes's *Don Quixote*, the first essentially modern novel, the paintings of El Greco and Velazquez, and the dramatic writings of Lope de Vega.

Charles's Habsburg domains went to his brother, Juana's younger son, the infante Fernando, who inherited the title of Holy Roman Emperor. He became a strong ruler in his own right, signing a peace treaty with the Ottoman Empire and supporting the Counter-Reformation. He died in 1564 and was buried in Vienna.

Beatriz de Talavera wed, bore children, and died in Spain. The admiral succumbed to a stomach ailment shortly after Juana's imprisonment. The handmaiden Soraya's fate is unknown.

Juana's eldest daughter, Eleanor, wed the king of Naples; after his death she became the unhappy second wife of François I of France. Isabella wed the king of Denmark, with whom she was apparently content. Juana's third daughter, Mary, married the king of Hungary.

Juana's youngest sister, Catalina, became queen of England and the first of Henry VIII's six wives. Her namesake, Juana's youngest daughter, remained with her mother in Tordesillas for sixteen years. In 1525, at her brother Charles's command, Catalina was stolen away while Juana slept and sent to marry King Juan III of Portugal. After giving birth to nine children, she died in 1578, twenty-two years after the death of her mother, whom she never saw again.

The loss of Catalina, Juana's sole remaining consolation, plunged the imprisoned queen into utter despair. According to the accounts of her current custodian, which I read firsthand, it was at this moment that she began to show the erratic, clinical signs of the manic depression that many scholars believe tainted the Trastámara blood.

In 1555, after forty-six years of captivity, Juana of Castile died at the age of seventy-six. Francesco de Borja, founder of the Jesuit Order, attended her in her final days. By this time, she had passed into myth, the unstable queen who went mad with grief, impotent symbol of Spain's suffering—Juana la Loca.

She was entombed with her husband, Philip the Fair. Today, the lovers who became mortal enemies rest in the cathedral in Granada, opposite the sepulchre of Isabel and Fernando.

JUANA OF CASTILE'S LIFE has been the subject of two award-winning films and several highly praised biographies in Spanish, in addition to an opera and a play. Yet she has been ignored in the larger scheme of history, known as the tragic, enigmatic figure whose incarceration caused scarcely a ripple. Nevertheless, she was the rightful queen of Castile and her refusal to abdicate did give rise to an empire under Charles V and his son, Philip II.

Legends are notoriously hard to research. Though a wealth of documentation exists about the period, much of the extant information concerning Juana comes from dispatches and eyewitness accounts, all written by men. Many of those who recorded her early years, praising her erudition and beauty, later denounced her as a deranged victim, while tales of her jealous behavior in Flanders and Spain veer from the lurid to the patently absurd.

Of course, such accounts reflect—as does much of written history—the prism of their era. The sixteenth century scarcely recognized spousal abuse or misogyny, much less mental illness. As for Juana herself, she has left almost nothing in her own hand. Thus, while I strived to stay true to the established facts, this novel remains a fictional interpretation of her life, and I confess to taking minor liberties with time and place in order to facilitate a difficult endeavor at best.

Among these liberties is an encapsulation of time toward the end of the book, to facilitate the story. I also have Fernando marry Germaine de Foix three years later than he did in actuality, again to facilitate the story and not further confuse an already complicated situation. I believe his motivations for marriage were as I describe them. I also have imagined much of the relationship between Juana and the admiral; while he is recorded as one of her most stalwart supporters, there is no account of them seeing each other after Fernando returned to Spain. It is comforting to think, however, that she did see him and knew him for a friend. Last, I have no verification that Juana might have had a hand in Philip's demise, though rumor was rampant he had indeed been poisoned. Of course, whenever a person of royal status died suddenly under such circumstances, poison was invariably suspected.

For those who might wonder, I assure you the wilder episodes of Juana's life, including her giving birth to Charles V in a privy closet, her rebellion at La Mota and attack on Philip's mistress, her frantic attempt to escape on horseback while pregnant, and the opening of the coffin, are corroborated by several contemporary sources.

Was Juana sane? Could she have ruled her country? Historians who've tackled her as a subject have struggled with these questions for centuries; they were certainly at the forefront of my mind. This novel consumed nearly six years of writing and research and, much like Juana, adopted different incarnations on its way to its present form.

In the end, I can only hope I've done justice to her passion, courage, and uniquely Spanish character. She was, if nothing else, an extraordinary figure for her time.

For those interested in further exploring Juana and her times, I offer the following brief bibliography of books, not all of which are available in English:

Alvarez Fernandez, Manuel. *Juana la Loca* (Palencia: Editorial La Olemeda, S.L., 1994).

———. *Isabel la Católica* (Madrid: Editorial Espasa, 2003).

Crow, John A. *Spain: The Root and the Flower* (Berkeley: University of California Press, 1963).

Dennis, Amarie. *Seek the Darkness* (Madrid: Sucesores de Rivadeneyra, S., 1969).

Hume, Martin A. S. *Queens of Old Spain* (London: Grant Richards, Ltd., 1906).

———. *The Spanish People* (New York: D. Appleton and Co., 1914).

Liss, Peggy. *Isabel the Queen* (Oxford and New York: Oxford University Press, 1992).

Luke, Mary M. *Catherine of Aragon* (New York: Coward McCann, 1967).

Miller, Townsend. *The Castles and the Crown* (New York: Coward McCann, 1963).

Prawdin, Michael. *The Mad Queen of Spain* (New York: Houghton Mifflin, 1939).

ACKNOWLEDGMENTS

...

Nothing is written in solitude, though it may often seem so to the writer.

I first wish to extend my heartfelt thanks to my partner, who's stood by me for sixteen years with humor, patience, and understanding. I might not have found the strength to keep trying if he hadn't been there to encourage me with his eternal optimism.

My incomparable agent, Jennifer Weltz, at the Jean V. Naggar Literary Agency, came into my life just when I needed her the most; with wit and sagacity she gave me shelter and restored my faith. My editor, Susanna Porter, first made a dream come true with her belief that my words were worthy of attention; then she and her assistant editor, Jillian Quint, improved those words with their insightful suggestions, keen eyes, and trust in my ability to revise. My copy editor, Jude Grant, scoured the pages with rare insight. Rachel Kind, senior manager of foreign rights at Ballantine, expressed her passion from the get-go and took on the book with style. The entire creative team at Ballantine conjured the book to life with their diverse talents. In the United Kingdom, my editor, Suzie Doore, of Hodder & Stoughton, made another dream come true when she enthusiastically took me under her wing, and Lucia Luengo of Ediciones B. brought Juana home. To all of them, and to the many others I cannot mention here who work every day to see books to the marketplace and who keep alive the flame of reading, thank you so much.

I owe a special debt of gratitude to the Historical Novel Society, true champion of the genre, and in particular to editors Sarah Johnson, Claire Morris, and Ilysa Magnus, for giving me my first break. Also to Billy Whitcomb, who designed the beautiful map; my friends Linda and Paula, who never doubted this day would come; and my writing group, led by the indefatigable Jean Taggart, who has provided caffeine, encouragement, and criticism for over ten years. Vicki Weiland has read more drafts of my work than I care to count and enhanced each one. My brother Eric, his wife, Jackie, and my niece Isabel cheer me along. Sandra Worth and I share a magical table; Wendy Dunn is a blessing from afar; and Holly Payne a staunch ally. In Judith Merkle Riley, I found a kindred spirit. She is a lady in every sense of the word, with a heart that is as magnificent as her pen.

Last but never least, I wish to thank all my readers. You are the reason I write.

About the Author

C. W. GORTNER, half-Spanish by birth, holds an M.F.A. in writing, with an emphasis on historical studies, from the New College of California and has taught university courses on women of power in the Renaissance.

He was raised in Málaga, Spain, and now lives in California.

He welcomes visitors at www.cwgortner.com.

About the Type

This book is set in Fournier, a typeface named
for Pierre Simon Fournier, the youngest son of a
French printing family. He started out engraving
woodblocks and large capitals, then moved on to fonts
of type. In 1736 he began his own foundry and made
several important contributions in the field of type
design; he is said to have cut 147 alphabets of his own
creation. Fournier is probably best remembered as the
designer of St. Augustine Ordinaire, a face that served
as the model for Monotype's Fournier,
which was released in 1925.